Seven Year Itch

Look for Amy Daws's next **Mountain Men Matchmaker** novel

HONEYMOON PHASE

available soon from Canary Street Press.

And check out the **Mountain Men Matchmaker**
and **Wait With Me** crossover novel

LAST ON THE LIST **(Max Fletcher's story)**

available now in ebook and audio, and coming soon
to paperback from Canary Street Press.

Also by Amy Daws

The Mountain Men Matchmaker series

Nine Month Contract

The Wait With Me series

Wait With Me
Next In Line
One Moment Please
Take A Number

The Harris Brothers series

Challenge
Endurance
Keeper
Surrender
Dominate

The Harris Brothers spin-off stand-alones

Payback
Blindsided
Replay
Sweeper
Strength

For additional books by Amy Daws, visit her website, amydawsauthor.com.
For exclusive news on upcoming releases and updates on all your favorite
characters, sign up for her newsletter at amydawsauthor.com/newsletter.

Seven Year Itch

AMY DAWS

CANARY STREET PRESS

**CANARY
STREET
PRESS**™

Recycling programs
for this product may
not exist in your area.

ISBN-13: 978-1-335-08161-2

Seven Year Itch

For questions and comments about the quality of this book, please contact us at
CustomerService@Harlequin.com.

TM is a trademark of Harlequin Enterprises ULC.

Canary Street Press
22 Adelaide St. West, 41st Floor
Toronto, Ontario M5H 4E3, Canada
CanaryStPress.com

Printed in Lithuania.

MIX
Paper | Supporting
responsible forestry
FSC® C021394

Dedicated to all those hotties with a body in every shape and size. Let's fall in love.

Seven Year Itch

Prologue

**ALONE AND LOOKING TO BONE!
LOUDMOUTHED MOUNTAIN MAN SEEKS FIERY
FEMALE TO STEAM UP HIS LOG CABIN**

Calder, 35 years old

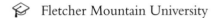 Fletcher Mountain University

Full-time cat daddy with a side-hustle
in screwing and nailing

14 miles away

Height: 6'3" at the doctor, 6'5" at the bar

Eyes: Blue and Full of Feelings

Body: Toned and overly inked to conceal
my real personality

Personality: My mom says I'm great

Size: Not as big as my brother Luke's
but honorable mention

What I do on a typical day: Mountainside
strolls with my cat strapped to my chest.

Self-summary:

I might be tall, tattooed, bearded, and all the classic things
one might look for in a rugged mountain man . . . but like

an onion plucked from the soil, you must peel back the dirty layers to see the moist inner belly that shows my true essence.

I'm not a "go with the flow" kind of guy. I catch feelings with direct eye contact. If you don't text me back within an hour, I'll probably cry a little before showing up to your house to see if you're cheating on me.

I once had a girl hold the door open for me, and afterward I asked her, "What are we?"

The other day, a bartender poured me the wrong beer and let me drink it for free . . . it was a weird way for him to propose, but I said yes.

If you like the taste of my potent onion, swipe right and let's giggle and make some soup together.

Chapter 1

CAT DADDY

Calder

"What the actual fuck," I state out loud, and my cat, Milkshake, lets out a high-pitched meow from where she sits on my naked chest. I sit up, clutching her black-and-white fur to me for comfort as I use my free hand to scroll through my Tinder account. "Have I been hacked?"

My eyes scan over the contents of my dating profile, knowing damn well I didn't write a single word of this. *Catch feelings with direct eye contact?* I don't catch feelings. I catch boners with a light breeze. I catch ladies' attention with my tattoos and muscles.

Feelings? Fuck feelings!

"Can Tinder profiles get hacked?" I ask Milkshake who tips her head up to me and drags her sandpaper tongue over my beard. "Who gives a fuck about someone's dating life enough to mess with their profiles? There has to be way cooler things to hack."

I quickly check my other hookup apps that I keep armed and ready at all times and see the same long-term relationship bullshit spewing out of every one of them. *Make some soup together?* My God. This is the complete opposite of what I look for in these apps. I'm very clear about that. Who the hell did this?

I reread the penis-size line, and my eyes narrow. *"Fucking Luke,"* I growl and stand up from the sofa to stomp across the knotty pine flooring of my small cabin. I glance out the window that faces uphill to see if his truck is here as I drop a soft kiss to my cat's ear. "Someone's gonna die today," I coo in a saccharine voice to my girl.

Without putting a shirt on, I throw the baby carrier on my chest and stuff Milkshake inside. That was the only part of the hacked profile that was true, but dammit, little fuzz loves being outside. And there's way too much wildlife around here to let her run free. So when my future sister-in-law, Trista, gave me a cat carrier to help Milkshake enjoy the great outdoors safely, that meant I turned into a big, tatted mountain man who wears a cat more often than not.

Come at me.

Fuzz gets to enjoy the fresh air and mountain scenery, and I get to sleep at night, not worrying she's going to get eaten by the coyotes that roam the dense forest surrounding us.

Milkshake secure, I storm out in the bristly early March temperatures, the cool air doing its best to cool down my fiery temper as I make my way to Luke's to tear him a new asshole, but an errant thought stops me in my tracks. I pivot to look downhill at the cabin on the other side of my place. Maybe the Luke dick-size comparison on my profile was a diversion to get me off my older brother Wyatt's trail. I certainly have payback coming from Wyatt after posting a Help Wanted ad for him last year at the local bar when he was looking for a baby mama.

But I'll be damned if it didn't work.

The fucker is probably tucked inside his architecturally obnoxious cabin cuddling his fiancée and their nearly three-month-old daughter, Stevie, in front of his stone fireplace, watching the snow melt outside the window.

Gives me the ick.

My brother went from never wanting a wife so much that he was looking for a surrogate to have a baby for him to now preparing to fly us all to Mexico so we can watch him marry his incubator-turned-fiancée in a couple of weeks.

It's enough to make a guy puke.

Not that I dislike Trista. She's cool, and I'm low-key obsessed with my niece that she gave birth to a few months ago. The two of them are fine additions to Fletcher Mountain along with the pick-and-mix assortment of farm animals that keep showing up in the red barn located down the drive.

But my two brothers and I made a pact nearly a decade ago: us three and this mountain. No one else.

Now we have a soon-to-be wife for Wyatt, a baby niece who has us all wrapped around her finger, eighteen random animals including a horse with a tongue deformity, and probably a fucking partridge in a pear tree somewhere in that barn.

Wyatt is a sellout.

My eyes shift to movement in the distance, and I see Trista emerge from the Dutch doors of the barn. She has a baby carrier strapped to her chest, and I decide to let Wyatt live for a few more minutes while I investigate.

Feeling Milkshake purr against my chest, I beeline straight to the barn, my boots crunching over melted snow as I intercept Trista walking back up toward her and Wyatt's cabin.

"What do you know?" I bark, my eyes narrowing on my brother's woman.

Trista smiles as she glances down at my pussy. "I knew Milkshake would love that cat carrier, for one."

I dig my calloused fingers into Milkshake's cheek, and her purr quickens as she nuzzles into my chest. "This isn't about my cat, and you know it."

Trista's smile drops, and she hits me with a scolding look. "Calder, it's barely nine in the morning. I had this feral little animal on my tits four times last night. You're going to have to spell it out for me."

"My dating profiles have all been fucked with, and I want to know who did it. My guess is your soon-to-be husband."

"What does it say?" she asks, her eyes narrowing curiously.

I pull my phone out of my pocket to show her the proof, and her face lights up as laughter bubbles out of her. "This definitely looks like payback from Wyatt."

"That's what I thought," I grind out as I turn toward my brother's house. He must pay for his crime. "Sorry, Stevie. Your dad is going to be out of commission for a while."

"Although you know who else it could have been . . ." Trista's voice stops me in my tracks, and I turn on my heel with a frown as she adds, "Your niece."

"Stevie's too damn young to be on Tinder," I exclaim, my eyes dropping down to the mound of chestnut curls sticking out from her little stocking cap. Her hair is wild and unruly just like Trista's.

"Not this niece, you moron," Trista bites back a bit too comfortably. She's definitely not the type of sister-in-law you can fuck with. She puts me and my brother Luke in our place whenever the mood strikes her. I kind of love that about her.

She pats her daughter's back and adds, "I'm talking about Everly."

My brows furrow. "Everly is at college in Ireland."

"They have the internet there, Calder."

My mind races with this new possibility I hadn't considered. How did my nineteen-year-old niece hack my dating profiles? In fairness, my password might be easy to guess. *Milkshake1234* isn't exactly a high-security option. And Everly was the one with the idea to do the baby mama Help Wanted ad for Wyatt last year when he was looking for a surrogate. I just helped her jazz it up a bit.

I shake my head and refocus. "But why would she sabotage my dating profiles?"

"Maybe she wants you to find a *nice* girl to bring to the wedding, not some rando from Tinder? I mean . . . we all have to hang with whoever you and Luke bring to this villa we're staying at in Mexico. Not to mention Stevie will be there, your mother, and your eight-year-old nephew, Ethan. A random Tinder hookup doesn't sound super family-friendly."

"Trust me, whoever I find won't be there for the family vibes." I waggle my brows suggestively.

Trista rolls her eyes and rubs Stevie's bottom. "Can you not speak that way in front of my daughter, please?"

"My daughter doesn't mind one bit." I match Trista's protective stance with my own fur baby. I move closer to lean in and whisper into my sleeping niece's ear. "It's best you learn young, lil Steve-meister, that your uncle Calder is a stallion."

Trista groans and makes her way up toward their house. "Calder, I don't know who messed with your profiles, but if you have to go to Tinder to find someone to bring to our wedding, maybe you don't really need to bring anyone at all."

My eyes narrow on my retreating future sister-in-law. She might have a point about Tinder not being the right place for me to find a date for a destination wedding. But she's wrong about me not bringing a date. Luke already has his plus-one lined up, and our oldest brother Max down in Boulder has been wifed up for years. Wyatt will be busy being a groom. If I don't bring a plus-one, that means I'll be my mother's date, and as much as I love my dear mother . . . I can't stomach the idea of dancing with her or my niece all night long. I need to find someone to bring with me on this damn trip.

I turn and gaze at the tiny mountain town that rests at the bottom of our long and winding gravel lane. Perhaps Tinder is casting too wide a net. Maybe it's time to look a bit closer to home. Jamestown ain't much to look at. It's a little hamlet of Boulder—an isolated and somewhat dilapidated sanctuary for weirdos who want to stay weird. It's full of loners. Trailblazers. People who don't want to be found and don't mind a bit of inconvenience—be that limited grocery supplies, weather that snows us in for a week, or cell service that goes in and out. Jamestown is our sanctuary. And it's the place Wyatt, Luke, and I have called home for over a decade now.

Unfortunately, the population doesn't even hit three hundred souls, so the pickings are slim. My brothers and I learned that quickly when we first moved out here. Things ended real messy back then, and the three of us made a pact to not test the waters in Jamestown ever again . . . but surely enough time has passed now. I mean hell, Wyatt's on his way to getting married anyways. Maybe it's time to shop local again.

Chapter 2

I'LL HAVE WHAT HE'S HAVING

Calder

"Here you go, boys." Judy's husky voice snaps my attention away from my phone as she sets three fresh beers down in front of me, Wyatt, and Luke.

My brothers and I are seated at the one and only food and drink establishment in Jamestown called The Mercantile, where everyone is a little feral. It's a hole-in-the-wall dive bar that's full of locals, but you see the occasional out-of-town cyclists stop through to fuel up for their rides.

Wyatt, Luke, and I used to stop here most nights after work to eat, although lately Wyatt can't get home soon enough. I guess fatherhood is more appealing than having a workday brewski with his brothers.

But today is a Wednesday, and on Wednesdays Trista goes to Boulder with Stevie and volunteers at the front desk of the Humane Society, so Wyatt can magically make time for us.

I'm not bitter at all.

"Your food should be out in ten," Judy adds before turning to leave.

"Thanks, Judy," Luke says, adjusting his backward hat before taking a fortifying sip.

"Hey, Judy," I call out before she gets too far away. "Any outsiders move to town recently that you know of?"

"Outsiders?" Judy asks with a frown.

Judy is a Jamestown lifer. She's owned the Merc for as long as we've lived here and has turned into a second mother to us . . . if our mother smoked a pack a day and wore Wranglers. She knows everyone who comes in and out of our little mountain town, so she's the best source for the latest news.

"I thought I saw a moving truck roll by one day last week. Wondered if any single ladies might have moved in?"

I feel Wyatt's eyes on me from across the table as Judy hits me with a punishing glower.

"Didn't you learn your lesson the last time with Robyn?" she asks in her gravelly voice.

I feel both my brothers tense at the mention of her name. The *she* who shall not be named. Except Judy mentions her name anytime she damn well pleases.

I wrinkle my nose and shrug. "Ancient history."

"Ha!" Judy barks out a haughty laugh. "Tell that to these two whose shoulders are pinned to their ears."

Wyatt and Luke both instantly relax their posture, only now realizing how edgy they got with the mention of our past fling's name. Yes, I said *our*. Robyn was the dark queen who moved into town just as we were building up on the mountain. She messed with all of our minds, pinning us against each other in a stupid competition for who she'd fall for first. And when she ended up being pregnant with the baby of her husband back home . . . that meant all three of us were the losers. And my relationship with my brothers at the time suffered greatly for that.

Judy presses her hands to the table and eyes me seriously. "Don't you go messing up a good thing now, Calder. No one new has moved to town, and you've burned the bridges of all the available options already."

I sit back in my chair with a frown. "Bridges can be rebuilt."

"Not in Jamestown." Judy hits me with a withering stare that has me shrinking in my seat.

"Point taken," I mumble and take a long, pouting drink of my beer.

Judy walks away, and Luke jacks me in the ribs with his elbow. "What the fuck are you thinking?"

"What?" I ask, shoving him in the shoulder.

"We don't date local. You know our pact."

"Our pact." I point an accusatory finger at Wyatt. "This one pretty much ruined our pact."

Wyatt grunts and sips his beer, refusing to dignify my accusation with a response.

"The pact was that we choose mountain life over traditional lives," I remind him even though I know he knows this. "We didn't even do our annual Dark Night tradition last year because of you."

Wyatt's eyes sharpen. "Do you have something to say to me, Calder?"

"Maybe I do," I reply, pressing my elbows to the table. "But first, do you want to tell me why you've been fucking with my dating apps?"

Wyatt's face twists in confusion.

"I know it was one of you," I growl and turn a menacing glare to Luke. "Every time I try to change them back, one of you jumps in and just fucks them up even more. Just tell me which one of you did it, and save me the effort of pounding both of your faces in."

"I don't even know what the fuck you're talking about," Luke replies, scratching his beard.

I open my fucked-up Tinder profile and show it to the two of them. They stare at it long and hard before throwing their heads back to laugh.

"That is epic," Luke exclaims with a whack on my back. "Whoever wrote that is fucking hilarious."

"It wasn't you?" I ask with a frown. "That means it was . . ." I stare at Wyatt who shakes his head, making it very clear that it wasn't him either.

"Then, it has to be Everly." My teeth clench before I take another swig of my beer. The student truly surpassed the teacher. I'd be proud of her if her evilness wasn't directed at me. "Damn that kid. Isn't she supposed to be busy at college and shit?"

"She must think you're desperate." Luke laughs, and I see that twinkle in his eye that he gets anytime he talks about Everly.

We all get that twinkle, even when she's being a pain in our ass. She's the kid our oldest brother, Max, had when he was still in college, so we were all barely teenagers when she was born. In an instant, she became the apple of our eyes and turned us from boys to men.

Now she's all grown-up and off to college in a foreign country and still managing to stir up trouble from across the pond.

Atta girl, Evie.

And her brother Ethan is going to be ten times worse. He's eight and recently got in trouble for taking his bicycle to Walmart without permission. Little fucker wanted Pokémon cards and his mom, Cozy, said no, so he just took his bike and pedaled his ass there all by himself. Didn't even have enough money at the cash register to buy what he wanted, but a sweet old lady in line spotted him the difference. He was halfway back home with his stash before Cozy and Max even realized he'd left. He had to cross a major highway twice on his journey!

I was equal parts horrified and impressed.

Once upon a time, I thought Max's kids were going to be the only little ones in our lives. Me, Luke, and Wyatt all vowed to stay single and live off the mountain after Robyn fucked with all of our hearts.

Now Wyatt's messed everything up.

"We didn't do our Dark Night last year because you wanted us to go to a sex club." Wyatt's deep voice reverberates in my ears. "It was a fucked-up suggestion for many reasons, but our pact still stands. Brotherhood, family, and mountain life over all else. Trista and Stevie don't change that. They've just been added to the pact. Unless you have a problem with my fiancée and daughter being a part of our family?"

"You know I love Stevie," I snap, my hand tightening around my beer. "And your wife gave me Milkshake . . ." My voice catches in my throat as I think of my little fuzzball waiting for me back home. "You know I love her for that."

"Then, what the hell are you whining about?" Luke asks, losing patience with me.

"I need a fucking date for this wedding trip. You're bringing the lumber chick. What do you call her? Roe?"

"That's just a nickname. Her name is Addison," Luke corrects smugly, naming the girl he locked in weeks ago.

She's the daughter at the company we buy most of our building materials through. I'm tempted to give Luke the *don't shit where you eat* speech because if he fucks with our lumber supply, we're going to have big business problems that we don't need. But I don't have the energy to tell my younger brother what an idiot he is. I'm too depressed.

"Can I bring my cat?" I ask, feeling desperate and mopey. "Maybe if I could bring Milkshake, I wouldn't care if I don't find a date."

"You know how creepy you sound, right?" Luke asks pointedly.

"Yes."

"Begging to bring your own pussy to Mexico?"

"Shut the fuck up, Luke."

"Just saying . . . people are going to think you're fucking that cat the way you're being so weird with it. First the baby carrier, now you want to take it on an international flight? What kind of fucked up shit do you get up to at that sex club, anyways?"

My chair scrapes loudly on the floor as I lunge for Luke and yank him out of his seat. He laughs and holds his hands up defensively as I pull back my fist to sock him in the nose.

But before I can send my fist of fury flying, I make eye contact with Judy who is approaching with our three plates of food. She says nothing. She just gives me *that look*. It's a look that only a mother can give. A look that silently says *Throw that punch and it will be the last thing you do, Calder Fletcher.*

I growl my frustration and release a chortling Luke back into his seat, dropping into my own to accept my food in sulky silence.

I'm supposed to be the hot, charismatic brother. The one who has no problem finding pussy that isn't of the four-legged variety. What is happening to me?

I need a new place to look for a date. Somewhere that's not in my backyard and not on my screwed-up dating apps. I need a viable option. Someone with well-defined expectations. Someone who understands clear-cut rules and boundaries and accepts that there's zero chance of a relationship at the end of the trip.

My eyes light up as an idea comes to mind. It might just be crazy enough to work.

Chapter 3

WE DON'T FUCK THE DEVIL

Calder

The familiar scent of vanilla and antiseptic permeates my nose as I walk into the dark and moody lounge of Lexon Club just east of Denver. This is a members-only spot for sex-positive individuals looking to exercise all sorts of kinks. Judgment-free. And with very strict rules.

Both male and female eyes turn, and I feel my body heat as their gazes move over every inch of me. I roll up my flannel sleeves to reveal my inked forearms because the bad-boy persona serves me well here. And hell, it serves me well pretty much anywhere. I got my first tattoo when I was only sixteen, and my three brothers were so scared of what my mother's reaction would be, they all went out and got tattoos as well to try to soften the blow for me.

We were all grounded for the entire summer.

At the time, I thought the Flatirons on the inside of my bicep were worth the punishment. I was in my rebel teenager phase. But as I grew older, I began reworking the ink to add more meaning. My most recent addition was my dad's favorite saying . . . *We're not here for a long time, we're here for a good time.* It's etched around mountain peaks on the inside of my forearm, and every time I look at it, I'm hit with memories of my dad. It's been almost three years since he passed now, and it still stings to think about him. Grief is a fucking bitch. And thoughts of my dead dad are not something I should be entertaining when walking into a sex club.

"Well, where they hell have you been, Calder?" A deep voice rumbles from behind the bar, and I turn to see Tyson, the bartender that's been here ever since I first stepped foot in this club years ago. "It's been years, I swear."

I nod at that comment. I haven't been back to Lexon since my dad passed. Guess I just wasn't up for it. It's probably why I wanted my brothers to come with me last year, to help shake me out of my funk. But they refused.

Pussies.

I frown at that thought . . . calling them *pussies* feels derogatory now that I'm a proud cat daddy. Then again it should have felt derogatory to women for all the years I've used it. Self-awareness is an embarrassing bitch sometimes.

"I've been busy, I guess," I reply as Tyson hands me a bottle of beer. I glance around, not recognizing any faces. "It's packed in here tonight."

"It's newbie night," he offers with a twinkle in his eye. "Non-members can check out the club, get a tour of everything, try some things out, and see what they think."

My brows lift. I remember my first tour. Glory Hole Alley and the Milking Station were not on my bingo card that night, but there they both were . . . staring back at me with various stations of towels, lube, and washrooms to clean up afterward.

Talk about baptism by lube.

My eyes scan the various couples and singles all mingling and having drinks. There's often theme nights at the sex club: couples night, single females, single males. Newbie nights, however, are a free-for-all. You'll get all types in on a night like tonight, and I spot several pink wristbands indicating the first-time visitors. The pink bands are to serve as a bit of warning to the regulars of the club. Go slow, be gentle, and request consent twice. This club is good at rule-following. Which is why I think it could be the perfect spot to find a plus-one for this tropical getaway coming up soon.

My gaze drops to the floor where I spot a curvy blonde on her knees in a collar and leash. She's wearing a leather mask, and her long hair spills out below it. I drink in the lines of her body dressed in a super short black corset dress that reveals a few dimples in her thighs. She has pale, supple skin, and the large globes of her ass capture my attention. She looks good enough to eat. I wonder if her Dom would share her for the night, and then I spot the pink wristband. She's a newbie, so it's not likely.

My eyes widen when the Dom jerks the woman's leash and yanks her back toward him. Her hands slip out from under her, and she stumbles, her face nearly connecting with the heavily lacquered wood. I cringe and force myself to look away. I don't like to yuck anyone's yum, but BDSM isn't my favorite of all the kinks, even if a sub would make a good date for Mexico.

In all the years I've been coming here, I still haven't really figured out what my kink is. I guess you could call me an equal opportunity participator. I'll try anything once. Even tried dabbling in dick during a pretty heated group session once. A masculine set of lips wrapped around my cock wasn't all that different from a woman's. But by the end of the night, I deduced being with a man wasn't something I needed to explore again.

The female body is just far more alluring to me. Soft and compliant. Strong yet still supple. Big, medium, small . . . I appreciate it all. Only sampling one body type is like picking one food to eat for the rest of your life. A damn shame. I crave a mixture—a buffet of flesh in all shapes and sizes. Variety is the spice of life, after all.

"I can't breathe in this fucking thing!" a female voice shrieks, and I freeze with the bottle of beer between my lips. I think I recognize that voice.

Jerking around, I gaze back at the blonde on the floor to see her sitting back on her heels and struggling with the strap of the mask. Her outburst is drawing the eyes of the people at the Dom's table, and he doesn't look pleased.

"I didn't say you could take that off," he growls and yanks her chain again to bring her to heel.

"I don't give a shit. My knees are killing me," she retorts as she struggles with the strap. "And this mask smells like ass. Who wore this before me? I hope you washed it."

"That is none of your concern." The Dom looks around the room as everyone watches the scene escalate with rapt fascination. A Dom with no control of his sub isn't a familiar sight this club. "Leave it on and sit down at my feet, or you will be punished."

She laughs and presses her hands to the floor to stand, revealing her garter belt and thigh highs. She's stunning.

"Lambchop."

"What?" The Dom's eyes go wide.

"Lambchop." She props her hands defiantly on her hips. "That's my safe word, right? Lambchop, lambchop, lambchop."

The man looks up at her completely flabbergasted. "You're only supposed to use your safe word when I'm pushing you to your limits, pet. We haven't even gone upstairs yet."

"I don't care. This isn't my thing. I don't know what my thing is. But this isn't it. This is just . . . hard on the knees."

She finally rips her mask off and confirms what I suspected to be true. The bratty sub is none other than Dakota Schaefer from my hometown of Boulder, Colorado. She's my oldest brother's wife's best friend, a T-shirt shop owner downtown, a former client whose house I renovated many years ago . . . *and the biggest pain in my ass for the past seven years.*

She removes her collar and plunks it loudly on the table. "I'm going to go check out some of those voyeur rooms. Have a good life, sir." She gives him a cheery salute, and I watch in awe as she turns on her heel and confidently marches up the staircase that leads to the themed sex rooms.

With a frown, I chug down my beer and struggle with what to do next. The reason I've appreciated this damn club all these years is because I'm anonymous here. My brothers and I have a sordid past with women back home, and I thought I was safe here. Invisible.

Leave it to Dakota-fucking-Schaefer to prove me wrong.

Without realizing it, I've carried myself up the stairs over to the theater room. It has one-way glass wrapped around three walls for voyeurs to watch, and from the crowd gathered, I suspect there's some heavy action going on inside already. My eyes scan through the watchers in search of Dakota, and there's not a blonde in sight. I begin to worry she took a wrong turn. I can't imagine Dakota at the Milking Station or, worse yet, Gangbang Lane. Before turning to leave, I glance at the sizable orgy going on down inside the theater, and my fists clench when I spot her.

"No fucking way," I say under my breath and am immediately shushed by the couple beside me.

I press my face to the glass and watch in rapt fascination as Dakota stands in the middle of the U-shaped sofa, watching the group around her nervously like she's not sure where to insert herself.

She's in way over her head.

There's at least six couples and trios going at it. Hard. Women eating out other women, men taking women from behind over the arms of the sofa. A pair of men sucking on a woman's breasts as she holds another man's mouth at her cunt.

Normally . . . I'd be hard right now.

Normally this would work me up into such a frenzy that I'd be desperate to find someone to join in on the fun with.

Tonight is not normal.

I'm too laser-focused on the bane of my existence looking nervous and unsure. Something I've *never* seen that girl look like a day in her fucking life.

Dakota is . . . well, if I'm being blunt, she's a bitch.

She knows it all, she doesn't want anyone else's opinion, she's demanding, impatient, nagging, and just . . . yeah, a total fucking Karen. The biggest mistake of my life was agreeing to help renovate her house years ago, and I swear she has made me pay for it ever since.

Yet still, I can't look away.

A half-naked older male approaches her from behind, and I feel my shoulders tense as he grips her wrist and plays with the pink band wrapped around it. He presses up behind her and whispers something in her ear, and I watch her recoil and shake her head, yanking her hand away.

"Come on, now . . . put him in his fucking place," I murmur and wipe the fog off the glass that my voice caused. "Where's the woman who turned a Dom into a sub just five minutes ago?"

When the man leans in to whisper in her ear again and she recoils for a second time, I see red. Heart hammering in my chest, I rush around the corner for the door and push my way through a swarm of sweaty, naked bodies, getting a handful of gropes with every step I take.

"Back the fuck off her," I growl at the dude as soon as I'm within spitting distance of him. The old geezer clearly failed to accept *no* the first time from a newbie, so he deserves no pleasantries from me. Using my shoulder, I insert myself between them and turn to face Dakota, who stares back at me with wide, horrified eyes.

"We are not here to play." I grab Dakota's hand in a claiming sort of way and add, "We're just watching."

"I didn't realize she was part of a couple." The man coos as he moves around me to take a full look at the two of us. I level him with a glare, and his brows quirk. "Maybe you both—"

"The answer is *no*," I bark and note that Dakota's breathing has picked up. I don't know if it's me or the guy freaking her out, but I expect I was breathing the same way when I spotted her kneeling at some asshole's feet five minutes ago.

Thankfully, her shock keeps her compliant for a rare moment, and she allows me to tuck her under my arm and move her through the crowd toward the exit. We have to step over a woman going down on another woman directly in front of the door, but when we're greeted with the quietness of the hallway, I sigh with relief.

Glancing around, irritation pricks the hairs on my neck as I spot all the voyeurs' eyes on us. I grab Dakota's wrist again and pull her away from the theater while fighting the strange urge to yell at all of them to look the fuck away. I don't even like this girl, but right now she's a newbie and she seems uncomfortable, so I'm trying not to read too much into my overprotective reaction.

I find a closet-size private room at the end of a hallway. It's poorly lit, but at least it has a door with no windows for gawkers.

"What in the fucking hell are you doing here?" I hiss, trying not to draw the attention of the security cameras as I close the door as calmly as possible.

"What the hell are *you* doing here?" she repeats my question and struggles to cover her body, clearly mortified to be so naked in front of me. Her curves glow in the dim yellow light overhead, and I feel my body reacting carnally to her. It's hard not to be turned on in a place like this, even by someone I can't stand.

Jaw clenched, I begin unbuttoning my flannel—and feel all the air escape my lungs when Dakota's small but mighty palms shove me across the room until my back hits the wall.

"I am not fucking you, Calder Fletcher," she exclaims, her voice shrill as her fingers gouge into my pecs.

"I am not fucking *you,* Dakota Schaefer," I roar back as I rip the last few buttons on my shirt in haste. I stand before her in nothing but my faded jeans and black boots as I hold my flannel out. "Would you cover yourself up, for fuck's sake?"

She looks at my shirt like it's covered in fleas. "Why? Am I that disgusting to you? Well, get the hell over it because I can wear what I want here. I don't give a fuck if my body disgusts you or not."

"You think your body is disgusting?" My jaw drops at her insane response.

Her head yanks back. "No, but you obviously do, or you wouldn't be trying to cover me up right now."

I bite my lip, holding back the irritation billowing up inside of me. In all the years I've known this woman, she never fucking *hears* me. It's like we speak two different languages. Every damn decision she had to make on her house with me felt like we were trying to solve the square root of pi. It was excruciating.

"I'm offering you my shirt because I can't talk to you when you're half-naked."

My eyes have a mind of their own and move down her body a little more slowly this time. This isn't the same body she had when I met her seven years ago as the best friend of my niece's nanny. Back then she was a slip of a thing but still just as spunky. In the years that have passed, she's been married and had some changes in her form. None of which are disgusting.

Noticeable, yes. Disgusting . . . hell no.

Her body is just as annoyingly delectable as it always has been. I'd be half-attracted to her if she didn't speak. Maybe that's my kink: a silent partner.

"Well, that's good you can't talk to me when I'm half-naked because I don't want you to talk to me at all." She flips her hair as she moves to open the door.

"Just tell me what you're doing here," I command as my hand flattens on the wood to press it closed again.

Her arm brushes against my abs as she struggles with the door-knob, and I feel my body tremble at her proximity. She turns and looks up at me, her nostrils flaring in defiance.

God, she'd make a stunning brat.

"You tell me first," she quips.

"I'm a member here," I answer through clenched teeth.

"Of course you are." She rolls her eyes. "You couldn't be more predictable."

"You couldn't be more annoying." I step back and toss my flannel into her chest and eye her firmly. "Aren't you married? That guy in there definitely wasn't your husband."

"I'm divorced, you idiot." She flings my flannel back in my face. "I haven't been with Randal for over a year."

My jaw clenches at the mention of his name. If I hate Dakota by ten, I hate Randal by a million. However, it was easier to file Dakota away in the Married and Gone Forever category after we first met. Otherwise I might have been tempted to engage with her during my fuckboy phase when we first met. The woman drives me batshit crazy, and when she was married, she was a lot less bothersome.

"So, what . . . you're here to find a new husband?" I ask with a quirk of my brow.

"Are you here to find a wife?" she volleys back.

"I come regularly for fun. You sure as fuck don't."

"Well, that's true, this was my first time, but if you're a member here, then don't worry about it. I'll just find another club."

"Another club?" I feel breathless at the thought. "Why do you want to go to another club?"

"To stay away from you, ya creep!"

"I mean why are you suddenly so desperate to hang out at a sex club?"

"It's none of your damn business, Calder," she snaps and then shoves me against the wall to thrust her finger in my face. "And if you tell Max or Cozy about this, I will dismember you, got it? Your dick will be so fucked-up, the club will kick you out for scaring away their other members."

Her chest presses up against me, and I can't help but smile at her spark. God, I really do love to hate this woman. This raging nag was impossible to please on her house reno. I bet she's impossible to please in the bedroom too.

"Tell me why you're hanging out at sex clubs and your secret is safe with me, boss." I quirk my brow at her. "Is this a midlife crisis?"

"I'm thirty-three, you asshole." She jerks away from me.

"Exactly, you're too young for this shit."

"You're like two years older than me!"

"And a hell of a lot more experienced, which is why I know that a place like this isn't for a girl like you."

"Like you know what kind of girl I am."

"Oh, I've got some ideas," I state with confidence. You really get to know someone when you work together on a renovation. And all it took was one damn setback to send her over the edge.

Recalling that epic blowout we had all those years ago still gives me the chills.

"What did that guy say to you in there, anyways?"

"In where?"

"The theater room," I snap, my patience wearing with every passing second. "What did he say to you to make you uncomfortable? I need to know."

"Why?"

"Because I will beat his fucking face in and get him kicked out of this club if he was inappropriate." I feel my shoulders tense as I grip my flannel in my hand and prepare for whatever comes out of her mouth next.

Dakota's brows furrow, and I feel my own face falling in confusion. Why am I so worked up over this? *Inappropriate* is kind of the name of the game here. Yes, people are allowed to have boundaries and ask for consent, but coming to a place like this is designed to push you outside your comfort zone. I need to chill the fuck out.

"Won't beating someone's face in get you kicked out of this club too?" Dakota asks, her head tilting like she's trying to figure me out.

I close my eyes and lick my lips. "Just tell me what he said to you. Please."

"A *please* from Calder Fletcher. Has hell frozen over?" Her gaze moves down my naked chest and lingers over my abs, and I feel my cock stir with interest. Down, boy . . . She's the devil. We don't fuck the devil.

Dakota must take mercy on me, because she finally answers my question. "He asked if he could take a dump on my chest."

My lips curl with disgust. "Are you serious?"

"Yes, and I swore I'd keep an open mind here tonight, but poop play is a hard limit for me."

"Poop play?" I repeat her words and feel my shoulders begin to shake as I use my shirt to cover my smirk.

"Is that not what it's called?" she asks, deathly serious, and that tips me over the edge.

My body erupts, and I brace my hands on my knees as I buckle over with laughter. "Only you."

"*Only me* what?"

"Only you would attract the one and only scat-kink guy in the club."

"Go fuck yourself, Calder," she says and makes a move to leave again. "I'm going back in."

"The hell you are." I force my shirt back over her chest and grab her shoulders, making a motion to open the door for her. "You're coming with me."

"Where?" she asks, and I swear I see a flick of desire shoot through her eyes. Does she want to go somewhere kinky? With *me*?

I swallow the knot in my throat. "I'm taking you home."

"No, you're not." She yanks out of my grasp, and her voice is loud in the small room. "I paid to be here."

"I'll pay you back."

"I don't care." Her eyes flare with determination. "You're not my daddy, Calder. You're just the guy who fucked up my house seven years ago. House-killer!"

"Would you stop throwing that in my face every time you see me?" I growl, stepping close to loom over her. She's maybe five foot seven but still feels small compared to my six foot three. Even tinier in a place like this. "Let's fucking go."

I wrap my arm around her waist and she pulls back, staring at me with a look that gets right under my skin. I rumble a curse under my breath as I step close and bend at the waist, throwing her up over my shoulder in one fell swoop.

"Calder Fletcher, put me down!" she exclaims, kicking her feet and batting her hands on my back.

"Not a chance," I grunt as her knee connects with my gut. "You're practically family, and you're not getting shit on on my watch, no matter how much I can't stand you."

When I swing the door open to carry her ass out of here, I come face-to-face with one of the security guards. The big one.

"Put her down," the guy booms, his voice leaving no room for interpretation.

"She doesn't belong here."

"She signed all the documents."

"I don't care," I reply, feeling anxiety creep up inside me if he doesn't let me get her out of here. "She's coming with me."

"If you don't put her down, you will be permanently banned from this establishment."

"I know her!" I argue and try to move past him.

"Don't care," he grinds back and continues blocking my path. "Put her down, or we're calling the cops."

I growl angrily and drop my flannel as I place Dakota back on her feet. She hobbles in her heels, and the giant man moves between us to grab my arms and cinch them tightly behind my back. Dakota moves back to allow him room to manhandle me out the doorway.

"Dakota, tell him you know me. We're . . . *friends*." The word is a complete lie, but I'll say whatever I must to not get kicked out. If Poop Play guy gets to stay, I sure as fuck should get to stay.

The guard stops shoving me down the hallway long enough to face Dakota. She's leaning back on the doorframe holding my flannel shirt over her shoulder like she's posing for some fucked-up catalog called Cunts and Cowboys. Honestly, it's not a bad look. Except for the fact that she's watching me struggle with a gleeful twinkle in her eye that I do not like.

"Miss . . . is that true? Do you know this man?"

Silence falls between us as Dakota's brows lift and I wait for her to save me from this guy's death grip, which is definitely going to leave a bruise. Finally, after what feels like hours, she replies, "I've never seen him before in my life."

Chapter 4

FLYING SOLO

Calder

"God, I love having a rich big brother," I state grandly as I stretch my long legs out on the luxury leather seat of the private plane Max upgraded the whole family to for this destination-wedding trip to Mexico.

"This is all free too?" Trista asks the flight attendant around a mouthful of cheese. She stands in the aisle by the table where a charcuterie board and various fancy prepackaged snacks are laid out all neat and tidy. The flight attendant tells her yes for the third time while refilling her champagne flute. She smiles over at me and Wyatt. "Holy shit, this is awesome!"

Trista stuffs some snacks in her purse, and Wyatt laughs and shakes his head from his window seat facing directly across from me. He's holding a sleeping Stevie in his arms, but that doesn't stop Trista from shooting him a dirty look when she sits down beside him. "They're for after we land. Max said it's a long drive to the villa."

I glance back at Max in the window seat behind me, with his wife Cozy tucked comfortably beside him. Those two look much more natural in this posh setting. Max in the business suit that he apparently wears even on vacation, and Cozy in some loungewear set that probably cost more than all the clothes in my closet.

Max is a big-shot businessman in Boulder. He took a very different path in life from us younger three Fletcher brothers. Wyatt, Luke, and I all chose to work for my dad's construction company pretty much straight out of high school and never wanted much else. It wasn't until Dad passed away that we had to get our shit together and start managing more than just punching the clock and taking orders from him. Now we all have our own niches.

Wyatt is the second oldest of us and is crazy passionate about renewable resources. He has us building new smart homes all over Boulder instead of the typical house-flipping we used to do. He's already bitched about the excess carbon emissions from this jet five times since we boarded. He's real fun at parties.

Luke is the youngest of our family and always took a shine to the business side of construction. He's our estimator and works with the vendors we buy our materials from. He manages our payroll too, or I wouldn't have a clue how much we profit on the projects we complete.

Me? I like to fuck off. Still.

In my younger years, my big, delusional dream was to go pro in hockey, but I blew out my knee sophomore year and never got back full function. Now I hobble around with Luke in an over-forty league that drinks more than it skates. I stay in the league to keep active, though. I'm not a big gym rat, and after our reasonably fit father died of a heart attack out of nowhere, we all worry about our health more than ever.

And sex just so happens to be a great workout, which is why I stay active on the apps. Or did . . . before someone fucked with my shit.

Mostly, I'm the muscle of our business and do all the heavy lifting. However, I have a small passion in outdoor furniture design. I make the odd chair or bench or end table when the mood strikes. Even did my first custom crib for little Stevie that didn't turn out half-bad.

But the most grown-up thing I ever did was build my own cabin on Wyatt's property. Luke and I worked our asses off helping Wyatt develop the land and make it as self-sustainable as his little eco-heart desired. Once all that work was done, Wyatt ended up offering up small plots for us to live up there too.

Fletcher Mountain is a fucking dream. We could survive an apocalypse on that peak, and to know we built it all with our bare fucking hands like pioneers feels meaningful. It was an incredible gift for Wyatt to let us build up there. And he only throws it in our faces once or twice a year.

Holidays are stressful.

Aside from a few brotherly brawls, the three of us are living the family-compound dream. We carpool into Boulder for all our construction projects, our mom brings lunch to the job sites regularly, and Max joins us for our monthly poker nights. Everly and Ethan visit often, or we come to town to spend time with them. We see Ethan more than Everly these days for obvious reasons. But overall, there's not much more a man could want in life.

Except maybe a private plane.

And a helicopter. A helicopter would make the times we get snowed in a hell of a lot easier.

I turn around and reach back for a fist bump with Ethan. He's seated behind Max and Cozy with my mother, Johanna. I can't help but notice how much he looks like his mother Cozy with her dark hair and eyes. Everly got her lighter features from her biological mom, Max's first wife, Jess. But Ethan's going to be a heartbreaker with those dark lashes. And his wild side will be attention-grabbing, for sure. I like to think the little shit takes after me, which drives my uptight brother crazy.

Across the aisle from them in the way back is Luke, who's looking real comfy with Addison. I'm a little worried about shit being awkward between these two after this trip . . . but as long as he doesn't fall in love with her, we'll be just fine. I can't lose another brother to a woman.

Everly is currently on her own first-class flight from Dublin to meet us. She's on Easter break from university, and I'm excited to see my little shithead niece, even if she did singlehandedly sabotage my chances of finding my own plus-one. I've been texting her for the past week asking why she's fucking up all my dating apps, and she acts like she has no idea what I'm talking about. I'm still not completely certain it wasn't one of my brothers who fucked with my shit. But I even feel like my sister-in-law Cozy has been acting weird around me. I don't know who's to blame, but someone is going to pay when I find out.

Because now I'm going on a sexy, tropical vacation . . . with my hand. Apparently, this villa Max bid on at some charity auction last year is in a remote location, so I won't even have fellow resort guests as potential for random hookups.

Fucking kill me.

If Dakota hadn't got me kicked out of Lexon, then maybe I would have a nice little submissive plus-one in the open seat next to me. Someone who could call me *Master* when we get back to our room at night. Someone who's a lady in the streets and a freak in the sheets. I would have loved to play that game all week.

Trista leans into Wyatt to check on Stevie in his arms, dropping a soft kiss to her chestnut hair. "Baby's first plane ride at only three months old, and it's private. This little girl is going to grow up to be such a brat."

"Speaking of brats," I murmur as I spot a burst of blond hair climbing up the jet steps.

"Who is it?" Wyatt asks, looking over his shoulder.

"Calder." Cozy reaches around from behind me and pinches my arm. "Dakota is my best friend, and she's been through a lot lately, so you will be nice to her this week? Plus, this is Wyatt and Trista's big trip, and none of us want to hear you two bickering all the damn time."

"They're like an old married couple," Max adds with an amused harrumph.

"Yeah," Trista adds with a smirk and kicks me lightly in the shin. "Be good or I'll go bridezilla on you."

I frown at the sudden gang-up, irritated that I'm automatically pegged as the bad guy. I swear I could be living in a foreign country and everyone would still ride my ass about something. I pull my hoodie up over my messy hair and slump down into my seat as Dakota boards the plane. Glancing at the spot open beside me, I quickly grab my backpack off the floor and toss it on the seat so she doesn't get any bright ideas.

She sees my movement and hits me with one of her punishing Karen glowers.

"Seat's taken," I mutter in a Forrest Gump accent.

"Real mature, Killer."

"I'll sit next to the jerk," Trista offers, jumping up out of her seat and carrying her bag of stolen free snacks with her. She tosses my bag to the floor and sits down next to me, jabbing me pointedly with her elbow.

"Don't you want to be by the baby?" Dakota asks, glancing down to Wyatt with an uneasy look. "I'm not great with babies."

"I'm right across from her. It'll be fine."

"Plus, it's my turn anyways!" my mom coos, appearing with her grabby little hands to take my niece from my brother. "Nanna is on duty all this week! You two are supposed to be enjoying yourselves." She mushes her lips into Stevie's cheeks, stirring her from her sleep.

"I was enjoying myself," Wyatt mumbles with a scowl.

Mom rolls her eyes and heads back to her seat.

The minute Dakota lowers herself into the spot across from me, I realize I have made a grave error. Images of her in that black corset dress last weekend flash through my mind: the garters, the thigh-high stockings, the way her icy blue eyes were bright even in that dark closet. The way she smirked when she let the bouncer throw me out. My chest feels heavy in her presence, and I turn to look away before she can read the dirty images racing through my head.

"Sit by your fiancée, Wyatt, you asshole," I grumble and grab my bag up off the floor to move over to his seat.

Wyatt looks at me like I'm a moron as he stands and I quickly drop down into his seat, pinning my eyes to the window and ignoring the faint smell of Dakota's perfume that I remember from the other night. The pilot begins talking over the loudspeaker now that everyone has boarded. Let's get this damn trip over with.

Chapter 5

Everly

"No hay habitaciones adicionales disponibles, ¿verdad?" I say to the house manager for the fifth time in my rough Spanish. I took it all through high school, so it's not the best, but I'm hopeful it's getting my request across.

"Sí, señorita," the short butler with a thick mustache replies with a wink. "No hay habitaciones adicionales disponibles."

"Big, tattooed, bearded guy? Him and la señorita rubia en la palapa, sí?" I point to the thatched roof covered in dried palms peeking out at the back of the villa on the oceanside. I arrived an hour before my family to get the lay of the land and decided that was the perfect spot.

Carlos nods and smiles, giving me a hearty thumbs-up and a big wink. Okay, good. I've got him on board with my plan.

What is my plan, exactly?

To force my uncle Calder and my stepmom's best friend, Dakota, to share a suite at this stunning villa in Puerto Vallarta, Mexico.

Because I am a mastermind!

I smile and sip the margarita the house greeters presented me with when I arrived. This trip is already off to a great start. That is, until Calder and Dakota learn that due to a supposed pipe leak, there are no longer enough bedrooms at the villa, and unfortunately, two people are going to have to share. And since I'm sharing a room with my grandma and little brother, Calder and Dakota are the only other two singles left to share a room.

Insert evil villain laugh.

A large black sprinter van turns down the lane that leads to the property, so I quickly set my drink down to jump up and wave as they traverse around the giant courtyard fountain to park in front of me. I was home over Christmas, so I got to meet my new cousin Stevie when she was born, but it's been nearly three months since then, and I'm dying to see how much the little squirt has changed.

Uncle Luke and Calder are the first off the van, and they both stretch their arms out to me for a hug.

I sprint toward them only to swat their arms away and dive into the van for my cousin. I find Trista in the back struggling to get her car seat unlatched.

"Oh my God, she's huge!" I exclaim when I lay my eyes on her. "And look at all that hair!"

"She is growing so fast. She loves the tit," Trista replies with a laugh.

"She's not the only one," my uncle Wyatt murmurs quietly causing my nose to wrinkle.

"Gross, Uncle Wyatt," I groan and quickly make an executive decision to unbuckle my cousin and pull her into my arms. She smells like baby, and I love her.

"Be careful," Wyatt chastises, and I roll my eyes as I slowly step out of the van behind him with his arms outstretched like I'm going to drop her.

"I got her."

"Hey there, kid," a voice says from the other side of the van, and I smile as I step into my father's familiar embrace, unsurprised he's wearing a suit and tie in Mexico. He's always on the clock.

Cozy appears beside him and reaches in to join the hug just as my brother Ethan whizzes past us.

"Ocean!" he screams, taking off for the beach.

My grandma laughs. "Good thing I wore my tennis shoes," she calls back with a wave as she chases after him. "Hi, Everly. I'll get my hug later!"

Once released from my dad and stepmom, I turn to see my three bearded uncles all standing in a line with their arms folded over their chests. Only these three weirdos would wear jeans to the beach. They all glower at me expectantly, and with a heavy sigh I pass Stevie off to Trista and make my way over to pay the toll.

The three of them crush me in a giant group bear hug, and I squeal when Calder begins ruffling my blond hair and yanks it out of the loose braid I tied it back into.

"Stop!" I exclaim with a laugh, pulling away and shoving at the three of them as they continue messing with me. "God, you guys are obsessed with me."

"Damn straight," Uncle Calder says without any humor in his voice.

"Missed you, Evie-girl," Luke adds shamelessly, pulling the brim of his baseball cap down low to hide his eyes.

I smile warmly. The truth is, I've missed all of them too. Growing up, they were constants in my life. We had weekly uncle date nights in town, and I got to hang out on the mountain whenever I wanted. I tended to Wyatt's pet goat, Millie. We even all saw Taylor Swift together! I mean, if that doesn't bond a niece with her three uncles for life, I don't know what could.

They're the best.

Being all the way in Ireland for school is a lot harder than I thought it would be. I miss the comforts of home, and I feel like I'm missing out on so much. Uncle Wyatt has become a dad and a soon-to-be husband, and I only get glimpses of it! And I'm pretty sure my brother has grown an inch since Christmas. I don't even know who this woman is that Luke brought to Mexico. I miss everyone something fierce, but I will *never* tell my dad that. He'd be all too willing to say *I told you so* and bring me back home for good.

I need to see this abroad experience through, even if I do cry myself to sleep on a pretty regular basis.

"Hola, señoras y señores," Carlos says, joining us out in the courtyard. "Welcome to La Casa de los Pájaros . . . the House of the Birds. I am your butler for the week. Mi nombre es Carlos."

"Did he say *birds*?" Dakota murmurs from her spot by Cozy as she gives me a quick squeeze.

I inspect Dakota with fresh eyes, since it's been a while. She's dressed in an adorable linen matching short set, and her blond hair looks like it's curling from the humidity already. She's gorgeous.

We first met back when Cozy was my nanny and not my stepmom. Dakota does these tie-dye classes out of her T-shirt shop, and I always admired how easy she made running a business all on her own look. She's the total package, beauty and brains.

But it wasn't until I saw her and my uncle Calder fighting at my graduation party last year that I knew she'd be perfect for him. Calder needs a strong female figure to settle him down. And no one fights with someone that much if they don't have some level of underlying passion. A matchmaker notices these things.

"We hope you had a pleasant journey," Carlos continues, snapping my attention back to the moment. "I have keys to all of your individual suites, and our staff is here twenty-four seven to help you with your bags, schedule you for relaxing massages, make you fresh guacamole, take you on drives into town. Anything you desire . . . you just ask one of us and we will make your dreams come true. Okay?"

As if on cue, a couple of servers waltz out of the house with trays of margaritas to greet everyone. I grab a fresh drink, and my dad scowls at me.

"Hey, I'm legal drinking age here," I state with a shrug. "And I'm legal in Ireland."

My dad shakes his head. "God help me."

"These are free too?" Trista exclaims with a smile and covers her mouth like she didn't mean to say that part out loud.

I've missed her too. She literally barreled into all of our lives like the most unexpected miracle . . . giving me a cousin, filling my uncle's barn with all sorts of amazing animals, and making my grumpy, quiet uncle Wyatt happier than I've ever seen him. The fact that I brought them together brings me so much joy I could burst.

Now it's Calder's turn.

Carlos begins to pass out keys, taking special care to make eye contact with me to ensure he's giving the right keys to the right individuals.

When he comes to give me my key, I eye him warily. "Carlos . . . you could have mentioned you spoke English when I arrived."

"Oh, but your Spanish is very good, señorita."

I hit him with a look.

He winces. "Good-ish." He winks and gestures to everyone. "You all can follow the staff inside the main house, and they will see you to your room. You two . . . please follow me."

Calder and Dakota both freeze in place, looking at each other and then back to Carlos, confused for being singled out.

"You two have a different oceanside room. Right this way," Carlos says reassuringly as he leads them toward the cobblestone path that wraps around to the back of the house.

"What are you up to, Everly?" Cozy murmurs into my ear when she spots me watching them with a knowing smirk.

"Oh, ya know . . . just mastermind shit."

Chapter 6

PALAPA FOR TWO

Calder

The house is fucking stunning . . . not that I get to see much of it because this Carlos guy is taking me and Dakota and our bags around to the back of the damn house. Though the view of the ocean we're walking toward definitely isn't going to suck.

"You are in the palapa," Carlos says excitedly. "Very nice accommodations. Wide-open walls so you hear ocean all night long. Most guests' first choice."

"Then, shouldn't Wyatt and Trista have it?" Dakota asks, her voice sounding unsure.

"They requested to be inside the main house to be close to la abuela to help with el niños."

I nod and roll my eyes. So, because my brother needs my mother to be his nanny for the week, I'm stuck in the bunkhouse with Karen.

Great.

However, when we round the corner to the back of the house, my jaw drops when I see where Carlos is taking us.

I guess I didn't know what a palapa was, but it's this cool, round, grass-hut-topped tower. Like a Mexican version of a castle turret or a really sick treehouse. He leads us up a winding staircase that goes past this tall, wrought-iron birdcage that's wrapped around a tree and full of exotic birds.

"You can feed the birds anytime!" Carlos says excitedly as he reaches into a container nearby and grabs some seed. As if on command, three birds dart toward the vertical bars.

"Cool," I reply in awe as their little claws wrap around the metal and slide down to meet his hands full of birdseed.

Carlos smiles and pats his hands clean before continuing up the steps. I gesture for Dakota to go before me, but she shakes her head and refuses.

"What's your problem?"

She swallows and holds her bag up like a coat of armor. "I hate birds."

"You hate birds?"

She nods. "Ever since I was a kid."

"Why? They're just birds."

"Are you kidding?" she snaps venomously. "They're gross with their beady little eyes. And did you see their giant talon feet wrap around those bars? Imagine those on your neck! Or gouging your eyes out! And I'm not convinced they're not all government drones eavesdropping on all our conversations."

I tip my head back and laugh at the grave tone of her voice. She's dead fucking serious, and it reminds me of my brother. "You and Wyatt should start a club."

"I'll be fine. I just need a minute," she says, shaking me off as she works to build up the courage to go up the stairs and walk right past them.

"Would it help if I banged on the cage to scare them back?" I whack the metal bars and send a couple flying.

"Knock it off, Calder!" Dakota screeches. "You're going to make them angry! God, you're such an ass."

"Stop being such a baby and come on," I reply with a laugh. "Or do you need me to carry you again?"

Her eyes snap to mine, and a flash of that night at the sex club plays in the irises of them. "Don't bring up that night. Not here. Not anywhere."

"Tell me why you were there in the first place and maybe I'll let it go." I tweak my brows expectantly, just dying to hear the nitty-gritty details of her decision to go to Lexon.

She crosses her arms over her ample chest. "I was there for the same reasons everyone else was."

"Nah, there's a deeper reason. There always is." I bite my lip and eye her. I know my reason. I started going there after the Robyn bullshit fucked with my head. I wanted an escape unlike anything I'd ever experienced before. Something to put her as far out of my mind as possible.

And it worked.

Dakota's clear blue eyes zero in on my lips when she replies, "I'll tell you over my cold, dead body."

"That'll be kind of hard when you're dead," I reply with a huff. "Then again, you're probably besties with the devil, so I'm sure you'll figure it out. Just like you'll figure out how to get up these stairs all on your own eventually."

"Señor? Señorita?" Carlos's voice calls down the stairs to us. "Are you coming? The room is just up here."

"Come on, you big scaredy-cat," I tease and let out a laugh.

With a tiny growl, Dakota shoves me face first against the bird-cage, using me as a human shield between her and the birds as she marches past me.

I pull back and rub at the indent the cage made on my cheek as she scampers up the stairs to get as far away from the feathered beasts as possible.

I feel used.

But then I tilt my head and take in the view of her ass in those tiny linen shorts and feel mildly less bad about it.

My eyes flinch when I realize what I'm doing. I might need a little solo session when I get tucked away in my room because I'm way too horned-up if I'm willingly checking out the devil.

Carlos uses Dakota's key to open the first door we come upon, and I stand back, waiting my turn and admiring her room. It's huge. It has a big, round bed centered at one end with gauzy canopy hanging over it from the ceiling. There's a small, attached bathroom, and a sofa in a decent-size seating area beside a wide-open balcony that overlooks the ocean.

The suite looks like it takes up the whole damn floor, and I glance around, wondering where my room is going to be.

"Come in, señor," Carlos says, gesturing to me.

"Nah, that's okay," I say with a wave and turn my eyes to Dakota. "I know better than to enter the snake's pit."

She narrows her eyes at me.

"This is your room too."

"What?" Dakota and I both ask in unison.

"We had an issue with one of the other suites. Big pipe burst. Lots of damage. You two must share. But it's okay. This is the biggest suite, so lots of space for your luggage."

"You expect me to share with him?" Dakota steps closer to Carlos. She's not a tall girl, but she's towering over the short Mario-looking guy.

"Sí . . . it's the only option, señorita."

"No . . . no way," she exclaims, crossing her arms over her chest. "I'll sleep on a couch in the main house."

"There is a nice, pullout bed here." Carlos points to the sofa. "Very comfortable. And if you want privacy . . ." He walks over to the balcony and pulls out a thin white curtain that spans the length of the living space, separating the living area from the bedroom area. "Complete privacy."

I bark out a laugh when I can see Dakota's irritated stance through the see-through fabric.

"This will not work," she snaps and yanks the curtain open. "Why can't you go share with one of your brothers?"

"Um . . . have you not heard about the infamous Fletcher libido?"

"No, señor? Tell me of this libido," Carlos says, blinking curiously back at me.

I smile at him. "We like to fuck, Carlos. A lot."

Carlos presses his lips together, his wide eyes turning to get Dakota's reaction.

"They have to fuck a lot because they only last a couple minutes on a good day. It takes a few tries before they can satisfy their victims."

"You wish you knew that fact."

"I don't have to experience it to know it. The Fletcher brothers' reputation around town as minute-men is very well known."

"Ha!" I bark out a laugh. "And what's your reputation? Besides being a total Karen."

"I'm a Karen? Well, you're a Chad . . . getting ridiculous tattoos every other month and walking around like the president of the douchebag fraternity."

"Doesn't she look like a Karen, Carlos?"

"Doesn't he look like a Chad, Carlos?"

"I think . . . I will leave you two alone to discuss your room situation."

"Nothing to figure out," I state firmly with a glower at Dakota. "I'm perfectly happy with this room. If prudish Karen doesn't feel safe sleeping next to a Chad, then she can find a couch somewhere in the main house."

"You think you get the room before me?"

I shrug. "I don't have any issue with this situation. You seem to."

"Bullshit," Dakota snaps and steps into my space, her head tilted back to glare up at me. "You're just hoping if you act like you're fine with this, you'll get the room. I'm not giving it up."

"Well, neither am I," I thunder back, looming over her. Ignoring the way her perfume invades my nostrils and causes my body to react.

"¡Bien!" Carlos chimes, clapping his hands between us. "Enjoy your stay at La Casa de los Pájaros."

Chapter 7

FUCK YOU, FORREST GUMP

Dakota

God, I hate him. I hate everything about him. I hate that stupid beard he's been sporting for years. I hate his brown hair that's always sticking up all over the place. I hate those tattoos that completely cover his arms and make him think he's God's gift to women. I hate the way his greenish-blue eyes look like a disgusting, infested lake. I hate the way his square jaw always looks clenched like he needs to take a shit. And I hate how his brother is married to my best friend, and now I'm stuck with the asshole until the end of time!

I especially hate that he thinks I'm a Karen just because I don't want to share a room with him. "I'll show him a Karen," I mumble to myself as I yank my clothes out of my suitcase and begin hanging them in the closet.

"Gonna leave any room in there for me, Big K?"

I jut my chin toward him. "There are three hangers left. Here you go, Killer."

I walk over to where he stands by the balcony, and just as he reaches for the hangers, I toss them out the window onto the sandy beach below.

A slow smile creeps across his face. "Now who's the mature one?"

"That's for the Forrest Gump line on the plane."

"Did I hurt your feelers, Karen Kay? Is there actually a soul inside your big black heart?"

"Ugh," I growl and turn on my heel, whipping my hair in his stupid smug face. "Can you just go away and let me unpack in peace?"

"Sure thing, Snookems. Can I go to the house and get you anything? A snack? A fresh drink? An enema to help you get that stick out of your ass?"

"Yes, and why don't you get a personality for yourself while you're at it? You've obviously killed yours at some point in your life."

Calder grumbles under his breath but shockingly does leave the room for a moment. As soon as he's gone, I text Cozy a huge SOS message to come to the palapa asap.

I inhale a cleansing breath as I stare out at the ocean view, willing it to make this situation better. But a white sandy beach and turquoise water is no match for the rage that man evokes inside of me.

My head jerks around when I hear a knock at my door. I march over and swing it open to reveal my best friend. "Did you know about this?" I point to Calder's bag on the sofa.

"Everly told me there was some room mix-up." Cozy steps into the room, taking in the space with wide, impressed eyes.

I am less impressed. "Room mix-up? What the hell? I don't want to share a room with Calder. I'd rather share a room with your mother-in-law!"

She winces. "Johanna snores like a trucker."

"Cozy!" I cross my arms and stand with ten toes down to indicate how unfunny I think this all is.

I didn't even want to come on this trip because it was clearly all just family, but Cozy and Trista wouldn't take no for an answer. They both said I needed to celebrate the fact that my divorce is final, and what better way than a private jet and an all-expenses-paid trip.

And after what my divorce cost me, it sounded pretty good.

Randal and I separated over a year ago, but coming to terms on our assets was a deep, deep hell that I never want to think about ever again. He hired some big-shot lawyer out of Denver and tried to take half of my business. A business that I started all on my own before I even met him. A business that supported us for the seven years we were together. A business that he tried to mansplain to me on a regular basis!

"Why do you only sell T-shirts, Dakota? You should sell pants."

"Your business name should be catchier."

"Maybe you should hire a new designer and change your logo?"

"If you moved locations, you'd have more street traffic."

He had so much input on a company that he refused to ever work in, even after he was let go from the bar he managed. I asked him if he wanted to help out at my mail-order fulfilment center until he figured out his next steps, and he said no. He didn't want anything to do with The T-shirt Shop until the end, and I paid dearly for that, paying him a huge settlement to keep the things I bought with my own money. How I ever thought I was in love with that asswipe is beyond me.

And while celebrating my divorce being final with this trip sounded good in theory . . . I had other plans. Bigger plans.

Like visiting a sex club for the first time.

Which I haven't had the guts to tell my best friend about yet . . . and now I really don't want to tell her because of fucking Calder.

Like seriously, of all the sex clubs in Colorado, what were the odds that I would walk into the one he's a member of? It's not like going to sex clubs is a common thing. It's not like running into each other at the supermarket. There I was just browsing for dick, and then bam, the Calder Daily Special was announced on the loudspeaker.

Talk about completely mortifying.

I'm normally a pretty confident girl. Granted, I've gained some weight over the past five years, and my size-four jeans have been collecting dust for ages, but arguably this is my body now, like it or not. Or at least that's what I keep telling myself.

However, as I dip my toe back into the dating scene in a different body than when I left it seven years ago, insecurity needles at me. I'm older now, things aren't as perky as they once were, and the brazen confidence that was my bread and butter in my twenties has dulled in recent years. Which is why I felt good in the little outfit I painstakingly picked out for that night. A new outfit was the boost of confidence I needed for my big foray into the sex club.

That was until I found myself standing in front of Killer Calder Fletcher. The guy who literally leaves a wake of destruction wherever he goes. Ugh.

But I refused to let him see me squirm. The ass.

He totally fucked with my post-divorce plan, and now I'm too embarrassed to tell my best friend that her brother-in-law saw me nearly naked . . . at a sex club.

Double ugh.

I'm not so sure Cozy would understand my reasons for going there either. She knows of my struggles with Randal: the constant fights we'd have when he was drunk, and so on. But there's a lot I've kept from her. I didn't want to pop the love bubble she's been living in. She's all happy and domesticated now. A mother of two, a fledgling charcuterie board–making business she does for fun while being married to a millionaire who can charter private jets and take his family to Mexico. She doesn't need my drama.

We were childhood best friends who grew up watching *Family Feud* together and eating nutty bars in each other's living rooms. Me going to sex clubs isn't the life we dreamed of as kids. Maybe that life doesn't exist for me anymore.

"Don't hate me for saying this, but this room is huge and gorgeous. You can hear the ocean all night long." She pulls the curtain that separates the spaces. "Is it really that bad to share?"

"Yes, it's that bad," I whine. "Your brother-in-law is disgusting. I bet he doesn't shower the whole time we're here."

"It's not like you have to hang out in the room with him all day. You just need to sleep."

I roll my eyes and cross my arms, feeling stubborn about this.

"Okay, okay. Maybe Calder can bunk with Max in our room, and I can stay here with you."

My face falls. "I'm not about to rob you of a sexy getaway with your husband. Max will hate me! And he's pretty much the only civilized one of all the Fletcher brothers."

Cozy laughs at that and rubs a spot on her neck. "He has his caveman moments, but you're right. Those three living on the mountain together still kind of weirds me out. I can't imagine ever liking my sister enough to live next door to her on a remote property."

I cry in "only child syndrome" but agree, even though I have no context to compare to it. "They all kind of look the same too. Do you notice that?"

"Bearded, tattooed, flanneled, and shockingly well-scented? Yes, I do notice that."

My cheeks heat as I recall Calder's scent in the small closet at the sex club. It was unlike anything I'd ever smelled before. If he was a different man with that scent . . . who knows what would have happened in that tiny room.

Shaking off the heat rising up my cheeks I murmur, "I didn't notice the scent part."

"Max smells amazing too, don't get me wrong. But the others have a different musk to them."

"Can we stop talking about their musk, please? They're still all knuckle-dragging animals," I say with a harrumph. "Poor Johanna had to give birth to all those giant meatheads."

"She does kind of walk funny now that you mention it." Cozy giggles.

I give her a playful shove. "You're gross."

With a sigh, she drops down onto my bed. "Seriously, though . . . we'll figure this out. Carlos said there's some resorts down the road a ways. I can book you a room there, no problem."

I exhale heavily as Cozy begins checking out resorts on her phone. I really don't want her worrying about me on this trip. I'm already here free of charge, and I know she and Max won't let me pay for my own room somewhere else. The last thing I want to do is cost them more money just because of Calder's . . . musk.

Plus, if I could live with Randal for seven years and whatever version of himself he came home as at night, I can handle Calder Fletcher for a few days. He's child's play compared to my ex. And it's not like we'll be spending ample time in this room together like we're a couple. I've got this.

I grab her phone to stop her from looking. "Don't bother with a room. I'll be fine."

"Are you sure?" she asks with concern etched all over her face. "I want this trip to be nice for you."

"It will be, don't worry. But I swear if Calder does anything creepy, he doesn't get to come home on the plane. Deal?"

"Deal!" Cozy smiles triumphantly.

"And I get the big bed."

She nods in solidarity. "Cavemen are used to sleeping on the ground, anyways."

That brings a small grin to my face. I can handle this. It's just a few days. I can handle anything for a few days.

Chapter 8

BUMP, SET, SPIKE

Dakota

Welcome to the Fletcher/Matthews Wedding Extravaganza.
We hope you enjoy your time in Puerto Vallarta.

Here is the schedule of events:

Day 1: Poolside Fun & Wedding Planning
Day 2: Hen/Stag Night
Day 3: Excursion Day: Jet Skis
or Local Food Tour
Day 4: Rehearsal Dinner on Beach
Day 5: Wedding
Day 6: Home

I stare in awe at the itinerary Carlos hands me as I walk through the main house to join everyone by the pool. It's light and airy with floor-to-ceiling windows displaying the stunning foliage and ocean views all around the property. It's clearly recently been renovated because it's much more modern than the palapa. The palapa is a bit more of that rustic Mexican style. Still luxurious and beautiful, but with a homey feel to it.

Either way, these aren't bad digs for the next few days. I'm glad I let Cozy and Trista talk me into joining them, even if that means I have to deal with an annoying mountain man.

The annoying man in question had to come back to the room earlier to change into his swim trunks. I tried to look busy when he walked out of the bathroom shirtless with all his muscles and ink on full display, but I have to admit to sneaking a peak when he was digging in his bag for some sunscreen.

I've seen Calder shirtless before. Max and Cozy have a pool, and I've been to enough gatherings at their house throughout the years that it's not like I didn't know he was jacked.

But seeing him at that sex club last week changed things between us. It's like a veil has been dropped, and we're not just looking at each other like mortal enemies. Now I know the sort of sex Calder is into, and if it's anything like what I saw in that club, *holy fucking shit.*

I mean, the woman-on-woman stuff didn't do it for me, but seeing multiple men pleasuring one woman had me trembling. Is that what Calder could be into? Would he share his woman? Would I like wearing that smelly mask if it was Calder holding the leash?

The stirring between my legs is unmistakable, and I have to brace myself on a nearby wall to maintain my balance. What am I doing? The last thing I need rolling through my brain are visuals for what Calder would have looked like on his knees—oh my God, I'm disgusting!

Stop thinking about Calder and sex, Dakota! He's gross, and you're gross for letting your mind wander like this! It's only going to make the vibe between us even more irritating.

I walk through the wide-open doorway out to the infinity pool that overlooks the ocean. The air blows my caftan around my legs, cooling me down as I spot Cozy and Trista on the far side of the pool. They're seated on loungers with Addison, who I met on the plane. She's stunning in that sporty, athletic tomboy girl-next-door sort of way with her black hair tied up into a casual ponytail. Vibes with her seem good, but if she's canoodling with Luke, I hope she knows what she's in for. The Fletcher brothers' reputation with women is pretty infamous around Boulder. Most of us were shocked when Wyatt actually settled down.

That was until I got to know his bride-to-be.

Trista is a force of nature. I've enjoyed getting closer to her the past several months. We've been working on a logo design for her animal rescue nonprofit that she's fundraising for, with plans to open and manage her own facility. I have a handful of designers I work closely with at my T-shirt store, and I'm happy to help for such a good cause.

It's incredible how she seems to fit into the Fletcher family like she was always meant to be there. And Wyatt has definitely changed for the better since meeting her. He went from this grunting, surly mountain man, to a soft, tender daddy and soon-to-be husband. Their love story is one for the books.

I head over to the open lounge chair by Trista, and she smiles up at me, adjusting a linen blanket over her chest that's covering Stevie while she feeds her.

"You are impressive," I state honestly as I pull off my dress and drape it over the back of my chair. "Bringing a three-month-old on vacation is brave."

"Have you met this family?" Trista laughs and glances out to the pool where the guys are in the process of playing volleyball with Everly and Ethan. "I have a whole swarm of people who would do anything for me and this baby at the snap of my fingers. And there was no way was I missing out on the opportunity to do a destination wedding . . . for free!"

"Is any of your family coming for the wedding? Or are you celebrating with them in another way?" Addison asks from her seat parallel to us.

Trista shakes her head. "Nah, no one else is coming. I'm not close with my family."

"No word from your sister?" I ask with a frown, glancing over at Cozy, who told me she was going to try to reach out to her. "I thought you said she was going to try to make it."

"It's a long flight from Hawaii to here. I didn't expect her to come." Trista shrugs and lifts the blanket to peek at Stevie, a small smile teasing her lips. "I have all the family I need right here."

"Yes, you do," Cozy says and reaches over to rub Trista's leg.

I smile as I spot the redness around both of their eyes. Trista has a complicated family and doesn't talk about them much, but I've seen a lot of growth in her since she became a mother and embraced the Fletcher family. It's beautiful how she found her own happiness and is content to leave her past behind. I hope I can do the same.

"Is she done yet?" Johanna's voice snaps me out of my musings as she appears with outreached hands.

"Yes, and she's totally passed out." Trista reaches under the blanket to clip the strap of her maternity bathing suit back on. "Milk coma."

"I'll take her inside," Johanna says, leaning over Trista to scoop a scrunched up and sleeping Stevie into her arms.

"And make sure she—"

"Burps," Johanna finishes Trista's sentence. "I got you, sweetie."

Trista smiles warmly. "Thanks, Jo."

She winks back at her future daughter-in-law and takes Stevie back into the house.

"See what I mean?" Trista says with a sappy smile as she stretches out. "I didn't even have to snap my fingers."

My brows lift in appreciation. "Maybe I could come around to the idea of kids if I knew my mom would be as good a grandma as that."

"No one is as good a grandma as that," Cozy says with a laugh. "My parents are great, but Johanna Fletcher is saintlike."

A round of margaritas is delivered by Carlos, and we sip and enjoy some much-needed girl talk and vitamin D. Colorado winters tend to turn me into a vampire, so this sun is life-changing.

"Why do you keep messing with your swimsuit top?" Cozy asks as I adjust the breast cup of my black bikini for the hundredth time.

I huff in frustration. "This suit used to fit me, but my boobs are bigger now, and I haven't worn this one in years."

"You're not pregnant, are you?" Trista asks with a pointed look.

"No, I just had my period two weeks ago," I reply confidently. Not to mention it's been almost a year since I've had sex. "I've just gained weight. Some of my old clothes don't fit like they used to."

"I think you look amazing," Addison says sweetly.

"Thanks," I reply with a laugh. "And you can look as amazing as me for the low, low price of a divorce that costs you six figures and twenty extra pounds!"

Silence descends as all three ladies stare awkwardly back at me.

"Oh God," I groan and push my sunglasses up on top of my head. "I sound like a bitter divorcée, don't I?" I gasp and clutch my chest. "I've turned into my mother. Someone kill me!"

"You are not your mother," Cozy corrects me.

"Here, have the rest of my margarita," Trista says sympathetically as she passes her drink over. "You've earned it."

I drink it all too willingly and give myself a mental pep talk. I will not be this scorned woman who only talks about her divorce like my mother was most of my life. I will get back to my former happy-go-lucky, confident self. I'll turn my lemons into margaritas, dammit!

I stare down at my breasts spilling out of my bikini. "But hey . . . a little divorcée weight gain gave me bigger tits, so at least I saved money on a boob job."

"Cheers to that!" Cozy clinks her glass with mine.

"Are you four going to get in the water anytime today?" Max asks from inside the pool, eyeing his wife like a piece of meat. "We want to play a real game of volleyball and could use the numbers."

Cozy looks to me with a challenging smile.

"We're in," I state confidently. I'm on vacation, and it's time I start acting like it.

Calder

As I watch the four ladies make their way into the water, I feel my body tense when Dakota struts across the pool deck in a black string bikini that she has no business looking that good in. Her nipples are pebbling through the thin fabric, and I have half a mind to cover poor Ethan's innocent eyes.

Honestly, I'd like to cover every man's eyes in the pool. And Carlos too! No one should be looking at her when she looks like that. I glance around to see if they're all staring at what I'm staring at, but shockingly, they're not. They're gawking at their own ladies, and here I am ogling Dakota like the pervert I clearly am.

Am I a sadist? Is it sadism to be attracted to someone who makes you miserable? Either way, this is a family vacation, and that is not a family-appropriate bathing suit.

"What's wrong, Uncle Calder?" Ethan says, splashing water at me.

I wipe the water off my face and tear my eyes away from the bane of my existence as she steps into the pool. "Nothing's wrong, buttface. Why do you ask?"

"You look grumpy."

"I don't look grumpy."

Ethan jumps up and pokes me on the forehead, nearly gouging my eye out. "Right there. You look mad. Like Angry Bird."

"All right . . . stuff it, or I won't give you those Pokémon cards that are in my suitcase after this match."

He thrusts his little fists up in the air and cheers as I swim over to Everly, who seems to be dividing up the teams. "Calder, you're on my team."

"Who's on your team?"

"Me, Wyatt, Cozy, and Dakota," she answers, pointing for me to move to the other side of the net. "Luke, Addison, Trista, Max, and Ethan will take that side."

I frown and turn on my heel to swim over to Max. "Switch teams with me."

"No way," Max says as he stretches his arms out, preparing for the match. "My wife sucks at sports."

"Switch with me!" I growl and shove him lightly.

"Forget it," he splashes me like I'm a pest and starts doing jumps in the pool to warm up. Psycho.

Feeling desperate, I move over to Luke. "Let's trade teams."

"Why?"

"Because I don't want to be on this side."

Luke smiles knowingly. "You're already sharing a room with her. You can't share a team too?"

"Just quit being a douchebag, and switch with me."

He sighs heavily and turns to talk to Addison for a moment before finally trading with me.

"No switching," Everly yells as Luke ducks under the net.

I rush up behind him and thrust my finger through the net at my niece. "Everly, knock it off or I'll tell your parents about the time I picked you up drunk at that party and snuck you back home so your dad wouldn't find out."

Everly's eyes go wide. "It was homecoming!"

"Do you think your dad will care?"

She frowns and glances over at her dad who just literally put on a sweatband. Where the fuck did he even get that?

"Fine, you and Luke can switch."

Damn these kids. No respect.

The volleyball game begins, and it quickly becomes way more intense than I anticipated. Teaming up with Max was a bad idea. I forgot how crazy competitive that fucker is. Not to mention a ball hog. I've taken elbows and fists to the gut, back, and arms because he's diving for every ball that comes to our side. Poor Addison and Trista are hanging onto the wall for dear life trying to keep themselves safe. Ethan's nearly drowned twice! One time

I swear to God Max stepped on his own son's head to spike the volleyball.

And we're on the same team!

But he's not wrong. Cozy is pathetic on the other side of the net. I glanced underwater at one point to make sure she wasn't wearing flippers because the girl can barely move in the water. At one point, she was just singing along to the music on the patio speakers when a ball smacked her right in the chest. How did she miss that? Everly isn't much better. You'd think at six feet tall, she'd have some athletic intuition, but she's more interested in drink refills than playing a lick of defense. Luke, Wyatt, and Dakota have the front net completely covered and are setting each other up like they're trying out for the fucking Olympics. I want them drug-tested after this match!

"Get your shit together, Calder!" Max screams at me with veins popping out of his neck. "This is game point, and you're blowing it!"

My eyes are wide because the psychopath is dead serious. We don't even have stakes. There was no bet, no money wager . . . nothing. This is literally a *for-fun family game*, and you'd think his multimillion-dollar company was on the line with the way his nostrils are in a permanent flare.

"You need to calm the fuck down, or I'm going to call for Mom," I call back over my shoulder.

"Pussy," Max grumbles as he prepares to serve.

"That's an offensive term, you know."

Max looks at me like I have two heads before he tosses the ball up to launch it over the net. When I turn back to see what happens, everything starts to move in slow motion.

The serve falls perfectly in front of Luke who easily bumps it into a soft pass to Wyatt. Wyatt makes eye contact with Dakota, whose eyes light up with fire as she nods and points up to the sky.

What the fuck does the point mean? That doesn't seem good!

Wyatt nods back and lifts his hands to the ball, launching it into a high set. My body tenses when I watch Dakota sink shoulder-deep into the water, her hair sticking to her temples as she bursts up out of waves like a phoenix rising from the ashes. She pulls her arm back as she catapults a solid two feet over the net, and I look left to see if Max and Ethan are seeing what I'm seeing.

But Max isn't watching the ball. He's staring at me with murder in his eyes. "Loook ooout!" he yells, his voice also in the slow-mo mode that's playing in my head.

"You're gonna diiieee!" Ethan squeals while pointing directly at me, and I swear I see all signs of childhood innocence leave his eyes.

My head jerks back to the match as I launch myself up to try and block the spike she's about to send my way. But instead of focusing on the ball, my gaze drifts down her body, and my jaw drops when I see that one perfectly large, D-cup breast has completely exposed itself. It's sprung free from the tiny black bikini triangle that everyone knew was no match for the power and athleticism radiating through her veins during this match. Her pale pink pert nipple winks back at me as water sluices off its large peak, and I feel my traitorous cock twitch as my eyes flash back up to Dakota. A devious smirk brightens her clear blue gaze before sparks burst through my vision, and the ball smashes into my face causing the lights to go out.

"Is he going to have to go to the hospital?" I hear Ethan's frantic voice cry as my body is being dragged through the water.

"No, Ethan." Max sighs. "But we're going to have to get out of the pool because Calder ruined it with his blood."

"Blood?" I croak and lift my hand to my nose. I pull my fingers back and see that yes, that is in fact my blood, and it seems to be pouring from my nose and leaving a trail behind us. That doesn't seem good.

"Help me out, Luke! Calder's ruining the pool," Max barks.

"I don't want Uncle Calder to ruin the pool!" Ethan cries.

"It's not ruined," Cozy says, finally bringing in some voice of reason. "They're just going to have to treat it with chemicals, so we'll have to take a break for a couple hours."

Ethan continues crying as Everly says, "We still won, though, right?"

"Hell yes, we won," Wyatt replies, and I look up to see them both high-five over my lifeless body. "Who wants to play pickle ball?"

"This is my nightmare," I mumble as the string from the tampon currently shoved up my nose sticks to my lips.

"It's stopping the blood," my mom says as she touches the bridge of my nose.

"Mom, that hurts!" I jerk my head away. "Why do you have to keep touching it?"

"I'm trying to make sure it's not broken, Calder. I can't imagine you'd want to have plastic surgery here in Mexico." She huffs indignantly. "You boys always play too rough. Almost forty years old and you still all act like children."

"It's Max's fault."

My mom hits me with a scolding look and stands to place her hand on her hips. "I'm going to go check on the baby. Just sit still and try not to stain anything."

I close my eyes to rest for a bit until darkness descends over me and I hear a faint "Hey, Killer" poke through my slumber.

When I look up, the devil appears in a vision, and I hold my hands up and scream, "No, Satan! It's not my time yet. I have so much more life left to liiive!"

"Would you knock it off?" Dakota scolds and chucks a bag of ice onto my naked chest. "I was coming over to apologize, but you're making me glad I did it."

My smile hurts my nose as I set the ice off to the side. "Don't act like you're not happy about this." I yank the tampon out of my nose, grateful to see that the bleeding has stopped.

"I might be a little happy," Dakota confirms with a spark of glee in her eyes. She sits down on the lounge chair beside me and turns her muscular legs in my direction, giving me a nice view of them and her long valley of cleavage.

"You have a lethal spike," I offer, and I swear my nose aches at the mention of it.

Her brows lift. "Is that a compliment from you?"

"Whatever," I shrug noncommittally and cross my ankles. "Did you play a lot of sports growing up or something?"

"Just volleyball all four years of high school." She shoots me a cocky wink, and it hits me right in the gut. "And track."

"Lucky me," I grumble, looking away because her skin is glowing in this light, and it's highly distracting.

After a moment she says, "I *am* sorry, Calder."

I shake my head and shoot her a look from the corner of my eye. "I'm not."

She frowns, clearly not understanding my response.

I turn to look at her, and my eyes drop shamelessly to her chest.

"What?" She covers herself protectively.

I shrug. "Oh nothing . . . I just saw your tit."

"You did?" She covers herself up like her breasts are still hanging out. "When? During the volleyball game?"

I laugh and nod. "Oh yeah . . . before it was lights-out, it was high beams on . . . or *beam* because only the one tit popped out. What's the other one look like? Now I'm curious. Are they identical twins? Or fraternal?"

"Shut up," she grumbles and yanks her dress up over her chest. "Did anyone else see? I thought it just popped out when I landed in the water."

"I don't know who saw, but that image is locked in the vault forever now, along with some other images of you."

Her face drops in horror. "What other images?"

I turn so my legs straddle hers, taking in the view of her fully now. Her blond hair is in a high messy bun on top of her head, and the pieces that have fallen out around her face are tight little coils.

I tap my temple as my eyes flare in blatant challenge. "You on your knees at the club."

"Stop," she snaps, jerking her head back.

"What?"

"Don't bring that up." She yanks her legs away from me and sits back in the lounge chair to face the pool, her jaw taut with irritation. "We are not discussing that."

"Now is the perfect time." I shift down in my seat to recapture her attention. "I'm probably concussed, which means the swelling in my brain will make me forget whatever you tell me."

"Why do you care so much?"

She frowns and folds her arms over her chest, and I watch her for a beat, trying to figure her out. What I've learned about Dakota the past several years as the best friend of my sister-in-law is that she dives headfirst into whatever she puts her mind to. First it was her T-shirt shop, then her house renovation, then as far as I could tell, it was her marriage—though, admittedly, she hated me during most of that, so I didn't see as much of her once we were done with the house business.

But Sex Club Dakota? That seems like a big dive, even for her.

"A sex club doesn't seem like something you'd enjoy. You like control too much," I reply honestly. "I just want to know why you had the desire to try it out so bad."

"You don't know me that well, Calder."

"I helped you with your house renovation," I offer. "You get to know a person a lot when you have to pick out paint and flooring together."

"We're not discussing the house or my sex life, so just stop." She shakes her head and loses all good humor on her face.

"Bossy as always." I narrow my eyes on her. "No wonder you couldn't be a Sub."

With a growl of irritation, she gets up out of her seat. "I just came over to make sure you weren't dead. You're not. I'm going now."

"It'll take more than a vicious spike to take me down."

A hint of a smirk ghosts her lips as she storms off, which has me sitting back in my seat with a smile. The devil ain't so scary after all. But she does have secrets. Secrets that I am annoyingly intrigued by.

Chapter 9

BED OF NAILS

Dakota

"Dinner was excellent, thank you," I say to Carlos as I bring my plate out to the kitchen in the main house.

"Gracias, señorita."

"Can I help with the dishes?"

"No," he chuckles and shoos me away. "We are okay. Please, go to the beach with everyone so you don't miss the sunset. Enjoy yourself!"

I set my plate down and slowly make my way out back toward the beach where everyone walked after dinner. Dinner was the best fresh crab I've ever tasted. I could get used to living like Max and Cozy. And thankfully I was seated on the end of the table by Cozy and Trista, so I didn't have to worry about making more small talk with Calder. But I could feel his eyes on me most of the meal, and it was unnerving. He's like a dog with a bone and doesn't seem to want to let this sex club thing go, but I'll be damned if I tell him the truth.

The warm salty air blows through my hair as I kick my wedges off and squish my toes in the sand. Glancing down toward the water, I see that everyone is coupled up. Max and Cozy are on a moonlit stroll, Wyatt and Trista are wading their feet into the water, and Luke and Addison are sitting in the sand talking quietly. It makes me lonely for the first time in what feels like ages.

Randal and I have been separated for over a year, and I haven't felt the least bit interested in dating. He ruined a lot of things for me when it comes to my relationship with men. Things that I am desperately trying to unpack now so I can start living my life again.

Watching all these couples today makes me realize I'm ready to put myself out there again. I still believe in love and happily-ever-afters. I just made a huge mistake on my first shot at it.

Feeling exhausted from a long day of travel and not really wanting to be a third wheel, I decide to turn in early. I twirl on my heel to head up to the palapa that I can see from where I'm standing and startle when I spot Calder walking toward me.

He attempts to pass me in silence, but I hesitate in front of him because I have something I want to ask. "Hey, um . . . Calder?"

"Yes?" He frowns and turns back to look at me.

I swallow nervously. "Are you going up to the room soon?"

"Wasn't planning on it," he says, glancing up at the palapa. "I'm going down to the beach for a bit. Why?"

"No reason," I reply in a rush and try to walk away but stop as anxiety bubbles through my veins.

"Just say whatever you need to say, Ace."

"Ace?" I turn back to face him, tilting my head curiously.

He points to his nose.

"You know technically they use the term *ace* for serves that get a point, not spikes."

He hits me with a flat look, and I shake my head. "Sorry, not the point. I just . . . I don't want to walk by the birdcage alone in the dark."

A lascivious smirk spreads across his face. "If you want to kiss and make up, all you need to do is ask."

"There will be no kissing and no making up. I just . . . need to use your face as a human shield again," I rush out, frustrated by this exchange. Inhaling sharply, I turn and wave him off. "Never mind. I'll just go back to the house and ask Carlos."

"I got you, Ace," he groans dramatically as he turns to make our way up to the palapa.

"At least you're not calling me Karen anymore," I offer, glancing over at him.

"Much nicer than Killer Calder, don't you think?" He pins me with a devilish look, and I feel my insides clench with the direct eye contact.

I make a noise. "Well, *asshole*, *douchebag*, *whiney baby*, and *dramatic loser* were already taken, so . . ."

He tips his head back and laughs at my joke. It's a deep, rich sound that makes me smile, and the wave of butterflies that erupt in my stomach is embarrassing. What is going on here? Why do I like making Calder laugh? Why is he actually laughing at me instead of poking me back? These aren't the normal Calder/Dakota vibes I've grown accustomed to. I call him Killer Calder because he ruins everything he touches and he doesn't care about anything. I can't forget that. Is this tropical air shifting things between us? If so, I am not a fan.

He stretches his arms out wide by the birdcage, and I stop myself from shoving him against the iron bars this time. When I hear his footsteps following me to the door, I turn and look over my shoulder. "You're coming in?"

"Not for kissing, relax," Calder huffs. "I'm just going to pull my bed out and set it up now, so I don't wake you up later when I come in."

"Oh." I watch him begin to pull the sofa bed out and make my way over to the closet to grab the bedding I saw in there earlier.

"Thanks," he says, and our hands brush as he takes them from me, causing a tingle to run up my spine.

"Thanks for giving me the big bed," I reply coyly.

He hits me with a knowing look. "Didn't really have a choice, did I?"

"I did win the volleyball game."

"Oh, is that why you get the bed? I didn't know we had stakes in the game. I would have quit taking it easy on you."

"Whatever you have to tell yourself to help sleep at night, Killer."

I shoot him a wink, and he laughs that deep throaty timbre

again, and I have to turn away from him before he sees my cheeks flush. This is really stupid. Why am I acting like this? It must just be because he looks good in that white linen shirt, and I'm not used to seeing him outside of flannels and jeans. It was hard not to stare back at him all night at dinner. That sun he got today gave him a bronze-god glow that suits him well.

I inwardly curse myself as I realize I'm fawning over *Calder Fletcher*—the asshole who ruined my wedding dress and my house. *Get your shit together, Dakota.*

I grab my toiletry bag and shut myself away in the bathroom and am relieved when I come out to find he's gone. Whatever that laughing, flirty exchange we had a moment ago was needs to stop. He saw my tit earlier, for God's sake. I should be mortified, not making him laugh and enjoying it.

My brain is obviously foggy from the travel, and I'm not thinking clearly. Just a few more days of this. I can do this. A hot shower and a good night's sleep will help clear my mind. Everything will look normal in the morning.

Calder

I'm going to kill her.

I'm going to take a pillow and make the nickname she's pegged me with a true story. At least if she's dead, she won't need the bed, and then I can get off this fucking bag of rocks they call a sofa bed in this godforsaken palapa.

I've been lying here for hours trying to will myself to sleep. I've moved pillows, I've lain on pillows, I tried the floor. I even attempted putting the bed back into the sofa position to see if that would help.

Nothing helps.

At one point, I just stared through the curtain at Dakota as she slept on one side of the giant circular bed. She was barely using twenty percent of the mattress! I considered sneaking onto the bed quietly because she wouldn't even notice I was there.

But knowing her, she probably has fucking pepper spray tucked under her pillowcase, and my tender nose wouldn't be able to handle that kind of assault.

I'm in hell.

And as the sun begins to peek up over the horizon of the ocean, I think I've gone completely mad.

"Motherfucker!"

"What is your problem?" Dakota exclaims, and I see the outline of her shoot up from her bed behind the curtain. "I haven't slept a wink all night because you won't stop wiggling around and making noises!"

She marches over and yanks the curtain back, revealing herself to me in a T-shirt (no bra), silky shorts, and a sleeping mask. But not even her nipples pebbling through that thin top can improve the mood I'm in.

"Oh, pardon me, madam!" I roar, shooting up out of the bed to match her irritated stance. "Was the *bed of nails* that you stuck me on all night a little too noisy for you and your football field of a mattress? Tell that to my back that's had to suffer through hours of involuntary acupuncture with rusty screws!"

"Oh my God, you're such a diva." Dakota walks over and pushes down on the mattress with her hand. "It's not that bad. Carlos said it was very nice."

"Go ahead, Ace. Give it a try."

She jerks back and wraps her arms around herself. "I'm not going to lie down in all your . . . musk."

"Scared you'll catch something?"

"Yes!"

"Well then, you'll just have to take my word for it. That bed is shit. I'd be better off sleeping on the beach all night."

"Then, maybe you should!"

"Maybe I will! Because heaven forbid I sleep on the eighty feet of mattress you're not even touching."

"I am not sharing a bed with you."

"Oh . . . I'm aware! My *musk* might be catching!"

We both stare at each other with fury in our eyes, and I realize that brief moment of truce we had last night is gone before I even had a chance to get used to it. And I have the aching nose to prove it.

"Fuck this. I'm going for a run," I growl as I dig into my suitcase and throw a pair of shorts on over my boxer briefs. I yank a cutoff T-shirt over my head and stuff my feet into some shoes. "Maybe if I run hard enough, I'll be so exhausted, I won't mind catching tetanus and dying from this bag of metal."

"You are so dramatic."

"Back at you, Karen."

I slam the door and crack my neck before jogging down the steps past the loud-ass birds and toward the beach where I hope to find my sanity again after one of the worst nights of my life.

Chapter 10

LAST FLING BEFORE THE RING

Dakota

"Let's do another shot!" I cheer as I stand beside Cozy on top of a local bar in town.

"Hell yes!" Cozy throws her hands up and turns around to signal to the bartender we need another round. "None for you, though."

"But I'm legal!" Everly argues from her barstool beside Trista and Addison.

"It took some major convincing for your dad to even let you come out with us tonight, and that's only because we have our own security detail." Cozy points to Carlos who is serving as our driver for the evening. "If I bring you back drunk, there will be hell to pay."

Everly pouts, but Trista puts her arm around her encouragingly. "I'll sit this one out with you. I am not that big of a drinker." She sticks her lip out as she touches her boobs. "Plus, if I drink much more I'm going to have to pump and dump."

"But it's your bachelorette party!" Cozy drops down on her knees to give her full attention to her almost sister-in-law. "You only get to do this once."

"Theoretically," I add, dropping down beside Cozy as the bartender pours four shots in front of Trista.

"You know what I mean." Cozy waves me off. "We'll dance the booze off before we head back to the villa, okay?"

"I'm all for more dancing!" Everly cheers excitedly.

Trista smiles as she sniffs her shot and wrinkles her nose. "I really hope I don't throw up tonight."

"No one is throwing up." I slide awkwardly off the bar, very aware that I'm not the party girl I used to be.

Back when I met Randal—he was a bartender at Pearl Street Pub, a quaint little dive bar in downtown Boulder—I dove head-first into the bartender's girlfriend role. Staying out late, waiting for him to finish his shift. Going out with other service industry people until all hours of the morning. It was a work hard, play hard mindset back then, and I had the high alcohol tolerance to prove it.

I am not that woman anymore.

In my mid-thirties now, I find myself annoyed if I'm not in bed with a book by nine o'clock. But tonight, I'm single and on vacation. This is the time to cut loose, and I need these ladies to get with the program!

I glance over at Addison. "How are you feeling?"

"I'm not even drunk." She takes a shot of tequila like she just took a drink of water. "You three are lightweights."

Impressed, I down my own shot, trying to be tough like her but wincing like a little bitch.

Trista follows suit and coughs as she downs the spicy liquid. "I wonder what the guys are doing?"

"Who cares!" I groan and set my glass down on the bar. "This is ladies' night. No guy talk!"

"But aren't you single and ready to mingle?" Cozy asks pointedly.

"Yes, but not with a Fletcher brother. Ick." I shudder at the thought. "I'd rather go for short King Carlos over Killer Calder."

"What's the story with you two?" Addison asks, noting my irritation.

"Who? Me and Carlos? I don't know." I glance over at Carlos, and he offers me a flirty wave. "There does seem to be a connection, doesn't there?"

"Not Carlos," Addison laughs. "I mean you and Calder. Why all the tension? Did you two used to date or something?"

"God no!" I exclaim defensively. "And there's no tension. I don't give a shit about Calder Fletcher. I'm totally chill."

"Totally," Cozy sputters out a laugh.

I glare over at my soon-to-be former best friend. "He just fucked up a lot of stuff in my house years ago, and we've never got along since then."

"That was seven years ago," Cozy groans and sips her shot of tequila with a gag. "When are you going to get over it?"

"And he fixed it, right?" Everly asks innocently. "I can't imagine my uncle wouldn't fix something he broke."

"Yes, he fixed it," I sigh, irritation crawling up my back. "Or he fixed what he could. But some of the stuff was irreplaceable. He was careless as he's always been, and my house . . ." My voice catches in my throat as emotion sweeps over me. I've clearly had too much to drink if I'm reacting this way about my house in front of everyone. "I had so many dreams for that renovation, and Calder didn't give a shit."

"I don't know if that's true," Cozy argues.

"Whose side are you on?" I stare back at my bestie who looks just as intoxicated as me. "I know you're related to the Fletchers now, but I knew you first!"

"He paid for your wedding dress," she volleys back.

"He *what*?" Trista, Everly, and Addison both snap their attention to me, waiting for me to elaborate.

My eyes blink heavily. "My wedding dress was part of the collateral damage of the house screwup. A pipe burst in the attached bath of my bedroom. That room shared a wall with my closet where the dress was stored, and my dress was ruined a few days before I got married. It was an original design by one of my closest friends who's a fashion designer in Aspen. It was one-of-a-kind. Irreplaceable."

"So, what did you do?" Everly asks, concern etched all over her face. She was just a kid when I got married so she wasn't aware of any of this stuff that went down.

"I went to some random bridal store and bought something off the rack. I hated it, but there was only one I could find that didn't need to be altered, so it was what it was."

I wince as I recall the wedding photos from that day. I looked bad. Randal looked bad. It was just altogether . . . bad. To say that my wedding day wasn't all that I hoped for would be a huge understatement.

"Maybe it was a sign," Everly murmurs, and all eyes turn to the young girl who just said the quiet part out loud. "I only met Randal a few times because you never brought him around that much. Maybe the universe did that for a reason."

"The universe is Killer Calder?" I roll my eyes. "Let's not give him too much credit, okay, kid?"

"Accidents happen, though, right?" Addison offers innocently.

"Yes, but it wasn't just the dress and the house. It was what he said when it all went down."

"What did he say?" Everly asks, and I feel all four women staring intently at me, but it's Everly I pause for.

Despite absolutely loathing the man, I know he's an excellent uncle. I don't want to spoil her good opinion of him—and that's for her sake, not his.

I press my lips together and inhale sharply through my nose. "It's not worth rehashing. This is a hen party. We should be having fun, not talking about my drama with Calder Fletcher. Let's do another tequila shot!"

Cozy shakes her head. "I'm out on this round."

"Fine, but your ass is still dancing!"

Calder

"And the prize for the lamest bachelor party goes to . . ." I murmur under my breath as I cast my fishing pole into the water that's glowing from the lights on the boat.

"Did you say something, Calder?" Wyatt asks, his voice deep and threatening.

"Is this really what you wanted to do for your big stag night?" I ask with a laugh. "Night fishing?"

"You can literally see the fish," Wyatt replies, like that's somehow supposed to make this lame experience better.

I scoff and shake my head as I prop my rod on a holder and head to the cooler for another beer. We've been out here for hours, and while, yes, we've caught our fair share of fish, I didn't realize this was going to be our entire evening. My brother is a pathetic groom.

"This is Wyatt's night," Luke argues in his defense. "When you get married, we'll do whatever freaky thing you want to do."

"Ha," I bark out at that notion as I point accusingly at Wyatt. "Unlike this fucker, I actually take our pact seriously. Marriage ain't never happening for me."

Max laughs and shakes his head but says nothing. A rare occurrence for him. Usually, he loves the opportunity to judge us and our mountain-life ways. Point out everything he thinks we're doing wrong. He's a real treat.

"Where were you all day today, anyways?" Wyatt asks as he casts his pole out into the darkness. "You missed a great afternoon on the beach."

"I was taking care of your baby," I grumble.

"I didn't ask you to do that."

"No, but Mom deserved a break, and I needed a nap." I cross my arms and sulk a bit. "I sleep better with Stevie on my chest. She reminds me of Milkshake."

"Cat-fucker." Luke coughs out his remark from where he's standing at the bow.

I narrow my eyes at my baby brother. "Call me that again and you're going for a swim."

The boat lights cast a glow on his face as he smirks behind his beard. "Cat. Fucker."

I set my beer down real calm and collected before I lunge, snatching him up by the collar as he howls with laughter. It takes both Max and Wyatt to pry me off him, and after a good scolding from our fishing guide about the importance of boater safety, I sit down and drink my beer in stony silence.

"Luke, stop pushing Calder's buttons," Max states firmly after we've all settled down. "You know he's testy when he doesn't get a full eight hours."

I down the rest of my beer. "I'm in hell. Mexico is my hell."

A couple hours later, after about six more beers and a dozen more fish, we make our way back to the villa, the ocean breeze and booze marginally lightening my mood. When we walk toward the main house, I can hear the girls cackling from the kitchen where they are going to town on some late-night munchies.

Wyatt instantly makes his way over to Trista, Max to Cozy, and Luke to Addison. I can't quite tell if he's fucking Addison or not. I tried to get some details out of him earlier tonight, but he wouldn't spill—the asshole.

Then there's Dakota, who intentionally turns her back on me like she has a reason to be pissed about me sleeping on the shitty sofa bed. My eyes drink in her back on full display in a pink-orange-ombré sort of dress with a fringe skirt that goes all the way to the floor. She looks like sherbet fucking ice cream, and the second that comparison comes to mind, I imagine licking dessert off her very smooth-looking back.

What the fuck am I doing? I am mad at Dakota. She was a bitch about the sofa bed this morning, and I should not be lusting after her.

Feeling feisty, I walk over and stand directly beside her so my shoulder brushes hers. She shivers but doesn't acknowledge my existence, so I grab a chip and dip it into the bowl of guacamole directly in front of her. I lean over the counter to make an obnoxious crunch right in her face.

"This is good." I grab another. "Don't you think this is good, Dakota?"

Her hooded eyes narrow as she sways in her heels. "Did you have any luck finding an air mattress today?"

"No," I snap and grab another chip. "Wyatt took us fishing, so we didn't go into town for me to do any shopping."

"Well, I looked when I was in town and didn't see anything, so we're screwed."

"We?" I mumble around another mouthful. "I'm the only one suffering on that bed of nails."

"I'll take the sofa bed tonight," she offers casually as she sips her margarita.

"Come again?" I ask, my brows distinctly furrowed.

She shrugs. "We can take turns."

"I thought you didn't want to roll around in my musk."

"I don't." She nibbles delicately on a chip. "I'll swap the bedding out."

I shake my head. "You must be drunk if you're offering to do something nice for me."

"I am a nice person, Calder," she snaps defensively, her blue eyes stunning against her sun-kissed cheeks. "Outside of you . . . I am a nice person. Sometimes."

"She has black-cat energy," Trista says and hiccups loudly.

"What is black-cat energy?" Cozy asks curiously.

Trista smiles as she replies, "Black cats don't seek attention, but somehow, they still always get it. They're really independent and know their worth. I have animal labels for all of you."

"What am I?" Cozy asks, her jaw dropped in rapt fascination.

Trista giggles. "You're a pug. Loveable, chill, cute, and cuddly but marches to the beat of her own drum."

"Do me!" Everly chimes in excitedly.

"You're a terrier mix. Endless energy and always up in everyone's business. Wyatt is a German shepherd, Calder is a rottweiler, Luke is a golden retriever, and Max is a Doberman."

"Oh my God, these are scarily accurate," Cozy says, her eyes scanning the room as she takes it all in.

"Addison, I need a bit more time to get to know you, but I'm toying with the idea of a border collie after our chat on the beach today. Big herding dogs . . . hard workers and hyperfocused on their task."

"Why am I the only nondog label?" Dakota asks with a puzzled brow.

Trista giggles. "I don't know. It's just a feeling."

"Don't sweat it, Dakota." A shit-eating grin spreads across my face as I lean in close to her. "I love cats."

She shoves me away. "Are you ready for bed?"

The entire group gasps and hoots and hollers at that very pointed question.

"Do you want me to be ready for bed?" I waggle my brows suggestively, leaning even closer to her to bathe her in my musk that she loves so much.

She rolls her eyes and waves off the group. "Forget it, I'll just have Carlos walk me by the cage of sky rats."

The birds. How could I forget? She can't walk by the birds at night by herself. Some black cat she is.

"I'm at your service, Ace." I stand to salute the group my good-night and can't help but notice the curious looks I'm getting from Trista, Cozy, and Everly. Especially Everly.

As we make our way down the cobblestone path toward our palapa, I realize Dakota is a tad more drunk than I thought because she nearly trips at least three times before I have to offer her my arm.

"Will you just take my arm before you break your ankle?"

Dakota's brows lift. "Calder Fletcher being chivalrous. Hell hath frozen over."

"You would know since you live there."

She rolls her eyes but takes my arm as we make our way up the steps. Her skin is cool against mine, and I see her staring intently at my inked arm wrapped around hers.

Her long lashes blink up at me as she scowls. "You know . . . I used to think you were hot, before I hated you."

The grin that I make is embarrassing, so I quickly deflect. "I still think you're hot, even though I hate you."

"You think I'm hot?" she asks with a deadass serious face, as we make our way past the birdcage. Last night, she was a wreck walking by them. Tonight, I think my compliment has helped her totally forget them.

I roll my eyes as we stop in front of the palapa door. "You know you're hot."

"I used to be hot." Her face falls as she tugs at the top of her dress.

"Used to be?" I hit her with a disbelieving look, certain she's fishing for compliments.

"Yeah . . . I've changed." She sighs and turns to open the door, stumbling into our room that's illuminated by the lamp she left on beside her bed. "I'm not the hot little thing I used to be. It's fine. I know I'm not a dog. But I'm not what I once was."

She begins to kick off her heels like she didn't just say the most fucked-up thing on the planet.

"Are you high?" I snap, irritation crawling up my skin.

"No, I'm midsize."

"Mid-what?"

"Midsize." She points to her midsection. "I have a little more here than I used to. And I don't even have the excuse of having babies. I just . . ." she shrugs ". . . gained weight. Hormones, age, whatever. It is what it is. Randal said I went from an eight to a six." She points her thumbs down and buzzes her lips.

I close my eyes and lick my lips, taking three deep breaths before I respond. "I'm going to need you to never say his name in my presence again."

"Why?"

"Cuz I hate him." My teeth crack as I clench them to stop myself from saying more.

"Why do *you* hate him? You barely even knew him. If anyone should hate him, it's me."

I hit her with a glare. "You should hate him. You should want him dead for multiple reasons, but he should definitely be six feet under for thinking he could ever put a number on you."

"Like you're one to talk," she scoffs and starts taking off her earrings and setting them on the nightstand by the lamp. "You don't care about anything."

"It's not about caring," I say, feeling strangely out of breath as I stare at her lush frame illuminated in a halo of light that makes every inch of her look alluring. "It's about not letting yourself be numbered by anyone when you're fucking infinite."

Dakota stops what she's doing and stares back at me, lips parted, breasts heaving under her tight dress. She looks like she's not buying what I'm saying, so I walk over and make direct eye contact, so she knows I'm not fucking with her.

"From the moment I met you, I could see that. You had the world by the fucking balls . . . and you did whatever you wanted. Only a guy with zero fucking common sense would somehow miss the fact that you are limitless."

She blinks up at me, her long lashes hooding her eyes in a way that makes her look really sexy. Like how she'd look when I'm buried deep inside her. But my dirty thoughts are thwarted when she finally replies, "He's the reason I went to the sex club."

I inhale sharply at that swift change of subject.

"What do you mean?" I ask, stepping closer to her. "He made you go? I thought you said that was your first time. Haven't you guys been apart for a while?"

The idea of her still being involved with Randal makes me want to punch something. Watching her with him the past seven years hasn't been easy. Not because I've been pining for her or anything. Just because he's the fucking worst.

There are two types of people who never leave Boulder. There are people like my brother or my dad who make a name and a business for themselves. They contribute to society in a mature and adult way. Then there are people like Randal. Randal is a man-bun, lame-ass fucking calf-tattoo hipster who thinks he's big shit because he became the manager of Pearl Street Pub for a hot second. How a guy like him landed a girl like Dakota is baffling, and

I don't even like Dakota, but I respect her. I respect her hustle and her drive, and I know she's a good friend to Cozy. And I respect the hell out of what she's done with her life . . . aside from that douchebag.

Sure, I might be a fuckup like Randal. I can see that most of my life has been handed to me: my job, my social life, my mountain view. Hell, even my mother gave birth to my best friends.

But at least I don't have the audacity to try to tie down a girl like Dakota Schaefer.

"Are you still with your ex?" I ask, stepping closer to her as she starts doing the heavy blinking thing a person does before they fall asleep.

"No . . . he just . . . he . . ." She sighs and presses her hands to my chest for some space. Her fingers knead into my pecs through the T-shirt. "Good lord, you're buff."

"Dakota, finish what you were saying."

She turns away from me and makes her way over to the sofa bed. "I need to go to bed, Killa Cal."

"But wait. Did he force you to go to that sex club?" I ask as she flops face-first onto the sofa bed and the sound of creaking metal echoes through the room. "Was he there that night?"

I hate how tight my chest feels over the thought of them at that club together. Why do I give a fuck? Seriously. I wait for her to reply with bated breath and frown when I notice she's completely lifeless on the bed. I press my knee down beside her and move hair off over to see that she's passed out. Just like that.

With a heavy sigh I check her pulse and feel relief when I confirm she's not dead. Just has a magical ability of falling asleep within two seconds of speaking complete sentences.

I stare at her ass for far longer than is appropriate before I head over to her bed and pull the covers back. She can sleep for now, but that's definitely not where this story ends with us.

Chapter 11

CALLING DINOSAURS

Calder

"Rise and shine, sleepyhead," I say cheerily as I walk into the palapa with coffee, toast, eggs, and bacon on a tray. I snuck into the kitchen early this morning to put in the request before anyone in the house woke up. If they saw me bringing breakfast in bed to Dakota, I'd never hear the end of it. But I need to butter her up to get the rest of that whopper of a story she left on a cliffhanger last night.

"Oh my God, nooo." Dakota rolls over and covers her face, a halo of tangled golden locks around her head.

"Wakey wakey, eggs and bakey." I lower the plate of food down to the end table beside her.

She takes one whiff of the bacon and bolts upright in the bed, her hair a rumpled mess. "Get that away from me." She slaps a hand over her mouth, black streaks of makeup all over her face. "I'm going to be sick."

"You need to eat."

"I need to throw up." She frowns and looks around the large round bed. "How did I get in this bed? I was going to take the sofa bed last night. I thought I went to the sofa bed."

"You did, but there was no way in hell I was letting you stay passed out on that death trap, so I moved you over here."

"You moved me?" Dakota stares up at me like I'm from another planet. "How exactly did you move me?"

I shrug. "I carried you."

Her eyes widen in horror. "I did not give you consent to carry me."

"Jesus, Karen, chill out. I didn't cop a feel or anything . . . and believe me, you wanted me to."

"What?" Dakota stares back at me in horror.

I smirk. "You asked me to spoon you."

"I did?" She presses her hands to her cheeks. "Did you?"

I laugh and shake my head. "I may be a pig, but I'm not a monster. I knew you were in no state to make those kinds of requests, so I just tucked the pillows in behind you really good and pushed your hair out of your sweet little face."

She frowns and shakes her head, clearly not enjoying this little walk down memory lane.

"I may have used my own pillows to spoon you with, though. I think you'll start to enjoy my musk once you get used to it."

"Oh God." She crawls off the bed and begins pacing in the dress she wore to bed last night. I wanted to throw a T-shirt on her to make her more comfortable, but I'd never hear the end of it if I did that. She grips her sides and points to the door. "You need to get out of here."

"Why? Because I made you sleep with my pillows? It was just a joke."

She sucks her cheeks into her mouth and presses her fist to her lips. "I think I'm going to be sick, and I don't want you to be here when that happens."

"Why? Are you planning to not make it to the toilet?" My nose wrinkles at that thought.

"I will make it to the toilet," she snaps, her face twisting up in pain. "But I don't want you on the other side of the door when I do."

"Why?"

She hits me with a lethal glare. "Because I'm not one of those delicate female pukers who spit up quietly."

"What is that supposed to mean?"

Her eyes flash in horror as she slaps her hand over her mouth and scurries to the bathroom. I run after to help, but she slams the door in my face, and I hear a splash of liquid hit the toilet water.

"Dakota? Sweetie?" I coo softly at the door.

"Calder, get out!" she cries, out of breath.

"I am out. I'm on the other side of the door."

"Get out of the palapa," she says on a groan. "I don't want you to hear this!"

"Come on, we've all been sick before. It's not that bad." My face falls when a horrific prehistoric-sounding cough reverberates off the tile floor, shaking the frame of the door. "Okay, maybe it is that bad."

"I mean it. Go down to the beach. Get far, far away. This is—" Another round of retching hits her full force. She coughs and sputters, and I hear more liquid hitting the toilet water followed by a strange animalistic belching noise.

"Oh God," she cries and coughs loudly.

I wince. "Do you need a doctor?"

"Go . . . the fuck . . . away!" she screams with more strength than I expected her to have as another wave hits her.

"Whatever you say, Ace," I reply before heading out, shivering at the faint sounds of the horror show that's sure to be our communal bathroom upon my return. That certainly didn't go as planned.

Dakota

I am never touching tequila again.

My stomach roils as I exit the bathroom. The dry heaving finally ceased, and after a scalding-hot shower, I'm feeling as miserable as I deserve. I even had to dress myself in one of Calder's T-shirts that was sitting in his bag in there because I had no clean clothes in the bathroom to change into after I dried off.

Our suite door opens, and my towel-wrapped head turns at a

snail's pace to see Calder walking in with a tray of supplies. He really needs to stop with the trays.

I wince when I catch him eyeing his Colorado Rockies T-shirt. "Sorry, I got vomit on my dress, and this was all I could find in there. I'll give it back."

His eyes flash to my legs. "So, you're uh . . . naked under there?"

"Yes." I frown and glance down like I need to check.

His Adam's apple slides down his throat. "Cool. Totally naked in my shirt. Cool, cool," he murmurs to himself as he sets the tray down on the bed and struggles to make eye contact with me. "Now who's sharing whose musk?"

"Chill out, I'll wash it," I offer as he continues to make it weird.

"Just keep it," he says with a punch that reveals just how much he hates the idea of me in his clothes. So much so that he doesn't even want his shirt back. The dick. He turns back to the tray and begins pouring some ginger ale into a glass of ice. "I brought you some stuff to help your stomach."

Frowning at the swift mood swing, I join him by the bed to watch him attempt to be domestic. It's a confusing sight on Calder Fletcher. I huff out a laugh as he hands me the fizzy liquid.

I accept the glass with a pinched smile. "I read something once that ginger ale doesn't actually help you when you're sick."

"So you're calling my mom a liar?" Calder stares blankly at me.

My eyes fly wide. "No, I'm not calling your mother a liar. I was just stating something I'd read."

He continues to stare at me with zero signs of teasing on his face, so I murmur my thanks and quickly drink the ginger ale. It actually does taste really good, and Calder seems mildly appeased once I've accepted his offering. God, he's acting weird.

He walks over to one of his bags and pulls out his laptop, kneeling on the floor as he flips it open on the round bed.

"What are you doing?"

"Looking for something for us to watch. I assume you're not up for the excursion today, right? I think they're doing Jet Skis and a food tour in town."

My stomach heaves. Neither of those sound good at the state I'm currently in. Lying in bed in a palapa with the ocean breeze blowing in from the balcony while I watch a movie sounds divine, though.

"Did you say something for *us* to watch? Don't you want to go do the excursion?"

He shrugs. "I don't want to leave you up here all alone."

"Are you messing with me?"

I stare at his back in shock, and he stops scrolling on his computer to look over his shoulder at me. "No, I'm not messing with you. I've been sick in a foreign country before, and it sucks. It's like an intense kind of loneliness. Plus, I didn't sleep the best last night either, so watching a movie sounds good to me. But it might involve me getting some of my musk on your bed. Are you going to be able to handle that?"

I stare at him kneeling in front of me and it reminds me of the club. *Again.* I inwardly cringe because I need to stop associating Calder with sex. It's not healthy for my sex-starved brain! Calder Fletcher has been nice to me today, but it doesn't mean he's not still the jerk I've argued with for years.

Even if he does look incredibly sexy on his knees in front of me.

God, my hangover is really messing with my hormones apparently. I need to be cooler than this.

"It's fine." I shrug and pull down his T-shirt currently covering my body. "I think it's safe to say we've evolved past the cooties stage of our hatred."

A soft smile tugs at the corner of his mouth as he hops up from the floor and makes himself comfortable like a dog who was just invited onto the bed for the first time. He settles in and narrows his gaze at me. "I get to pick the movie."

"No way," I snap, joining him on the bed and pulling his T-shirt down as it rides up on my thighs.

His eyes snap from my legs to the screen. "My laptop, my movie choice."

"I'm the one who's sick."

"Self-induced sickness!" There's a spirited glint in his eyes that feels different than the other times we've argued before.

I scowl over at him. "Maybe I was drugged. This is a foreign country, you know."

"Nobody would dare drug you."

"Why is that?"

He pins me with a challenging look. "Because you're far too formidable to mess with."

"That doesn't seem to stop you." I quirk a knowing brow.

"I'm built of stronger stuff than most, Ace."

He winks, and I roll my eyes and fight the smile spreading across my face. Even when he's being nice to me, I still want to beat the hell out of him.

"Fine, pick the movie, but if it sucks, I will kick you out of this bed."

"I would expect nothing less," Calder replies with a sexy smirk that gives my roiling stomach a fresh injection of butterflies.

I nibble on one of the crackers from his tray as the beginning credits of *The Call of the Wild* begin. It's an interesting choice by Calder. It's been a while since I saw the film, but if I recall, the dog is sort of too big for his own life and seeks adventure outside of it. Not unlike the boisterous man sitting next to me seemingly fumbling through his own life a bit.

I shift down to get comfortable when Calder's voice stops me in my tracks. "So now that you're no longer violently ill, are you going to finish your story from last night?"

I swallow nervously and glance over my shoulder at him. "What story?"

His brows tweak. "The one where you told me the reason you were at Lexon Club was because of your ex."

He turns to give me his full attention while the beginning movie credits roll and the serious look in his eyes cause my throat to constrict.

I'd been having flashbacks of my big mouth last night while in the shower earlier, but I was hoping I'd dreamed the part where I mentioned Randal.

"Come on, Ace," he urges before pausing the movie. "Just spill it."

"Why do you care so much?" I ask as I wipe away an imaginary crumb on my lip.

"Because it doesn't seem like your kind of place. It's not your thing."

"You have to quit acting like you know me so well, Calder," I argue because I'm done letting men think they know what I can and can't do with my own damn life.

My throat tightens as Calder stares back at me in that intense way he has about him, and I feel a flashback to the first night we met.

It was seven or eight years ago, and I was picking up Cozy for a night on the town. She was nannying for Max at the time, taking care of little twelve-year-old Everly, and I knew full well that I could text her and she'd come out from the guest house she was living in for the summer and meet me in my car. But I wanted to see this boss of hers who had my best friend so stressed that she needed a night out. I saw that and a whole lot more.

"What do we have here?" I ask when I walked into Max Fletcher's house to see a plethora of hot men seated around the table with cards and poker chips.

"You got any money?" Calder Fletcher waggles his brows at me, and my stomach swirls. All of his attention is focused directly on me. This guy has a way of making you feel like you're the only person in the room. It's really annoying.

"I do, but I usually make the man pay for me." I reply with a coy smile,

feeling all my feminism vacate via my loins. "It's possibly antifeminist of me, but I figure taking a man's money is also a way to fuck the patriarchy."

"What's a patriarchy?" a little voice asks, and my eyes widen in horror as I spot a little blonde girl with braids at the end of the table.

"Oh my God. I'm so sorry. I didn't see you there."

"It's okay," Max replies dropping down into his seat. "Everly knows what words aren't for her."

"Is patriarchy a bad word, Daddy?"

"Kind of? But it's not really a curse word, so you can feel free to use it."

"You want me to deal you in, Blondie?" Calder asks, pulling my focus back to him like we're the only two people in the room as he adds, "I like to fuck the patriarchy too."

My chest tightens as I swallow the knot in my throat and shake my head, even though all I want to do is sit on his lap and debate whether sex is a need or a want, and maybe go through some exercises to draw our own conclusion. It's the beard and ink combo that's doing me in . . . which is a bit surprising because he's not my typical type. I'm usually drawn to dressier hipsters who can pick out a good bottle of red at a restaurant. Calder Fletcher looks like he leaves the toilet seat up.

But tonight isn't about me. It's about my best friend, and ogling her boss's younger brother is not a good idea.

"Not tonight," *I reply, feeling my loins weep at the lost potential of an ideal one-night stand.* "Cozy and I are meeting some people in a little bit, and I wouldn't want to be late."

The look of disappointment in his eyes is unmistakable, and the confidence that surges through me over that reaction is better than sex . . . and makes me think perhaps sex is a need. A need that I should be thinking about with the man I've been seeing for weeks now, not this bearded new guy.

I better stay far away from this Fletcher brother if I know what's good for me.

"Enlighten me, Ace. Tell me something I don't know about you." Calder stares back at me with a severity that I feel squarely between my legs, stoking the fire that little flashback already caused. Couple that with my foggy hangover brain, and the way his eyes keep dropping down to my legs, and I feel like I'm going to upchuck again.

"I'm too hungover for this conversation."

"Just tell me if he was there," Calder presses further.

"If who was there?"

"Your ex."

"Randal?"

"Obviously!" The muscle in Calder's jaw flexes under his beard as he looks away from me.

"Randal was not there." I laugh at the thought. "If he was, I certainly wouldn't have been there."

Calder shakes his head with a confused frown. "You said you were there because of him."

"I was, but that doesn't mean I was with him there. We're divorced. Completely."

"Good."

"Good?"

"Yes, good. He didn't deserve you, but that still doesn't explain why you were there."

"Calder, I'm not getting into this with you."

"Why not?"

"Because no offense, but it's really none of your business." I shift in the bed as the sensation of walls closing in on me hits me the more we discuss this.

"Fine, forget it then." He resumes the movie, refusing to make eye contact with me, even though I *know* he knows I'm looking at him.

I stare at his brooding profile for a moment and feel a pang of guilt. He's being so nice to me, and here I am with all my black-cat energy ruining his attempt at being decent. But this is such a personal thing that I haven't even talked to Cozy about yet. I can't confide in Calder of all people.

It's better this way. Calder doesn't need to know how crazy I really am. Maybe no one needs to know.

Calder

I am one sick motherfucker, I think to myself as I stand under the scalding-hot shower of our attached palapa bathroom. The grip I have on my hard shaft has me trembling as I press my forehead against the shower wall, bracing myself.

Dakota Schaefer completely shut me out after I went above and beyond to make her feel better. Something I've never done. And now what am I doing? I'm in here stroking one out like a teenager because I couldn't take my eyes off of my shirt riding up her legs after she fell asleep beside me. Or how I could see the hard buds of her nipples through the thin fabric and knew she was completely bare under there.

A smile teases the corner of my mouth when I recall the moment she started snoring.

She fucking snored.

And I got a boner.

Sick. Motherfucker.

I squeeze the tip of my dick and bite back a moan. Fucking Dakota. Those curves. Her breathy groans as she snuggled closer to me and her warm skin touched mine. Felt like I was on fire in that bed with her.

Maybe I need to go back to Club Lexon and find a Domme if this is the kind of shit that gets me hard. A rude, off-putting nag who snores like a trucker . . . Is there a room at the sex club to exercise that kink? I'm guessing not. Little too niche, I'd bet.

But it wasn't just her snoring, it was the way her face softened in her sleep. So peaceful. Like she finally let her guard down and just let herself breathe.

So fucking sexy.

And I'm so fucking stupid because I let my mind wander as I watched her sleep like a creep getting myself so worked up. I had to ditch the movie and come in here to relieve myself.

I tremble as I thrust harder into my fist, eyes closed, picturing what Dakota's face would look like if it was her I was thrusting into. How her full lips would part as I bury myself balls-deep. Her breath would become ragged as I thrust in as deep as she'll take me. The picture my mind conjures is so fucking hot, I have to relax my grip before I blow, not wanting this fantasy to end just yet.

A small laugh escapes me, echoing off the shower walls as I think of how her scowling Karen barrier would vanish forever if she gave me one fucking night. Just one night to cure her of her bristly attitude. One night to erase whatever that fuck-wit Randal did to inspire her to visit a sex club by herself.

My fist squeezes my shaft at the rage I feel over Randal entering the fucking chat. I hate that he had her. I hate that she let him see her naked. I hate that I care that he saw her naked. I fucking hate her. I hate that the more I hate her, the thicker my cock gets. I hate that the more I admit I want her, the harder I feel myself thrusting into my hand.

I rise up onto my toes as the tingles of climax begin to heat my balls and I can't stop it now. Pressing my head against the tiles, my grunts reverberate loudly in my ears, and I don't even try to quiet myself as I visualize her body in the pool, at the sex club, in our bed.

A primal rush of heat floods my tip when I think of her waking up, covered in my scent. "Oh God," I grunt, and like a fucking animal my climax rushes from me, spurting over the walls of the shower as I shudder and pant and jack every last drop from my length with a punishing grip.

I groan and shake my head as my aching fingers release my cock and I come down from the most intense orgasm I've had in ages. The hot water scalds my raw shaft, vibrating at the lingering tingles and making my whole body quiver. And as my sanity returns, I realize with a heavy pit in my stomach that I really hate myself because I don't actually hate her.

I want her.

And I hope she heard me just now.

Dakota

You know those delicious naps where you feel like you want to get up, but the sleep keeps pulling you under? You're stuck in this delirious state of oblivion getting some of the best rest of your life, and it takes every ounce of willpower to rip yourself out of it?

That is the best way to get rid of a hangover.

And when I finally rise from my movie-induced slumber, I glance to the other side of the bed to see that Calder is nowhere to be found. I sit up and rub my eyes, noticing the door to the bathroom is closed with the faint sounds of the shower running.

I check my phone and reply to a couple requesting-proof-of-life texts from Cozy. She wants to make sure Calder hasn't taken me hostage up in our little palapa. If I told her that once he quit pouting about me not sharing my innermost thoughts and feelings with him, we willingly watched two movies together and ordered room service, she'd never believe it.

I'm not sure I believe it myself.

I glance over at all the empty space he left on the bed, my hand reaching over to the space he was lying. We made it through this afternoon without killing each other. I suppose there's really no reason we can't share this bed the last two nights we're here. It's tainted with his musk now anyways. As long as he stays on his side, we'll be just fine.

An odd noise echoes from behind the bathroom door, and my lips part. Is Calder with someone in there? Surely not. He wouldn't bring some random woman into our shared room, right? Even for Calder that would be bad.

A masculine grunt sounds off, and I listen intently, my entire body erupting in goose bumps when I consider what might be going on in there. Is he . . . jerking off? Would he have the nerve to do that? In our shared space? While I'm sleeping just feet away from him? That seems way too audacious, doesn't it?

Then again, this is Calder Fletcher we're talking about, and he probably assumes I'm still asleep.

An image of his inky forearm flexing as he strokes himself hits me out of nowhere, and I duck under the covers, horrified at my intrusive thoughts. Images of my time at the sex club replay in my mind. Of all the people I saw going at it that night, nothing aroused me as much as the moment Calder appeared in front of me.

My thighs clench as I squirm in the bed and picture him naked and wet and grunting as he masturbates just ten feet away from me. I glance down at his shirt covering my body. His scent enveloping me in the sheets and in his clothes has my breasts heaving through the thin fabric. My nipples pebble at the thought of Calder touching me over his shirt. Claiming me.

My God, I really do belong in hell. And he'd be right there with me if he thinks it's normal to jerk it in a bathroom you're sharing with someone.

Then again, he's a sex club expert. Jerking off with someone nearby is probably par for the course in that world he's clearly experienced in.

The blood in my veins hums with intrigue as I consider that thought.

The water shuts off, and I stop the ridiculous writhing I was doing in bed and sit up, straightening my hair to look cool and collected . . . like I wasn't just thinking about touching myself over thoughts of Calder at a sex club.

When he emerges in a puff of steam wearing nothing but a white towel, his sculpted muscles glistening with moisture, I feel my lips part. Like the devil sent him from the depths of fiery hell to fuck with me.

"Morning, Ace," he says, offering me a dazzling smile. "Or should I say good evening."

I hold my hand up to avoid the sight of his chiseled body and the ink scrawled across his chest. "Is there a reason you didn't get dressed in the bathroom?"

"Didn't feel like it." He shrugs and walks over to one of his bags before shamelessly dropping his towel and giving me a view of his ass.

I slap my hands over my eyes. "Calder! What the hell?"

"I saw your tit the other day. Seems only fair you get to see my pocket python."

"Pocket python?" My face twists in disgust.

"Yeah, do you think it looks like something else?" he asks, swerving back toward me. "What would you name him?"

I peek through my fingers to confirm that he's now facing me fully with his hands proudly on his hips, his dick swinging in the ocean breeze.

"I'd like it covered up, please. God, Calder. I was just coming around to the idea of sharing this bed with you tonight, but this kind of ridiculous behavior has me reconsidering."

"Aw, come on, Ace. The human body is a wonderful thing. Don't be ashamed."

"I'm not ashamed. I just don't need to have your unit looking me in the eye."

"He likes to look."

"Calder!"

He chuckles and thankfully throws a pair of shorts on. "Not to rush you, but the rehearsal dinner is starting in an hour, so if you're feeling up for it, you might want to start getting ready."

Shit, he's right. I need to get ready. I guess our little palapa siesta is well and truly over, and it's back to reality.

And the reality is . . . Calder Fletcher has an anaconda.

Chapter 12

BED BUDDIES

Calder

There are two words on my mind as I watch my brother and his fiancée rehearse their wedding vows with the civil officiant at sunset on the beach with all of us watching them.

Sex. Club.

I glance over at Dakota who's standing in the audience section of the bride's side while I'm standing in the audience section of my brother's side. It took a lot of fucking willpower all afternoon not to pester Dakota for more details about her sex club interest. And my mind has scrolled through endless possibilities ever since.

First of all, I'm relieved Randal wasn't there. I wouldn't have put it past that asshole to have his kink be to divorce someone and still sleep with them afterward. The fucking twat.

And I'm not ashamed to admit I breathed a little easier after she confirmed he wasn't with her there. I'd rather see Dakota fuck a stranger than Randal.

I close my eyes and try to shake any thoughts of him out of my head. I really shouldn't be thinking about Dakota either. I should be focused on this wedding. On my family. On the reason I'm here.

I glance at Luke, who's standing beside me, and my mom, who's adjusting Stevie's floral dress. There's no groomsmen or bridesmaids standing up with Wyatt and Trista. They said it felt unnecessary since this is such an intimate ceremony, and there's something kind of beautiful about just the two of them up there, starting their journey together.

Not that I want to ever get married. Honestly, I don't see the need for it. I'm comfortable in my own skin, and people typically irritate me. I get all the human contact I need by living next door to my brothers and working with them every day. And when I'm horny, that's what the dating apps are great for . . . *when they're not being hacked, that is.* You can clearly lay out what you're looking for, and for me, it's always just sex. So the boundaries and expectations are out there on the table.

The one woman that I considered opening my heart to ended up fucking over me and both my brothers, so who's to say love is worth all that hassle?

Truthfully, I'm not sure I knew what love was back then. I just assumed the fact that I considered more with her at all meant love. That was until we found out the truth about her, and goddamn if that didn't fuck me over in more ways than one.

If I stay single, then I get to continue to do all the things I want without needing to factor someone else's schedule into the mix. And for what? So you can have someone to watch a movie in bed with? I have Milkshake for that. I'm good.

Though, there was something mildly comforting about how easily Dakota fell asleep next to me this afternoon during our second movie. She has this soft little snore that reminded me of Milkshake's purr.

I guess a little extra human contact isn't all bad. But I don't need to get married to have it.

Trista turns to look out at us in the audience and gasps at something off in the distance. All heads turn, and my forehead wrinkles when I see an unfamiliar couple walking down the beach toward us.

The man is a giant bear of a guy with brown skin and black hair. The woman walking with him looks familiar, but it isn't until she draws closer that I realize she's the spitting image of Trista.

"Vada!" Trista squeals and runs down the sandy aisle to wrap the woman in a hug.

I glance across the aisle and see Cozy's eyes filling with tears. I frown my silent question at her, and she mouths "Trista's sister" back at me.

Oh shit, Trista's sister? The one she hasn't seen in years? The one who she doesn't have the best history with? We've all grown close to Trista the past year, and she's opened up about the thorny past with her family. Her parents abandoned both her and her sister when they were teenagers, and Trista's sister did the same thing when she met some guy and moved to Hawaii with him. Trista was only sixteen years old at the time and had to basically finish raising herself.

I hate to say it, but I'm not real excited about this new wedding guest.

Trista drags her sister and the man around to everyone, introducing the guy by the name of Kai. She seems happy, with tears in her eyes, but I feel protective of my soon-to-be sister-in-law. Her family has fucked her over more than once, and I don't want to see her hurt again.

When she makes her way over to my mom and Stevie, I feel my fists clenching at my sides. Stevie is ours. Not theirs. They don't get to claim her the way we do, and if they try, I'm going to have a real problem with that.

Luke elbows me, snapping me out of my brooding. "Chill the fuck out, man."

I frown and shake my head. "Why are they here?"

"I flew them in," Max hisses from the other side of me. "It was Cozy's idea, and Wyatt was good with it."

"I don't like it."

"You don't have to like it," Max says firmly. "Trista clearly likes it."

Trista holds her daughter proudly in front of her sister, pressing soft kisses to our girl's head of curls as her sister leans in close and touches her cheek. She looks like a proud mama bear showing off her cub, and I guess if having her sister here makes her happy, I'll try to chill the fuck out. But I'm keeping my eyes on both of them.

The rehearsal resumes, and I glance over and see Dakota watching me curiously. Honestly, I've been trying not to look at her since the moment she stepped out of the palapa earlier this evening. She's dressed in a long emerald green and pink floral satin dress that dips low in the cleavage. And the slit that shows off her muscular legs when the wind catches her dress is enough to make me salivate. After lying next to her earlier, seeing those smooth legs, hearing her breathe, visualizing her naked under my T-shirt, it was no wonder I needed to jerk one out in the shower.

Tonight, she looks good enough to eat, and it's going to make sharing a bed later even more uncomfortable. If I wake up with morning wood tomorrow, I know for a fact she will never let me hear the end of it.

Dakota

"So where were you all day?" Cozy asks quietly as we sit down at dinner being served by the pool.

"In bed fighting for my life. Please tell me you felt the same."

She winces. "I don't think I did as many shots as you did last night."

I roll my eyes. "A true friend would have stopped me."

She shrugs. "You needed to blow off some steam. You earned it. This trip is as much for you as it is for the bride and groom."

I laugh and glance over at Wyatt and Trista who are all heart eyes at each other tonight. Wyatt is supposed to be the grumpy one of the four Fletcher brothers, but he's been smiling nonstop.

"Trista seems happy her sister is here."

"Thank God," Cozy says with a sigh. "It was a bit of a risk flying them out here for this, but Wyatt really wanted to make it happen for Trista."

"God, they are so cute and in love." I sigh as I look back at them again. "Did I ever look at Randal that way?"

"You sure did." Cozy looks almost sad and contemplative at that answer. "But don't worry. You'll find love again."

I bark out a laugh and wince when all heads turn to look at me and Cozy at the end of the table. My eyes snag on Calder's, and he frowns quizzically at me. Like somehow our shared afternoon of peace entitles him to know my innermost thoughts.

I clear my throat and take a sip of my water. "Trust me, girl. I'm not looking for that again."

"What are you looking for?"

My traitorous eyes move to Calder. Damn them. "Just . . . myself again."

I turn back to find my best friend frowning at me.

"I lost a lot of myself, and I'd like to find that girl again. The one who opened her own T-shirt shop fresh out of college and renovated her house all on her own and just . . . killed it at life, ya know?"

"How will you find her again? Do you have a plan?"

I lick my lips as I ponder her question. This is not the time or the place to get into the specifics of my post-divorce plan with my best friend. I'm not sure Cozy would approve anyways. She's in such a different place in her life. Cozy is in busy-mom mode and sister-in-law mode, and I love that for her. But it makes me sharing the inner workings of my crazy plan a bit awkward. It feels seedy and dangerous and like it might taint the perfect bubble she's living in. And I don't know if I really want advice from someone who's smack-dab in the middle of her happily-ever-after. Hell, I'd probably get more relatable advice from Everly these days.

I have to figure this out on my own. I'll plan to find Cozy on the other side when it's all said and done, hopefully feeling more like myself than I have in years. Not this tired, insecure, splintered shell.

The clinking of glass on the other side of the table draws my eyes as I see Johanna stand up from her seat, holding her flute of champagne and waiting for everyone's attention. Everly holds a sleeping Stevie in her arms beside her, and Trista tears her attention away from her future husband to grin up at her future mother-in-law.

"I think it's customary for the father of the groom to make a toast at the rehearsal dinner, so I hope you don't mind 'ol Ma doing it instead."

Trista reaches up and rubs Johanna's arm encouragingly as her lip quivers. Both of their eyes fill with tears as she pauses and focuses her attention to Wyatt and Trista. "First of all, I want to welcome Trista's sister Vada and her partner Kai here with us this evening. Thank you so much for making the trip all the way here from Hawaii. We love your sister very much, and she means the absolute world to us."

Vada smiles and nods, her eyes finding Trista's across the table before refocusing on Johanna who breathes heavily, as if preparing herself for the next bit.

"And Trista . . . my little mountain woman. The number of times I've thanked my lucky stars you came into Wyatt's life is insurmountable. Of all my boys, he was always the toughest one for me to crack."

"Grumpy bastard," Calder says with a cough into his fist, and the whole table chuckles, grateful for the moment of levity.

Wyatt scowls at his brother, but when he looks back to Trista, his eyes sparkle with adoration.

"But for you . . . he fell completely apart. You did more than just love my son and turn him into a father. You turned him into *his* father." Johanna pauses as her voice catches in her throat, but she smiles gallantly through her tears. "And I know you never got to meet Steven, but he was one for the books. I see so much of him in Wyatt tonight, and I can't thank you enough for bringing a piece of him to us this evening."

Wyatt's eyes are red-rimmed as he pulls Trista's hand up and presses a chaste kiss to the top of her knuckle. She leans in, wrapping her arm around him with tears falling freely down her cheeks.

"My whole life I wondered what it would be like to have a daughter. And now I am about to have two daughters and two granddaughters." She raises her flute to Cozy and then back to Everly and Stevie. "It feels good to even out these wild Fletcher boys at long last."

"Hear! Hear!" Everly peals excitedly, and everyone laughs.

"Welcome to the family, and if Wyatt ever screws up, don't you worry because I'll always be here for you like you're my own."

That last comment sends Trista over the edge, and she releases a soft sob as she stands and wraps her arms around Johanna. The whole table is filled with tears; I even spot Calder wiping away some moisture. Trista's sister watches everyone with rapt fascination, clearly still getting her bearings with this family her sister has found.

And what a family it is.

Perhaps my life would have turned out very differently if I'd had unconditional, unwavering support and love. And good examples of love. Maybe then I wouldn't have been so hyper-focused on getting married and finding my HEA that I would have seen the red flags Randal waved.

The ocean waves crash onto the darkened beach outside as I stand on the other side of the big round bed in the sexiest pajamas that I packed for this trip.

Don't get me wrong, it's not a negligée or anything. Just a pale green tank top and matching boy shorts. But admittedly, the built-in bra makes my boobs look good. And while, yes, I know nothing will happen between me and Calder, I still feel the urge to look good in front of him. Especially after getting a look at his body after his shower earlier today.

There is no denying Calder Fletcher is insanely hot. I knew it from the first time I met him at that poker night at Max's house over seven years ago. Cozy was the nanny living in the guest house out back, and I was stopping by to pick her up. I didn't have to go through the main house to let her know I was there, but I wanted to get a look at the man my bestie was working for.

And I got a look at all those men.

The Fletcher family is well known in the Boulder, Colorado community—mostly Max with his ever-growing company. But the other three Fletcher boys have developed a good reputation for their house-flipping and development projects around town. My house issue with Calder would be an exception to that reputation, I suppose.

Their reputation with the women of Boulder is just as well known.

Calder steps out of the bathroom in a pair of black boxer briefs and no shirt, causing butterflies to erupt in my belly the instant our eyes connect. I quickly slip into the bed before he can get a good look at me, feeling suddenly foolish for being dressed in such revealing sleepwear.

"What is that?" Calder points to the line of pillows I put down the center of the bed.

"A boundary," I state pointedly sitting up to gesture to his half of the bed. "My side, your side."

"Your side is bigger."

"Well, I'm a girl," I reply with a shrug. "And I wanted a little extra buffer in case you have wandering hands in the night."

"Wandering hands?" He points to his sculpted chest with an offended look. "Do I look like I'd have wandering hands?"

"Do you want to sleep in this bed or not?"

"Hell yes." He jumps onto the mattress like a child. "I'm going to sleep like a rock in this thing."

"Just stay on your side and everyone will have a good night."

"Whatever you say, boss."

I lean over and click the lamp off, bathing us both in complete darkness, save for the moonlight streaming in through the open balcony. The sea breeze blows the canopy that hangs around the top half of the bed, and the longer we lie in silence staring up at the ceiling, the more nervous I begin to feel.

"I'm still trying to figure out your sex club shenanigans," Calder says, his deep voice breaking through my racing thoughts.

"Why do you care?"

"Because I'm a curious cat." He turns over to face me but I can only see his shoulder because of my pillow wall. "Do you have some fetish that he didn't satisfy?"

"No!" I bark out a dry laugh as my body tenses defensively.

"Are you trying to meet someone? Put yourself back out in the dating pool?"

"No." I groan and roll away as I feel him drawing closer. "Just let it go, Calder."

"I can't," he exclaims, and his voice is almost panicky. I hear the rustling of sheets and look over my shoulder to see he's moved to the head-barrier pillow. "Just tell me. It's killing me."

"No," I snipe and look away. "Just drop it."

Silence descends on us again, and my stomach is in knots over the thought of actually telling Calder why I was at that sex club. It's unfathomable. Unimaginable. Too horrifying even to consider having the full conversation with him.

"Hey, Dakota . . ." Calder says in the dark.

I sigh heavily. "What, Calder?"

"You're not a six."

"Huh?" I frown and turn to see his profile as he's stretched out with his arms behind his head, staring up at the ceiling.

"You're not even an eight."

"What are you talking about?" Flashes of what I said to him prick back into my mind.

He turns, and his eyes sparkle in the darkness as he hits me with a serious look that tells me I revealed a lot more than I intended to last night. "You said Randal told you that you used to be an eight but now you're a six."

I cover my face in horror. "I shouldn't have told you—"

His warm hands grab my wrists as he pulls them from my face. "You're neither of those numbers."

I inwardly curse myself for blurting out whatever drunken, self-deprecating, stupid drivel I must have said last night. I had to do those extra tequila shots, didn't I? Vacation Dakota is a moron. A stupid, stupid moron.

I cast my eyes down and brace myself for whatever numerical value Calder is going to peg me with. "What am I, then? Come on . . . get it over with."

"You're a ten," he says quickly, his eyes fixed intently on me. His focus drops to my chest before flicking back up to my eyes. "You're a pain-in-the-ass ten."

He turns away from me like he didn't just say the most shocking thing I would ever have expected him to say. And after a few seconds of silence, he offers a cheery "Good night" that stuns me even further.

"Good night," I reply breathlessly as my head spins. How the hell am I supposed to sleep after that?

Chapter 13

Dakota

I wake the next morning to the feel of something strange moving on top of my head. My eyes crack open to sunlight streaming into the palapa, and it takes a second for me to understand what exactly is going on.

It's Calder's hand toying with my hair. I roll over to discover he's lying on top of my pillow barrier, ass up and completely invading my space.

"Calder, you're on my side," I hiss, shoving his arm away from me. "And were you just . . . petting me?"

"What?" His voice cracks as his eyes blink away the sleep, flinching when they open to the bright sunlight bathing our entire bed. He frowns and shakes his head violently as he shifts back to his side.

"Were you just touching me?" I ask again, my hand smoothing my hair as I sit up to assess the situation more properly.

"Of course I wasn't touching you," he adds in a deeper, more masculine tone as he adjusts the covers over his body. "I just . . . forgot I wasn't at home."

"What do you touch at home?" I hold my hand up, my face twisting with disgust. "Never mind. I don't want to know."

"It's just my cat," he exclaims with a snarl. "It's nothing weird."

"Unless that's a euphemism for something."

"I have a cat, Dakota. It's a literal feline. I have a heart under all this chiseled, godlike muscle, and I was obviously sleeping so hard, I forgot where I was and thought you were Milkshake." He shoves his sleep-tousled hair back off his forehead and murmurs to himself, "Though, I can't believe I didn't open my eyes to confirm that first because Fuzz burned me once before when I thought I was snuggling her face, only to realize I was nuzzling her asshole." He shakes his head, his nose wrinkled. "That memory still haunts me, if I'm being honest."

"Stop being so honest." I shake my head, unable to process everything I'm seeing right now. "This is too weird."

"It's only weird if you make it weird. At least I wasn't petting your tit."

"I could understand that more, coming from you. The fact that you're a ten with a cat, Calder, is just . . . unnerving."

"Well, pardon me for paying you a compliment. You've definitely never had a kind word to say about me."

"That isn't my fault. Your reputation kind of proceeds you."

"And what reputation is that?"

"You're a screwup!" I squeal indignantly. "You don't take anything seriously, and the notches on your bedpost prove that. You and your brothers had to move out to Jamestown because you slept your way through the population of Boulder already. I'm not going to let your silver-tongued compliments and talks of being a cat daddy fool me into thinking you're a decent guy."

"Jesus Christ, I've been awake for sixty seconds, and you're already starting." He gets up out of bed and stomps over to the closet, grabbing the suit he hung there earlier. "I can't wait for this fucking nightmare of a trip to be over."

"The feeling is mutual!" I call out as he slams the bathroom door.

Guilt niggles at me as I hear the shower kick on. That escalated quickly, and it was all my fault. I didn't intend to pick a fight with him right away, but honestly, I was up for hours last night fretting over what he said to me. I don't know what Calder is after exactly, but whatever it is, I don't trust it. It's better for both of us to just continue hating each other until we get off this beach and back to the real world.

Calder

I'd forgotten what a head case Dakota Schaefer was.

You're a screwup! You don't take anything seriously, and the notches on your bedpost prove that. You and your brothers had to move out to Jamestown because you slept your way through the population of Boulder already.

While she's not altogether wrong, I didn't deserve to wake up to her black-cat claws—way too much before coffee. I certainly won't be trying to erase her ex-husband's words again anytime soon.

The mood swings, the temper tantrums, her capacity to change her mind on a dime . . . all of this is giving me flashbacks of the girl I worked with years ago when I was renovating her house.

It was supposed to be an easy project, one that didn't require my brothers. Occasionally the three of us picked up solo side gigs for a little extra income when work for our dad's business was slow. So when Cozy said her best friend needed a contractor to help update her old Victorian, I thought why not? I needed the cash, Dakota ain't bad to look at. Win-win.

More like lose-lose.

It was a miserable experience from start to finish. She was constantly blowing up my phone with things she had changed her mind on, and she wanted me to explain every part of the job to her, like I could somehow teach her how to build a damn home. I nearly quit on the spot when I was laying tile one day and she wanted to handpick every piece before I placed it. She even had me return all the ones that didn't make the cut in exchange for new boxes. One day I overheard her on the phone with someone saying she couldn't leave me there to work alone because if she did, nothing would be done right.

She was wild.

And I know she thinks the accident that happened was intentional. She probably invented some sort of villain story where

I sabotaged the project because I'm careless and didn't check something properly. And I'll let her keep thinking that, because it doesn't make any difference anyways.

We are oil and water. Fire and ice. Hot or not, I need to re-member one thing the next time I want to be nice to her.

Don't.

"Calder . . . the photographer said to smile." Luke elbows me and I force a grin that I don't feel as I pose with my brothers be-neath some palm trees with the ocean front at our backs.

"Jesus, man, you're in a mood," Luke says as the photographer resets his camera, barking orders at his assistant.

I quickly take off the cream jacket. "It's hot as hell in this coat."

"It's a linen jacket." Max frowns over at me.

"I'm sweating my balls off."

Wyatt eyes me with a threatening look. "Do I need to throw you in the ocean before the wedding to get you to cool the fuck down? You've been a pain in the ass all afternoon."

"Yeah, what is your problem?" Luke adds, taking Wyatt's side. "These suits breathe really nicely."

"Maybe you guys aren't hot because you're staying in a nice, air-conditioned house, while I'm stuck in a wide-open palapa with the spawn of Satan trying to boil me alive!"

"Dakota isn't that bad," Max scoffs and shakes his head at me.

I huff out a laugh. "Then, you share a room with her."

A slow smile spreads across Luke's face. "You're just pissy because she won't fuck you."

"Oh, like Addison is fucking you?"

His eyes turn to slits. "We're just friends."

"And who's decision was that?"

Luke steps up so we're standing toe-to-toe. "Are you looking for a fight today?"

"All right, knock it off," Wyatt thunders stepping between us and pressing his hands to both of our chests. "You were the morons who demanded plus-ones."

"Dakota is *not* my plus-one," I snap, my shoulders tight as I point back to the house where the ladies are all getting ready. "Someone sabotaged my plus-one plans, and now I'm stuck with her."

"If you had some semblance of control, you wouldn't have asked to bring someone anyways," Max says with a harrumph, adjusting the cuff link on his sleeve.

"Stop acting all holier-than-thou, Max. You and Wyatt are no picnics to be around these days."

"What is that supposed to mean?"

"I mean you're both shoving your happy love bubbles in all our faces, and it's a fucking lot, okay? It's enough to make a guy puke."

"My fiancée and daughter make you want to puke?" Wyatt steps up close and bumps chests with me.

"They're fine, it's you that makes me want to yack."

"I'm going to fucking kill you," Wyatt lunges for my neck as Luke and Max dive into the mix, trying to break up our brawl.

"Boys!" a loud voice shrieks from the distance, and we all freeze in place, knowing that tone all too well.

We turn and see our mother standing there in her powder-blue Mother of the Groom dress. Her short blond hair is curled, her makeup is done, and her flat sandals thwack loudly on the cobblestone sidewalk as she marches toward us.

"Wyatt, let go of your brother's throat," she snaps, swatting him on the arm.

I inhale a deep breath as I relax my shoulders and crack my neck.

She turns her pinched lips to me. "Calder, what did you do?"

"Me? You think I'm the problem?"

"You're usually the problem." She closes her eyes and sighs heavily. "What did you say?"

My teeth crack as I clench my jaw, refusing to answer the question that she obviously already knows the answer to.

"You know what? It doesn't matter what you said or what any of you said." She flails her arms at all of us. "This is your brother's wedding day, and you're all down here acting like a bunch of animals!" she hisses. "Your father would be ashamed of you."

Fuck.

She could say anything but that.

"Mom, I'm sorry."

"I don't want to hear it, Calder," she says, holding her hand up to stop me from speaking. "All I want to hear is you turning to your brother and telling him you love him."

I roll my eyes and shake my head. "Seriously?"

"Yes, seriously," she sighs, crossing her arms over her chest. "Go on."

My lips thin as I turn to Wyatt and stare at his brooding face all grumpy and stern, like a dad. Like *our* dad.

He's a dad. My throat tightens as I let that thought settle over me. My big brother is a dad. And about to become a husband. Of course I love him. Of course I'm fucking happy for him. I'm being a dick because of reasons that have nothing to do with him. Mom is right: this is his wedding day, and he doesn't need my shit. He's a good brother. A good man. *Just like Dad.*

My eyes soften as I inhale a deep breath. "I love you, man."

He huffs and looks away, clearly not believing me.

I step closer to him and grab his shoulder. "I mean it. I love you, Papa Bear."

He turns back to me, frowning as he silently asks me what the fuck all this is about.

"This is a me thing. Not a you thing. I love you, and I love Trista. And I love—" my voice catches in my throat "—I love lil Stevie. No matter what bullshit I might say in the heat of a moment, please don't ever doubt that."

Wyatt finally relaxes and nods, cupping his hand behind my neck and yanking me in for a hug. He claps my back, and I hate how much he even *feels* like our dad. It makes me wish he was here more than ever. When I pull away, I look down to hide the tears in my eyes.

"We all miss him," Max says, stepping in close and putting his hand on my shoulder.

And in a breath, I'm wrapped up in a hug by all three of my brothers as we mourn the man who should be here still to knock some sense into us.

"Dammit, now I have to go touch up my makeup," Mom blubbers from behind us.

We spread apart as she wipes away the tears running down her face. I reach out and yank her into the center of our group embrace, causing her to squeak as we all squeeze her tiny frame a bit too hard. We're dysfunctional at times, but no matter what, we're still always family.

Dakota

"I, Trista, take you, Wyatt, to be my lawfully wedded husband . . ."

Trista and Wyatt exchange vows in front of a stunning pink-and-purple sunset. They stand beneath an archway draped with hanging white flowers and twinkle lights. Everything is perfect. From Trista's simple, yet stunning white dress that showcases her beautiful body, to baby Stevie in a white fluffy dress lying in a wagon wrapped in flowers and tulle parked right beside her. Even Ethan is on his best behavior as the ring bearer, standing up by his uncle proudly in a matching cream linen suit and holding the rings in an adorable mini toolbox that Everly decorated for the big day.

It's all so beautiful.

And if I continue gaslighting myself like this, I can even believe that maybe these two got it right. Maybe they will make it the long haul. Maybe they won't end up like me, hating everything about the person they married because somehow, he made you lose sight of the person you once were. The person you were proud to be.

I will definitely not be giving a toast at the reception tonight.

"You may now kiss the bride."

A low rumble sounds from Wyatt's chest as he pulls Trista in close to his side in a dramatic dip. She squeals, her foot kicking up just before their lips connect in a passionate kiss that isn't at all like the one I had on my wedding day.

Randal winced when we kissed. Literally winced because he had a split lip and a black eye. And there I was in a mediocre wedding dress purchased off the rack that countless other brides-to-be had tried on before me.

If those weren't signs that our marriage was doomed from the start, I don't know what was.

We make our way from the wedding ceremony area on the courtyard over to the black-and-white checkered dance floor that's laid out by the pool. The sun is nearly gone as the music swells for Wyatt and Trista's first dance.

He sweeps her into his arms, pulling her close as we all huddle around to watch them. My eyes find Calder's across the floor and look away when he looks at me. We haven't spoken a word since that ugliness this morning, and it's probably for the best. We don't need our negative energy to ruin the beautiful evening ahead of us.

Stevie lets out a wail from her grandmother's arms, breaking through the music, and Wyatt and Trista both turn with big smiles on their faces. How a crying baby makes them both happy is a bit puzzling, but Wyatt twirls his bride over to her daughter where Trista scoops Stevie up, holding her close as he takes both his girls out on the dance floor. Stevie settles instantly.

Okay, no gaslighting here . . . That's cute as shit.

My eyes sting as I watch Wyatt press his lips to his daughter's head and then to his wife's temple. He's the grumpiest of all the Fletcher brothers, but the grin on his face right now seems to be healing whatever scowl that man has had most of the years I've known him. Maybe these two will be the lucky ones.

Max and Cozy sure seem to be making it work, too.

They married around the same time as Randal and I. I thought the four of us would be best newlywed friends, but with Cozy having Ethan so soon after they were married, and Randal working evenings while Max had his corporate day job, we were all on very different schedules and life patterns.

Perhaps another sign I ignored.

I turn on my heel and make my way over to the bar, desperate for a drink. Going to a wedding before the ink was dry on my divorce papers probably wasn't the brightest choice I ever made. Self-reflection is a painful bitch.

"Champagne, please," I say to Carlos who's manning the bar. That guy is everywhere.

"I'll take a beer when you have a sec," a deep voice says from behind me, and goose bumps erupt over my skin.

I turn to take in the sight of Calder standing far closer to me than is necessary. His scent of soap, cologne, and whatever natural musk he emits draws me in, and I have to force myself to look away because, dammit, he looks good in that cream suit. His white shirt is partly unbuttoned to show off his tan, and his eyes are sparkling with mischief that I cannot get sucked into.

"Evening, Ace," he says, reaching around to grab both of our drinks from Carlos. He hands me my champagne flute and holds his bottle of beer in front of his lips as his eyes drift down my body. "You look very nice tonight."

I fight the urge to tug at my deep blue off-the-shoulder midi dress. It's formfitting, and the ruffles around my arms add a touch of drama to go with my long blond curls and wedge heels that bring me up to Calder's chin. I evaluated myself in the mirror today and knew I looked *good*, which is good because I need all the confidence I can muster around this infuriating man.

"You look nice too." I sip my drink and look out at Wyatt as the music shifts, and he begins dancing with his mother.

Calder mock-gasps. "Holy shit balls, was that a compliment?"

I narrow my heavily made-up eyes at him. I did a smoky brown shadow to make my blue irises pop—not that I want Calder of all people to notice.

His shock turns into a lascivious smirk as he matches my pose on the bar to watch Wyatt and his mom on the dance floor. "Is that compliment your pathetic excuse for an apology?"

My brows knit together. "What do I have to be apologizing for, exactly?"

"For waking up on the wrong side of the bed this morning."

I take a deep breath, trying to keep my cool because we're in public and Carlos is perched at the end of the bar listening to our entire conversation. "I woke up on the right side. It was you that woke up on my side that set me off."

He grunts and takes a long drink of his beer. "So I suppose I've lost my coveted thirty-three percent of the bed and it's back to the mattress of nails for me."

"You can have the bed. I'll take the sofa."

A deep noise vibrates in his throat. "That's not happening."

"Yes, it is."

"No, it isn't."

"Calder."

"Satan."

"Hi, guys!" Everly's voice chimes in as her blond, bubbly energy interrupts our quiet squabbling. "It's time for all of us to join them on the dance floor. Let's go!"

"Oh . . . you two go ahead." I wave Everly and Calder off as she begins dragging him out by the wrist. "I'll hang back here with Carlos." I turn around and frown when I see that Carlos has vanished.

"Just one dance," Everly says as she uses her free hand to grab my arm, barely giving me a chance to set my drink down.

I smile stiffly at Cozy as she walks out onto the dance floor with Max. She gives me a sympathetic smile as she threads her hands around Max's neck.

With a devious grin, Everly puts my hand inside Calder's. "You two go ahead and get started. I need to go track down Ethan! He's probably over by the cake."

I fight the urge to yank my hand away from Calder's big paw.

I don't want to look like a petulant child as all eyes focus on us. Wyatt is with his bride, Max with Cozy, Luke with Addison, and Johanna is sitting at a table feeding Stevie a bottle and smiling at all the happy couples on the dance floor.

This is so embarrassing.

Calder laughs and jerks me in close, causing me to fall into him as our bodies press together. His breath is warm on the shell of my ear as his other palm snakes around my waist. "Now is your chance to run, Ace. I'm getting my cooties all over you again."

The chill that runs up my spine at the warmth of his body next to me is unnerving, but I give a surrendering exhale and allow myself to embrace the man who drives me crazy and put on a show for the sake of the happy wedding. "Just try not to pet my head again, cat daddy."

His chest vibrates against mine as he laughs and moves me around the dance floor with more grace than I would have given this meathead credit for.

After a moment of awkward silence, he asks, "Was today hard?"

"What do you mean?" I pull back so I can look up at him for explanation. His green eyes smolder and make my stomach flip, so I quickly move in close again to look over his shoulder.

"Watching them get married today," he murmurs into my ear. "Did it remind you of your wedding?"

I frown at that pointed question. "No."

He pulls back to look at me, his silence speaking volumes.

"My wedding was nothing like this."

He nods and resumes our dance. "What was your wedding like? Your contractor's invitation must have got lost in the mail."

I roll my eyes up to the starry sky. "You wouldn't have come anyways."

"Sure, I would have."

"Oh really?" I quirk a brow up at him.

"Yes," he replies with a sexy smirk. "Weddings are a great place to meet chicks."

"Jesus." I shake my head and laugh. "Always on the prowl. I should tell Trista you're more of a tomcat than a rottweiler."

"Definitely," he hums in my ear, and the shiver that runs down my spine has to be obvious to him.

Silence descends for a moment, and I lick my lips, fighting the weird sensation humming in my veins. Being in this man's arms should be giving me hives, and yet, I feel good. Which is so nuts because I lashed out at him viciously this morning. Seriously, you can tell my period is coming because I was feral.

But right now . . . I don't hate being pressed up against him. Not that that *means* anything. It's just because Calder isn't disgusting to look at and it's pleasant to be held by a non-disgusting man after going so long without.

Objectively, all four Fletcher brothers are handsome in their own ways, so I could feel the same if any of one of them were dancing with me.

Though admittedly, Calder is the most striking of the four. Sharp chiseled facial features, narrow striking eyes that pierce right through you, and a body that could put fitness trainers to shame. And his musk . . . it's shamefully growing on me.

It's a damn shame all that beauty is wasted on such an obnoxious personality.

"So . . . what was your wedding like?" Calder asks, resuming his earlier inquiry.

"Messy." I reply honestly.

He looks down at me with a frown.

"Randal got into it with some drunk guy at the bar a couple days before our wedding, so he was all banged up."

"Really?" Calder huffs, his brows furrowed.

"Yeah, the asshole was belligerent and took a swing at him as Randal was kicking him out. Made for some really nice wedding photos that we never got around to retaking. On top of that, my parents were at each other's throats . . . and well . . . you know about my dress issue."

He tenses at the mention of that.

I shake my head because I promised myself a few nights ago: I am not going to be that whiney divorcée making comparisons about a day I'd rather forget. It was a day I deeply regret, and today is nothing like that, so why taint it with memories of mistakes? "I'd really rather not talk about this."

"Fair enough," Calder agrees as he moves in close again, swaying to the music. "You know, if you want, we could cut out of here early and go find a sex club. I bet Carlos could point us to some wild fucking haunts around these parts. He's probably a wicked Dom."

I burst out laughing and when everyone's heads snap in our direction, I quickly stifle my amusement into Calder's shoulder. "Maybe your mom could give us a ride."

He shakes in silent laughter, and it feels good. *Too good.* Calder is a man I need to keep at arm's length . . . which is hard to do when I feel incredible wrapped up in his ink-draped arms on this dance floor. But I need to remember that tomorrow everything will go back to normal, and I have to pick up the pieces of my life. Letting someone like Calder get under my skin isn't a good idea. He's definitely got a case of Peter Pan Syndrome, never wanting to grow up, and I'm all done raising boys.

The music ends and we pull away, both of us staring curiously at the other. Calder opens his mouth to speak, but the music shifts to something fast, and I breathe a sigh of relief when Cozy pulls me away to dance with her.

Dancing is good. Not talking to Calder is good. Keeping my distance from him . . . is good.

But damn, do I have a tiny urge to be bad.

Chapter 14

YOU DON'T HAVE TO LIKE ME TO FUCK ME

Calder

Food was ate, cake was cut, Carlos even took a spin on the dance floor with Everly at one point. It was a killer night, down to the toasts. Max made us all cry. Luke made us all laugh. And I wasn't sure what to say . . . so why not quote the man I looked up to most?

"We're not here for a long time, we're here for a good time."

I plagiarized my father tonight, but I'm pretty sure he didn't invent his favorite catchphrase, so he likely stole it from someone first. But they're words we've all taken to heart since his passing, so it seemed a fitting way to end the evening.

And as I walk Dakota back to our palapa, I can't help but think of how much he would have loved tonight. He would have danced with Trista since she didn't have a father show up for her, which is why my mother demanded a dance with her. That inspired me to grab Max and Luke and tell them we were going to do a dance with our new sister as well. She deserved all the special moments her own family is too crazy to appreciate, and my brothers were all too willing to make this a night she'd never forget.

The three of us surrounded her and swayed to a song that had her wiping tears from her eyes the entire time. She was blaming her postpartum hormones, but I knew our gesture meant a lot to her. Trista is tough on the outside and likes to act like she doesn't need anything from anybody, but that only makes us all want to show up for her even more.

Even Dakota managed to let her hair down and have some fun tonight. At one point, she danced with me again. It was a fast song so I didn't get my hands on her like I wanted to, but I enjoyed the view of her body moving to the music.

Those hips are a sight to behold.

Her blond hair got curlier as the night drew on, and now it has this wild, untamed quality that makes me think of how she would look after being fucked. Hard.

It makes me hard just thinking about it.

Need pulses in my groin, and I take some deep breaths to calm myself down. There's a palpable shift between us that's happened on this trip despite our little tiffs, and I think she feels it too because she hasn't yelled at me for something in at least ninety minutes.

I'm wearing Dakota down. And apparently I *want* to wear her down because it's becoming harder and harder to fight my attraction to her.

Something else is getting hard as well, since I can't stop myself from imagining what it would be like to fill her mouth with my cock so she can't annoy me anymore. *Something tells me she would be a very good girl.*

"Who are you going to miss more? Me or these birds?" I ask, trying my hardest to slow my heart rate down as I drag my hand along the rails of the cage as we climb the steps to our room.

"Oh boy, that's a tough call." She laughs as she picks up the pace, glancing nervously at the cage like the birds are going to dive-bomb her through the rails. She stops at the top of the steps and puckers her lips. "I think I'll be glad to be rid of all of you."

My brows lift as she turns to walk into our room and heads over to the bed to flick the lamp on.

"Admit it, you had fun with me tonight."

She rolls her eyes and props her hands on her hips. "You were less irritating tonight than you have been other nights, but I still can't stand you."

I laugh and shake my head as she perches on the edge of the

bed to take off her heels. She's stunning with the warm yellow lamplight bathing her body. She looks almost as good as she did the night I saw her on her hands and knees inside that sex club.

Speaking of which . . . "So are you really going to let us go back to Colorado without telling me the truth about why you were at Lexon?"

"This again?" She sighs as she tosses her heels toward the closet.

"Yes, this." I cross my arms over my chest and drop my chin. "We fly out tomorrow, and I know you'll go back to pretending I don't exist once we're back home. So it's now or never, Ace."

"I don't pretend you don't exist." She stands up rubs her palms together as she walks out to the balcony of our suite.

My eyes shamelessly drink in her backside as she stands at the railing and gazes out to the ocean. She looks like a wet dream all barefoot in a sexy dress with moonlight shining down on her and the ocean providing an erotic soundtrack.

I walk over and prop myself on the edge of the door. "You're either yelling at me or acting like I don't exist."

She rolls her eyes at me. "It's not like you're trying to be my best friend."

I slide my hands into my pockets. "I can take a hint."

"Like you're my biggest fan!" She turns to lean her ass against the railing and shoots me a teasing scowl.

I smirk as I stare back at her. The truth is, I love to hate her. It ignites something inside of me that feels . . . invigorating. Unexpected. Like you never know when things are going to shift between us. And if I'm not mistaken, that spark in her eyes right now tells me she likes it too.

"Just tell me what you were looking for at the club, then." I pin her with a serious look, trying to lose all sense of humor so she feels safe. "You weren't going there for romance. You said you weren't looking to explore a kink. So, what was it, then?"

She blows a strand of hair out of her face, the moonlight casting a blue glow around her shoulders as she hits me with an irritated look. "If I finally tell you, will you leave it alone and promise never to bring it up with me again?"

I make an *X* over my chest. "Cross my heart and hope to die."

She smiles like she enjoys that thought. The freak.

But then her face sobers, like she's got to psych herself up to spill her guts. She grips the railing and stares down at her bare feet as she answers. "I was there to learn some different stuff in the bedroom because Randal said some things to me—"

"What did he say?" I stand up straight as my hands clench into fists at just the mention of his name.

"Nothing. I mean . . . something, obviously, but I'm trying to forget it, which is why I want to put myself out there and try some new things. Have some casual sex and figure out what I like and don't like before I dive back into the dating pool. I refuse to do the hooking-up thing on the dating apps because I don't want Randal to find out I'm on there. He knows too many people, and it would get back to him which would make it feel like I'm announcing to him that he was right . . . I'm boring in bed."

"He said you were boring in bed?" My head has to be the picture of the mind-blown emoji.

"Among other things." Her voice is strained as she pinches the bridge of her nose. "So I figured sex clubs are anonymous and adventurous. Win-win. Maybe a sex club can help get me back to the person I used to be . . . the brave one who knew her own voice and how to use it. The one who was up for trying new things. I'm trying to find my lost confidence." When she looks up from the floor to make eye contact with me, she shows me something in her that I've never seen before.

Vulnerability.

I stare back at the stunning woman before me. From the day I met Dakota, confidence never seemed to be an issue. But if I really think about it, the light in her eyes has dimmed the past few years.

And knowing it was fucking Randal that did that to her makes me see red.

"So, what you're saying is you want to get laid." I smack the railing obnoxiously, trying to lighten the mood and the agitation humming in my veins.

She scoffs and rolls her eyes, turning to look back out at the ocean. "Of course that's all you hear."

My eyes drop down her body, lingering on her ass. "I heard everything you said, but the end result is still sex, right?"

She shrugs sadly. "I guess so."

I nudge her with my arm and nod toward the bed. "So, let's do it."

"Do what?" She frowns up at me.

My brows lift. "Let's fuck."

She sputters out a nervous laugh as she snaps her head to look at me. "Don't be stupid!"

I drop my chin, allowing her a moment to process what I've just said. It's something I've been thinking about this entire trip, and the idea feels even more valid now. She needs to get laid. Needs to forget that fucker ever existed and find that confidence she had the day I met her.

"You want a casual fuck?" I let the last word linger in the air for a moment before I shrug and add, "I'm right here, Ace."

She scoffs, annoyance dripping in her tone as she replies, "We don't even like each other!"

"You don't have to like me to fuck me." I lick my lips and smirk to show her this isn't as serious as she's making it out to be. She isn't weak. She is strong. And that dickhead made her forget that. *And I am more than happy to help her remember.*

"Of course you would say that." She crosses her arms over her chest and shudders. "Have you ever liked anyone you've slept with? Like genuinely liked them?"

"Sure, I like 'em." I slip out of my jacket and drape it over the railing.

"That's real convincing," she says as her eyes watch me unbutton my sleeves to roll them up. "You probably don't even remember most of their names."

"Is there a reason you're so judgmental about someone who enjoys sex?" I quirk a brow and her eyes brighten with a million questions. "You were literally just talking about wanting casual sex."

"I know but . . . how do you even know what the person likes or doesn't like if you don't know them at least a little bit?"

"I'm a quick study, baby." I wink.

"Don't call me *baby*." She holds her hand up, and her grossed-out expression amuses me.

God, what would be like if she really let her hair down? Really let go? I bet she would be magnificent.

"This is your big chance. A one-night stand with a guy who only does one-nights."

"But what happens when we get back home? It'll be awkward for sure."

I tilt my head. "What happens in Mexico stays in Mexico."

"So we'd never speak about this again?"

I make another *X* on my heart, and her eyes linger on my chest as a look of longing casts over her eyes. I'm wearing her down. The ice queen is melting before my very eyes.

She licks her lips and then chews them, intrigue brightening her features in the moonlight. With a flash of brazen confidence, she looks up at me and says, "Where do we start?"

Hell yeah. "Why don't you start by telling me what you want? Nothing stokes a person's confidence like being in control when the clothes are off."

"I don't want to be a Domme," she blurts out, her chest rising and falling in rapid succession. She turns on her heel and rushes into the room to begin pacing in front of the bed. "And I know I'm not a submissive either. That first experience at Lexon did not go well."

I laugh and watch her wring her hands in front of her as she cracks her knuckles.

"Don't worry about the labels. Just tell me what you want me to do to you."

She barks out a laugh. "Oh yeah, right. Like you'll just let me make demands. You didn't take kindly to my demands during the house reno."

"This is different. I'm a very open-minded person when it comes to fucking. And the sexual frustration I've felt in every cell of my body since the moment I saw you at the club tells me that I will give you whatever you demand."

She shakes her head, clearly unsure how to process that comment from me. "Oh sure . . . like if I asked you to crawl to me, you'd actually do it."

A dry laugh bubbles up from her lips as my brows shoot to my hairline. That is a very specific and unusual request which indicates to me that she's thought about this already. About what it would be like to have a man crawl to her.

My dick thickens in my slacks.

I stare back at her without an ounce of humor on my face. "Say the word."

She sucks in a sharp breath as her lips part. Her breasts heave with a huge gulp of air, and I wonder if they might try to pop out of that dress she's wearing. "You're messing with me."

The blood in my veins heats as I lick my lips and utter, "Try me, Ace."

She lifts her fingers to her mouth, her long nails tapping on her ruby lips as she contemplates this moment.

I really would do anything to bite that lip.

She takes four large steps back, and her eyes sparkle with desire as she says, "Crawl."

Chapter 15

HOW BAD DO YOU WANT ME?

Dakota

Holy fucking shit, I have lost my mind. My entire brain has evaporated into the moonlight. It's all air up here because I seriously just told Calder Fletcher to crawl to me.

Who the hell am I?

I have no idea. That's the point of this. A sexual awakening. A journey of self-discovery. A guess-and-check experiment where I try something out and see what the end results are . . . like a science project.

Calder's eyes twinkle with wickedness, showing no signs of defiance or humor. I half expect him to make fun of me for this, but he doesn't. He's doing it. This cocky bastard is doing what I asked him.

My head wars with what my body is telling me I want, and a wave of heat spreads through me as he takes his giant six foot three body and lowers it down to the floor. His linen shirt tightens around his sculpted shoulders as he presses his palms to the tile and slowly slides a hand forward on the floor, never taking his eyes off me.

I shuffle my feet as nerves rock through me. Watching him slide his other hand forward. He's taking his time, perhaps giving me the opportunity to stop this if I want to.

But I don't think I do.

This crawling request started as a test to make sure Calder wasn't fucking with me because I still don't fully trust him. I'm not sure I can trust any man ever again. But if Calder wasn't serious about this, there would be no way in hell he'd be down on his hands and knees right now. His ego wouldn't allow it. Right? And then I recall what he said about me the other night.

You said Randal told you that you used to be an eight but now you're a six. You're neither of those numbers. You're a ten.

He didn't have to say that to me. No one forced him into it, and Calder doesn't pass out compliments for free. Which means . . . Calder Fletcher thinks I'm sexy.

Maybe it's time I let myself believe it.

As I watch him, I realize there is something incredibly erotic about a tall, rugged, bearded, muscular man crawling to his woman. I may have been the one to ask him to crawl, but I feel like the prey as he makes his way closer, and that scares the shit out of me in the most exciting way possible.

Clenching my dress, I take a deep breath, trying to calm my rapid heart that's fixing to burst out of my chest as he sits back on his heels in front of me, waiting for what I will ask him to do next.

I have no idea, honestly! I didn't think we'd get this far. I meant what I said . . . I could never be a Domme. I don't want control. I want freedom and surprises and possibility. And I want to feel alive again and not view sex as an obligation.

We stare at each other for several long seconds, and I fight the urge to break the spell and push him away. I search his expression for a tell that this is all a joke to him, that he doesn't want me, isn't attracted to me. Something.

"What next?" he asks, and I watch his Adam's apple slide down his thick neck as he appears out of breath. He's enjoying this. The arousal in his body is palpable, and I want to reach out and touch it.

I shake my head in disbelief. "You're crazy."

"I'm not crazy for wanting to fuck you," he replies without a glimmer of humor in his eyes.

Liquid heat pools between my legs, and my voice is trembly when I ask, "Are we really doing this?"

"That's up to you."

Feeling unsteady, I drop down onto my knees in front of him, needing to be level for my next request. The crawling was hot and all, but I'm having trouble understanding where reality and fantasy exist here. My eyes sweep over his face before zeroing in on his lips.

They are good lips.

"Maybe we should kiss first. Make sure we have a connection? Or is that weird? Too intimate? Should this be like a *Pretty Woman* hookup where we don't touch lips?" I snap my mouth shut. I'm rambling. Super hot, Dakota.

Calder's eyes drop to my mouth, and he pulls his lower lip in, chewing it hungrily before replying, "I'll kiss you anywhere you want."

His words create an instant throb in my core. Well, shit . . . maybe I shouldn't have started with the lips. I shake those dirty thoughts out of my head. Lips are good. Let's make sure we can actually kiss before I get naked with the man who I was literally calling an asshole this morning.

I point to my mouth and croak, "Just here for now."

Before I can take a breath, Calder's large hands reach out and grab my face. He pulls me into him, both of us rising up on our knees as he captures my lips with his shooting liquid heat straight through my core. He pulls back after only a second, his eyes fierce on mine with a look of shock that feels like throwing a glass of water in my face. A wave of disappointment descends upon me when I think he's going to call it, and before I have a chance to speak, he's kissing me again with ten times more passion.

A whimper escapes me as I tilt my head and allow his tongue to part my lips, sending a riot of tingles through my whole body. I grip his sculpted arms to steady myself, shivering at the feel of his rough beard against my face. The edginess of that sensation, the grit, makes the kiss that much better. Dirtier, more elicit. The swirling in my groin is unbearable.

His body shifts closer, and my eyes pop open when I feel the ridge of something hard between us. His eyes are still closed tight as he consumes me, and my muscles weaken as his hands move from my face, down my back, mapping the shape of me.

He must sense my hesitation and pulls away. "What is it?" he asks, his eyes searching mine.

"Nothing," I mutter, trying to tame down my stupid thoughts. "I'm just . . . surprised."

"At what?"

I swallow the lump in my throat as my gaze trails down.

The corner of his mouth tugs up into a smirk. "This isn't the first time your mouth has made me hard."

What the hell does that mean? I wonder but am distracted when his palms wrap around to my ass and he pulls me into him, making it very clear he's happy to see me.

"This too," he murmurs, smiling against my lips. "I've wanted to get my hands on your ass since the first day I met you."

I think back to the body I had all those years ago, and my heart sinks a bit.

"But never more than these last couple of days. You're a fucking tease."

Flutters, stars, sparks, sizzles . . . all of those flippity emotions that happen in the human body are happening to mine at the same time. And we're both still fully dressed!

He continues to grip my ass and grinds my center against the length of him, and my heart and my vagina both feel like they're on the brink of explosion as my arousal shifts into overdrive. The man who's an ass to me most of the day is attracted to me enough to be hard within seconds of our kiss. What is this life I'm living?

I comb my fingers through his hair and kiss him back, my nails scratching lightly against his scalp. The low growl that vibrates in his chest gives me signs that he likes what I'm doing, and I swear I want to swallow him whole.

"My turn," he says, pulling away, his hot breath on my lips as both our chests heave with desire.

I feel the loss of him as I struggle to see straight. "Your turn?"

"To make a demand." His hands slide from my ass to my thighs, his thumbs skating up the skirt of my dress. "I'm not going to make you crawl. But I am going to make you beg."

He stands and holds his hand out to me, helping me up with all the grace of a burly mountain man. He turns me around so my back presses against his front, and he finds the zipper of my dress.

"This was a beautiful dress, but it wasn't my favorite outfit of yours from this trip," he says softly as his lips dance along my shoulder and neck.

"No?" I squeak, clutching the unzipped dress to my chest as anxiety pools in my belly. A man hasn't seen me naked in a very long time. I didn't even get a chance to strip down at the sex club I so brazenly waltzed into. But somehow being naked in front of a bunch of strangers seems less anxiety-inducing than stripping down in front of Calder Fletcher. What am I thinking right now?

"That black bikini of yours has been haunting me since night fucking one." He slides his hands up my arms to my wrists and gently urges me to release my dress.

Swallowing the lump in my throat, I let go, and it pools around my waist. My eyes shut tight as I fight the urge to cover myself from his fire-blazing eyes as he rakes them down my body.

His masculine fingers trail lightly on my belly, up my ribs and around my chest, gliding slowly down the slopes of both my breasts eliciting goose bumps across my whole body.

Licking his lips, his mouth dances against my neck again. "I had to jerk off in the shower yesterday."

I moan and drop my head onto his chest as he traces his finger over my nipples, causing them to pucker even tighter.

"I think I heard you," I admit, my voice not even sounding like my own as his large hands cup my breasts, testing the weight of them.

His breath is warm on my neck, and I can feel his smile against my throat. "Can I tell you a secret, Ace?"

I swallow the knot in my throat, feeling desperate for the bed because my legs feel like they're going to give out any second. "Sure."

His voice is hot on my ear as his teeth bite lightly down on my lobe before he whispers, "I wanted you to hear me."

I gasp as he tugs slightly on my nipples, sending shock waves of pleasure through me, and wetness pools between my thighs.

In a flash, Calder turns me on my heels, capturing my lips with his again as he yanks out of his shirt, crushing my bare breasts to his chiseled front. I struggle to shimmy my tight dress over my hips before he hooks his fingers into my panties and slides them down, kneeling at the apex of my thighs as he does.

When he leans in and presses his nose to my center, I fight the urge to push him away. Oral sex is so nerve-wracking and intimate. Randal never did it, and I developed a bit of a complex over that. Plus, I've been dancing all night and I don't feel fresh down there and—*holy shit, that's his tongue on my clit.*

I wince as I brace myself for him to pull away, but he doesn't. In fact, he shifts me so I'm forced to sit on the bed as he stays on his knees and yanks me to the edge toward his face. He throws my legs up over his shoulders and ravishes me, his tongue deft and punishing while his rough hands knead my bare breasts and twist my nipples with the perfect amount of gentle pressure.

I throw my head back and moan when he sinks a finger inside my wet heat, pulling out to slide my arousal over my clit in a punishing rhythm. Thank fuck I got waxed before this trip. Since separating from Randal, I'd let myself go down there, fully intent on collecting cobwebs. But with my sex club shenanigans and this trip, I'm very glad my black-cat energy is more like bald-cat energy.

"Calder," I cry his name as I feel the climb of orgasm hitting me quicker than I expected. I haven't come from a man's mouth, let alone a man's dick, in so, so long. "I'm going to—"

"No, you're not," Calder growls and stands up, yanking his pants down to release his painful-looking erection. It bobs toward me, and I clench my thighs together in agony as he takes his time rolling a condom over his swollen tip. His dick is huge. Even bigger now that it's hard. His voice is low and sinister when he says, "I told you I was going to make you beg."

He holds my legs apart, spreading me wide as he stares down at my sex. It's unnerving having a relative stranger stare at you like that, but he seems fascinated by the sight of it. And even though every part of me wants to crawl into a hole and die, I don't want to feel insecure. Steeling myself, I push those voices far, far away. He found me at a sex club for Christ's sake. Act like you're used to this, Dakota!

He puts two of his fingers into his mouth, wetting them before bringing them down to my center to coat my opening. "You're so ready for me, aren't you?"

I nod, soaked, desperate, and starving for him. For release. For all of it.

"You are so fucking sexy. So fucking beautiful," he continues, his eyes full of lust. "I want you so damn bad."

Insecurity has left the building and every cell in my body is on fire as I yearn for him to just slam into me and give me a break from this pain coursing through me.

But the asshole doesn't do that.

He grips his length and presses his tip into me and then pulls it back, rubbing the head over my clit before teasing me with just the tip again and again and again.

I squirm under his hands, writhing for more. "Just fuck me, Calder."

He smirks. Cocky bastard. "Not until you beg."

"I just did!" I snap back at him, smacking my hands on the bed in frustration.

His abs tighten as he chuckles. It's a good look. "Tell me how bad you want me."

"I want you," I exclaim, out of breath and frustrated by his games. I'm finally out of my head for once and he wants to prolong the process? "Please, fuck me."

He inches in just a tiny bit more, still toying with me. Of course this man would do this. He can't just make it easy and let this be what it is. A hard, fast fuck. He has to make a game out of it. A power play.

Well, two can play at this game.

I reach up and grab his hips in an attempt to pull him into me. He laughs and presses his head into my chest. "So fucking demanding."

"Calder, this isn't funny anymore," I snipe, my center throbbing with need. "Just do this or get off of me."

"I'll get you off, baby. Just need to hear how bad you want it first."

Irritation hums in my veins at the *baby* remark and the way his eyes are on me as he says it. It's too much. Too intimate. So unlike him. Unlike us. It's better when we're fighting. I understand that. But it's been so long since I've been fucked, and I need this.

After more edging than I can handle, I shove his shoulders and catch him off guard, rolling him onto his back. He laughs and the crinkles in his eyes cause butterflies in my stomach as I straddle him to position his tip at my entrance.

With my breath high in my chest, I sink down, pulling him all the way inside of me, deeper than I've ever had a man. *Oh. My. Fucking. God.* It feels otherworldly, like I've entered another dimension, one where pain and pleasure work hand in hand to create the most euphoric sensation.

His eyes roll to the back of his head as he mutters, "Fuck Dakota . . . *fuck.*"

He sounds completely unmanned, and that coupled with the unreal pressure between my thighs has my body wanting to coil up into a ball. I press my chin to my chest, my hair curtaining my face as my fingers dig into his pecs for support while I try to adjust to his girth. It's so tight. *Unbelievably tight.* A year of no sex and a big dick will do that to a body, I guess.

I shift up to try and relieve the pressure, but the ache building inside me is too strong. I slam back down on him, and the tension shifts from a burn to a pulse that ripples through my body and needles that spot inside of me that's been deprived far too long.

I undulate over him, my wetness dampening his length and making things a bit more bearable. His hands are bruising on my hips as he tries to slow me down, but I'm beyond reproach. I'm taking what I asked for . . . what he crawled on his hands and knees to offer me. I am not just breaking my dry spell, I'm blowing the fucking roof off it.

In mere moments, I'm cresting, my insides exploding into a warmth of erotic ecstasy as I climax over top of him. Calder calls out my name over and over, thrusting up into me as he prolongs my pleasure, dragging out my orgasm as he chases his own.

When I feel him rupture inside of me, I fall over top of him, completely overstimulated and out of breath as I lay in the warmth of him, feeling strangely comforted by his scent. Quite a change for where we started this trip.

When I roll off, I feel Calder's eyes burning a hole in me, so I look over with a frown. "What?"

"Care to answer for your crimes?"

I pull a strand of hair off my lips and dab at the sweat on my brow. "I don't like asking for things twice. I thought you would have known that about me."

We fall into a comfortable, satiated silence, and I feel myself drifting to sleep with a smile on my face. Let's hope I can keep this sense of satisfaction when we head back to the real world tomorrow, because it feels good for a change.

And it's a real punch to the gut to admit that of all the people in my life, it was Calder Fletcher to help get me there.

Chapter 16

PUT THAT ON A T-SHIRT

Dakota

My smile feels permanent as I walk the three city blocks from my old Victorian house to my old 1950s historic downtown store. I catch a glimpse of my retro signage before cutting down the back alley to enter through the back.

"The T-shirt Shop" isn't the most original name for a business, but I was twenty-two when I came up with it and thought it was gloriously meta of me. It's located in downtown Boulder near the Pearl Street Mall area, which is a redbrick pedestrian-only thoroughfare. The storefront is on the back side in one of the original redbrick shops so the foot traffic is decent but not crazy busy.

I unlock the back door and set about my daily routine. Make coffee, water plants, check to make sure the online sales have all been fulfilled, and rearrange anything that isn't quite up to my standards. I'm always rearranging in my store. No matter how I display my T-shirts, I can never seem to find the perfect layout for everything, and the employees I hire to work here when I'm busy don't quite have the eye that I do when it comes to displays. Plus, I'm always getting new shipments in, so just when I find a display I like, I have to change it to make room for more.

My store has an artsy and eclectic vibe, different from the stuff on the main roads. It even has the original creaky wood flooring and retro lighting to match the decade the property was built. A lot of my T-shirt designs have a vintage feel to them, so it all fits really well together.

I really do have my dream job. And the only reason I even scored this incredible location was because of a grant I received from the city of Boulder years ago. I was fresh out of college, and the city was trying to revitalize its downtown area. One of my graphic design professors showed me an application where you can receive a three-year grant for a storefront downtown. So I put together a pitch, complete with logos and expense-and-income projections, and I gave a presentation on the value a T-shirt shop would provide to the city of Boulder. And how it won't be just a T-shirt shop but a timeless boutique shopping experience with a casual, more approachable aesthetic.

Next thing I knew, I was a twenty-two-year-old business owner.

The store has grown tremendously in the past decade, from offering basic Colorado-love shirts to hoodies, thermals, and even a super popular knitwear line. The majority of my product is made locally by a factory in northern Colorado too, which is an important part of my branding. Made local, sold local.

And I have a huge online store presence, thanks in part to my college bestie, Tatianna. She's a high-end designer out of Aspen who specializes in plus-size formal wear, but she has a line of graphic T-shirts here that keeps my online store booming. So much so, I had to pay for a fulfilment center in Denver to manage it all. It's like I have my own little workhorse over there that continues chugging along without me doing the heavy lifting.

Here in Boulder, it's a much more chill vibe. There are three college student employees that rotate in and out when I need time off, but otherwise I can run the business almost entirely on my own. It's busy but manageable. And then, because I just can't help myself, a few years after I opened, I expanded my back room to offer tie-dye classes. The T-shirt Shop is a popular spot for birthday parties, bachelorette parties, day cares, and preschools. It's a nice boost of income that helped me purchase my own home before I got married . . . which isn't easy to do as a single person.

This store is my baby and feels like the one thing I did right in this world. I work hard for it, and I love what I do, which is not something many people can say in their careers. And the fact that

I opened the store and purchased my house before I met Randal makes me even more bitter over the fact that he tried to take half of it in the divorce. *Tried* being the operative word, thank God. Though he still came out smelling like a rose when it was all said and done.

I shake away those negative thoughts because I told myself on the plane ride home that I was going to hang on to this post-vacation, post-sex high I'm on. I do not need to let the negative vibes continue to drag me down.

I shuffle through my mail, and my eyes zero in on an envelope from the Best of Boulder Business Bureau, and I frown curiously as I open it. I'm a member of all sorts of business groups around town and I get mail from them all the time . . . but this isn't one of them, so I'm curious what they might be contacting me about. My jaw drops as the letter that starts off with . . .

Dear Ms. Schaefer,

The Best of Boulder Business Bureau has hand-selected you as this year's winner for outstanding service and contribution to the city of Boulder. With over 40,000 businesses in Boulder County and 8,000 businesses in the city of Boulder, this is a prestigious award that we want to honor you for . . .

My eyes gloss over as I read about the selection process and an award gala they want me to RSVP to. I've heard about this award, but never expected my little T-shirt shop to ever be considered, let alone win. Holy shit! This is so unexpected.

My phone starts ringing from the desk, and I see a FaceTime call coming in from my friend Tatianna. I prop it up and sit down at my desk, attempting to collect myself before accepting the video call.

"Oh my God, you had sex!" Tatianna squeals as she jumps on the video chat for our monthly meeting.

"Wait . . . wait . . . what??" I shake my head, my mind on information overload right now. "Why would you say that?"

"Your face!" Her round features move closer to the screen as she squints at me. "You look so different. Like the weight of the world is off your shoulders."

"Or I just got a little sun." I laugh and shake my head.

"Are you sure?"

"I mean . . . I did have sex, but my face right now is because I just found out I won the Best of Boulder award."

"Oh my God, Dakota. That's incredible!"

"I know." I hold my hands to my cheeks, feeling flush and over-whelmed and crazy excited. "I can hardly believe it."

"I can! You're a badass, and this is well deserved."

My mind reels with that praise because if anyone is a badass here, it's Tot. We met in college, and from the moment I met her, I knew she had more creative genius in her pinky finger than I did in my entire body.

However, she's one of those creative types who must be guided or nothing would ever get done. I always had a bit more business sense than creative sense, which is why we made a great team. I don't see her as much as I'd like since she moved to Aspen, but these monthly calls end up being 90 percent girl talk and 10 per-cent business so we're still well informed on each other's lives.

"I'm just so shocked." I shove a hand through my hair as I look over the letter again to make sure I'm not dreaming.

"I'm more shocked by the fact that you had sex. We can get back to singing your award-winning praises later. That's not nearly as shocking as you getting laid! Did you find someone at that sex club? I've been dying for details about that night, but you've been on fricken vacation, so I was trying not to bother you."

"Well . . ." I turn the letter over and focus on my friend, trying to reset my brain from business to personal. "I guess you could say I found someone at the club."

"Holy shit, I am dead," Tot squeals. "I still can't believe you had the guts to go to a sex club in the first place. I still can't believe sex clubs actually exist. I still can't believe you went to a sex club!"

She repeats herself, and I have to hold my hand up to stop her rant. Tot has a tendency to get carried away sometimes. She's the best.

"I ran into Calder Fletcher there."

That silences Tot real quick. "Is that Max Fletcher's brother?"

I nod and tell her the whole awkward encounter all the way down to getting him kicked out of the club. Which maybe was a little cruel in the moment, but he was being completely overbearing and ridiculous.

"So then we get to Mexico and end up having to share a room . . . and he just wouldn't let it go. He kept begging me to tell him why I was there."

"Oh, he's obsessed with you," Tot says with wide, exhilarated eyes.

"No, he's not."

"Puhleeease." She waves her hand at me. "He sounded jealous. Like he didn't want anyone to see you like that."

"No, he didn't!" I argue. "He wasn't jealous, he was just overprotective. Like a big brother."

"A big stepbrother who wants to fuck you, maybe."

"Tot! Can I finish my story please?"

She presses her lips together, and I give her all the dirty details from Mexico. The bloody nose, the dancing, the movie watching, the fighting, the flirting, the fighting again. And then . . . the finale.

What a finale it was.

A flash of Calder crawling to me has my cheeks heating so much that I pray Tatianna can't see it through the zoom video.

"He got me out of my head, Tot. Like I swear I wasn't thinking, I was just doing and feeling and feeeling. Jesus, he has a magic penis, I swear."

"Put that on a T-shirt," Tatianna giggles.

I giggle too. It feels good. It feels like the old me. Like the free, confident me that I used to be.

"So how was the next day and the plane ride home? Awkward?"

I shrug. "Fine, I think. We shared the bed but didn't cuddle or anything. He was quiet in the morning and didn't say much, but he helped me with my bags and stuff and slept most of the plane ride. It was a little weird but not horribly."

"Wow. That sounds like a successful one-night stand."

"I know. He's such a confident guy . . . I fed off that, you know? I think I was faking my confidence so much I actually started to believe myself."

"Amazing."

"It kind of pisses me off that he found a way to help me let go so easily. Like I hope some of these guys that I hope to meet at the sex club are able to give me that too."

"So you're still planning to go back to the club?"

"I mean, maybe?" I inhale deeply and feel anxiety prickle back into my mind. "But I'm nervous. I realized it's hard to be in those places alone. A lot of people come as couples. I don't know if it's just a strong swinger community there or what, but it's not easy to approach people when you're on your own."

"Man, if only you had a big, tattooed mountain man you could go there with."

My brows furrow. "What do you mean?"

"I mean Calder. Why not ask him to go with you?"

My eyes widen. "I can't do that."

"Why not? You guys have already seen each other naked."

"I know but . . ."

"But nothing. He'd probably jump at the chance. I know I'd sure feel a lot better if you took him with you. It always scared me to know you were going there alone."

"I know but it was a one-night thing between us in Mexico. He wouldn't want to see me again, I'm sure," I state firmly for Tatianna to hear . . . *as well as myself.*

The truth is, I've been thinking about my night with Calder nonstop. It was obviously mind-blowing sex. And shocking on so many levels . . . not just because of how good it felt physically, but how good it felt emotionally too. Calder wasn't Calder. He was like . . . taken over by some person who passes out compliments and listens to a woman's voice.

I'm used to Calder just being a dick or a misogynistic asshole who leads with his penis. And he did lead with his penis . . . he could knock over a stack of books with that giant thing swinging all around.

But for him to admit that he's been attracted to me all these years? That he noticed every outfit I wore on the trip? That took guts. He was vulnerable. And it's what made the sex that much hotter.

I have to hand it to him, he's got game.

But it was a one-night thing. We were both very clear on that. And I can't let one night of mind-blowing sex with a tattooed mountain man derail my plans.

"You don't have to have sex with each other," Tot says, snapping me out of my inner musing. "You said he's casual. You're casual. So just use each other as wingmen to find that with other people."

"A wingman." My head jerks back as I ponder this idea. A week ago, I could never have dreamed of Calder being my wingman. But he's shown me a different side to him recently, and the idea isn't as ridiculous as it once might have been. He *was* very sweet and helpful during my hangover day on the trip.

My stomach swirls over the potential of being with Calder again in that night club. The dark lighting, the mood music, the erotic vibes you get entrenched in when you walk into the space. My breath comes out a little shaky as my libido enters the chat, and I have to squeeze my thighs together.

But there is no way in hell I'd have the nerve to ask him. He'd probably laugh in my face and use it as ammunition against me for the rest of our lives. No. No way. No way in hell. I need to stick with the plan. What happens in Mexico stays in Mexico. The more space I maintain from Calder Fletcher, the better for everyone.

Tot bursts out laughing, ripping me out of my inner musings. "Listen to me . . . I've had sex like a handful of times in my life, and now I'm sitting on a video call giving advice on sex clubs. Delulu, party of one, please."

My brows lift as I refocus on my friend. "Maybe you could be my wingman? You know what they say . . . nothing bonds some besties like a visit to a sex club."

"No one says that." She laughs and shakes her head. "And sex clubs aren't ready for a body like this." She slides her hands down her curves with a giggle. Tot is the most confident curvy girl I know, and I desperately need to take a page out of her book. She's beautiful, self-assured, successful, and famous in the fashion world . . . yet still, she's thirty-three and single like me. It ain't easy out there. Maybe we're all doomed to live alone.

"This is your sex quest, not mine," Tot adds with a pointed look. "You'll figure something out."

"Yeah, I will." I nod and begin shuffling through the stack of mail on my desk.

"Okay, let's go back to discussing your big award. Or do you want to hear about my shitty Bumble date first?"

"Duh . . . shitty Bumble date, please."

I listen intently as Tatianna shares her wild tale of assholery, and it reinforces my decision to do this sex club thing. I'm at the top of my game professionally. It's time to give my personal life some TLC as well. And really, I'm not asking for too much. No deep, personal connection. I just want to do what I did with Calder a handful of times before I put myself out there again.

I know it's crazy, but I have to find my mojo again, and that one little moment with Calder got me closer than I've felt in a long time.

Chapter 17

WHO WORE IT BETTER?

Calder

"Hey, I'm at your house, and no one is answering," I say to Cozy over the phone.

"Why are you at my house?"

"It's my night to take Ethan." I pull my phone away to look at my calendar to make sure I have the right date. My brothers and I alternate weeks where we take Ethan out for some fun and bonding—and to give Max and Cozy a break. We did the same thing with Everly for years . . . even while she was still in high school. Wyatt usually just brings them up to the mountain and lets them play with the animals. Or his goat, before Trista joined the scene and brought her assortment of wildlife around. Luke does something lame like a movie. Me and E-Man, we go for high impact.

"I was planning to take him to that trampoline park tonight. Does he still want to go?"

"Oh God, yes, he would love that," Cozy responds, sounding out of breath. "I'm sorry. I must have had my days mixed up! I'm at Dakota's shop with him. Can you just come here and grab him?"

"What?" I cringe as pressure instantly builds in my chest at just the mention of her name.

"Yeah, he's making a tie-dye shirt, but he's almost done. Just swing by and grab him. The front door says Closed, but you can walk right in."

"Okay . . . sure. I'll see you in a bit."

I feel stiff as I make my way back to the truck, running a trembly hand through my hair. It's only been a few days since Mexico, and I wasn't really prepared to see Dakota so soon. She's been occupying way too many of my thoughts since we got back, and coming face-to-face with her isn't really going to help me with that problem. And it is a problem because our night in Mexico was . . . unexpected.

I guess I knew the sex would be good.

I didn't know it would be fucking spectacular.

And that frustrates the shit out of me.

I'm an experienced man, and I've had loads of great sex. But hardly ever with someone I know well, aside from Robyn. And Robyn is the fucking worst and not worth another thought in my head. Dakota on the other hand . . . I don't know what to expect when I see her.

She was fine with me the next day in Mexico. We didn't really speak because I took a page out of my brother Wyatt's silent, classic mountain man book. I was quiet on our flight home. Quiet in our palapa as we showered and packed up. Quiet when I walked down the steps, staying on the side to serve as a barrier for Dakota and the birds. I was quiet because I was afraid of what I would say if I opened my mouth. It'd probably be something crazy like . . . *Being with you was fucking aces. Fuck me again, please?*

And that is not something I say to women. Ever. One and done. That was the deal. So I need to get my shit together and stop stressing out over seeing her again. She's not stronger than me. She doesn't have a magical vagina that beckons to me like a siren calling her ships home.

She's just a chick that I fucked.

I repeat that last sentence over and over as I park next to her storefront and make my way inside. An old bell jingles above the door, and I feel my heart rate increase as I look around her shop for the first time. I've known Dakota for seven damn years and managed to never step foot in this place . . . and now I know why.

It looks just like her. Loud, colorful, and stylish with a touch of midcentury aesthetic. She had a similar vibe for her house re-model too. A mix of modern with classic elegance. She has a way of finding unique clunky-looking pieces and making them shine in a space. One of the chandeliers she ordered took twelve fucking weeks to arrive, but she refused to look at anything else because that light was "the one."

God, she's high-maintenance.

My eyes look up when I see someone emerge from the doorway in the back of the store. She's carrying a giant box that covers her face and when she drops it loudly on the floor by the cash register, I think my heart skips a beat.

She looks good. Tanned and busy in a take-no-prisoners sort of way. Her hair is tied up in a messy bun, and she blows a wisp of it out of her face before she finally notices me. Her cheeks flush when our eyes connect, and I hate that my cock twitches. It's a fucking traitor.

"What are you doing here?" she asks, looking nervously behind her like someone is going to come out of the back room.

I stand awkwardly by a table covered in hoodies, my fingers toying with the strings on one of them. "Ethan—" I blurt out after the longest, most awkward pause of my life.

I hear the sound of running footsteps, then "Uncle Caldy!" and Ethan emerges out of the backroom door wearing what looks like a dye-splattered apron and rubber gloves.

He makes a beeline toward me, and I see Dakota's hands fly up as she cries, "Don't touch anything!"

As soon as he gets close to me, I clamp my hands around his wrists and hold his dye-soaked gloves straight up above his head. "You're under arrest!"

He laughs and squirms to get closer to me. "I want a hug, Uncle Caldy."

"No way, dirt ball," I gruff, walking him back the way he came, his little legs fighting me every step I go. "You need to finish whatever you were doing first."

Cozy appears in the doorway next, looking out of breath. "Did he ruin anything? I'll pay for it, I promise."

"Calder caught him," Dakota answers, her eyes dropping to look at the ground when I draw closer.

"I looked away for one second." She marches over and takes Ethan's wrists from my hands. "Thanks. I'm really glad you're doing this tonight, Calder. He seriously needs to burn off some energy. I'll go get him cleaned up, and then he'll be ready to roll."

"No rush." I slide my hands into my pockets as Cozy walks Ethan back through the door they came out.

I take a moment and walk along the counter, noticing that Dakota is doing a bad job of looking busy back there, like she's completely unaffected by my presence. I stop at a rack of shirts and slide the hangers over, one by one.

"I like your shop," I offer, trying to break the tension a bit.

"It's been here for ten years, and you never managed to stop in?" She pushes back from the front desk and leans on the counter behind her, watching me through her narrow sapphire eyes.

"I'm not a big shopper." I walk around, perusing more of the clothes. "Plus, I don't think you sell the kind of clothes I wear."

"Sure, we do." With a frown, she walks around the desk and makes her way over to me. My heart rate increases with every step she takes, ratcheting up even higher when the scent of her perfume hits me as she reaches past me and pulls out a T-shirt. "This would look good on you."

She hands me a shirt that has the outline of a hairy man's physique wearing a neon green mankini. I can't help but smile. "This?"

She fights back her own amusement and nods. "Yep. We have dressing rooms if you want to try it on."

I chuckle and shake my head. "You don't think the real thing is better?" I pin her with a look, and that flush in her cheeks is back. I move closer to her to return the shirt to the spot she pulled it from. "Come to think of it . . . I am short a Colorado Rockies T-shirt, so maybe I do need to find something here."

Dakota licks her lips, pulling the lower one into her mouth to chew on for a second. "I thought you gave that one away."

I glance down at her lip as it goes back between her teeth. "Oh yeah, I think you're right. That's a shame. I kind of miss that shirt."

I lean over her, resisting the urge to touch her like I want to. This is why the silent thing worked after our night together. When she does the talking thing, I have to do the looking thing. And the looking thing makes me want to do the touching thing. And the touching thing makes me want to do the naked thing.

When did we get so close together?

The sound of footsteps approaching rips both of us out of whatever fucked-up trance we're in, and we split apart like a couple of horny teenagers caught kissing at a church dance.

"All clean!" Cozy sings as she walks Ethan over to me. "Thank you again, Calder, and sorry for not being home when you stopped by."

"No worries." I ruffle Ethan's dark hair. "Ready to go, poop stain?"

"Ready!" he cheers and links his hand in mine to head out.

When we're about at the door, Cozy calls out to me. "Oh wait, Calder."

I turn around and frown, trying to keep my focus on Cozy when all I want to do is look at Dakota again.

"Dakota was asking me today if I could build her some custom shelves for these two corners of her store. And it's just too big of a project for me . . . you know I'm more into the serving boards and small woodworking stuff, but I think you could make something perfect for it."

"What?" Dakota and I both say in unison.

Dakota laughs nervously. "Cozy, it's fine if you can't do it. We don't need to bother Calder with this."

"Oh come on, Dakota!" Cozy waves me off. "You were telling me earlier how hard it's been for you to find something to fit those two awkward spaces. You need a custom build, and Calder is super talented at that. You should see some of his furniture pieces. He's way better than me. Aren't you, Calder?"

She turns her big eyes to me, and I shake my head like a moron. "No."

"Nonsense. He's great. Send her some pictures of your stuff, and I'm sure he can figure something out."

I swallow the knot in my throat. I'll figure something out, all right. I'll figure out how the hell to get out of having to spend more time with the woman I can't get off my mind.

Chapter 18

GOT WOOD?

Dakota

I hate to say it, but the photos Calder has texted me the past few days of his outdoor furniture pieces are intriguing. Damn Cozy and her damn good ideas and her damn meddling bullshit. I swear she knows something happened with me and Calder, because why else would she spring him on me at my store? She could have mentioned he was coming by to pick up Ethan . . . That's a common thing to tell a friend, right? That you've invited a hot mountain man into my business after hours?

But no, I had to be assaulted by his devastating good looks without warning. I would have gone to the bathroom and fixed my hair, maybe freshened up my makeup. Instead he saw me in leggings, an oversize T-shirt, and a fair share of lip sweat from hauling inventory up from the basement.

Mortifying.

But not as mortifying as my thoughts. I actually wondered if he was there to like . . . I don't know . . . ask me out or something? It was so silly of me because the man has never stepped foot in my store, even when we were working on a house renovation together. Of course he wasn't there for me.

But if Cozy had told me he was coming, I would have tidied up more. Made the store really shine. I have this irritating urge to one-up Calder. He's like the asshole from high school who never gave you the time of day, but now as an adult, you're wildly successful, and all you want to do is impress him and let him know all that he missed out on. That's the vibe I have with Calder. I want him to see me as more than just a bumbling sex-repressed divorcée with lip sweat.

Maybe that's what he wants from me too. Maybe that's why he texted me the photos of his work. He could have easily just dropped the ball and let the deal fall into the oblivion of nothing. Does he want to work with me? Does he want to see me again? What does this mean?

It means that I am hauling my ass up to Fletcher Mountain to see his stuff in person because the photos just don't fully do it justice, and I need to touch everything to really get a sense of what he can do for me. And while I'm doing the touching of wood, I'm going to forget about the touching of Calder's body because, as it turns out, he could do more for me than just make some shelves.

What can I say? I'm a control freak.

I drive up the winding gravel lane flanked with pine trees toward the top of the peak, feeling like I'm disappearing into another universe. I'm a born-and-bred Boulder girlie, and while I can enjoy the view of the Flatirons from time to time, it's always been city living for me. Driving into the rural mountain areas freaks me out. There are some suspicious mountain towns off the main highways that I would not want to be caught alone in at night. I will admit, though, that Jamestown is the exception. It's got that perfect amount of small-town vibe with civilization just a stone's throw away. I can see why the Fletcher brothers choose to live up here.

I've been up here a couple times before with Cozy throughout the years and just last year for Trista and Wyatt's gender-reveal party. Though, originally it was a gender reveal for Wyatt because Trista was just the surrogate at the time. My, how quickly things change.

Maybe not quickly enough when it comes to me.

The big red barn comes into sight, and I stop when I see Trista stepping out of the Dutch barn doors and waving violently at me. She has Stevie strapped to her chest, and she's holding a bucket in one hand. I stop and park in front of her, hopping out to say hello.

"Oh my God, Dakota! To what do we owe this unexpected visit?" Trista sets her bucket down and walks over to me, kitted out in overalls and knee-high rubber boots.

"Look at you, country mama!" I smile at how calm and at peace she looks with a baby strapped to her in front of a barn.

"This is like my permanent uniform these days." She laughs and turns so I can get a look at Stevie who's wide-awake and blinking up at her surroundings. "Although, I prefer the *mountain mama* label over *country mama.*"

"Both suit you just fine," I reply, crossing my arms and fighting off a feeling of jealousy over how happy she looks. "Married life suits you too. You and Wyatt·thinking about going on a honeymoon?"

Trista shakes her head. "I feel like that trip was our honeymoon and wedding all in one."

"It was all so beautiful. Thank you again for letting me tag along."

"Oh please, I was glad you were there!" She waves me off. "It wouldn't have been the same without you. And it was nice to have someone else around to help me keep Calder's ego in check."

I grumble knowingly. "I'm actually here to see Calder." I glance up to the log cabin up the lane past Wyatt's house to see if I can spot him before refocusing on Trista.

"Calder? Really?" Trista gets a coy look in her eyes that's so obvious it's not even funny.

"He's hopefully building some custom shelves for my store. Cozy kind of forced him into it, I think."

"Sounds like Cozy." Trista pats Stevie on the back when she begins fussing. "Actually, it sounds like Everly too."

"Everly?" I ask with a frown but get cut off when Trista gasps.

"Cozy was just telling me about some award you won!"

"Oh," I feel my face heat with anxiety. "Yeah, it's just the Best of Boulder business thing. It's no big deal."

"She said they only pick one business a year to receive that award."

"Yeah . . ."

"That's a really big deal!"

"Thanks," I murmur running my hand through my hair.

I've been feeling kind of weird about the award since I found out. Cozy was so excited for me, but I still couldn't shake the feeling that it was depressing not having a partner to share the news with. Not that I wanted to tell Randal. But it would have been nice to have someone special to tell me they were proud of me. And someone to go with me to the ceremony. I refuse to let Cozy be my plus-one. My pride couldn't take it. I would rather go on my own.

I inhale a cleansing breath. "I have to go to an award ceremony thing, so I guess I'm just nervous."

"Don't be. You're amazing. And you so deserve this. I have really appreciated all the logo work you're doing for my rescue center. You're the shit."

"Well, it's my pleasure."

A loud whistle sounds off behind us, causing both Trista and me to turn and look. I spot Calder standing up by his cabin. He sticks his hands out like he's wondering what I'm doing down here with Trista.

"What's his problem?" Trista asks with a frown.

"I guess he wants to get our meeting over with." I roll my eyes and sigh. Some things never change. "I'll talk to you later, okay?"

"Okay."

"Bye, baby Stevie." I wave and hop back in my car to continue my journey up the mountain to park directly in front of Calder's place.

The view of Calder standing in front of his cabin in a Carhartt coat and jeans elicits butterflies in my stomach, even if he looks irritable and impatient. I internally scold myself to chill out because this is just a business meeting. You've worked with Calder before. Yes, you were engaged at the time, so completely unavailable, but still. You've been around this man loads of times before and not thought about sex.

Much.

"I have plans tonight so we need to hurry up," Calder says gruffly as I walk around my car to join him. "You can gab with Trista later."

"Jeez, sorry," I murmur, falling into stride with him as he walks past the side of his house toward a well-worn path deeper into the woods.

We pass by some weird metal hot tub–looking thing located right behind his house, and I wonder how many women he's had sex with in it. Then I wonder what his plans are tonight and then shake that thought away. It doesn't matter what his plans are. You probably know what he's doing, Dakota, and you don't need to think about it.

"How much farther is this workshop? I feel like you're leading me to my death."

He huffs out a laugh. "I thought Satan was already dead."

I stop midstride, feeling the cut of that remark deeper than before. I didn't think sex would change anything, but apparently it has.

He notices my absence and stops to turn on his heel, his face falling at the sight of me. "That was a shitty joke. I'm sorry."

"If you don't want to do this, just say so," I snap, crossing my arms protectively over my chest. What was I thinking having Calder do work for my shop? Our time together on my house nearly killed me. I start to turn to leave, chastising myself for this dumb idea when he rushes over to stop me.

"I want to do this," Calder says, walking over to stand in front of me.

"Are you sure?" I hook my thumb back the way we came. "Because I have no issues driving my ass right back down that mountain."

"Don't, please. I really am sorry." He gets a pensive look on his face as he glances down the mountain toward Wyatt's cabin. "None of this is about you. I got into it with my brothers at work today, and I'm in a bad mood. I didn't mean what I said."

I lick my lips and stare into his eyes, noticing how much greener they look next to the pine trees all around us. "What happened with your brothers?" I can't help but ask. Calder has never really been this vulnerable, so I find myself curious.

He exhales heavily and shoves a hand through his hair, mussing the brunette locks into a perfectly tousled mess that hairstylists would spend hours trying to achieve. "They use me to do the grunt work on our job sites a lot, always assuming I have nothing better to do. I'm getting sick of it."

"Why don't you tell them that?"

"Because the shit still has to get done, so I just fucking do it." He shrugs and hits me with a disappointed look, but his eyes suddenly soften around the edges. "I really do want to show you my stuff, though. I've been looking forward to this."

My eyes widen at that rare sign of vulnerability. It's unexpected but very appreciated, and I consider the fact that we all can have bad days from time to time. Even happy-go-lucky guys like Calder.

I resume our walk, appreciating the silence between us for a change until we reach our destination. It's a small cedar-sided outbuilding with a green metal roof and tiny little windows. And when Calder opens the double doors, it feels like an entry into his mind.

It's woodsy and messy and still strangely beautiful. It feels like the essence of him in a workshop form. Exposed bulbs hang from the rafters with a small TV mounted to the wall. There's a stack of notepads filled with sketches of designs for various furniture pieces and power tools and hand tools and nails, and wood chunks scattered everywhere with a layer of sawdust clinging to it all. He has a huge assortment of beautiful, completed pieces placed everywhere, even some stored up in the rafters.

"What did you make all these for?" I ask, walking over to check out what looks like the porch swing he sent me a photo of the other day.

He slides his hands into his pockets. "I don't know yet."

"You just made them for fun?" I blink back my shock as I notice the intricate detailing along the arms.

"Yeah, I guess," he replies, gripping the back of his neck. "I built this shop after my dad died. Woodworking was kind of our thing together, and I just sorta . . . never stopped making stuff. I watch game shows while I work, so the time flies out here. My dad loved game shows."

My eyes soften at this unexpectedly sentimental side of Calder. To build an entire shed dedicated to a hobby he had with his late father makes my heart squeeze in a way that it never has for him. I only met Steven a few times, but he left a mark.

If you looked at the Fletcher family as a whole, you would have thought they lived a charmed life. Two married parents with four sons who all worked for their father's construction business. Max eventually paved his own path, but the other three stayed strong in the family business. And by all accounts, Wyatt, Calder, and Luke are the best of friends. Willingly working and living next to each other every day.

The death of Steven a few years ago rattled them. I remember seeing Calder at the funeral. I was showing up to pay my respects to Cozy and Max mostly, but it was Calder who drew my eye. He looked like a deer in the headlights. Like his entire world had been rocked. The normally outgoing, outspoken, life of the party, nothing-gets-me-down giant mountain man was truly broken. I'm guessing he built this shop to help himself grieve.

"What game shows do you usually watch?" I ask with a soft smile, trying to lighten the mood. "Me and Cozy used to watch *Family Feud* together all the time when we were kids. I was kind of obsessed."

"That's one of my favorites too," Calder replies with a genuine smile. "But I like *Wheel of Fortune* too."

"That's so funny." I blow some dust off the swing to feel the smooth wood beneath my hands. "I must have applied to be on *Family Feud* like ten times but never got picked. You don't see too many divorced families with just one kid getting selected for that show."

"Huh," Calder frowns, fiddling with a tool he'd left out. "I guess I never noticed."

I shrug my shoulders. "I always imagined what it would be like if my family got along like the ones you see on the show. Everyone works together and laughs and teases each other. It's sweet. My family functions are like personality-disorder festivals. Your family would be a riot on that show."

Calder chuckles as he props himself on a sawhorse in the middle of the space. "We could probably compete in a personality-disorder festival too."

"Nah, you guys are solid," I hear the longing in my voice while I muse over the image of all of the Fletcher brothers standing behind the table and answering those questions from Steve Harvey. They'd probably surprise me and be really good. I was always terrible at that game. I don't think quick enough on my feet. I need to ponder something for a bit before I can decide on an answer. Impulsiveness isn't really my style.

Except in Mexico, apparently.

I refocus on the furniture. "Do you think you'll ever decide to sell these pieces?"

Calder grips the back of his neck, looking uncomfortable with my fondling of his work, which just makes me want to fondle it more. "Yeah, for sure. I just haven't got around to it yet."

"Have you sold anything before?"

"Nah, I just give them away usually. Gave Trista a chair for their gender-reveal party thing last year. She has it outside the barn and sits in it a lot. It's nice giving them to people I get to see use them."

He reminds me so much of Cozy. She loves making charcuterie boards, but it took a lot of convincing to get her to do them for money. What is with these people having talents and not wanting to monetize off them? I understand some things are just hobbies, but this level of talent goes well beyond that. Calder has to spend hours on these, pouring himself over them. They'd sell for a hell of a lot more than one of my T-shirts, that's for sure. And he just . . . gives them away?

He moves over to his workbench and picks up a notebook,

wiping some dust off it before flipping it open to a page. "This is what I was thinking for your shelves."

My boots scrape on wood shavings as I walk over and look at a drawing he's done. I grab the notebook from his hands for a closer look, my fingers stroking over his sketch, amazed that he drew this himself. I wouldn't have pegged Calder as the artistic type.

"It's a rotating cube shelf with a space on the left to display your graphic shirt design and a shelf beside it to hold the inventory. I want to do some rotary wheels at the base so people can spin it and see everything without having to walk around it. We can do two to fill those spaces you have open right now. I'm thinking maple to match the floors in your shop."

"You noticed the floors in my shop?" I look up at him and he frowns back at me.

"Yeah, why?"

"Nothing, I'm just . . . surprised."

"I notice things." His eyes tighten, and his nostrils flare with irritation. "And I know you want these to match everything you have going on in there, so I kept the detailing simple."

"But I like your detailing," I argue, looking up at the pieces he has in the rafters. I could find a place for all of them in my house.

"But it should match your vibe."

"But I wouldn't need to hire you to make this if I didn't want your vibe. Otherwise, I could just buy something off Wayfair."

"Wayfair?" he snaps, his severe eyes turning to slits. "No fucking way you want a mass-produced unit from a discount store in your shop. It would look like shit."

I jut my chin up at him in defiance. "I know it would, which is why I'm paying you to make something nice with your style in it."

"Jesus fucking Christ, Dakota. It'll still be my style." He steps closer to me, his arm brushing against mine as he points back to his sketch. "See? These curved angles I drew here are kind of my thing. And that works well with the vintage aesthetic in your store."

He flips back a page, and my lips part when I see a sketch of my store. It's a rough drawing, but it's undoubtedly my place. He's got my funky globe chandeliers and the curves of my stained-glass windows. He even did a good illustration of my front counter with the vertical slat boards and rattan accents. And he's drawn his shelf idea into the space that I wanted it for. He's put a lot of thought into this.

I smile and look up at him, disarming his sour disposition with my change in mood. "Our styles look good together."

"That's what I was fucking saying," he grumbles under his breath, and my chest shakes with silent laughter.

It feels like old times. Like the house reno all over again, only this time . . . the arguing feels different. More stimulating. Back then it was just exasperating. Maybe it was just sexual frustration we were dealing with all that time. Maybe that's what we're still dealing with now.

"Have you ever had sex with anyone in here?" I blurt the question and stop myself from clapping my hand over my mouth like a moron.

"Excuse me?" Calder's expression is unreadable, and I hate it. God, what must he think of me asking such a stupid question out of the blue like that? Especially when he told me he built this place after his dad died. I'm hopeless!

I shake my head and try to recover. "I was just wondering if you bring girls back here."

"To my workshop or the mountain in general?" he asks, not avoiding my question, just requesting more clarity. His eyes dart to my lips before moving back up to my eyes.

I chew my lip and shrug. "I'm curious about both, I guess."

His eyes crinkle as he chuckles, and the sound ignites a fire in my loins. "*Yes* to women in my house, but not as many as you might think. I don't like bringing them up here if I can help it. But *no* to the workshop. This place is my escape, you know? Where I get away from all the noise." A pensive mood casts over him as he looks around at everything, but then he shoots me that playful smirk again. "Plus, power tools and sex aren't really a kink I need to explore."

"Probably wise," I say under my breath, turning away to hide the blush I feel running up my neck. "I was just curious."

I snap the notebook closed and march over to the furniture like I need to see it one more time to make my final decision. "To get back to business, I think your design is perfect. I need two of them so just text me a quote for the price and estimated turnaround time, and we should be all set."

I clear my throat and push my hair out of my face before steeling myself to turn back around and face him. And when I do, the butterflies in my stomach become a serious problem because he's standing there, in his masculine workshop with his trim beard and rumpled hair, looking so utterly mountain man perfect. It's making me wish he didn't have a rule about not sleeping with women in here . . . because I would probably consider a repeat performance right now if he was interested.

He stares back at me with a look I can't decipher, something totally different from the teasing, mocking one that I've grown accustomed to. I want to say it's like lust or hunger but doubt that's true. He's probably just itching to get me out of here so he can get on with his plans for the night. I bet he has a girl he's going to go see. Someone easy and uncomplicated who he hasn't had a one-night stand with before. Someone who's not me.

Chapter 19

HALF-MILLION-DOLLAR MISTAKE

Dakota

My mouth goes dry when I see his name pop up on my phone as I sit in my house on a sad, boring Friday night. I shake my head in irritation because all communication is supposed to go through our lawyers. But I'm already paying an insane amount to my lawyer so the urge to save myself the legal fee overcomes me.

"Hello?"

"Hey, Dee, how you doing?" he drawls in his smarmy bartender voice.

"What do you need, Randal? We're not supposed to talk to each other directly."

"Oh, come on. The divorce is final. We can talk again." He chuckles, and I can tell just by the sound of that laugh he's been drinking.

"What do you need to talk about?" I wince when I realize what I just did. Asking Randal a question is never a good idea because I almost never like the answer.

One time after we were driving back from a birthday party for Ethan, I asked him how he thought I looked that day. I'd been kind of experimenting with my wardrobe, doing some more fashion-forward things I always envy on the influencers I follow, and he cut me the worst look and asked, "Do you want to fight, or you want me to say you looked fine?"

My stomach dropped because he gave me the answer without giving me the answer. So like a fool, I poked him more about it. Finally, he said, "Well, Dee, your arms looked fat, and your belly was sticking out. It's obvious you put on a bit of weight."

I'd never been more crushed in my entire life. The man I shared a bed with just fat-shamed me with very little effort.

I iced him out for days, giving him the cold shoulder and expecting him to come crawling to me for forgiveness, but he never did.

When we finally did talk about it, he just shrugged and said, "If your husband can't be honest with you, who can?"

I should have left him then and there . . . but I didn't . . . because I'm an idiot.

Randal's voice cuts into my horrid walk down memory lane as he says, "Listen, I know we set up installments for you to pay me on the settlement or whatever, but I just found a really great place here in Denver, and I'm going to need more cash to put a down payment on it."

My throat tightens with every word he said. "What are you talking about?"

"Can you hit me up with two installments instead?"

"Randal . . . no, that's not the deal we signed up for."

"I knooow, but you have to see this house," he drags his words out like he's talking to his best friend over beers, not his ex-wife of a few weeks.

"I don't want to see the house. I don't care about the house. This isn't like me Venmo-ing you for pizza, Randal."

He sighs heavily. "Fine, I'll just bring it up to the lawyers."

"Bring what up?" I hop out of bed, putting my book down to pace my bedroom. "There's nothing to bring up. Everything is final. I'm paying you half a million dollars spread out over four years. That's what we agreed upon. You agreed."

"I know, but things changed. We might need to reopen the case."

"This isn't fucking *Law and Order*, Randal. We've already paid a fortune to our attorneys. Opening this up would be insanely expensive. Aren't you sick of paying a lawyer?"

"Yeah, but I just think I got the raw end of the deal."

"Then, you shouldn't have signed the deal!" I shriek, feeling my blood pressure surge to levels beyond healthy.

He makes a weird noise in the back of his throat. I *hate* that noise. That noise is like nails on a chalkboard to me. "Dee, you got the business, the house, Boulder. I'm having to start a whole new life here. That takes money."

"You grew up in Denver. That is your home. It's not like you've moved to a foreign country! And I had the business and the house before you and I even got engaged. That's why I want to keep them."

"I know, but I contributed to the household expenses."

"Barely," I exclaim, my voice rising in pitch. "Your name isn't even on the home improvement loan. Maybe you contributed to the groceries and utilities, but Randal . . . you know I covered the mortgage and the renovation. We've been over this."

He makes a clicking sound with his teeth, and I feel my body shrink. "You always sound so tense, Dakota. You need to get out and live a little. Exercise, or maybe even try dating. I know sex isn't really your thing, but you should try something to help you stop being a victim of your own life." He laughs as if he's the funniest person on the planet, and I'm ready to hang up when he adds, "I've met someone, and I'm happier than I've been in years."

"I don't care!" I snap, my hand griping the phone so tight I think it might crack.

"She's young but she is real fun. Adventurous too. Will try anything. No problem keeping the spark alive here."

Tears sting my eyes because I know what he's doing. He's reminding me of everything he said I wasn't. *Young, thin, pretty, confident, sexy.* I felt like I was finally clawing my way out of the abyss. My night with Calder made me feel sexy. Like my old self again. Then with one manipulative phone call, Randal's put his boot on my face and pushed me back down.

"Have your lawyer call my lawyer," I hiss and hang up before I blow a gasket.

I walk into the bathroom and stare in the mirror, willing myself to see the girl I was before I met him. Not the smaller, size-four jeans girlie. The size-twelve girlie who likes how she looks.

Unfortunately, the only thing staring back at me is a sad, thirty-three-year-old single woman who did a great job pretending to be a ten on the outside but let a small man make her feel like a six on the inside. And I know Randal's opinion of me shouldn't matter. He's awful, and this is why I divorced him. But it still hurts to know the man I chose to live my life with thought so little of me in the end.

My eyes catch on a lacey red dress hanging in the attached closet behind me, and I turn around to stare at it. It was an outfit that I bought before Mexico that I had big plans for and never followed through with.

Stop being a victim of your own life.

Randal used those words to belittle me, but I am no victim. *I am a ten on the inside and out.* It's time I get back to my plan.

Chapter 20

KNOCK KNOCK ... WHO'S THERE?

Calder

"You have to chill out, Fuzz," I bellow to Milkshake who's been crying at the door since I got home from work an hour ago.

She's been a whiney brat lately. Clearly starved for attention because it's been all work and no play since we got back from Mexico. I had Judy pop up the mountain to take care of her while we were gone, and she gave her plenty of loving. But the needy girl has been dying to get outside since we returned, and I'm pretty sure Judy would have laughed in my face if I asked her to wear the cat pack and take her for walks.

Wyatt, Luke, and I have been busting our asses lately because we're majorly behind on a custom build for a high-maintenance client in Boulder. Behind on deadlines means late nights in town, which really put Milkshake in a mood. And me for that matter. She weaves between my feet as I button up a clean flannel. I barely had time to shower and clean up after work, never mind eat because this cat is up my damn ass to go outside.

I stuff my feet into my boots and throw on the harness and before I can even hold my hands out, Milkshake leaps up into my arms, vibrating with excitement.

"High-maintenance, pain-in-my-ass brat," I grumble as I swing the front door open and work on securing her in the harness.

"Well, hello to you too," a voice says, and my jaw drops as I do a double take, unable to process the person standing on my front porch.

I usually hear cars coming up the gravel, but maybe I was in the shower when she pulled in? I lean out the door to look around, wondering if anyone else is here. Maybe she's hanging out with Trista, but all I see is Dakota's green SUV parked directly in front of my house. So odds are she's here to see me. Again.

When will her being up here on my mountain ever stop feeling weird? It was weird the other day when she was in my workshop, and it's extra weird now that she's on my porch, standing before me in a tight pair of leggings, a graphic sweatshirt that says *Boulder-Bred*, her long coat, and snow boots with the mountain backdrop behind her.

My cock likes how she looks up here.

Down, boy.

"What's going on?" I ask, clearing my throat as Dakota's eyes fixate on my cat. "Did you have a change of heart on your shelving units?"

"What? Oh gosh, no. All good there. Take as long as you want on those. I'm in no rush." The smile on her face is tight as she points to my chest. "Did you lose a bet?"

"No," I grumble defensively, clutching Milkshake to my chest. "This is my cat, and we were just going to go for a walk."

"You walk your cat in a baby carrier?"

"Yes, I do." I narrow my eyes at her. "And if you're going to make fun of me, just know that Wyatt and Luke have already come up with all the lame-ass fucking cat dad jokes you can imagine. I'm immune to you cat-haters of the world."

"I don't hate cats." She steps closer to me, and my heart rate spikes as she bathes me in her spicy perfume. She reaches up and pets Milkshake and my eyes drift down her neck, catching the way the shirt shows off her collarbone.

Milkshake purrs like a traitor, leaning away from me to accept the affection from this perfect stranger. "You call her Milkshake, right?" Dakota looks up at me, and her blue eyes do nothing to slow my heart rate down.

"Milkshake or Fuzz," I say gruffly, trying to sound unbothered. "Or Little Witch sometimes because she can be that."

Milkshake meows, punctuating my point.

Dakota smiles, but it doesn't reach her eyes. She clearly has something on her mind, and I'm kind of nervous to find out what it is. "Can I walk with you?"

I swallow. "I guess so. I mean . . . sure."

I close my cabin door and glance up the hill to Luke's, and I swear I see the ass duck down from the window. Fucking creep. I'm sure Wyatt and Trista have their noses pressed up against the glass at their place too with little Stevie enjoying the show. Moments like this make living next door to family a big pain in the ass.

I've brought women up on the mountain before, so that's nothing to take note of. But Dakota Schaefer twice in one week? That is newsworthy in the Fletcher clan.

I point toward the trail we walked the other day. "Your boots okay to get a little muddy?"

"Yeah, these are good." Dakota strides beside me, crunching through the melting snow like this is a normal fucking occurrence, but the tension is palpable.

"So, you really are a full-fledged cat daddy."

"Yeah. She showed up as a stray on one of our job sites last year, and Trista kind of helped me figure out how to take care of her."

"And that includes walking her?" She turns to watch me as I make my way through the worn, muddy trail.

"Well, the first couple months I had her, she kept trying to bolt out the front door. She was successful a couple of times, and my brothers and I didn't particularly enjoy chasing her around the peak."

Dakota laughs. "Picturing the three of you chasing a cat is a pretty amusing image. I hope Trista took videos."

"God, I hope she didn't." We were a hot fucking mess chasing after her. Milkshake zipped down the hill to the barn and riled up all the chickens. At one point, Luke dove for her, falling into a pile of horse shit while I tried hopping a fence, busting it and my ass in the process. Wyatt just stood there and laughed. Asshole only cares about his goat, Millie.

"Could she run wild? Do you think she'd return home?"

"I don't have the heart to test it." I pat Milkshake's belly in the carrier before giving her paw a little squeeze. "There's too much wildlife out here that she could get into scraps with. Not worth the risk."

I feel Dakota's eyes burning a hole in the side of my face, but I'm trying not to look at her. She looks too good in this golden setting sun with the backdrop of snowcapped pines all around her. Being attracted to her in Mexico was one thing. Entertaining fantasies of her back here in reality is quite another.

What happened in Mexico stays in Mexico, and I need to remember that.

"I want you to come to the sex club with me," she shouts out, and my boot catches on a tree root. I stumble a bit before I regain my footing. This woman needs to stop blurting her intrusive thoughts out to me or I am going to have a heart attack. Why can't she just ponder them in her own mind like the rest of us?

"Hear me out," she rushes, moving to stand in front of me with an excited bounce to her step. "We don't have to sleep together again or anything. I know Mexico was a one-off. I just want you to be my copilot there, a wingman, a partner in crime. It's only men that come alone as far as I could tell, and I think if I go with you, it'll help give me a bit more confidence."

"Confidence to do what?"

"To explore my options . . . have some new experiences. Just . . . be free!"

My heart lurches in my chest. "You still want to do that?"

"Yes," she replies, her forehead creased in confusion. "What do you mean? Why wouldn't I?"

"I guess I thought our night in Mexico would have helped scratch whatever itch you needed scratched."

Dakota pauses for a moment, her brow pinched tightly between her eyes before she bursts out laughing, causing Milkshake to jump against my chest. Her little paws straighten like pegs, and

I have to hug her to calm her down. Dakota buckles over, holding her stomach as her blond hair fans around her face.

"Take it easy, okay? We don't need your cackling to cause an avalanche."

She straightens and presses her lips together as she struggles to get control of herself. "Sorry, Calder, but did you really think one night with you would ruin me for other men?"

Kind of, my inner voice says with a surly pout. Maybe if she would have let me fuck her how I wanted to fuck her, we wouldn't be having this conversation. But no, Miss Control Freak had to take charge and basically force my premature ejaculation.

My dick thickens in my jeans at that memory. *Hottest fucking moment I've ever had with a woman.* Not that I'd tell her that. See? Intrusive thoughts stay inside the brain. Dakota should try that.

What I'd also never tell her is that I wanted a rematch, but she was exhausted and fell asleep too fast afterward. And morning sex is too intimate and would have blurred the lines of a one-night stand too much.

It didn't stop me from stroking myself in the shower before we flew out, though.

"So like . . . how many dudes are you wanting to fuck?" I ask, my shoulders tightening at the mere thought as I begin walking again.

"It's not about quantity, it's just about experiences," she says, falling into step with me. "It's about being comfortable in my own skin. I only had sex with two men before I met Randal. I kind of missed the boat on my slutty twenties, and I guess I want to make up for that now."

"And you think sex clubs are the best place for that? People who go to sex clubs are really experienced."

"Exactly," she says excitedly. "The women in those clubs are so uninhibited. It's so admirable. And heck, even when you and I were doing it . . . I felt my confidence growing just because you were so confident. It's just crazy enough of an idea to work."

I feel the corner of my mouth turn down as I glance over at her. "You should be confident, Dakota. You're fucking beautiful."

She stills, and her cheeks flush with my praise as her eyes blink with a softness that I rarely ever see on her. She's quiet for a moment before finally she says, "I just know I don't want to end up in another relationship where I'm insecure and letting a man get in my head. And I think a little foray with some sex-positive individuals will help me with that."

"All this because some ass fuck called you boring in bed?" My head jerks when I notice that Dakota is no longer beside me.

I turn on my heel to find her frowning, her eyes filled with way more emotion than they were just a second ago.

"Fuck, I'm sorry. That was harsh." I walk over to her and stand awkwardly, unsure what to say or do to get myself out of this. Even Milkshake feels the tension as she stops purring and stares up at me like *You put your foot in your mouth there, you idiot.* "I don't know shit about you and Randal. I shouldn't pass judgment. I just really don't like that guy, and my mouth does the talking before my brain does the thinking. I don't know anything about your marriage to him."

She offers me a weak shrug. "On the surface, people would probably call our split the classic seven year itch."

"Seven year itch?" I frown, unfamiliar with the term.

"They say seven years is the point in a marriage where the steam starts to fizzle, and they can't hold their mask up anymore. The *real them* is revealed." She sighs before adding, "Usually someone in the relationship cheats."

"He cheated?" My teeth crack as my hand tightens around my cat.

"No, that would have been too easy. Instead, Randal said our marriage failed because I lost the confidence I had with my smaller body, which in turn, ruined our sex life. He literally said I let myself go."

I drop my head to my chest as dread washes over me. It's moments like this that I really hate being a man. "What a fucker."

"He usually only said it when he was drunk. But they always say the truth comes out when you're drunk."

"It's not true . . . You're just as beautiful now as the day I met you."

"In my right mind, I can believe that," she says, her eyes looking up at me with an introspective glint to them. "I see the girls in a size ten–twelve body on Instagram and think they are so hot. I see myself in them and feel good in a lot of the clothes I wear. But when the man you choose to share your life with gets drunk and starts making digs at your body, it really fucks with a girl's self-esteem."

My chest contracts at the stricken look in her face. "It sounds like he's an alcoholic and an asshole, which is a him problem, not a you problem."

"He would quit drinking sometimes and things would get better, but as soon as he'd let himself partake again, the same stuff would come out of his mouth. Somewhere along the line, he developed all this pent-up resentment toward me that he could never communicate in a healthy way. It's no wonder he thought I was boring in bed. Never wanting to have sex with your partner *is* pretty boring."

"Sex is about give-and-take," I state confidently, desperate to shift Dakota back to the positive, bubbly girl she was when she knocked on my door ten minutes ago. "Him asking for something you weren't comfortable enough to give means he wasn't giving you what you needed to feel safe. That's not boring, that's just expected."

Her lips part as she stares up at me, her eyes swimming with a million different emotions I can't all place. "Have you gone to therapy or something?" she asks, staring intently at me.

"No . . . but I do read a book on occasion," I admit, leaving out the bit about them being audiobooks. Audiobooks count as reading, right? They sure make the long days on the job sight a lot less monotonous. Thrillers are usually my book of choice, but I listen to some self-help ones when I'm feeling down.

I have my father to thank for that life hack. He always said *why pay a therapist when you can rent an audiobook from a library for free?* I'm not sure that was the most emotionally intelligent advice he ever gave, but it's not bad for a guy like me who would never take the time to go see a doctor.

"I wish Randal had picked up a book here and there because toward the end, he thought a baby would fix all our problems, and I know there's no literature that would make that claim."

I wince and attempt to brace myself for what she says next.

"I told him we needed to fix our relationship before we added another human to it, but he kept bringing it up. Said I was unhappy because I was stagnant. Working the same job, in the same house, with the same guy. He said we needed a change. But the thing is . . . I love my store. I started it straight out of college, and I *still* get an endorphin boost every time I step foot inside. Why would I want that to change? I'm proud of what I built."

"You should be proud." I feel my temper rise over the thought of Randal, a bartender, ever trying to tell Dakota anything about her business. That'd be like me telling her how to curl her damn hair.

She inhales a shaky breath and looks down at the ground when she adds, "Then there was the condom mishap." My eyes burn into her as she continues to look down at the ground. "He took off the condom in the middle of sex once and came inside of me without asking."

"Fucking hell." My hands forming tight fists at my sides. "Are you serious?"

She crosses her arms and turns away from me with a nod. "I've never reacted well to birth control, so condoms were our only form of protection all the years we were married. It was dark, and he said he was just adjusting it, but he wasn't. He took it off on purpose, and I didn't notice until it was too late. He even admitted it. Said he was letting destiny decide for us."

"Jesus fuck," I spit, wishing Randal was here right now so I could rip his head off.

"I felt violated, like my decision to have a family with him was taken from me. It was awful. That entire month was hell waiting to see if I was pregnant or not. When my period finally showed up, I don't think I'd ever felt more relieved in my entire life. I literally cried tears of happiness in the bathroom at my shop. So much so, one of my employees knocked on the door to make sure I was okay."

I move closer to Dakota. She looks raw and bare in this moment surrounded by the heavy pine and quiet hush of nature. Different from any other time I've seen her. I swear, the mountain has this weird ability to lower your guard. The solace of it gives you the confidence to really lay yourself out bare.

I place a hand on her back to offer her some comfort. I grew up with only brothers, so I'm not great at the soothing thing . . . but watching my mom grieve my dad has taught me that sometimes physical touch is all someone needs.

"I'm sorry he did that to you," I offer, and she looks back at me, forcing a big toothy smile that doesn't reach her eyes.

"It was the kick in the ass I needed to make a change. The same day I found out I wasn't pregnant, I boxed up a bunch of his shit and set it out on my front lawn. I even peed on a stick, those digital ones that say Pregnant or Not Pregnant and put the negative test result on top of his box. I said I was filing for a divorce and would send him the name of my attorney as soon as I hired one."

The corner of my mouth lifts into a proud smirk. "Very savage and very you."

She takes a moment to collect herself, fluffing out her hair and gripping her coat around her abdomen. "So that's my divorce sob story. Not even a very good one."

"No, it's good," I reply, unable to take my eyes off her. She looks like a fucking goddess in this lighting after just opening herself up like that, revealing her darkest truths and holding her chin up high despite everything.

"How is it good? Were you even listening?"

"I heard every word," I reply firmly. "And it's good because you got the fuck out of there. You cut your losses, and that takes guts."

"I wasted so much time with him, though." Her chin trembles, and her eyes are glassy as she sniffs. "I'm thirty-three and starting over."

I have to hold back a laugh. "Yeah, you better call the nursing homes and save a room."

"Shut up, you know what I mean."

"What I do know is that you have a lot of life still to live and that spark you had the day I met you is still burning strong. Maybe even stronger now that you've dumped the deadweight."

An errant tear slides down her cheek, so I reach out to wipe it off with the back of my finger. Her breath stutters with the contact, but she doesn't pull away. She shoots me a wobbly smile that hits me right in my gut. Dakota might be the strongest woman I know—and that's saying something, because my mom and Trista both rank pretty high up there on my list of badass women.

I step closer to her and grab her by the arms, dipping my head so we're eye level and she can really focus on what I'm about to say. Milkshake's extended feet press against her chest and Dakota pets her behind the ear before looking up at me.

"Just please promise me you're doing this sex club thing for *you* and not for him."

"I am," she replies a bit too quickly, her head jerking away from me.

"Cuz that fucker doesn't deserve any more space in your head."

"I know." She nods solemnly before peering up at me, her brows knitting together as she searches my face for something. "Do you have history with Randal that I don't know about? Because every time his name is brought up . . . your nostrils seem to permanently flare."

I release my grip on her and step back to resume my hold on my cat. "I don't have history with Randal. I just hate to see you doing anything for a guy like him."

"See? A guy like him." She points at me. "That makes me think you have a beef with him."

"I don't give a fuck about your ex-husband, Dakota," I snap a bit too viscerally.

"Fine," she snaps back.

"Let's just stop talking about him."

"Great idea."

Silence descends over both of us as we turn and resume our cat walk in a brooding mood that's much more familiar than the gushing heart-to-heart stuff we were exchanging a moment ago.

We ventured way off topic because the reason she's here is that she wants me to take her to a sex club.

I hate the idea. I hate everything about it. But I hate the thought of her going back there alone even more. She's right: they're not really designed well for single women. But does she really know what she's asking?

"Going back to your proposition." I take a long breath, mustering my strength for the next question. "What if I take you to Lexon and we meet a couple who wants to swing with us, because people are going to assume we're together?"

"That sounds great," she exclaims, her sour mood quickly replaced with excitement. "We've already seen each other naked so it's not really that big a deal, right?"

"Riiight," I murmur, my eyes moving to the ground. My mind kicks into overdrive as I picture Dakota naked and fucking some guy right beside me. It'll be some other man touching her flesh, some other man making her moan. Not me.

The lump in my throat is damn near painful as I feel my palms grow slick with sweat, but I quickly wipe them off on my jeans because this isn't a big deal. This is just sex. I'll be fucking someone too, not just watching. I can handle this. Casual fucking is my way of life.

"I was thinking we could go Friday night after work if you're up for it," she chirps, ripping me out of my mind fuck.

"This Friday?" I snap, my eyes wide. "So soon?"

She shrugs. "Yeah, why not?"

Why not, Calder? Why the fuck not? Get your goddamn balls back and stop being such a pansy-ass-feelings fucker.

"I'll call Lexon and make sure I can get your membership reinstated. I'll explain it was just a misunderstanding and hopefully they'll be cool with it. If they are, are you available to come with me?"

She states this all like she's setting up a damn business meeting, and I wonder how the hell we ended up here. This isn't at all what I expected. Honestly, I was hoping to just walk my cat, work on some shelves, and attempt to forget how good Dakota's lips felt on mine. How lush her breasts felt in my hands. How goddamn life-changing it was seeing her naked on top of me.

That was the plan.

But this bossy woman always has a way of fucking up my plans.

Chapter 21

PLAYTIME

Dakota

"What are you wearing under that coat?" Calder asks as he traverses through the busy Denver traffic.

"A dress."

"What kind of dress?"

Frowning, I unbutton my coat and pull it open to reveal a red, long-sleeved lace bodycon dress with a nude underlay. It's a little slutty but also a little demure. I'd never be caught dead wearing something like this in Boulder, but that's the fun of this place. You get to be someone else.

I spent hours on Reddit threads researching sex clubs before I ever stepped foot into Lexon. It's how I figured out what to wear, how to act, and when the best nights were to go. I would have never known about newbie night if it weren't for Reddit.

Calder clears his throat and looks away, shifting in his seat. "That'll work."

I close my jacket and buzz my lips. "God, I'm nervous."

"Why?"

"Because last time did not go well, and I don't want a repeat."

Calder nods and turns into the parking lot, sliding his giant truck into the first open spot. He's dressed in the same kind of clothes he's always wearing. Men like him have it so easy. Hot and tattooed is all the style he'll ever need. He could be wearing a garbage bag and the women would still come panting at his feet.

But the flannel and denim look isn't a bad choice on him. It's rustic and cozy and so utterly masculine, you just want to just curl up in his arms and never let go. It was weird seeing him outside of his mountain gear in Mexico. And it's annoying how even in a cream suit or swim trunks, he looked just as hot as ever.

My palms are slick with sweat as we make our way inside. Flashbacks of the first time I came here are on Replay in my mind. I hadn't even been in the bar area five minutes before I was approached by the last guy. The Dom or Sir or whatever he wanted me to call him. I felt so uncomfortable being alone, I was just grateful someone was finally willing to talk to me. And when he handed me the mask to wear, I wanted to say no, but I told myself to keep an open mind.

I kept it open as long as I could. That guy was not my vibe. Hopefully tonight with Calder by my side, no one will ask to take a dump on my chest.

"Let's get a drink," Calder says as he hands my coat off to the coat check gal. She's wearing a skimpy black dress, and her eyes rake up and down Calder like he's the hottest thing she's ever seen. He doesn't notice her, but I do. She chances a glance at me, and I feel her scrutiny deep in my bones.

I tug on my dress. Maybe this was a bad choice. Maybe I should have gone for something skimpier. It's not enough to be tight. It needs to be revealing too. Is *demure-sexy* even a thing?

But I would have needed Spanx in all the other dresses I bought. I can't imagine Spanx are seen in a place like this. Unless that's someone's kink? Ripping women out of their medieval shapewear. Could be hot. I'd probably try it.

"Stop fidgeting with your dress," Calder growls in my ear as he presses his warm hand to the small of my back and leads me toward the end of the bar. His hot breath on my neck sends a riot of goose bumps all over my skin. I am super sensitive tonight.

He sidles up to the glossy black counter and waves the bartender down ordering himself a beer, and I tell him I'd love a cosmopolitan. A cosmo seems like a sexy drink to have in a place like this. Last time I had a wine, and whatever happens, I do not want a repeat of last time.

I glance around at the women peppered throughout the club. They're all showing a lot more skin and seem at least five years younger than me, further fueling my insecurity.

"I made a bad choice." I tug on my long sleeves. "This dress isn't slutty enough."

"It's slutty enough." Calder takes a sip of his beer, barely looking at me.

"Even the coat check girl looked hotter than me."

"Would you stop?" He frowns at me as his eyes drift down to my chest. "The dress is good."

I try to sip my drink, but a hot brunette is staring at me and not in the *you go, girl* kind of way. "Maybe we should leave. This was a bad idea. I don't know how I made it in here the last time." I make a move to walk back toward the coat check, but Calder's hand wraps around my wrist, and he yanks me back into him.

"I'm fucking hard already, okay?" he growls, irritation all over his grumpy face as I stumble into him, my leg brushing against something in his groin area that does feel a bit firm.

"What?" I sputter, my hand flat on his chest as I try to regain my balance and stop myself from pressing up against his dick. My eyes drop down to his crotch and widen when I confirm what I just felt. But how do I know he's not turned on by the coat check girl? Hell, *I* was turned on by the coat check girl.

"I've been hard since the truck." He sits down on the barstool and turns away from me, his jaw taut with irritation as he glances back at me. "The dress is hot. Now, shut up and sit down and have a drink."

I've never been happier to have a man tell me to shut up in my entire life.

With a smile I can't even remotely hide, I slide onto the stool next to him and grab my cocktail glass. "Yes, sir."

A rumble vibrates from his lips, and I can't help but giggle.

"You're going to fucking kill me, Ace." He turns to look at me, and his grumpy mood lightens as I continue smiling and fighting back a laugh. The corner of his mouth tugs up, and he looks away again.

God, we are dysfunctional.

One second we're getting along and then, bam . . . back to bickering. I don't know why it's so easy for me to fight with Calder. It's like we're wired to pick at each other until one of us cracks.

The only time I ever really fought with Randal was when he was drunk. It was a different kind of fighting than what I do with Calder. With Randal it was mostly just him being a bully and me being too stunned to really fight back. Then the next day, everything would be swept under the rug, which meant that by the time we went into divorce proceedings, there was loads of dirt for us to clean up.

I swallow the uncomfortable knot in my throat as my mind slips back to the yucky place I'd been living in for the past few years with him. The place he yanked me back to with one stupid phone call the other night. It's no wonder my body changed, I was living in a nightmare I couldn't wake up from. An endless loop of Randal coming home from the bar and picking a fight with me. Literally even waking me up to do so.

But putting my depression aside, my body could have just changed because I'm not as young as I once was. It's entirely possible it was always going to change because that's just life! And obsessing over a dress size is so uninteresting to me. I know in my bones that my worth and my beauty are not tied to my weight, no matter how many assholes like Randal want to make me believe it is. Those aren't the men I want in my life anyways. I want a man I feel confident enough to fight with.

That is what this experiment with Calder is about. To find the girl I once was, who doesn't give a fuck what anyone thinks because loving herself is enough.

"What was your first time here like?" I ask after sipping my drink and allowing the alcohol to calm my nerves.

Calder inhales deeply. "I guess you could say I was on a warpath."

My brows lift. "What does that mean?"

He licks his lips, and his eyes tighten. "My brothers and I had just found out that this woman we knew was pregnant with another man's child."

I frown. "Why would that bother you?"

"Because we were all sleeping with her at the time."

My eyes nearly bug out of my head. "Like . . . together-together?"

"No." Calder rolls his eyes and takes a drink. "She was sleeping with all of us separately . . . but at the same time."

"And you didn't know?"

Calder shakes his head. "Not really. I think we might have suspected, but we were all sort of vying for her attention. It was kind of a game, and we are all way too competitive."

I need to process this. Three Fletcher boys after the same woman . . . She must have been something truly special. "Most people are competitive when it comes to sports, not humans."

Calder winces. "I'm not proud, okay? We were new to Jamestown and excited to finally be out of Boulder."

"I'm not judging," I reply, taking a big drink and waiting for him to continue, wishing I had some popcorn. "I'm just really intrigued."

"Well, it gets even more fucked-up. It turns out a construction company out of Colorado Springs called Pristine Contractors was owned by her husband, and apparently, he and my dad were both bidding on a project, and my dad ended up getting it. The guy hated us for it. Said my dad got a hold of his bid and underpriced ours to edge him out. He's a fucking whack job."

"Sounds like it."

"Anyways, I guess at some point, he cheated on Robyn, and that's when she left him and moved to Jamestown and met us."

My eyes are dry from how wide they are. "Did she know who you guys were?"

Calder licks his lips and sighs. "Yep. But we didn't know her connection to Matt."

"Wait . . . wait, wait, wait!" I hold my hands up, unable to fully process this. "Did she sleep with all three of you to get back at her husband?"

"She sure did."

"Holy shit."

"*Holy shit* is right." Calder huffs out a self-deprecating laugh. "And I've never felt more embarrassed than when I had to give a sample of saliva for a paternity test to find out who the father of the baby she was pregnant with was."

"Holy ever-loving God, I am going to pass out!" I press a hand to my chest, struggling to get my heart rate under control. I had heard rumors about something scandalous with the Fletcher brothers years ago, but I always assumed it was gossip. And it wasn't like I even knew those guys at the time. I just knew of the family business, so it didn't really matter much to me.

It wasn't until Cozy fell for Max that I ever even met them, and they all seemed relatively normal at the time. Weird for living on a mountain compound together, but Cozy approved of them, so I did too. To know this whole soap opera happened in the little mountain town of Jamestown is wild.

Calder's jaw muscle ticks as he drinks his beer with very little emotion after the story he just shared. Either he has a great poker face, or this really doesn't bother him as much as I would think it should. I suppose it's been a while, and time heals all wounds, but a wound like this has to leave a scar. Right?

Weirdly, it impresses me how close the Fletcher brothers are despite that crazy time in their lives. It takes a strong family to repair after this woman came in and wreaked havoc on all of them. I can't help but wonder what their father thought of it all.

"And the baby turned out to be this Matt-guy's?"

"Yes, thank God," Calder huffs and shakes his head. "That was the one silver lining that came out of all of this, because it would not have been pleasant being tied to her with a kid. Although, I feel bad for the kid. Her and Matt are still together last I heard."

"Wow." I feel a bit silly that I can't offer anything more profound after that bomb was dropped. "I can see how visiting a sex club after all of that felt like no big deal."

Calder chuckles softly. "I don't know about *no big deal*. I just wanted something different with no connections. I was used to going out with my brothers all the time, but I wanted a place where I could meet someone on my own that would help erase her from my mind. First time here, I found a female Domme, and she worked real hard to help me forget about all my problems back on the peak." His eyes dance with mirth as his mind drifts down memory lane. He clearly enjoys this memory much more than the Robyn one.

"So is that your kink?" I lean in, my voice a whisper. "You like a bossy type?"

Calder shrugs. "I like lots of things. Can't seem to ever find a favorite, and believe me, I've tried."

"Hmm." I turn on my stool to survey the crowd. "Do you think everyone is here because of some fucked-up past trauma?"

"Don't we all have trauma in one way or another?" Calder asks, and I tilt my head to watch him for a moment, wondering which trauma affected him more. This Robyn chick or the loss of his dad?

Maybe it doesn't matter. He's right. Trauma is trauma. It's how we work through it to come out the other side that matters.

My thoughts are distracted when I spot a couple from across the room staring in our direction. They whisper to each other, never taking their eyes off of me or Calder. I can't quite tell. They look relatively normal. Like a couple who would walk into my shop . . . whatever that means. The man is tall, dark, and handsome. Clean-shaven and wearing a suit. The woman is a petite redhead with large breasts. They're both beautiful.

I nudge Calder with my elbow and nod. "I think something might be happening."

"What?" he murmurs, more interested in his beer than the action of the club.

"Would you stop being such a grump and look?" I grab his face and turn him to look out into the club, and at the same time, the couple stand and begin to make their way over to us.

"Oh my God, they're coming over here!"

"Chill out, Ace."

"Holy shit!" I swivel on my stool back to the bar to down my drink. "Can I get a shot?"

"No," Calder bites out. "There's a two-drink maximum anyways."

"Exactly why I want that shot. What do you think this means?" I glance over my shoulder. "Do they want to hook up with us?"

"I'm not a mind reader."

"Would be nice if you were."

"Hi," the woman purrs from behind me, and I take a moment before turning around to face her.

"Hi," I repeat back, wondering if I can get away with just copying everything she says all night. That would take a lot of pressure off.

"You guys want to play?" the man asks, his arms wrapped around the woman's waist as his eyes move from Calder to me. He licks his lips as his gaze drifts down to stare at my chest, and I have to fight back my look of shock. I suppose in a place like this, everyone is here for the same thing, so there's no need to be shy about it.

I look to Calder, waiting for him to take the lead. That's what an experienced wingman does, right? But he says nothing. He just stares up at the guy with an expression I can't fully read.

"What did you have in mind?" I croak, surprising myself with that very smooth response.

The man releases the woman, and they cross paths with each other, the woman sitting down by Calder and the man sitting down by me. Both of them instantly sweep us up into light conversation, making it very obvious they're pros at this sex club mingling game.

"So, what do you like, beautiful?" He trails his fingers down my arm, sliding into the crook of my elbow and practically lighting my vagina on fire with desire.

"What do you like?" I ask, mimicking the question again. Honestly, it's some of my best work to date.

"Bondage," he says firmly. No hesitation. "I like to tie women up and give them the most mind-blowing orgasms of their life. Do you want me to tie you up, beautiful?"

My face heats as I picture myself tied up and being touched by a perfect stranger. It sounds both terrifying and exhilarating at the same time. And I'm intrigued not only by what he likes to do, but how good he'll look doing it. The man is attractive, there's no way around it. He's not Calder-level hot, but he's up there. And the fact that he picked me out of a room full of women is validating in so many ways. I love how this place allows people to speak freely about what they want too. No preamble, no will they, won't they. You lay your cards right on the table, and it's up to you to play or not.

I'm ready to play.

I smile and feel myself nodding, my body humming with nerves as I agree to this man's offer. I'll make sure I have a safe word so if it gets to be too much, I can dip. Hopefully I can come up with something more clever than *lambchop* like last time. I can do this. This is what I'm here for.

Plus, I'm not really interested in hanging around and watching Calder do his thing with the woman he's talking to. There's something strange about watching a man you slept with flirt with another woman. I know it was casual and this is what I asked him to do with me, but seeing it close-up is a lot more unsettling than I expected. I need to just focus on myself and this guy who just asked to tie me up and get Calder Fletcher far out of my mind.

The man holds his hand out to me, and my back brushes against Calder's as I stand up off my stool and let him lead me toward the steps. We're going to go find a playroom.

Holy shit, this is exciting. I remember catching a bondage scene between a couple when I got a tour on my first visit, but I was kind of on information overload at that time, so seeing it with this man will be an entirely different experience.

I turn back to look at Calder, and he's watching me walk away with a deep scowl on his face. Oh no. It looks like he's maybe not getting along with the woman as well as I am with the man. But I'm sure he'll have no problem finding someone to hook up with. He is a pro, after all. But admittedly, I get a secret thrill over the fact that I scored before Calder Fletcher. Maybe I am competitive with humans after all.

Calder stands as I reach the steps and I give him a thumbs-up, silently telling him I'm good. I am good. I got this. It's time to "play."

Chapter 22

WHEN FANTASY BECOMES REALITY

Calder

My eyes are on Dakota's ass as she climbs the giant staircase. It took her all of five minutes to ditch me for some other dude, and I'm equal parts horrified and impressed. And as the young girl who sits in front of me natters on about how her husband loves to share her, my mind races over everything Dakota has revealed to me in the past week.

I knew Randal wasn't a good guy. I only ever saw him in passing when I was in and out of Dakota's house during the reno, but there was a feeling about him that I could never shake, and having her confirm that feeling shrouds me in shame.

I should have said something to her.

Instead, I stood back and let them get married. Whatever he did, whatever he said, or didn't say, to her in the bedroom and during their marriage . . . I feel responsible somehow. Which is ridiculous because she's a grown-ass woman, but seven years is a long time to be with somebody who treats you like shit. Is this really the best place for her to rediscover herself?

The woman beside me slides her hand up my thigh, and my dick has zero reaction, which is honestly fucking ridiculous. She's beautiful. She's obviously experienced. She's the perfect choice. But I can't stop thinking about the annoying blonde who just disappeared upstairs.

"What else is your husband into?" I cut the girl off midsentence.

Her brown eyes widen. "Are you into men? Do you want me to see if he—"

"No . . . just . . . what's his thing? What do you think they're doing up there?"

She smiles knowingly. "If I'd have to guess, he's got her strapped up to a St. Andrew's cross with duct tape on her mouth. He loves the red mark tape leaves on a face when we're done."

My stool scrapes loudly on the floor when I stand up, drawing the eyes of several patrons around us. "She's not ready for that."

The woman chuckles. "She seemed to go up there pretty willingly, didn't she?"

"Yeah, but if she can't talk, how will she use a safe word?"

She shrugs and slides her hands up my chest to pull me toward her. "I don't have a safe word." She peers up at me like that's going to be my go signal to take her upstairs, but it has the opposite effect.

Immediate fear courses through my body. If he's used to a woman without a safe word, how will I know he'll honor one from Dakota? Dakota knows to advocate for one, right? Fuck.

I grab the gal's hands and remove them from my chest. "I have to go."

She sees me bolting for the steps, and I hear her gasp. "I'll come with you!"

"Don't bother," I call back as I take the steps two at a time, flying to the upper level. I hang a right to go toward the bondage hallway where I've seen the St. Andrew's crosses before. Dakota never said she was into bondage. And I thought she didn't like BDSM. Why did she agree to come up here with this guy?

My heart rate spikes when I see them talking quietly in the hallway. Still both fully dressed, thank fuck. She's leaned up against the wall, and the man's hand is splayed out on the wall by her face, his other sliding across her cheek as he leans in to—

"We gotta go, Ace," I state loudly, stopping him just before their lips connect.

Dakota turns half-hooded eyes to me, and my jaw clenches at the aroused look on her face. The sense of betrayal that slices through me makes no fucking sense, and I want to scream at her for some unknown fucking reason.

"We're leaving." I grab her wrist and pull her away from this dude, my chest vibrating with barely concealed rage.

"Whoa, whoa, whoa. Let's make sure she wants to leave." The man moves closer to Dakota and touches her arm, which makes me see red.

I step up into him and bump my chest against his. "You have a death wish, buddy?"

He lifts his hands up in surrender, his eyes dilated with desire as he stares up at me. "No death wish. Just wanting to make sure the girl can advocate for herself. What is it you want, big boy? I'm open to ideas."

"She can talk just fine," I grind out, stopping myself from adding the fact that she usually never shuts up. I turn to look at Dakota. "You ready to go?"

She frowns at me, and I see a million unanswered questions cross her face before she does the unexpected and nods. "Okay, we can go."

I slide a cocky grin to the suit and lace my fingers through Dakota's, pulling her behind me at a pace she can barely keep up with in her heels. Meanwhile I can barely keep up with the thoughts racing in my head. Thoughts I am really fucking confused about.

We stop at the coat check, and I cover her up, exhaling slowly as I attempt to lower my blood pressure. We make our way out into the cold darkness toward my truck, and I open the passenger door, waiting for her to jump in.

"Mind telling me what that was all about?" she asks, crossing her arms and looking up at me, refusing to get in the truck.

"What do you mean?" I roll my eyes and gesture to the vehicle. "Can you just get in the truck?."

"No, I want to know what is going on." She pushes her hair out of her face and pins me with a defiant look that is much more on-brand for the Dakota I know. "Was there something wrong with that guy that you ripped me out of there like that? He didn't ask me to shit on him, which felt like a step up from last time."

"Nice to know you have such high standards," I scoff.

"Hey!" She pokes me in the chest. "What do you know that I don't?"

My lips thin as I shake my head. "I don't trust him."

"Why? Did his wife say something bad about him?" She searches my face with anxiety before glancing back at the club.

"He likes to tape women's mouths shut."

She looks back at me, her lips twisting in confusion. "I already knew that."

My eyes bug out of my head. "You did?"

"Yeah, that's what we were discussing in the hallway."

"How are you going to utter a safe word with your mouth taped shut?"

"That's what we were discussing," she replies, acting like she's talking about a casual encounter. "He said there are other ways to signal a safe word. A dropped item or blinking."

"Blinking?" I roar, stepping closer to her until her back is pressed against my truck. I cage her in so she can feel the full wrath of me as the steam of our breaths dances in the darkness. "You think when a guy has you naked and strapped to a fucking cross he's going to notice you blinking your safety notice? Goddammit, Dakota!"

"Why are you so mad?" she snaps, looking at me like I've got two heads.

I jerk away from her and shove my hands through my hair. "Was it so easy for you to jump to another guy? I was just inside of you less than two weeks ago." My voice is guttural and doesn't even sound like me. I thought I ripped her out of there because of what she told me at the bar . . . but clearly, my cock is doing all the talking for me right now.

She blinks back at me, her expression unreadable. "But you agreed to this. You said you would be my wingman."

"I didn't know you'd jump on the first dick you saw. Did you even like that guy?"

"Why do I have to like him? It's just sex. I thought you of all people would understand that."

"I don't." My tone is acidic.

"You know what?" she snaps, poking me in the chest again until she backs me all the way up into the parked car beside us. "It's completely misogynistic for you think casual sex is okay for you but not for me. If I was a dude, you wouldn't have any issues with this."

"Oh bullshit."

"It's true! You probably got laid the other night after we met up to look at your shelving designs. You were so stressed because you had big plans you had to get to."

"Plans?" I rack my brain to remember what it was I had going on that night last week.

"Yes, plans. You yelled at me to hurry up because you had to go somewhere. Tell me you didn't hook up with someone later that night."

"You would think that." I can barely restrain my anger. "That's all you see in me is sex, isn't it?"

Her mouth opens and closes before she shrugs. "Pretty much."

"Well, you're one to talk. You were all horned-up for that guy in there in within like two seconds." I wince as I picture her face in that hallway again.

Her lips part as she takes a step back. "I wasn't *horned-up*. God, who speaks like that?"

"I saw your face right before he was about to kiss you. You looked like you were about to come."

"No, I didn't."

"Yes, you did," I shout like a psycho. "I know that look on you. I saw it in Mexico, and you just met the guy. How the hell—"

"I was thinking of you, okay?" she exclaims, stomping her heeled foot into the ground.

"What?"

"God, this is so embarrassing." She waves her coat out and paces back and forth, like she's boiling hot all of a sudden, and the glimpse of her curves straining under that dress has my cock swelling in my jeans. "But you're acting nuts, and I don't know how else to get you to shut up." She stops by the bumper of my truck and turns back to look at me. "I was thinking of you and our night together, when I was with that guy. That's why I looked so turned on. I was . . ." she stutters, completely helpless ". . . I was fantasizing about you. I've been doing that a lot lately, and it's annoyingly effective."

I exhale heavily, my breath puffing a cloud of steam in front of me as I stare at her, watching her chest rise and fall in that tight fucking dress that's been driving me nuts since the moment she popped open her coat in my truck.

"I wasn't in a hurry that night on the mountain because I was going to have sex with someone."

She frowns back at me and rolls her eyes.

"I had old man's hockey practice." I flop my hands to my side in blatant surrender.

Her head snaps up to look at me. "What?"

"I play on an over-forty league where men who are old enough to be my father fucking humble me on the ice every goddamn week. I tried out for the over-thirty league, but I was too damn slow."

Dakota stares back at me, her brows twitching with shock, then bemusement, then disbelief, then humor. Unfortunately for me, humor is the one that sticks.

She erupts into a fit of giggles, holding onto the tailgate for balance as she folds over laughing, her eyes filling with tears over the sheer comedy of my pathetic-ness. I don't blame her for laughing. I am pathetic.

"I'm so bad I don't even let my mother come to watch me

play . . . and she tries to, but I refuse. It's too embarrassing. But God, I love skating with those old dudes. I have my entire retirement plan in place, thanks to those humbling assholes."

I can't help but smile as I drop my chin and walk over to her. It's good to see her laughing. I like it a lot more than the yelling. But if I'm being honest, I like it all.

She reaches up, using me for balance as her giggles slow down. "Are you about done?"

She blows out a happy sigh as she finally regains control of herself and wipes at the tears in her eyes. "I needed that."

"Well, good. I am here to serve you, after all."

She blinks slowly and licks her lips, the smile on her face completely dazzling me as my intrusive thoughts spill out this time. "I really need you to take your coat off."

Her brows twitch as she gazes up at me. "What? Why?"

"Because when I fuck you inside my truck in about sixty seconds, it's going to get in my damn way."

My cock swells as all humor leaves her face, and her eyes dance over every one of my features as she tries to make sense of the words that just spilled out of my mouth. She's trying to make sense of them, and I suppose I'd like to make sense of them too. I don't know what the fuck is going on. I haven't fucked the same woman within a couple weeks in years. It's always just been about release, so I've been able to forget the girl I was with easily and move on to the next.

But Dakota is undeniably unforgettable. My mind has been consumed with her for far too long, and this isn't about her confidence or her insecurities or her ex or even that douchebag bondage guy. I'm done playing wingman when I want her in the cockpit.

I turn on my heel to open the door to my truck, pointing silently at the cab. Her eyes move from me to the truck and back to me, and the minute she strides over to me and tosses her coat inside, it's like the puck has dropped.

I grab the back of her neck and seal my lips over hers, swallowing her needy whimper as she kisses me back. Our tongues dance as my hand shifts down to grip two fistfuls of her tits, squeezing them together, fighting the urge to grab the dress and rip it down the front so I can taste her skin on my lips. Lick the flesh that's filling my hands so perfectly. She moans, and my cock pulses at the sound of her.

God, she makes the best fucking noises.

"Get in the back seat and take off your panties." I drop down to press against her so she can feel my erection on her center.

"I'm not wearing any panties," she breathes, her eyes on my lips as she fists my shirt.

"Good girl." I pull away and smack her ass, shutting the front door and helping her into the back. She slides to the center, and I move in next to her. But before I even get the door closed, her hands are on my dick, her lips are on my neck, and she's rubbing my length over my jeans, thickening the painful bulge in my pants. My head falls back as I pump into her palm, reveling in how good the friction feels. How good her hands look on me.

Thank fuck this parking spot is dark so no other pervert gets to see this. *Her.* Because she is mine and mine alone right now.

"What do you want me to do?" she asks, pulling back and staring at my dick. She bites her lip and I feel my cock pulse over the sight of her slowly losing control.

"What do you want to do?" I watch her mind whirl with possibility as my body hums with desire, my cock begging to feel her skin on mine.

As if she reads my thoughts, a smirk lights up her face as she undoes my belt and pulls my length out, gripping my shaft tightly in her smooth palm.

"Ah," I grunt as sparks of heat fight against her cool fingers while she fists me. I want her so fucking bad. Have I ever wanted a woman this bad?

I don't have time to debate that as her hot lips wrap around my cock, her head dropping so low, my tip hits the back of her throat and I feel her gag.

"Yeah, baby," I croak, slicing my hand into her hair to ride her. "Choke on me."

She must enjoy my words as she picks up speed, her head relentlessly bobbing over me, her teeth catching around my tip in the most wicked way that sends shock waves through my entire body. My abs contract, and my chest pounds as my cock bulges and seeps into her mouth. I can feel her greedy tongue tasting me, lapping around the tip, and swallowing my precum drip by drip.

Fuck, I'm going to come already.

I grip her hair at the roots to gently pull her off, my cock aching at the view of her smudged lipstick and tear-filled eyes. "What did you want to happen tonight, Ace?"

"Huh?" she says, wiping the edges of her lips, her hooded eyes blinking back at me.

"In there." I nod toward the club. "What did you want that guy to do to you?"

Her chest heaves as she looks down at my soaked cock and swallows.

"Don't be nervous. Just tell me." I tip her chin, forcing her to look at me.

"I wanted him to tie me up." Her blue eyes sparkle in the darkness of my truck, and I can't help but smile back at her. She makes me proud when she speaks up for herself like that. I'm surprised every time because she says she lacks confidence, but her actions contradict that.

"Get on your hands and knees," I command, pointing to the bench seat as I reach into my back pocket for a condom, shoving my pants down my ass and pulling my shirt off over my head to get it out of the way.

I shift to the edge of the seat to make room for her legs as she gets into position, her heels kicked off, and her toes pointed toward me. She flips her blond hair over one shoulder to stare back at me as I roll the rubber over my length.

Hunched over and kneeling between her legs, I slowly inch her dress up over her ass, my cock straining at the view of her like this. Posed and waiting for me but still in that sexy-as-sin dress. *Seriously such a good fucking girl.* And when I spread her apart and spot the moisture pooled between her folds, my dick weeps with anticipation.

"You soaked for me or that guy in there, Ace?" I ask, dropping a soft bite to her right cheek.

She yelps and shifts back toward me. "Shut up."

"Answer me." I bite the other cheek.

"You know it's for you, asshole," she groans, dropping her elbows onto the leather seat, to pop her rear up higher. Her head bows, her hair a curtain all around her face.

A smile spreads across my face. "You want me to fuck you?"

"Yes," she cries, her hands little fists on the bench. "Please fuck me."

"Not quite ready," I tease as I reach to the floor of the truck. The sound of metal clinking causes her to crane her neck to look back at the neon green pickup straps in my hand. I shoot her a devilish smirk. "Put your hands behind your back."

"Seriously?" She sits back on her heels, and her voice has lost all sexual tones as she stares at the straps like they're murder weapons.

"Just trust me, Dakota."

Her eyes lift to mine, and she narrows them challengingly at me before hitting me with that sexy smirk again. With a squeak of irritation, she gives me one hand and then another, allowing me to wrap them with the end of a tie-down strap. One quick glance and I know there's too much slack to use the ratchet, so I take a deep breath and attempt to slow my racing heart as I tie them as best as I can, ensuring I can free her with one quick tug if needed.

She moans with impatience and wiggles her ass into me, so I grab the ratchet of the strap and slowly click it a few times to build anticipation. She stills to listen, and the sound of our heavy breathing before I've even entered her causes the blood to rush straight to my cock.

I grip her shoulders and bend her back over so she's chest down and ass up. Her cheek rests on the cool leather as she stares back at me. God, she looks incredible. Like a fucking wet dream all trussed up and waiting for me.

"I left it loose so you can slip out anytime," I state, leaning over and pressing my lips to her lower back. I want her to be able to free herself easily if she's ever uncomfortable. And with how hard I am right now, I am expecting her to get very, very uncomfortable.

"Okay," she gasps while still squirming against me.

"But just to be safe . . . we should have a safe word."

"Okay," she repeats herself, her body trembling with anticipation.

"Any preference?"

"*Lambchop*," she blurts out and I have to look away as I fight back my laugh.

"*Lambchop* it is." I shift up onto my knees and press my tip to her center, rubbing my head around her opening to get her primed. "You ready?"

"Yes," she pants, aching for relief.

She inhales sharply as I press myself inside of her, inch by inch, until I'm hunched over and balls-deep into her slick heat.

"Fuck, you feel so good," I grunt, grinding in and out of her at a slow, delirious pace. My vision blurs as I fight with my consciousness to not completely lose myself in the sensation overload happening on my cock.

She moans a delectable sound in the small cab of my truck as she attempts to rock back into me, clearly wanting more than what I'm giving her.

I grip the back of the seat as my body shudders with uncontrolled need. I hold her trussed-up arms by the straps, pulling her back as I thrust deep inside of her, hitting even deeper than before. She cries out, throwing her head back as much as she can with her

limbs otherwise engaged. Her dress rides up midback, exposing
the underside of her crushed breasts, and the sight of it all ignites a
fire in me, and I feel my control snap.

I pound into her, my pace relentless as our bodies grow slick
with sweat. I grip the front seat to keep my balance as I feel my
climax growing closer and closer.

She screams my name, and I think I scream hers, but my mind
is too busy whirring from the intensity of it all. Her scent, her
voice, the feel of her skin as I grip her ass. My eyes close tight, and
my muscles throb as I continue at a grueling pace while the blood
rushing through my shaft feels unbearable. I fold over top of her,
covered in sweat as the windows of my truck fog up.

"Ahhh!" Dakota screams, and I feel her center grip and pulse
over my length, her orgasm catching me off guard.

I quickly slip the straps off her, and she instantly pulls her hands
up, bracing herself on the bench as I continue slamming into her
sweet cunt.

I use the opportunity to grab a handful of her breasts, pulling her
up on her knees. Her hand streaks across the foggy glass as I thrust
upward, and her cries catapult me over the edge as heat floods to my
tip and I come, filling the condom with pulsating shocks of ecstasy.

Slick with sweat, I release her, my knees screaming as I drop
back into my seat and glance over at her. No wonder I came so
quickly. Look at her.

The dazed look in her eyes. The flush of her cheeks. Her wild
hair and frantic breathing. It's all so goddamn hot. And then I notice
the soft smile, as if she's completely sated. I like that look on her.
Maybe a bit too much because I want to make her look that way
again and again and again. *Fuck*.

She pulls her dress down and twists around, straightening herself up as I slip the condom off and wrap it into a napkin I retrieve
from the door.

I catch her rubbing her wrists and frown when I see faint red
marks. "Fuck, did I hurt you?"

I grab her hands to inspect for myself, and she shakes her head, trying to pull free from my hold. "I'm fine, I swear."

"Are you sure?" My eyes find hers as nerves fire off in my belly.

"I'm positive." She bites her lip, and a bashful look casts over her face before she erupts into a laugh.

"What's so funny?" *God, I want to kiss her.*

"I really don't know why *lambchop* is my safe word." She pushes away the hair stuck to her face and wipes at her eyes. "I think I need therapy."

My shoulders shake as I laugh with her. "I think I know what you need."

Chapter 23

CHANGE OF PLAN

Dakota

"I think we should be friends with benefits," Calder says as he drives down the interstate that leads back to Boulder.

"But . . . we're not friends," I blurt out as I turn to look at him to make sure he hasn't been possessed by a demon.

He shrugs. "Semantics."

My mouth opens and closes over and over like one of those silly singing bass wall hangings. He's got to be messing with me right now, right? He doesn't sleep with women more than once . . . at least not on purpose. "So instead of being my wingman, you want to be my fuck buddy?"

"If you're intent on a label, you can call us *enemies with benefits*." He smiles like he's casually talking about the weather. "It's honestly genius because if you're friends with benefits, feelings are bound to get involved because you both already like each other. You hating me makes this much easier."

"Don't you think we need to get along for something like this to actually work?"

"Got along just fine ten minutes ago." Calder shoots me a dark look that I feel squarely between my legs. "Just consider me your emotionally distant genital masseuse."

My mind reels with this proposition that I did not have on my bingo card in my postdivorce era. A sex-only affair with Calder Fletcher . . . the asshole who ruined my house and my wedding dress seven years ago. It sounds like a horrible idea that's sure to end in catastrophe. I call him Killer Calder for a reason.

Then again, it also sounds kind of poetic in some strange way. It's like revenge sex or something. And he's not the same guy he was seven years ago. I've seen that in more ways than one the past few weeks.

I shake that thought away, trying not to let my heart get too involved with this discussion. "I thought you never hook up with girls twice."

"I don't usually, but it's not really a rule I have."

"So I would be an exception?"

Calder's jaw muscle twitches. "Sure, Ace. You're an exception."

"Why exactly am I the exception?"

He exhales. "I just think you've been out of the game for a while, and jumping headfirst into a sex club is too risky."

"Risky."

"You have to walk before you can run," he adds with a sexy smirk that sends my belly into somersaults. "And with any luck, even walking will be hard when I'm done with you."

I turn away from him to stare ahead at the highway, my eyes fixating on the lights of the cars in front of us as I try to process all of this. I had a good feeling Calder would say yes to my wingman request because I knew he'd do anything to get his membership reinstated. But this . . . this is unexpected. And kind of appealing for obvious reasons.

The truth is, when I saw Calder stomping down that hallway toward me at Lexon, I had almost an out-of-body experience. I was already fantasizing about him so much when I was with that man, it felt like I was in some sort of sexual hallucination. I'd already been using our night in Mexico as content while I was using my vibrator at home and low-key hating myself for it, so I was certain my mind was playing tricks on me when he came striding toward me.

Then I realized it was really happening. Calder was stepping in between me and this guy who wanted to take me into the bondage room. Could it be that he was jealous? Did I want him to be jealous?

God yes.

But not for like emotional reasons. It's just lust. And hate. And there's something incredibly empowering about making a man like Calder Fletcher jealous. Whatever it was, it made for some seriously sizzling sex because we are two-for-two now with no signs of decline.

Randal and I never had sex even half that good in all our years of marriage. In our early dating days, the sex was good . . . but it didn't feel like what I'm experiencing with Calder. And the surge of confidence I feel over just the idea that Calder was jealous tonight is life-changing. Is this what a sexual awakening in your thirties is like? Maybe I wasn't just boring in bed . . . maybe I was just boring with Randal. And maybe exploring this newfound sexuality with Calder for a few weeks will help me take this into my future relationships.

"So how would this work?" I ask, turning to face him as he continues driving. His wrist is draped casually on the steering wheel, his other arm outstretched on the back of the seat behind me. All of this is so easy for him.

Calder's brows lift. "Just thinking off the cuff here . . . but I vote we *fuck* . . . a lot."

He turns and hits me with those green eyes of his and I have to look away as a blush crawls over my face. I run my hands over my lap as my thighs squeeze together to fight off the ache that radiates through my core.

Fuck is a good word from his mouth.

I clear my throat and refocus. "Okay, but I still can't get over the fact that you hate me."

"It was always you that hated me, Ace. I've just been defending myself around you for the past seven years. I don't hate you. I don't particularly like you . . . but I don't hate you."

I frown at that observation. Surely the hatred went both ways, right? Him calling me a Karen wasn't exactly nice. But me calling him Killer Calder every time I've seen him for the past several years isn't real inspiring for a friendship. Either way, it does neither of us any good to look backward.

"If you want, I can come up with some kinks or exploratory things we can try out." He glances over at me and waggles his brows. "A list of sexual activities you can consider."

"Oh please. You're going to come up with a list?" My tone is unapologetically ruthless. Calder is exceptionally talented with his hands, his tongue, and yes, with his anaconda. But his laissez-faire attitude toward the details I wanted in my home was partially the reason it was so hard to work with him. "You could barely put together a punch list for me on the house reno. No way you're going to come up with a list for this."

He sighs. "You know, Ace, I might just surprise you."

Chapter 24

Calder

"Hey, guys!" Everly's voice peals through FaceTime on my phone as Wyatt drives us all back to Fletcher Mountain after a particularly grueling day on the job site.

"Hey, Evie-girl," I call back over my brothers' greetings.

"How's it going?" she asks, her eyes bright and cheery as I hold the phone up to show her to everyone.

"Great. How's it going for you?" Wyatt replies, not taking his eyes off the road.

"I'm amazing!" She pulls a silly face as I look at her a little closer, clocking the heavier makeup and hooded eyes.

I glance at my smartwatch that shows the time in Dublin right now. "It's late there. Have you been out partying?" I ask, as Luke leans over the back seat to squeeze his face into the frame.

"I thought you'd still be recovering from Mexico," he adds with a big, cheesy smile as he twists his baseball cap backward to see better.

"The Irish know how to have a good time," she answers and giggles, revealing just how tipsy she is. "Actually, they call it the *craic*."

"You should not be doing crack, Everly," Wyatt thunders, nearly jerking the car off the road. "What are you thinking?"

"Yeah . . . even I'll judge you for that one," I add, frowning back at her.

She erupts into more giggles. "Not crack cocaine, you guys. Jeez. I mean the craic. C–R–A–I–C. It means a party. Like, the craic was ninety tonight," she says, doing a nice job at an Irish accent.

"I have no idea what you're saying," I deadpan, feeling like an old fuck. "I can't handle Gen Z lingo."

"This isn't Gen Z . . . this is old Irish stuff. Maybe you guys should come out and visit me sometime. I have a feeling you'd fit right in here."

Wyatt grumbles like the negative ass he is, but my brows lift. It could be a good Dark Night–bonding experience for us all in the fall when she goes back next year. None of us have ever been to Europe, but I doubt Wyatt will want to go with Stevie being so little. He only said yes to Mexico because our mom came with the baby and he was marrying the love of his life. Everly ranks high on his list of priorities, but I'm not sure if a trip across the pond is in his near future.

"So what have you guys been up to since Mexico? How's my baby cousin?"

"She's good. Home with her mama," Wyatt says, and I catch the proud smirk on his lips. God, he's such a happy fucker.

"Wyatt is working us like dogs," I grumble, and the sicko's smirk grows even wider. "He made me stay late last night to finish some sheet rocking on my own."

He harrumphs and I harrumph right back. I'm picking up all the slack these days because he's got to get home to the family. Luke usually has bookwork shit to do for the business, so that leaves me: the muscle, the trained monkey, the hired hand. They depend on me to not have a life and get the piddly shit done that no one else wants to do. It's getting old.

"Well, hopefully you can relax tonight," Everly says, her bright and happy tone piercing through all the way from Dublin.

"We had to hurry back to the mountain tonight because Calder has a date," Luke sings like an ass from the back seat so I swing my elbow back, connecting with his shoulder.

He laughs and rubs his arm while I reposition the phone to see Everly again.

Her eyes are saucers, and I think I can see the molars of her teeth as she grins back at me. "An actual date, Uncle Calder? With who?"

"No one." I clench my teeth and shake my head. "Luke is full of shit. It's not a date."

"It's with Dakota," Luke coughs out and slides across the back seat so I can't swing at him again.

"Would you shut the fuck up?" I bark and turn back to our niece. "It's not a date, Everly. Dakota and I just have a project we're working on together."

"What kind of project?"

"Yeah . . . what kind of project?" Luke repeats in a mock high-pitched voice.

Wyatt glances at Luke in the rearview mirror with a knowing smirk that I would punch off his face if he wasn't driving. "I'm building some custom display shelves for her store."

I can feel Luke's eyes burning a hole in the back of my head as I refuse to look at him. I didn't want to tell anyone about me and Dakota, but like a dumbass, I decided it would be a fun idea to be fucking neighbors with my nosy-ass brothers. When it's just random women I bring home from the bars, no one asks any questions. But I knew they'd see Dakota at some point, and Trista, Luke, and Wyatt would be like dogs with a bone until I cracked. So I did something shocking.

I told them the truth.

Well . . . part of the truth. The *casual friends with benefits* truth. If I showed them my list of kinky shit I plan to do to that maddening woman for the next couple weeks, I'd never hear the end of it.

And having to go public with this shit is Dakota's fault. My preference would have been conducting this little social experiment at her place for some privacy, but she axed that idea immediately. I guess having sex in the house she shared with her ex-husband brings up shitty memories or something. I didn't want to pry. I just focused on managing my douchebag brothers and new sister-in-law as best I could.

Trista was like a kid in a candy store when I told her, peppering questions at me left and right. It was so bad, I had to text Dakota to tell her she might want to tell Cozy, because this shit wasn't going to stay secret for long.

The downfall to a close family: no fucking privacy.

But what happens behind closed doors is for our eyes only. And I can't wait to see how Dakota reacts to everything I have planned. Just the anticipation of her coming over tonight has made my dick hard off and on all fucking day. Do you know how awkward it is to pop a boner while running a buzz saw next to your brother? *Fuck*. This woman has a way of messing with me even when she's not around.

I can't wait.

Dakota

"I have to tell you something," I say into the phone line as I sit on the countertop in front of the vanity mirror in my bathroom at home.

"You're pregnant." Cozy's voice is resigned.

"No . . . What the hell?"

"Well, you freaked me out in Mexico with all that big-boob talk."

"I'm not pregnant," I repeat firmly. "You have to have sex to get pregnant. I am currently on a year-long dry spell. Or I was . . ."

She gasps loudly into the phone. "You're finally going to tell me you had sex with Calder in Mexico."

I cringe and nod. "Yes, but seriously, how did you know?"

"Oh please, I think everyone knows."

"Everyone?" I drop my eyeliner into the sink as I press my hand to the mirror for balance. "Like who everyone?"

"Pretty sure Johanna was the first one who called it."

"Calder's mother?" I swivel around to hang my legs off the countertop, so I don't fall off. "Please tell me you're joking."

"I wish I was, friend. This is really embarrassing for you."

Heat floods my face, and I have to fan myself before I pass out. I hop down and begin pacing in my bathroom, trying to slow down my heartbeat. "Don't sound so smug! You were the nanny when you started screwing Max."

She gasps. "That's a low blow."

"Well! You're making me feel like shit."

"At least I married the guy. Are you planning to marry Calder?"

"God no, I'm not an idiot." I wince before I hit her with the next bit. "But I think I am going to have sex with him again."

So. Much. Gasping.

"I didn't think Calder ever slept with the same woman twice," Cozy says once she's caught her breath.

I cock my head and press my lips together because that ship has already sailed thanks to our little sex club visit a couple nights ago. "I think he's making an exception for me."

"This is big."

"It's not big." I wave my hand even though she can't see me. "It's chill, casual sex. We're fuck buddies. No feelings involved."

"Huh." Cozy laughs. "Fascinating."

"What?"

"I just didn't know you could do casual."

"What do you mean?"

"You've had sex with like three people. Your high school boy-friend, your college boyfriend, and Randal."

"So . . ."

"So . . . I'm totally into this, I think it's amazing. I just want you to be careful because this is new territory for you." I can hear the doubt in her voice.

"Getting divorced was new territory for me too, and yet . . ."

"And yet . . ." Cozy sighs.

"This just means it's a good time for me to do some things that aren't my norm." I resume my pacing because it seems to help my brain function.

"I fully support this. So what's the plan? When are you going to see him again?" I hear Ethan's voice murmur something about downloading a game on his tablet.

"Ask your father!" she hisses. "I'm on the phone."

"I'm headed to the mountain tonight," I reply when it's quiet again.

"Holy shit, this is juicy!" Cozy squeals excitedly. "Can I tell Max? I have to tell Max. Everly too. She's going to flip."

"Not Everly." I sigh and pinch the bridge of my nose. "But I think Calder already told Wyatt and Luke, so go ahead and tell Max, I guess. But jeez, we don't need the teenager knowing about this. It's weird."

"Calder told his brothers about you?"

"Yeah, I guess the shelving units he's making for me aren't a good enough front . . . even though it's true."

I walk into my attached closet and begin rifling through my clothes to figure out what I'm going to wear tonight. What does one wear to an enemies-with-benefits night of passion?

"The Fletcher family is relentless."

"I am gathering that," I reply with a huff. As an only child, I'm not used to all this sibling sharing-everything stuff. I rely heavily on my friendships for connections. But how to do you talk to your brothers about who you're banging? It's weird.

"Anyways, it's casual, I swear. And I'm not going to fall for him because we still bicker at each other pretty regularly, so you don't have to worry about me."

"I'm going to worry a little bit," Cozy says softly. "I'm a mother. It's what I do. Not to mention I'm your best friend, and I'm pretty sure you worried about me when I started hooking up with Max."

I smile at the memory of that love saga. The maternal softness in her voice is comforting.

My brows lift as I spot Calder's Colorado Rockies shirt hanging in my closet. I haven't washed it since Mexico, and even though I was the one who wore it, I swear it still smells like him. I press my nose to the fabric and feel my insides clench with desire.

It seems shocking to be doing this, but I literally feel like I don't have a choice. My vagina would revolt against me if I said no to Calder's proposition.

I'm not sure what he's getting out of it, though. Surely he can have any girl he wants. His reputation is proof of that. Maybe he really is just being overprotective of me and my sex club experimenting. But offering to have sex with me seems like a pretty generous answer to that question, right? I guess I'm easy because I've available. Maybe it's as simple as Calder likes sex, and I'm open for business.

That's probably it. A guy like Calder doesn't likely think very deeply about string-free sex.

"Well, just know that while you're busy being a mom and a wifey, I'm going to be getting railed by the hottest Fletcher brother."

"No way. *I* for sure have the hottest Fletcher brother."

"Oh, look at the time. I have got to go. Talk to you later!"

I hang up and smile as a surge of excitement rushes through me. I'm feeling better than I have in years, and I'm taking that all as a good sign. Let my sexual awakening commence.

Chapter 25

KAREN GETS HER FREAK ON

Calder

The fire crackles as I toss another log onto the fire and when I hear a car pull up outside, I swear my dick jumps with excitement.

God, I'm pathetic.

I assess my cabin one more time to make sure I didn't miss anything. I've been cleaning since the moment we got home and only took a break to shower and polish myself up. It's been a long time since I've had a woman over.

Since the birth of Stevie, it's felt kind of weird to go out and bring home a hookup. My brothers and I used to go out in a pack. We usually went into Denver and hit up some decent clubs or bars . . . We had our routine. But lately, it's felt different on Fletcher Mountain. Wyatt's busy with the family, Luke seems distracted with God knows what, and I've been stuck with my hand most snowy nights this winter.

I usually don't care what women think of my place because we're here for one thing. And that's the idea with Dakota too, but since we know each other outside this sexual arrangement, I guess I don't want to add more fuel to the fire of her thinking I'm a complete fuckup.

My house isn't much. It's a classic pitched-gable cabin with the log finish on the exterior and interior, so it definitely has that rustic, outdoorsy charm. It has two bedrooms and one bathroom on the main level with a small office in the open loft area above. The decor is nonexistent. I have a worn leather couch, an armchair, and a couple quilts that my mom made because it gets cold as fuck up here in the dead of winter. My kitchen is decent-sized with black quartz counters and a wood-burning stove.

What can I say? I'm really leaning into the mountain man aesthetic out here.

The sound of footsteps on my front porch causes Milkshake's head to pop up from where she's curled up on the couch. Ready or not, this is happening. I straighten my black-and-white checked flannel and walk across the knotty pine floor to swing open the door and find Dakota smiling brightly.

"No cat greeting this time?"

"Huh?" I swallow the lump in my throat as the image of her on my front porch sinks in. Again. It's such a strange dichotomy going from hating her to being excited to see her.

"You had your cat strapped to you last time I was here." She points to my chest, and I look down like an idiot.

"She's on the couch," I murmur and step back so Dakota can walk in.

She unzips her long parka, and when she turns around and pulls it off, all oxygen leaves my lungs.

"Surprise!" She laughs as she holds her hands up to show off her outfit.

It's my Rockies T-shirt and nothing else. Wait—not nothing else. Definitely something else. It's the something else that's sending my brain to my dick and making it difficult to form complete sentences.

She's wearing thigh-high black boots that remind me of the ones Julia Roberts wore in *Pretty Woman*. She has a pair of long white socks sticking out the top, and the strip of thigh exposed between the sock and the bottom of my T-shirt make my already struggling cock completely out of control.

"Nice dress, Ace," I reply, clearing my throat and trying to get my fucking man card back as I take her coat from her and hang it on the hooks by the door.

Every time I've seen this girl in my shirt, I turn into a bumbling moron. Women have worn my clothes before. This isn't a new concept. It seems to be a thing they like to do . . . take something of mine before they leave. I've lost more flannel shirts to the city of Boulder than I currently have in my closet.

But no one wears my stuff like Dakota.

"So this is your place. I didn't get to see much of it last time I was here." She turns on her heel to look around, her high ponytail swinging behind her as her boots click on the wood floor. She walks past the dining room table and into the kitchen, eyeing the random photos I have up on the fridge that I didn't even print. Everly did.

"It ain't much," I huff as I walk past her to grab a couple beers. Beers help most awkward situations, and the situation inside my jeans is very awkward.

I pop her cap off and hand it over to her, and she takes it with a curious look on her face. "Thanks."

I brace my hand on the island, struggling with what to say next, and then I see Milkshake slink over to wind herself between Dakota's feet.

"Milkshake, get lost."

"She's fine." Dakota sets her beer down and bends over to pick up my cat. "She's really pretty."

"Thanks," I grumble, feeling irritated for some reason. I don't like her being nice to my cat. I don't really like my cat being nice to her either. I kind of want them to hate each other for some bizarre reason. But Milkshake loves everyone. She's a whore just like her daddy.

Milkshake purrs and shoves her nose into Dakota's neck, practically fucking her in front of me, the traitor.

"Come here," I gruff and grab my cat out of her hands, setting her down so she'll buzz off. "Go on."

Milkshake struts over to the steps that lead up to the loft. She lies down halfway up to watch us, looking completely unbothered as silence descends and all I can hear is the crackle of my fire and my pulse rushing in my ears.

I take a sip of my beer.

Dakota does the same.

Finally, she says, "So let's hear this kinky list of yours. I assume you didn't write it down like you said you would."

I exhale with relief that we're diving right into this. If I had to make her a snack or ask about her day, I was going to fling myself out a fucking window.

"Oh, just you wait, Ace." I lift my brows, my mood brightening as we step out of the awkward date vibes and into a place I'm much more comfortable. "Come with me."

I walk into my living room and squat down in front of my TV where my laptop is connected. I use the remote to flick on the TV, and the words Karen Gets Her Freak On pops up on the screen.

"Did you make a PowerPoint?" Dakota asks, walking toward me in those hot-ass boots. From my vantage point on the floor, I can see a lot more thigh, and the fantasy I have of them wrapped around my face later tonight isn't an unpleasant one.

"You bet your hot legs I did." I gesture to the sofa as she laughs and sits down. Her T-shirt rides up and reveals even more thigh, so I turn back to the computer and force myself to focus on the task at hand. "You ready?"

"I'm ready," she says excitedly, crossing her legs and taking another sip of beer. I swear she knows what she's doing, and it's fucking killing my focus.

I sit down on the floor and lean back against my armchair, turning away from her to start my presentation as I click to slide one.

Primary Objective: To make Dakota Schaefer aka Crabby Karen less of a prudey bitch.

"I'm not a prudey bitch!" Her jaw drops, and she scowls at me.
"You sure about that?" I lift my brows and pin her with a look.
"If I'm a prudey bitch, then you're a lazy whore."
My lips turn down as I consider that. "Probably true."
She grumbles, and I click to the next slide.

Secondary Objective: To give Calder Fletcher's magical pocket
python a purpose in life.

"Oh my God . . . this is a joke."

"Not a joke. My dick has been looking for an inspiring way to
give back to the community, and this is just the type of charitable
endeavor he can excel at."

"In other words, you're happy because you get to have sex."

"Correct." I click to the next slide.

PROPOSED SEXCAPADES:
#1: Sex Store Shenanigans—Both of you go to a sex store in
Denver, pick out a toy that interests you, and bring it back to
Calder's snake pit to experiment

"Snake pit?" Dakota cackles and shakes her head as she laughs.
But the crimson that flushes from her neck into her cheeks is very
telling. "Okay, that's unexpected."

"Unexpected good or unexpected bad?" I ask, watching her
body language intently as she crosses her legs the other way.

She regains control of herself and bites her lip as she shrugs.
"Good, I think."

I smile victoriously. This is already going better than I expected.

#2: Exhibitionism

"What does that mean exactly?" she asks, her silliness replaced
with curiosity.

"Sex in a public setting, like in a restaurant bathroom or even
just at a party. Something with other people mingling around. Have
you done anything like that before?"

"Definitely not," she replies with a shy smile.

"Would you like to try it?" I ask, my heart hammering with

hope at having a little public fun. Our night outside of the sex club gave me a few ideas.

Her chest rises and falls, and she gives me an almost imperceptible nod.

I'm acing this fucking test so far.

#3: Outdoor Sex—See Calder's hot tub

"No way. How many women have you banged in that hot tub?" She points back to the tub we passed on our walk the other day.

"None."

"None?" She looks like she doesn't believe me.

I shrug. "It's just never happened. Honestly, I don't bring that many women up here if I can help it."

She sighs. "Okay."

Okay? Jesus, she said okay*!*

Next slide.

#4: Bondage Play

I click the next slide that shows an *X* over top of the text. "We can go ahead and cross this one off the list since we've already done that. But I'm happy to repeat if you decided you enjoyed it?"

Dakota's eyes blink, and she nods timidly, that flush returning to her cheeks.

I smile. Okay, then. Unscripted bondage play is still on the table. I am not mad about that.

#5: Have Sex in Dakota's house

She frowns at me, clearly unhappy with this challenge so I hold my hand up to explain myself.

"I think you need to get past your boundary there. Reclaim the home you bought on your own. When I started renovating it, it was just your house. You bought it without Randal. You shouldn't let him take that from you."

She chews her lip, and the pain I see in her eyes hits me in the gut. After what she shared with me the other night at the sex club, I can understand how hard this might be for her. But I still feel strongly she should do this. He doesn't deserve to have that much real estate in her mind and her home.

After a long pause, she gives me a resigned nod of approval, so I continue.

#6: Spontaneous Sex

"This is an exercise in confidence. Whenever the mood strikes you . . . even if we're not together. If you want to fuck . . . all you have to do is ask, and I will make myself available for you."

She sputters out a laugh. "How generous of you."

"I'm a giver, Ace." I state solemnly, pressing my hand to my chest.

She rolls her eyes in a way that feels like fucking foreplay, so I continue.

#7: Shower Sex

"Because who doesn't like to get dirty before they get clean?"

#8: Sexting

"Need I say more?"

#9: Role-playing

"Thinking a public place . . . something to help you get out of your comfort zone a bit. We'll workshop ideas as we get more comfortable with each other."

#10: Voyeurism at Lexon Club

"This will be our final test. We go together just as spectators. Walk around, get a feel for everything, enjoy the action. We can hook up if we want to, but only with each other. This will also give you the opportunity to decide if you want to go back to the club once you're all done with me. Win-win."

She arches one brow at me. "This is very thorough of you."

"See? I'm not a complete waste of space." I say it casually but this whole thing is anything but casual. She has no idea how hard I worked on this. She has no idea how hard I got when I worked on this. Jacking off in my shower didn't come close to the satisfaction I'll experience with her if she agrees to all this.

"How long is the arrangement going to last us?"

"I'm guessing a couple weeks."

Her eyes turn to saucers. "You think we can get through all of this in a couple weeks?"

"I may be part of the forty-plus hockey league, but I have very good sexual stamina, Dakota." I waggle my brows at her. "But if you need more time, we can extend it to three weeks. Any longer and we're basically in a relationship."

"Yeah, we don't want that."

"Exactly." I sit back and eye her carefully. "So what do you think?"

"I think by the end of this I will have had more sex with you than I did with Randal in the last few years of our marriage."

The joy that one sentence brings me is a little troubling, but I click to the next slide to stay on task.

RULES

—No mention of previous sexual partners

"We're trying to forget about your past, not bring it back up." Not to mention I'm maxed out on Randal stories already. No good comes from rehashing the past. I feel the same way about

Robyn. The further I can relegate that woman to the back of my mind, the better.

"Fair enough," Dakota agrees, so I move onto the next rule.

—No hooking up with other people: this is exclusive
—Condoms at all times, NO EXCEPTIONS

A grateful smile ghosts her lips, and it's honestly fucked that she even has to worry about that. Protection isn't something anyone should fuck with. Ever. My fists clench at just the memory of what he did to her in that regard. I redirect my focus to the next rule.

—Testing

"We've both been tested recently per the club's membership rules so we should be good there. Unless you want an updated test?"

"Um . . . no, that's fine. As long as you haven't been with anyone since your last test?" She shifts on the couch, struggling to maintain eye contact with me.

It's been a month since the sex club, the trip to Mexico, and the time we've been back from the wedding. And it was many months before that since I had sex. Honestly, I'm trying to remember who I even hooked up with last. Once Trista moved into the apartment above the barn last year, we all kind of went through a dry spell. I think we were adjusting to having female energy back on the mountain again. The last woman that lived up there was Robyn, and well, we all know how that ended.

"I haven't been with anyone," I reply gruffly, trying not to focus too much on my dry spell.

"Me neither, obviously," she says with a nervous laugh.

"Why is that obvious?" I frown up at her.

She shrugs. "I don't know. It doesn't matter. I'm just impressed with how detailed this all is. I'm surprised you don't have this all printed up in a contract with a notary person that's about to pop out of your closet."

"Oh, that reminds me. Debra . . . you can come on out now."

Dakota's eyes widen as she jerks her head to look down my hallway.

"I'm fucking with you, Ace."

"Jesus." She presses a hand to her chest.

"But I do have a doctor in the bedroom ready to do our STD exams if you decided you wanted an updated one."

Her eyes widen.

"Fucking with you again. Jesus, you need to relax!"

"Sorry, I'm just . . ." She inhales deeply. "This is just a lot."

"Is it too much?" I ask, moving my computer off my lap and hopping off the floor to join her on the sofa.

"Maybe?"

I shrug and stretch my arm around the back of the sofa behind her. "That's no problem . . . we'll cut some shit, then. I went a little overboard to try to show you I'm not as awful as you think I am."

Her eyes snap up to mine. "I don't think you're awful."

"You do too," I argue. "You call me Killer Calder because you think I ruin everything I touch."

She chews her lip. "I'm sorry. I'll try to be less of a . . . what did you call me, prudey brat?"

"Prudey bitch," I correct her with a grin.

She grins back, her eyes holding mine for a long, drawn-out moment that makes all the blood rush to my cock once again. All this talk about fucking and we still haven't fucked tonight is really messing with my head.

I pull back to break the sizzling spell we're under because we have other business to discuss. "Listen, you don't have to agree to this tonight. Give it some serious thought. I can email the presentation to you, and you can make changes or tell me to fuck off. I would totally understand."

"I'm not going to tell you to fuck off." She laughs and glances at the TV screen. "I'm impressed. You put a PowerPoint presentation together. Who the hell are you?"

My brows lift as I point back to the TV. "Refer to slide two. With great power comes great responsibility."

She laughs at my lame joke and gives me a little shove, her hand lingering on me for longer than necessary, which has me exhaling with relief. Knowing Dakota, this all could have gone a very different direction. I half expected her to tell me it was predatory and fucked-up and she'd drive away and never come back. And if that was her decision, I would respect it.

But the realization that I'd have been fucking crushed with disappointment is a little alarming.

Chapter 26

I WAXED FOR THIS

Dakota

If I leave here without sleeping with Calder Fletcher tonight, it would be a crime against humanity. There would be riots in the streets. Forest fires would erupt all around us. Tsunamis would wipe out towns. Tornados would decimate the Midwest. Earthquakes would crack the earth's core.

Perhaps I'm being a touch dramatic.

But there's a roaring fire in the fireplace for goodness' sake! I did not get another wax job and put on these sexy-ass boots just to leave his cabin and wait for an email from Calder to consider his proposition. Is he crazy?

I've been waiting my whole life for this. Not Calder specifically, but this moment. This opportunity to just . . . have casual sex. Something I never let myself do. I was always the responsible mom of the group, making sure my friends were safe during high school and college. Designated Dakota was my nickname, so I missed the fun, adventurous casual-sex time in my life.

I think that's why I was attracted to Randal when we first met. He was a bartender with long hair and stayed out late, and he felt like all the exciting things I hadn't experienced yet. Not unlike Calder and this sex-periment we're about to go on. The only difference with Calder is this has an end date, and there is zero chance of falling in love and marrying the wrong guy. Been there, done that. Threw out that T-shirt.

Steeling myself, I shift closer to Calder on the sofa, my legs making an awkward squeak on the leather. I place a trembling hand on his thigh, and he glances down, shifting underneath my palm.

"What was number six on that list again?"

"*Spontaneous sex?*" Calder answers, and a smile lights up his face in the glowing firelight.

I nod slowly and press myself into his nook, tipping my lips up to his as I fight my racing heart. "Maybe we check that one off tonight."

He stares at my lips like he wants to devour them. "I thought I was the one in charge here, Ace. I did make the PowerPoint, after all."

"You know I've never been good at giving up control." I wrinkle my nose with a smirk, and a low growl vibrates in his chest.

"Oh, I'm fully fucking aware." He eyes me for a second before reaching out and dragging his fingers along my jawline, tucking a loose strand of hair behind my ear. "Does that mean you're officially saying *yes* to all this?" His brows twitch ever so slightly. "I thought you of all people would have some notes at the very least."

"What can I say? You nailed it." I inwardly giggle at my double entendre. "But I reserve the right to make changes to this list whenever I want."

"It's a woman's prerogative." He nods solemnly.

I purse my lips before my tongue darts out to lick them as my body hums with desire. Just being this close to him is an aphrodisiac. I guess it's a fine line between love and hate. "On second thought, you didn't have orgasms listed in that presentation. I might need more clarity there."

He chuckles, and his hand slides from my cheek to my neck, gripping me in a claiming sort of way as he uses the edge of his hand to angle my chin up to him. "No need to promise what's already guaranteed, Ace."

And my breath escapes my lungs when he seizes my mouth with his, his tongue parting my lips as he thrusts into me, forcing my neck back to accept the intrusion. It's a wild, demanding kiss that sends a rush of desire rocketing through me.

My tongue attempts to catch up to his level as my neck pulses against his palm. How long has it been since I've been kissed like this? Well, except for Calder, that is. But when was the last time? Did my ex and I ever kiss like this? Fuck, it's good. I've missed this type of all-consuming kissing. Kissing that turns you on and feeds your whole body. Kissing that makes life worth living.

I grip the front of his shirt and lift one leg up around him, causing him to growl into my mouth as his hand releases my neck to grip my leg to his hip. His fingers are rough on my skin as he skates his hand up the outside of my thigh and wraps around to palm my ass. He kneads my flesh with harsh, punishing pressure that has my body rolling up into him.

He shifts so I'm on my back now, and he's over top of me. His leg catches between my thighs . . . directly on my clit, and I gasp, fisting his shirt in my hands as he breaks our kiss.

"You like that, Ace?" he asks, grinding his knee into me.

I struggle to breathe as my core throbs against the rough denim gliding over the thin silk of my panties.

I nod, unable to form words as he presses his knee farther into me, soaking my panties while his kneecap catches on my clit in the most mind-blowingly insane way that I want to stop and never stop at the same time.

I moan into his lips as he shifts so now his groin is flush against my center, his hard ridge a wicked promise of what's to come. My back arches up off the couch as I kiss him, pulling him into me with my booted leg as close as I can.

A desperate frenzy takes over both of us as he dry-humps me. It's been torture all night waiting for this to happen. Being friends with benefits or enemies with benefits is kind of weird. Both of us are here for one thing, but common decency forces us to act civilized, be polite, talk, have a drink, do all the mundane human things . . . when all I want to do is act like an animal. I'm a feral cat who just wants this tomcat to fuck me. God, please fuck me!

And as Calder reaches under my shirt to unclasp my bra, I realize how miraculous this all is. I want to have sex! I haven't wanted to have sex for the last several years. I was insecure with Randal, insecure of my body and our connection. With Calder, there's no need to worry. We're both here for the same thing and perfectly okay with it. This should be the definition of fucking the patriarchy.

He breaks our kiss, and I quickly slip my hands into my sleeves to pull the loose bra out from under my shirt. I fling it to the floor and my nipples are rock-hard and raw beneath the thin cotton.

Calder stares down at my chest. "I like you in my shirt, but I like what's under there even better."

I process his words for a moment, noting the sentimental undertone to them. He mentioned my outfits in Mexico too, and it's surprisingly sweet coming from a self-proclaimed playboy.

And incredibly validating.

Randal wasn't good at the compliments or affirmations. I think there was too much resentment there for him to ever see any good in me.

Calder watches me speculatively as he slides my shirt up my body, exposing every square inch of me in the warm living room lighting. I fight the urge to suck my stomach in or fret over all my imperfections.

It's not necessary to feel insecure . . . He's already seen me naked, and that was before we decided to do this.

"Fucking beautiful," he growls before capturing my hardened nipple and sucking it deep into his mouth. His beard scrapes against my flesh, causing goose bumps to erupt all over my skin as I comb my fingers through his hair and turn to stare at the crackling fire as a similar blaze stirs between my legs.

"Calder, I want you to fuck me," I beg, my panties growing more damp with each passing second.

He shakes his head against my chest. "Not yet, Ace. You've rushed me the last two times, and this time I want to see you. All of you."

A wave of pressure roils through me as he moves us to the fur rug on the floor and peels my shirt off before slowly unzipping my boots with dark, sinful eyes. He leaves my long socks and panties on as he kisses and nips and praises every exposed part of me, murmuring *fuck* and *beautiful* and *so damn sexy* against all my flesh.

When he's had his fill, he finally slides his fingers over the damp fabric of my panties, teasing my center. "Fuck, baby, you're soaked."

I whimper and close my eyes as he strokes my clit over the material, my fingers gripping his shirt as I try to control the lust shooting through my body. I knew I was wet. I felt it happening during the drive up the mountain. But the minute he sat on that sofa with me, basking me in his scent and heat and sex appeal . . . I was done for.

"I have to taste you," he growls and shifts downward, yanking my panties to the side before pressing his mouth to my sex.

I moan as his tongue licks and sucks my clit, stirring me up into a frenzy that I didn't know could get worse than it already was. I thread my hands through his hair as he grips my ass, pulling me into his face as he devours me like a bowl of ice cream. My release feels close, and it's as if Calder can tell, because he stops, pulling away just when I need him most.

With a wicked look in his eyes, he strips out of his own clothes and wraps himself in a condom, kneeling between my legs as I struggle to see straight.

His tip nudges my center. "I'm going to fuck you hard and fast now. You good with that?"

I nod again, unable to form words as my insides cry for release. I want an orgasm more than I want my next breath. And with that, Calder grips my hips and slams into me, lighting my entire body on fire.

I cry out, my voice guttural as I grip his arms, my body convulsing at the swift intrusion, while also welcoming it, pulling him into me to never let go.

"Fuck," he groans, pulling out and thrusting back into me. "You feel so fucking good."

I whimper as he pumps into me, my heart racing faster with each thrust of his hips, my nipples aching as my insides clench with the crest of my almost forgotten orgasm. He grinds against my clit with every deep drive, and it's the most tantalizing spark of pleasure every time.

Finally, he pauses his rapid pace, allowing me a second to catch my breath. He leans back, and I look down to see his fingers at my center, and when he runs his thumb punishingly over my clit I cry out, my orgasm ripped from me before I even realize what's happening.

"Fuck yeah, baby. Scream as loud as you want. No one to hear you up here."

He resumes his thrusts, and the orgasm suspends me into a state of ecstasy as he drags out the sensation, so it feels like a never-ending climax. Like toppling down a hill that goes on forever.

My heels dig into his back as I hold on for dear life, marveling over how good this is and how good he makes me feel. What a gift. And of all the men on this planet to possess this ability, I never would have guessed that man to be Calder Fletcher.

Chapter 27

CAT-O'-NINE-TAILS FOR THE CAT DADDY

Calder

"Where are you off to?" my mom asks as I step out of the guest bathroom located on the main level of her house in Boulder.

I finish buttoning up my flannel, wincing like I've been caught red-handed. She wasn't here when I arrived after work, and I was hoping to duck in and out without being noticed. Tonight is not my night, I guess.

I often stop at my mom's for a shower after work if I need to stay in town for something, so she's used to me letting myself in. But she's not used to me stopping by for a shower before a date . . . so to speak.

Not that tonight is a date with Dakota. We're just going shopping. Sex toy shopping to be more specific.

I'm not highly experienced when it comes to sex toys, but I've seen plenty of items at the sex club in the random times I've been there throughout the years. Vibes, dildos, butt plugs, anal beads, nipple clamps . . . you see all types of things at Lexon.

What will be the most interesting part of today is discovering what Dakota goes for. I feel like the type of sex toy a person picks out says a lot about their character. And for some reason I still can't fully comprehend, I'm enjoying learning more about Dakota.

The other night at my place was hot. She understood the assignment for spontaneous sex, and I was all too willing to help her check that task off her list. I can see her confidence growing the more time we spend together. Or maybe I should say I can see her confidence returning. She's always been confident. I think she just lost sight of it when things took a turn with Randal.

None of this shit is something I should be thinking about in front of my mother.

"Just going out for drinks," I reply gruffly as I roll up the sleeves of my shirt.

"With Dakota?"

My brows shoot to my hairline. "What makes you say that?"

"Word gets around in this town, Calder."

"You mean baby Luke opened his big fat mouth." I stomp over to the door and begin stuffing my feet into my shoes. "Nothing serious is going on with me and Dakota."

"But there is something going on?" my mom asks, her eyes wide and full of hope like I'm about to tell her I'm giving her another grandchild. Good God, this woman needs to get a grip.

"Don't get your hopes up, Mom."

She sighs heavily. "One of these days, you're going to see the light."

"What light?"

She shrugs. "The light that life is more than fun and games."

"But then who would be the family screwup?" I huff out a laugh and lean in to kiss my mother's forehead before opening the front door to leave.

"You sound just like your father."

This stops me in my tracks, and I turn on the front step to stare at my mom propped on the doorframe with a knowing look on her face.

"How do I sound like Dad?" I ask as a heaviness presses down on me. I always felt like Dad was a perfect mix of Max, Wyatt, and Luke, and I was this weird outsider that could have a different father if only I wasn't the spitting image of him.

Dad could be bossy like Max, somber like Wyatt, and generous like Luke. He was never the funny, boisterous one like me. Sure he'd laugh at my jokes, but most days, it felt like Dad and I spoke two different languages and he was constantly disappointed in me.

"Do you know how many jobs he screwed up before he made

the business what it was before he passed?" My mom says this with no emotion, no pain or regret or heartache . . . just matter-of-fact business.

The look on her face has my chest expanding with shock. Normally just the mention of my dad brings tears to her eyes and a tightness to her mouth that cuts me to the core. It's made it almost impossible to work through my own feelings over the loss of him, because I'm too busy worrying about hers and giving her a shoulder to cry on. Is it possible she no longer needs that from me? I'm not sure how I feel about that. It might mean I have to start reflecting on my own grief, and I am not prepared for that.

"Dad always had his shit together. We were nothing alike."

"Calder," she scoffs and shakes her head. "The truth is, your father was a mess until he met me . . . in his personal life and his business. If it wasn't for me, he would have been whoring around town and working road crew for that concrete company still."

My jaw drops. "Why didn't he ever mention that?"

"Because he wanted to be larger-than-life to you boys, obviously." She laughs, and her eyes twinkle with affection. "He never wanted to be anything less than perfect in front of you. But the hard truth is he needed someone to take him seriously before he could take himself seriously."

I frown and stare down at the ground, having a hard time wrapping my head around that. Even if I could believe this of my father, it doesn't mean I'm like him. "Lucky for me, no one takes me seriously."

"Pretty sure Dakota wasn't laughing at you in Mexico," my mom chirps with a glint to her eye. "Saw her looking at you a lot, but she wasn't laughing."

"She wasn't looking at me," I volley back defensively, feeling my neck turn hot under the collar.

"If you say so." She licks her lips and smiles like the cat that got the cream, and it's weird and uncomfortable. My mom is getting bizarre in her old age. She needs to focus on her sons that will give her grandbabies and leave the black-sheep middle child alone.

I say my goodbyes, and as I drive toward Dakota's store to pick her up, I do my best to reaffirm everything I know to be true in my head. I don't want a relationship. I don't want a future with someone. The one time I let myself consider that with a woman, it went to complete hell and I nearly lost my relationship with my brothers.

And it's a painful reality that my family is all I have in life. Losing my brothers is not an option. No amount of great sex with one person is worth that kind of risk. Even my dad would agree with that.

I shake off any thoughts of my family as I walk into The T-shirt Shop to pick up Dakota. The sounds of a screaming child draw my attention toward the back of the store as I look around. There's a college-aged girl at the checkout counter who eyes me curiously.

"Can I help you?" She scans me up and down, her lips curling in disgust at my appearance.

"I'm just picking up Dakota," I reply, shoving my hands into my pockets and glancing down to figure out what I'm wearing that's so offensive to this girl.

"She's just finishing up a day-care group. You can head on back." She points to the doorway in the back of the store, so I make my way there, adjusting my shirt and still puzzling over what that girl's problem was.

However, that interaction is completely forgotten when I step into the back room and see a group of moms and preschoolers running around the colorful space like animals.

Dakota has a white apron on that's covered in dye like the one Ethan wore last week, and her hands are gloved as she holds a wad of white fabric in her hands. "Okay, your tie-dye shirts will need to sit overnight, and moms you can pick them up by the end of the week."

"I want to take mine home now!" a little girl cries from beside

Dakota's leg, and her lower lip sticks out into a large pout before she erupts into tears.

Dakota looks around, clearly trying to find the child's mother who is nowhere in sight. "Anyone know where this one's mom is?"

"Bathroom!" another woman calls back.

Amused, I cross my arms and prop myself on the doorway to enjoy the show. The girl continues to cry, and Dakota grows more and more frazzled as she deposits the T-shirt onto a rack holding other wadded-up, dyed shirts and pulls her gloves off. She walks over to the little girl and sits down on the floor where she's throwing her fit.

"There, there," she says, awkwardly patting the little girl on the head. "You'll still get your T-shirt, but it needs to dry first."

"But I want it," the girl says, crying harder.

"I want a time machine, but I'm afraid that's just not how the cookie crumbles."

The little girl shoots Dakota a confused look before resuming crying, so Dakota tries another tactic. "Do you have a dog, Tay?"

She nods and wipes her running nose on her shirt.

"What color is your dog?"

"White."

"If you take your T-shirt home today, then your pretty white dog might get dye on his nice fur. You'd have a rainbow puppy, then. That's not good!"

The girl immediately stops crying, and Dakota looks relieved.

When the bathroom mom appears beside them, the girl jumps up onto her feet and smiles. "Mommy! We can make Rizzo a rainbow puppy!"

"What?" Dakota's eyes are wide as she stands up and shoots the mom an apologetic look. "That's not what I said."

"Rainbow dog! Rainbow dog! Rainbow dog!" the girl chants.

"I want a rainbow dog!" a little boy says from the other side of the room.

"Me too!" Two other kids join in.

All the kids begin whining to their mothers about wanting to bring home their shirts to make rainbow dogs. You can feel that the mothers are on the verge of their own meltdowns. Dakota presses the back of her hand to her forehead and murmurs a curse to herself as she turns around and spots me in the doorway.

Her arms drop, and she shoots me a glower as my shoulders shake with silent laughter. She walks over and drops her head down low. "How long have you been standing there?"

"Not long enough," I reply with a laugh. "I would have come earlier if I knew you were putting on a show. This is performance art!"

"The rainbow dog thing totally backfired on me," Dakota murmurs and crosses her arms.

"What makes you say that?" We both look out at the mothers consoling their crying children. I gently nudge her with my elbow. "You ready to get out of here?"

"God yes."

I can't decide what's more entertaining: watching Dakota Schaefer do a horrible job at consoling crying children, or watching Dakota Schaefer peruse a sex toy store.

It really is a toss-up. She's not good at either of them, apparently. With the kids, there's a lot of wincing and heavy breathing and some audible gasps.

Apparently she's the same way at the sex shop the moment she presses a button on a display item and jumps when it starts vibrating in her hand.

"Find anything interesting?" I whisper in her ear and delight over how she shivers at my proximity.

"You know . . . Cozy threw me a bachelorette party, and I got a few sex toy items, but they just collected dust for years until I threw them away."

"That's sad."

"Is it?" Dakota asks, eyeing me curiously. "Are sex toys needed at the beginning of a marriage? Isn't that when things are supposed to be easy?"

"Are sex toys hard?"

She holds up a giant purple dildo the size of my arm, and I laugh.

"I just think it seems like if you need these items at the beginning of a relationship, then maybe you're doing something wrong. Wouldn't most guys get offended if I say I need to add a vibrator to the bedroom?"

"I look at toys as teammates, not competition," I reply, propping myself on a shelf full of lube. "They just add a level of excitement and variety. They encourage open communication as you navigate the toy and figure out what works and doesn't work. They can prolong a sexual experience and help you bond with your partner."

"You really do fucking read!" She puffs out a noise of disbelief, and I frown, feeling wounded.

"It's audiobooks if that makes it any more believable."

"You know . . . it actually does." She smiles and turns to grab a flogger off the shelf, her fingers touching the leather before she slaps it onto her palm. "Sex toys just seem super intimate to use with someone you just met. How does all that open communication not make you catch feelings?"

"It's the open communication that keeps the feelings in check. I'm always crystal clear with my partners what this is. And not all of the women I sleep with are one-night stands."

"They're not?" Dakota's head snaps to attention.

"No. I have some repeat customers."

Her nose wrinkles.

"I just don't repeat them too close together. If I sleep with a woman multiple times within a couple weeks, that's when things get dicey."

She nods and chews her lip. "Fascinating."

"Okay, five more minutes of browsing, then pick your item, and let's get out of here."

"Okay, boss."

I stop in my tracks and turn to look at her. "Am I in charge again?"

She rolls her eyes. "As long as it doesn't go to your head, you can have a little control."

I shoot her a wicked smirk. "Oh, Ace . . . you really shouldn't have said that."

Dakota is on her third orgasm from this vibrator I bought for her, and my dick is so fucking hard it hurts. She's spread out naked on my bed, her body covered in a sheen of sweat as I lick and nip at her breasts, lapping them up like a starved animal. Her needy clit is raw from the sucking action of the device I grabbed for her.

I did my research before we went into the sex store. I read reviews, I found out what women like . . . and I have not been disappointed.

How can any man ever be threatened by a bedroom toy? Watching their woman orgasm is a fucking gift. Plus, sex can be exhausting. A helping hand here and there is just good business.

"No more," she moans and presses her legs together, rolling over on her side. "I need a break. I need water. I need . . ." she breathes heavily ". . . a hug."

I laugh and set the vibrator on the side table before wrapping myself around Dakota's trembling body. She rolls toward me and tucks herself into my arms, laying her head on my chest as I pull the sheet up over our naked bodies.

"Is this okay?" she asks after she's caught her breath.

"Is what okay?"

"Cuddling." She hits me with a curious look. "Cuddling wasn't on your PowerPoint, and I expect you haven't cuddled with many of your conquests."

I roll my eyes and stare up at the ceiling. "When are we going to stop making assumptions about each other?"

"Oh, come on!" She pokes me in the ribs and moves to sit up, pulling the sheet up over her chest to sit crisscross facing me. "Tell me I'm wrong. Tell me you cuddle every woman you've slept with and whisper sweet nothings into their ears as they fall asleep in your strong, inky arms."

I hit her with a flat stare. "It happens."

"How many times?"

My brows lift. "Doesn't happen a lot, but—"

"See!" She points an accusing finger at me. "I knew it."

"You know nothing," I grouse and sit up to prop myself against my wooden headboard, propping my legs up to conceal the tent I'm pitching. "That's why we're doing this whole thing. Remember? Now, come on . . . talk about what you liked."

She groans and covers her face with both her hands. After we hooked up in front of my fire the other night, I forced Dakota to talk through everything she liked and didn't like. The only way she's going to come out of this little experiment with some good takeaways is if she talks. "Reflecting helps give you confidence, and that's what you're looking for, so let's hear it."

She sighs and crawls over me to retrieve a bottle of water on the nightstand. She takes a few long swigs before pulling it down and dabbing at her lips. "Clitoral orgasms are different than vaginal."

I have to stifle my laugh. "How so?"

She shakes her head and shrugs. "The clit ones are like sparky and surface-level. Like getting burned by a pan."

"And vaginal?"

Her lips curl up. "Those are like deeper and more robust. They feel like sinking into a warm bath." Her eyes partially shut and her face relaxes.

"I take it you like the vaginal ones better?"

She shakes her head and giggles. "Nah . . . I like 'em all."

I chuckle, feeling a bit smug over how happy she looks. Far different than the woman who walked with me in the woods the other day, revealing her past relationship trauma.

"Are there different types of orgasms for men?"

My lips curve down. "In a way. It more just varies from intensity.

When I come for the first time in a day, it's always stronger and more intense than if I come for a second or third time in one day."

Dakota's eyes widen. "Do you have multiple orgasms in a day very often?"

"Do you?" I prop my hands behind my head and watch her curiously. She looks like a kid in a candy store, just discovering what sugar is.

"I've had two, but never three." She points to the bed indicating what I just did to her.

"Well, good. We can add this accomplishment to the Power-Point."

She nods and smiles. "We are overachievers."

"But to answer your question, multiple orgasms in a day for guys is different. It's easier for us I think."

"What's the most orgasms you've had in a day?"

Shit, she's playing hardball. "Do you really want me to answer that?"

"Yes. Why?"

"Because you're going to call me a pig."

"You don't know that."

I exhale. "I've had five."

"Five?" Her eyes nearly bug out of her head. "Holy shit . . . five? With who? That Robyn girl?"

"No," I snap, hating even the mention of her name. "You don't know her."

"I might know her."

"I don't even know her," I reply with a laugh.

Dakota's face falls. "The five-orgasm woman wasn't worth a second look?"

I shake my head. "It was years ago. A one-night stand with a woman in Denver. We never spoke again."

"That's sad. Why wouldn't you even consider seeing her again if the sex was that good?"

"Because I don't want to be in a relationship with anyone," I answer firmly. "No matter how good the sex is."

"Why?"

"Because I don't." My voice takes on a sharper tone than I intended, but I'm trying to be clear.

She watches me intently for a moment. "What is it that makes you so certain you don't want a relationship? I'm not asking for myself, I'm just asking for research. Did this Robyn person really mess with you?"

"No . . . Jesus. You're breaking the damn rules right now. We're not supposed to be talking about our past relationships."

She shrugs. "I like to know things."

I take a moment and exhale. "I'm not serious enough to be serious with anyone."

"Why do you say that?"

"Just ask my family. I'm the one always screwing things up, causing problems, ruffling feathers. I couldn't ever provide for a wife and kids either. My entire life is by default."

"What does that mean?"

"My job? Got it because of my dad. My house? Got it because of Wyatt. My best friends? They're my brothers. They are genetically forced to hang with me."

Dakota frowns over at me. "That's a sad way to look at your life."

It's not sad when it's accurate and confirmed by everyone around me. Even Dakota would agree as she's the one who pegged me with the Killer Calder nickname.

"How would you look at it?" I ask, frowning over at her.

"You live in a beautiful cabin on a secluded mountain with people you actually like, and you get to work with your best friends every day, and you have a cat who watches us have sex."

"I know, but I didn't earn any of it. Even Milkshake was kind of forced on me by Trista."

"So then, do something on your own. Something you can earn without anyone else."

"How?"

"What do you want to do with your life? What's your dream job?"

I laugh and shake my head. "It doesn't matter. I'm locked into the family business."

"So? You can have a side gig."

"No, I can't."

"Why not?"

"Because there's no time. Wyatt has us building smart houses all over town, and I'm the trained monkey that does all the grunt work, so I put up or shut up. My brothers would laugh in my face if I tried to tell them I wanted to break out on my own. And my mom would be heartbroken if I abandoned the legacy my father left behind."

She remains quiet for a moment, watching me speculatively. "But isn't that pile of gorgeous furniture in your workshop kind of your father's legacy as well?"

The impact of her words hits me right in my gut. I'm actually shocked that she's tied that hobby of mine so closely to my dad. I know I revealed a fair amount to her that day in my shop, but I didn't really share everything.

The truth is, I feel closer to my dad when I'm working out there. Even though he never stepped foot in that shed I built, I can feel him there with me when I work. I hear his laugh, and him bitching at me to sand with the grain of the wood, not against. He'd growl at me if I used the wrong vise for a softer wood. He really did teach me everything I know.

How did she read so much into that?

I shift awkwardly in the bed. "I guess I might have started de-signing the furniture pieces because of him, but it's not like it's easy to make a business out of it. Not all of us are entrepreneur badasses like you." She rolls her eyes like she doesn't believe me, so I continue. "Having a brick-and-mortar store in downtown Boulder for over a decade is nothing to sneeze at, you know."

"I know," she replies with a funny smile and then covers her face to add, "I'm actually getting an award."

"You are?" I pull her hands down to get a look at her. There's a red flush to her cheeks and she's biting her lip in an adorably shy way.

"It's just the Best of Boulder business award. It's like a committee-voted thing. There's this fancy dinner and award ceremony I have to go to. It's not really that big a deal."

"Bullshit, that sounds fucking awesome. Congratulations."

Her nose wrinkles as she squirms under my praise. "Thank you."

I'm a bit awestruck. My dad started the construction business, and my brothers and I practically got it handed to us. Wyatt morphed into the visionist, and Luke became the brains behind the operation. I'm just the brawn. So to see Dakota do so much all on her own is fucking wild.

"You really are kind of inspiring, though. You've been running your own business since college. That's so unheard of."

"I got lucky."

I chuck a pillow at her, and she shoots me an offended look. "You worked hard, and you earned that shit."

"Fine. I worked hard, and I earned that shit." She smirks and then squints at me for a moment, pondering something. "Hey, would you let me list your pieces on my website maybe?"

"What? Why?"

She shrugs. "Because I get a shitload of traffic, and it would take my web developer less than an hour to get them posted. We could price them really high just to see if we get any bites."

"I don't know . . ."

"Why not? What do you have to lose? They're just collecting dust out there as they are anyways, and that's a shame. Because they're really beautiful."

I make a noise of contempt in the back of my throat, but I will admit it's getting annoying having to shove stuff up in the rafters to make room. And my dad would be giving me so much shit for how cluttered my shop is. Maybe there's no harm in trying to sell a few.

"All we have to do is go out to your shop, snap a few pics, you write down some of the details of the pieces like type of wood, finish, et cetera, and I'll send it all off to my guy. Easy-peasy."

I feel myself giving in. Dakota is fun to watch when she's like this. I can see her brain churning with a plan and actionable items she can check off another damn list.

"We do this, and then I'll show you the sex toy I picked out," she offers, waggling her eyebrows suggestively at me. "A little work before a little reward."

"If it's that big purple dildo, I'm going to take a hard pass on it all."

"It's not the dildo." She laughs and leans over the bed and the sound of a rustling bag draws my eyes. When she pulls out a leather whip with nine braided tails on it, her smile turns devious. "Cat 'o nine tails for the cat daddy."

I pinch the bridge of my nose and sigh. This woman is going to be the death of me.

Chapter 28

IS THIS SEXTING?

Dakota

My phone pings with a text from my web developer, and I click the link to see that he's got Calder's furniture live on the site already. I scan through them, reading the details and proofing for any mistakes. They look amazing. A little out of place on a clothing boutique website, but my developer placed them on their own tab, so it works.

I send the link off to my social media girl and tell her to do a few posts, just to get the clicks going on it before I text to Calder.

Dakota: Check it out! You're live, baby!

Calder: That's trippy. And looks way too expensive. No way is anyone going to buy that shit.

Dakota: Hush. You don't know that.

Calder: Are you sure we shouldn't drop the price? Your T-shirts aren't that expensive. My shit looks way too overpriced next to your stuff.

Dakota: My friend Tatianna's line is higher-end, so I think it's fine. Just let it sit for a bit. You said yourself you weren't in a hurry to get rid of them.

Calder: You're the boss. My ass still hurts btw. Hockey should be interesting tonight.

Dakota: Maybe I should have sprung for the BPD.

Calder: I'll take a whip to the ass over a big purple dildo any day.

Dakota: I thought you like to keep an open mind when it comes to all things kinky?

Calder: Even I have my limits, Ace.

Dakota: Does this count as sexting?

Calder: I don't know. Are you turned on?

Dakota: A little.

Calder: Then, yes. And same.

Dakota: I love checking stuff off our list.

Calder: I know you do.

Dakota: Good luck at your game tonight.

Calder: Thanks, I'm going to need it.

The sound of a loud throat-clearing interrupts my texting and I glance up from my phone to find a stunning redhead standing before me with a teasing smirk.

She whacks my feet propped on the checkout desk and tuts, "Ma'am, I'd like some service, please."

"Kate! How the hell are you?" I pull my feet down and run around the desk to give her a big hug.

"I'm great! How are you?" She squeezes me back and hooks her thumb toward the door. "I was just signing some books at the store, and thought I'd pop over to say hi. It's been a while."

"It has." My lips purse as I take in the sight of her. She looks amazing.

Kate Smith is probably the most famous person in Boulder, but no one would ever know it. She writes erotic romance novels under the pen name of Mercedes Lee Loveletter and hits all the bestseller charts. She even has a movie and a Netflix show based on one of her series. She owns an independent bookstore just around the corner that specializes in these charity-book box subscriptions, and we collab a lot for T-shirt merch to go into her boxes. Kate's a mom, a wife, and a boss-ass bitch that I constantly admire.

"How are the boys?" I ask, leaning on the counter to catch up.

She blows a strand of red hair out of her eyes. "They're good. Playing all the damn sports and making it impossible for me to write. Oh, and Tucker broke his leg last week and is in a cast."

"Oh my God!"

"I know." She rolls her eyes. "We have to push him in a wheelchair everywhere. The other day at Target, he was so pumped because he got to use one of the electric wheelchairs. You'd have thought I took him to Disney World. And this isn't even his first broken bone at the ripe old age of nine. Landon isn't much better. Do you know how hard it is to write smut when your kid asks you to scratch his knee with a wooden spoon handle every other day?"

I let out a chuckle. "I'm afraid I don't."

She shakes her head and leans on the counter. "But enough about me. I was coming to check in on you. Your divorce is final now, right? How are you doing?" She gets a thoughtful look in her eyes as she reaches out to rub my arm affectionately.

"I'm great!" I beam and then flinch when I realize I actually mean it.

"Really?" Kate looks shocked. "How great?"

I'm just as amazed by my response as she is. "Like super great."

"Great!" she peals happily. "Is there a new man in your life that's contributing to some of this greatness?"

"Um . . ." I frown as I try to figure out how best to answer this. "Not really? I mean . . . kind of. It's complicated."

Her brows lift. "Girl, I'm a best seller of *complicated*. What book trope are we talking about here? Friends to lovers? Second-chance romance? Workplace relationship? Tell me you're hooking up with one of these young college kids you always have running around here. I would die for a juicy reverse–age gap sapphic romance right now!"

"God no." Before knowing Kate, I had no idea that there were different tropes or themes out there in romance. She's opened my mind up to a whole new world since I met her. I think for a moment and then chuckle. "Ummm . . . I guess you could call it enemies to lovers."

"My freaking favorite!" She rubs her hands together, and her eyes narrow as her writer brain kicks into overdrive. "The tension in those books is so much fun. And I love how the two characters constantly fuck with each other and you never know what's coming next. There's such brutal honesty in hate-to-love stories."

"There's no love happening, I assure you."

She rolls her eyes. "You know what I mean. It's fun because the hate makes it unexpected. And the ribbing and poking and the arguing makes the moment they say fuck it and bang that much more intense. Who's the lucky guy we love to hate?"

My mind races with her very astute reflection on what's happening in my life without even knowing exactly what's happening in my life. It's freaky how much romance novels can mirror real life.

"I can't tell you who it is. It's casual, so we're keeping it on the down-low. Sorry."

She purses her lips together. "Smart, smart. A secret affair is super hot too. Little taste of the forbidden. Rarr."

I wish it was more secret. Every time I have had to drive up the mountain, I pass Wyatt and Trista's house and it feels so weird. Like they know I'm just coming over to bang.

Calder is right: I need to get over my hang-up about him coming back to my house, but I just don't love the vibe there anymore. It feels tainted somehow . . . both by Randal and by the major blowout I had with Calder there seven years ago. I don't want our past to ruin our present.

Plus, I love the mountain. It feels like such an escape every time

I go up there, and Calder's cabin is the perfect love shack for us to explore each other's bodies. Like how I did last night with that whip.

My cheeks heat as images of Calder's perfect ass streaked with red lines flood my mind. That cat-'o-nine-tails was meant to be a joke, but Calder shocked me when he suggested I try it out on him. I don't think Randal's toxic masculinity would ever have allowed him to give up control like that, but Calder seemed more than happy to let me explore this kink.

There is something so insanely sexy about a bearded, tattooed, super alpha male giving in to his lady. And I think Calder knows what he's doing, because it made the sex we had afterward completely mind-blowing.

"Hey, congrats on the Best of Boulder, by the way!" Kate says, whacking my arm playfully. "I can't believe you haven't won that before."

"Oh, thanks." My cheeks flush with her praise.

"Miles and I are going to the banquet too as a part of the Boulder Business Bureau, and I can't wait to see you up there accepting your award in a couple weeks."

"Gosh, I need to look for something to wear to it." I run my hands through my hair, anxiety prickling in my belly. "Time has just flown by the past few weeks."

"Well, good sex does sort of mess up the space-and-time continuum." Kate laughs knowingly. "Will you bring your secret fling with you as a plus-one?"

"No way," I exclaim, shuddering at the thought. Calder would probably laugh in my face. "We are casual, so I will be flying solo."

"Mmm-kay." Kate eyes me skeptically. "Well, we'll be there with bells on and can't wait." She leans in to give me a tight squeeze. "I'm just happy to see you glowing, girl. Randal tried to suck all the joy out of you, but I can tell that you are in a really good space. Even if this enemy stays an enemy, at least he's helping you get your sex sparkle back."

I chuckle. That's one way to put it. But she is right. I feel satiated, not just sexually but emotionally.

I feel alive.

As she walks away, I think some more about what she said earlier about the enemies-to-lovers stuff. Calder and I have surprisingly been getting along lately, and I weirdly miss the teasing spark we used to have.

I never thought I'd yearn for the day he called me a Karen.

Is he just being nice to me because he knows all the dirty details about Randal? I don't want to be treated with kid gloves like I'm some kind of victim. That's not what this sexual awakening is about. Maybe it's time I poked the bear again.

Chapter 29

Calder

The ref blows the whistle signaling our first intermission is over, and I skate out onto the ice, girding my nut sack for another beating. The score is three to nil, and I'm a sweaty fucking mess as I hunch over and stare at the guy I'm facing off with. This is supposed to be a beer league, and I haven't seen one of these athletic assholes on the other team crack a single drink.

"God, I'm tired," the guy croaks from behind his plastic shield.

Finally! A human moment from one of these dudes. "Me too, buddy. Me too," I lament.

He stands up straight and flips his helmet up. "I'm seventy-two-years-old. What's your excuse?"

My face falls as I swallow the lump in my throat, feeling truly humbled by an old man.

"Can you just drop the puck already?" I snap at the ref, and before I can even get my stick on it the old man rams his shoulder into me and passes the puck off to one of his teammates.

They tear down the ice toward our goal, so I recover and bend and tuck, busting my ass to try to catch up to them, picking up a little more speed than I'm used to. When I reach the old man, I miraculously manage to steal back the puck and attempt to volley it behind our goalie to pass it off to my teammates. But a body checks me, and I feel myself hurtling toward the boards, unable to brake. I brace myself for impact, but my eyes catch sight of a familiar blonde right before I splatter across the glass.

"Dakota?" I murmur, my face smushed against the clear barrier as three guys press into my back, their sticks thwacking the ice by my feet, trying to steal the puck from me.

"Go, Killer Calder!" She claps her hands in front of her and cheers like it's totally fucking normal for her to be here right now.

"What are you doing here?" My voice is muffled by the barrier as I get ass-fucked by a seventy-year-old who really wants this puck . . . and my dignity.

"I'm here to cheer you on! You're doing great." She shoots me two very enthusiastic thumbs-up. "Go, sports!"

Finally, one of my teammates sweep the puck out from beneath my skates, and I topple backward onto my ass as the pack breaks away to the other side of the ice.

"Hey, Dakota!" Luke skates over and stops swiftly, spraying a cloud of ice shavings over my helmet.

"Oh hi, Luke! I didn't know you played too," Dakota says as Luke awkwardly helps me up off the ground.

"Yeah . . . they wouldn't let Calder on the team if I didn't join."

"Shut the fuck up." I shove my brother, and he chuckles before skating away to rejoin the game.

"This is the third ice arena I've been to in Denver," Dakota says, chatting animatedly like I'm not in the middle of a game. "You were not easy to find."

"That's because I didn't want to be found!" I seethe, irritation simmering in my veins.

It's bad enough Luke sees me suck ass on the ice, I don't need the girl I'm currently banging to witness my humiliation. I've considered quitting multiple times, but I keep thinking one of these years, I'm going to get better. It's just a shame everyone else seems to get better too.

"I gotta go," I bite out, skating away and hating the fact that I feel like I have to try harder, skate faster . . . suck less. This is why I don't do well with girlfriends. I don't like them to see me when I'm not at my best. And unfortunately, my best has never been hockey. It's too bad sex isn't a competitive sport. I'd nail that competition.

Irritation niggles at me as I trip and flounder on the ice, sucking like usual, and by the time the whistle blows for our second intermission, rage is simmering in my veins. The guys all haul ass to the bench for a beer, and I catch Dakota's eye and point to the hallway that leads to the locker room.

I unlatch the gate at the ice and make my way down the rubber-matted hall in an attempt to get out of earshot. When Dakota finally joins me, my temper boils over. "Why the fuck are you here?"

"To watch your big match!" She whacks my arm playfully, trying to be funny, but I do not find this funny.

I scowl back at her. "You know I don't like anyone to come to these things."

"Oh come on . . . this is fun! There are other spectators here."

I look up and see we're drawing the eyes of everyone around us, and I even spot Luke peering over, trying to eavesdrop on our conversation.

With a low growl, I tuck one of my gloves under my arm with my stick and grab Dakota's hand to pull her through the hallway until we're in the locker room. When the door closes and we're encased in the cold, smelly concrete space, I turn and narrow my eyes at her. "Why are you fucking with me?"

"I'm not!" She leans her back against the white brick wall, and I can't help but notice the low cut of her sweater under her long coat. She's wearing a plaid skirt and little ankle boots, and she looks fucking sexy, which just pisses me off more.

"I just wondered . . ." she begins, but stops as a deep flush darkens her cheeks.

"What?"

She bites her lip in a way that makes my dick react. Usually it's because she's thoughtful or nervous, but this time . . . "We could check something off our list."

My brows furrow. "Here?"

"Feels pretty exhibitionist to me." She smiles and lifts her brows, her eyes dropping to my cock that reacts very favorably.

"I'm a sweaty mess."

"I don't mind," she volleys back as she takes a step toward me.

"I'm wearing skates."

"I'll be careful." Another step.

"I . . ." I swallow the knot in my throat as my dick thickens inside of my pads, pushing against the compression shorts and my nut cup.

I have nothing else to argue. No other excuses. We're in the locker room . . . the team is out on the ice. I have maybe about ten fucking minutes before that whistle blows.

"Fuck it." I drop my stick and gloves before grabbing her neck and hauling her toward me.

She lets out an audible squeal as I crush my mouth to hers, pouring the frustration I feel in this moment right into this kiss.

"I don't like to be surprised," I grumble against her lips before moving to devour her neck, sucking harshly in one spot.

"Duly noted," she pants, gripping my collar as my hands roam down her body and steal under her skirt, wasting no time.

"Didn't like it at the sex club. Don't like it here." I slip past her panties and push my finger deep inside of her, my entire body shuddering when I feel her wet heat. She's soaked. And she's tight, and her silky channel causes my whole body to convulse as I slick her wetness around her opening, flicking over her tight bundle of nerves with harsh pressure. "What do you have to say for yourself?"

She whimpers and grips my shoulder pads as I walk in my skates and press her against the brick wall. She grabs my wrist and rides my hand. "I'm not sorry."

"Oh, you're going to be when I'm done with you," I threaten as I hook my fingers around the crotch of her panties and yank downward.

The fabric tears after a few more tugs, and she gasps when the cool rink air touches her hot sex. She blinks at me with hooded eyes, her brows pinched together as if she's in pain. But I know what that look means. She wants more.

I struggle to undo my hockey pants, and as soon as I toss my nut cup and grip my bare shaft I throw my head back in anger. "Fuck, I don't have a condom."

She smiles and digs into her coat pocket, revealing a foil square between her two fingers.

"This doesn't change anything." My eyes narrow on her as I take the condom and rip the packet open with my teeth. "You're still in the doghouse."

"Ruff, ruff." She giggles as she watches me roll the rubber over my angry cock, and I fight away a smirk as her playfulness pokes holes in my irritable mood.

"You want it rough, baby?" I ask as I grip her leg up around my hip and bend my knees to line my cock up with her center. "Is that what you wanted when you came here tonight?"

She nods silently, her lips parted as she holds her breath high in her chest and without any prep, I thrust up into her, my fingers digging into the meat of her thigh as a lightning strike of pressure rockets through my cock.

"Yes," she cries loudly, her body arching into me as I grab her other leg and hoist her up around my waist, fusing our bodies together. "God yes."

"Be quiet or you're going to get us caught," I command, looking at the door nervously. There's no way to lock it so if someone walks in, they're going to get an eyeful.

She licks her lips and wiggles against me, begging for movement. So I give her what she wants and fuck her hard and fast against the wall, thrusting into her at a pace that I have no business keeping up with after two periods of hockey. But that's what this girl does to me. She makes me fucking crazy. She shocks me and pushes me and manages to dig shit out of me that I haven't shared with anyone. God, she's a pain in my ass.

She cries out when her orgasm rips through her, her voice echoing off the locker room walls, and I look to the door, certain someone had to have heard that.

A dark thought invades my mind. Maybe I want them to hear. I've been humbled on the ice enough tonight. I deserve this fucking win. I want everyone outside that door to know I just fucked my woman delirious in the locker room at intermission.

Holy shit, did I just refer to Dakota as *my woman*? I better get my shit together because she is most certainly not *mine*. I mean, she is mine for the time we're doing this, but when we're done, we're done. That's what I want, and I know that's what she wants. She's newly divorced, for fuck's sake. She doesn't need any man staking a claim on her. However, a lump settles in the pit of my stomach when I think about the reality of that happening down the road.

Another guy is going to touch her like I am right now . . . My hips jack forward faster, enraged at the thought.

Another guy is going to hear the way her voice cracks when I'm buried balls-deep in her . . . I grip her waist, savoring the moans that escape her lips.

Another guy will kiss her lush, pouty lips that scream my name . . . I seal my mouth over hers, messily kissing her between my relentless thrusts.

Another guy will get to look at her stunning body . . . I gaze down at her supple curves, the perfect amount of soft and hard, relishing the moment she lets go, her climax squeezing my cock so tight I almost lose my balance.

Fuck.

My orgasm takes me by surprise, and I hiss through my teeth as I empty my balls into her. Into the condom. Shame washes over me as I realize just how fucked my thoughts were just then. I need to get my head out of my ass and back to reality. This is just sex. Dakota Schaefer and I are just fucking.

"Stick that in your pipe and smoke it, old man," I huff as I picture that old guy out on the ice drinking water while I just got laid by my casual fuck buddy. I toss my knotted condom into the trash.

"What was that?" Dakota asks, depositing her torn panties in the same receptacle.

"Nothing," I say, doing up my pants. "Are you going to stay for the last period?"

"Can I?" She hits me with wide eyes, clearly shocked by my invitation.

I nod. "Yeah . . . and sit by the visitor side, would you? Cheer real loud for me."

"Okay." She laughs and frowns up at me.

"And don't heckle me, or I will make you pay."

"Promises, promises." She tugs on her skirt and winces slightly.

"What's wrong?" I ask as we walk toward the locker room door.

She smooths her hands over her ass. "I'm cold."

My eyes heat with the knowledge that she is completely bare down there and heading out to an ice rink to sit on a cold metal bleacher. I lean in and press a chaste kiss to her lips. "You play stupid games, you win stupid prizes, Ace."

And the sound of her laugh echoes in my head as I play one of the best periods of hockey in my adult beer-league hockey career.

Take that, old man.

Chapter 30

MIDDLE CHILD SYNDROME

Calder

"Calder . . . can you run to the lumber yard tonight and pick up the shipment that just came in?"

My head jerks toward Wyatt who's standing in our Boulder workshop barking orders at me just like Dad used to.

"Why isn't Luke going? He always goes to the lumber yard."

Luke's head pops up from behind his computer, and the grimace on his face is unmistakable. "Roe and I are kind of in a fight."

"I thought you weren't fucking her."

"I'm not."

"Then how are you in a fight with her?"

"It's none of your damn business, okay?" Luke snaps, his jaw taut as he dives back into whatever the fuck he does on that thing. "Plus, I have to email these engineers about the ag land we're buying for the new development. They've been waiting on me all week."

I sigh and turn back to Wyatt. "I have shit to do tonight. I need to work on the shelves I'm making for Dakota's shop."

Wyatt cuts me a look. "I know what that's code for."

"It's not code for shit. I have to get them done." Which is partially true. Wyatt doesn't need to know the plans I have for later with Dakota. It's none of his damn business. He gets to cuddle up with his family and take a break. Why can't I have a moment to myself with Dakota?

"The shelves can wait," he barks, his eyes turning to slits on me. "We need that lumber tonight to get an early start tomorrow. Just take the shop truck and stop bitching. If you hurry you might get back up to the mountain before dark."

"Fuck." I slam my tools down onto the workbench, irritated as shit that he's just throwing this on me now. I stomp my way out of the shop, grabbing the keys off the hook before I head out. "Fuck, fuck, fuck," I grumble again as I swing open the shop door and turn on my heels to slam it shut.

It's only when I turn back around that I realize what a monstrous fit I'm throwing, because I am now staring into the eyes of a very unimpressed looking Johanna Fletcher.

"Calder Fletcher, what on earth has gotten into you?" I glance down at her hands to see she's holding a tray of cookies and a six-pack of beer. Mom often shows up after five with treats when she knows we're all working overtime, but I am not in the mood.

"Mom," I state woodenly and shuffle my way around her to head to the truck. "I gotta run."

"Stop right there."

I grip the driver's side handle and turn on my heel to face her. "What?"

Her brows lift. "Come again?"

I close my eyes and lick my lips. "I'm sorry. I'm just frustrated with my brothers, and I took my anger out on the door and a hammer I threw in there."

"Is there any blood?" she asks, her tone grave and overly dramatic.

"No, jeez. I didn't chuck the hammer at anyone. I just chucked it at the workbench. Everyone is fine. I'm sure if you go in there, you can have a nice chat with your two golden boys." I turn to open the truck door, but my mom zips over and forces it shut with her hip.

"What's going on?" She sets the beer down on the ground and opens up her container of cookies.

She hands me one, and I take an agitated bite, mumbling around a mouthful. "I have a lot on my plate right now, and I'm getting sick of always being the grunt boy around here. Luke is being Luke, aka a little whiney baby who can't do anything for himself. And Wyatt is busy being a family man, and I'm happy for him, I am, but I just feel like no one gives a fuck about what I need to do with my spare time."

"What do you need to do, honey?" She tilts her head, her eyes softening as she looks up at me.

And it's irritating as fuck that she even needs to ask. Like she needs proof that I have a life outside of this job and my family. "Just stuff."

"Does this have anything to do with Dakota?"

I hit her with a flat look. She's been riding my ass about Dakota ever since I showered at her place, and I'm sure she knows the truth by now. Luke has a big mouth, and he's always on the phone to our mother, gossiping like a little hen. Total fucking mama's boy.

"Don't get your hopes up." I grip the back of my neck and avoid eye contact. "Dakota and I are just friends."

"Sounds like you've been spending a lot of time with her," she offers, and I can feel her eyes burrowing into me, trying to read my mind.

"Not that much time." I shrug dismissively and stuff the rest of the cookie in my mouth.

"Not what Luke says."

"Luke needs to get a life," I mumble around a mouthful of chocolate chip.

"Maybe you're frustrated because you like her as more than just a friend." Her brows lift knowingly, and I feel my defenses rising with her words.

The thoughts I was having with Dakota at the hockey rink are not something I'm trying to give life to. I was able to kind of dismiss all that possessive jealousy as intrusive thoughts during sex. Just caveman bullshit and not something to be taken seriously.

But the way I looked for her in the stands as soon as I scored a goal in the third period?

I'm embarrassed.

Somehow, I've morphed from this sex-adventurous, mountain man playboy to a guy looking for a smile from his girl. It's crazy how having someone you want to impress in the crowd can motivate the fuck out of you. I never played hockey that good even in high school.

And the kiss I laid on her in the parking lot after we were done? Fucking fireworks.

And it was just a kiss.

I have to get my head on straight. This is a limited-time only arrangement. I can't keep thinking this is more than what it is: phenomenal fucking with a sexy-ass woman who will have no problems finding her dream man after we're done.

"Maybe you should see if she wants to be more than just friends?"

"I'm not going to do that, Mom," I answer firmly, because if I don't make this clear she will get her hopes up.

If it was up to my mother, all her boys would be married with multiple children each by now and she'd have a swarm of grandkids at her house every weekend. I could see how much baby Stevie has helped with her grief the past few months. She still tears up when she talks about Dad, but there's new purpose to her life. And her close relationship with Trista has been good for her too. Of course, we all still miss him, but the new additions to the family are things we know he'd be proud of, so that helps with some of the sadness. And since I have no intentions of giving her any grandkids, the one thing I can do is honor my dad's legacy for her by continuing the family business. So why am I being such a little bitch?

"You know what your father would say?" she says, pulling me from my thoughts as she hits me with a teasing smile. "He'd say 'Shit or get off the pot.'"

I laugh at those crass words coming from my sweet mother's mouth. It's unexpected, but she's so right. I can literally hear his voice in my head.

He never liked how casual me, Wyatt, and Luke were with women, but he always said that as long as we were clear and not stringing someone along, then he didn't care what we got up to.

In my heart of hearts, I don't feel like I'm stringing Dakota along. We both know what we signed up for, and it's way too early to cut and run. I have to see this through with her, if not for myself, then for her.

She needs this.

And I need her to be good when we end this, or the guilt will haunt me just like it already has for the past seven years.

I'm not going to fall for her. I'm just enjoying myself a bit. And with the bullshit I have going on at work with my brothers, I deserve this.

"Thanks for the talk, Mom, but I have to get going." I lean in and brush a kiss to her cheek, ignoring the way her pensive eyes follow me as I hop in the truck and get my ass back to work. That's clearly all I'm good for these days.

Chapter 31

Dakota

"Oh my God, it's freezing out here!" I shriek as I grip Calder's black-and-white checkered flannel around my body and dash across the worn path behind his cabin.

"Stop bitching and hurry up!" he snipes, reaching back to grab my hand and hurry me along.

We make our way through the woods to the metal capsule-shaped hot tub emitting steam into the cold night air. It's dreamlike as large wet snowflakes drop over us. That's the mountains in early spring for you. It's probably not even snowing back in Boulder.

Calder releases my hand as he steps behind a woodpile and fiddles with something while I kick off my boots and hang his shirt on a nearby branch. I adjust the black bikini I resurrected from our Mexico trip, and my lips part when string lights turn on overhead, casting the space in a warm glow.

"Holy shit, this is romantic!" I tease, making my way over to the tub. Are you sure you've never brought a girl out here?"

"Shut up," Calder grumbles, and when he looks up from what he's doing, his eyes snag on my body.

My chilled limbs suddenly flush with heat as his eyes score over every square inch of me, causing a bolt of desire to rush through me and settle squarely between my legs.

"Nice suit, Ace." His voice is guttural, and the irritable mood he had when I first arrived on the peak tonight seems to have vanished. "Been in my fantasies a lot lately."

Power to the bikini, baby.

If anything is going to help build up my confidence throughout all of this, it's Calder Fletcher adjusting himself inside his swim trunks. Because of me.

But as I stand before him, enjoying how beautiful he makes me feel, I realize that I feel beautiful without his eyes as well. I have felt more comfortable in my skin the past week than I have in years. Maybe this enemies-with-benefits challenge is actually working.

"Are you getting in, or are you planning to cut glass with those hard nips?"

And just like that, I'm thrust back to reality.

"This thing better be hot." I tiptoe over to one end of the tub and test the water with my hand before stepping inside. I moan as I ease my body down into the heat, my back pressing against the narrow end of the metal basin. "Oh my God, this feels amazing."

"A nice, balmy hundred and four degrees for you, boss," Calder says as he ditches his shirt and joins me.

My eyes drink in the way his inked muscles flex and bend as he lowers himself down into the tub across from me. Our feet tangle for a moment before he grabs my legs and puts them on his lap, holding my feet in a way that feels oddly affectionate. There's been a lot of tender moments between us in the past week since we've been doing this enemies-with-benefits thing officially. I guess seeing someone naked pretty regularly entitles you to a few sweet moments.

"This runs with no electricity or pump." He smiles proudly as he looks around the space.

"Really? How?" I peer out of the tub to eye the metal tubing swirled along the ground.

"All the magic is in the stainless-steel coil. It takes the cold water from the bottom of the tub, sucks it into the coil, heats up because hot water rises, following the curve of coil, then gets pushed back out into the tub. At the top there's negative pressure, so no moving parts."

I stare blankly back at him. "I have no idea what you just said."

The corner of his mouth tugs up as he rolls his eyes. "It's fine. You don't have to get it. This eco-friendly stuff is kind of Wyatt's thing. I remember him and my dad arguing about it when we were installing it. My dad hated all that shit."

I watch Calder as he glances around the space, taking it all in. He doesn't speak about his dad much, but I am curious about that comment he just made. "Are you like your dad and not into the eco-friendly stuff too?"

"I don't mind it, I guess." A thoughtful look falls over his face. "I just do whatever makes my family happy."

I watch him speculatively for a moment, so many things clicking into place at that simple comment. It's probably why he's never told anyone that his true passion is furniture-building, not house-building. He wants to be what everyone else wants him to be, not what he wants to be.

I open my mouth to say something but stop myself. He let me list some of his pieces on my website, and that's probably enough meddling from me for now.

"What was your dad like?" I ask, shifting the focus back to him. "I only ever saw him in passing a few times before he passed."

Calder smiles softly. "He was overbearing and pushy. Kind of like you." He squeezes the arch of my foot, and I giggle, splashing some water out of the tub as I squirm. "He was also thoughtful and motivated and always pushing us to be better."

"Better than what?"

"Better than we used to be, I guess." Calder shrugs, wiping away some of the snow clinging to his beard. "If I had known we were going to lose him so soon, I guess I would have tried harder to impress him."

"I'm sure he was proud of you."

"Yeah, I suppose." Calder slides deeper into the tub, immersing his shoulders as he rests his head on the metal edge and hooks his feet around my hips. "I really looked up to him, and it just sucks because now he's gone."

"You can still look up to him." I nudge Calder with my foot as I point to the sky.

He angles his neck up, squinting against the falling snow, and I do the same, feeling the wet flakes cling to my eyelashes. We fall into a comfortable silence as we both muse over our own thoughts. It's humbling being out here in the middle of nature, staring up into the big open sky. Makes you grateful for what you have and less focused on what you don't. Maybe I'm not as big a city girl as I thought.

"What's the deal with your parents?" Calder asks, and I look down to find him gazing at me. "You guys close?"

"Ugh, my parents." I wipe my face with my wet hands, feeling a sheen of sweat collect on my upper lip. "Divorced since I was in junior high and hated each other for years even before that. I grew up hopping between their two houses, and neither of them ever felt like a home. They both just felt like a place I stayed."

Calder nods, his eyes laser-focused on me as he rubs my feet in the hot water.

"It's why I was such a freak with you during my house reno. I had such big dreams for that house. I wanted it to be this perfect home where my husband carried me over the threshold, and I brought my first baby home in . . . a baby with two parents and a backyard . . . just . . . the dream, you know? Not split custody with alternating weekends, and parents arguing over who had to take me when the other one wanted to go have a life that wasn't kid-friendly. I felt like a commodity and a burden all in one go. I swore I would never be like my parents because I was going to choose the right person . . . and just look at me now."

"I'm looking," Calder says pointedly, his eyes never leaving mine. "You look pretty good to me."

I rub my lips together realizing he's not talking about my suit. "I just wanted things to turn out different, you know?"

He takes a deep breath and tilts his head at me. "Do you think that deep down you knew Randal wasn't the one, and that's why you never wanted kids with him?"

My brows raise at that keen observation. "Probably," I reply with a shrug. "I didn't want to put a child through the same shit I went through."

Calder nods. "So do you want kids at all?"

I wipe away the dab of snowflakes melting down my cheek. "I'm not yearning to have them really, but if I met the right guy and we were good, I think I'd come around to the idea. I still really want that happily-ever-after."

Calder licks his lips and turns to look away, and I notice the muscle in his jaw twitch.

I shift my foot in his lap. "Do you want kids?"

He laughs. "Considering I don't even want a girlfriend, I don't think I have any business wanting kids."

"Wyatt was planning to be a single dad before he fell for Trista, right?"

"Wyatt and I are very different."

I eye him and nod. "Yes, you sure are. But in a good way, I think."

Silence descends before Calder says, "I wish I knew all that stuff about your house. Your big dreams. Why the renovation was so important to you. I maybe would have . . . I don't know . . . had more patience with you or something."

I cringe when I think about what a nag I was back then. "I was no picnic either. I was under so much pressure with the wedding planning, and I know I took it out on you."

"I know, but I want you to know I am sorry. I said a lot of shit that day of the incident, and I hate myself for it."

A knot forms in my throat as my mind drifts back to that awful day.

Dakota

Seven Years Earlier

"Oh my God!" I scream from the floor of my bedroom closet. My knees and shoes are soaked in the three inches of standing water covering every square inch of the flooring. Now it's crawling up the walls.

Loud footsteps pound up the stairs, and I turn when Calder's wide frame fills the doorway. He has faded jeans on, a flannel, a tool belt, and a look of sheer panic all over his face. He's out of breath from running to the basement where he was shutting the waterline off after we discovered the disaster in my upstairs bathroom.

"My wedding dress is ruined," I cry, tears falling down my face as I hold up the stained, dripping wet skirt of my dress for him to see. The wet fabric fused to the wall during the flooding, and since the closet is covered in red floral wallpaper, the bottom of my dress now looks like a crime scene. Whoever chose to wallpaper a freaking closet needs their head examined, but that's exactly why we're in the middle of a giant renovation.

"I'll pay for it to be cleaned," Calder says, his boots thwacking across the wet floor as he comes to squat down by me.

"This is dye, Calder. You can't just spray some stain remover on it and throw it in the wash. And who knows how long it's been sitting here like this!"

"Can I pay for another dress?" he asks, shoving a trembling hand through his hair.

"This was a custom design from one of my best friends!" I cry, my blood pressure skyrocketing as that reality settles in over me. "And I'm getting married in three days."

"What do you want from me, Dakota? It was an accident." Calder's tone is harsh, and I feel the rage bubbling in my veins.

"I want to go back in time and never have hired you," I sob, shaking my head in disbelief. It's been such a nightmare working with Calder these past few months, and we were in the home stretch. I was finally going to be rid of him for good. My tone is bitter and harsh when I add, "There's *a reason you work with your dad and your brothers. You are so careless. Reckless! You need supervision. You're not responsible enough to do a solo job. Just look at this damage."*

I gesture to the warped trim and walls all around me.

His eyes flare as he grinds his jaw back and forth. *"Maybe if you didn't micromanage every goddamn thing I did, I could have done my job with a bit more confidence. And if you're going to melt down over every little setback, maybe you shouldn't be renovating a house on your own to begin with."*

"This isn't a little *setback!" I scream and chuck my dress away to stand up and face him. My finger jabs into his chest as the blood rushes to my cheeks.* *"I swear you did this on purpose. You're so antiwoman, anti-wedding, anti-relationships . . . you can't stand anyone to actually be happy."*

"There you go, Dakota. You got me all figured out!" he roars, flinging his hands out wide.

"Damn straight I do, Killer Calder," I roar, my tone lethal. "You've killed my house and my wedding, and I regret the day I ever agreed to hire you."

The silence is deafening as he stares back at me. "If your wedding can be so easily killed, then maybe you shouldn't be marrying this guy in the first place."

My jaw drops as I bark out a noise of indignation. "Like I'm going to take relationship advice from you. You've never even had a real girlfriend. You're too much of a joke for anyone to ever fall in love with you."

Calder's eyes darken, and his nostrils flare as he takes a step back. "I'd be shocked if the guy you're marrying actually loves you. You're too much of a nightmare to love."

My chest contracts at his cutting words as tears burn my eyes. "Get the fuck out of my house."

Calder

Shame blankets me as I look over at Dakota sitting in my hot tub looking completely at ease. Throughout the years, our hatred for each other has turned lighter and more playful, as time has healed some of those wounds. But if I actually replay the awful things we said to each other, there's nothing funny about it.

"Not that this is any excuse, but things between Wyatt, Luke, and me were kind of rough back then," I offer, scrubbing steam off my face as I shoot an apologetic look toward Dakota. "It was in the post-Robyn phase, and I wasn't even nursing a broken heart from her. That would have been easy. I was repairing what was broken between us three brothers. It was hard. We all broke each other's trust, and our dad was angry at us for bringing such a mess to the workplace. Max was pissed at us for being so careless. It was brutal."

I sigh as I think back to how ashamed our father and Max were for all of that. Max wouldn't let us see Everly until we all got along again. It weighed on me so much, I could hardly get my ass to work most days. It's why we created our Dark Night–bonding tradition. It's weird, but it's important. It helps us remember why family is so important.

I shrug my shoulders in the water. "I'm a player and didn't even know I was getting played. And it was reinforcing some hard truths that I wasn't ready to admit about myself. I really shouldn't have taken that job to work for you. I was in no position to be responsible for myself, let alone your renovation. The broken pipe was an accident, but what came afterward, well, that was just me being an asshole."

Dakota's brows knit together, and I see a brief flash of nerves flit across her face. "She must have really done a number on you."

"Honestly, Robyn doesn't bother me. It's the family stuff that nearly killed me." I pause as I think about the dynamic in my family. I love them. Fiercely. I genuinely appreciate living next door to Luke and Wyatt, even when I bitch about it. Being a package deal with them is a part of my identity, but we're not without problems.

"When the Robyn thing blew up in all our faces, we were all in pretty rough shape and not talking to each other for obvious reasons. My mom was all over Wyatt because he's so closed-off she can't help but smother him. And she was there for Luke because he's the baby and has always been a little smothered. My dad was pissed at all of us for being nightmares to work with. And I just kind of . . . existed. My family has a tendency to assume I'm always okay. *Oh, it's just goofy Calder. Nothing gets him down.* That's kind of the story of my life. It's assumed I'm always okay to pick up the lumber or stay late to finish drywall or share the room on a family trip with a woman who hates me."

Dakota makes a noise of understanding, her hand reaching out to touch my leg in a small sign of empathy.

"I hate saying *middle child syndrome* because I'm obviously a grown-ass man, but since we're all still so close, that birth order stuff is still really present. I just get sick of the expectation that I'll be fine with whatever the others don't want to do. Or can't do. There's just never a choice for me."

She nods, her eyes sweeping over my face filled with sympathy. "That would be extremely frustrating."

I hold her ankle, feeling lighter already after unleashing a decade's worth of family bullshit on her, and then another thought hits me. "Hey, now that we're hashing all this out, can I ask you a question?"

"Of course." Dakota smiles sweetly at me, and my chest tightens as I steel myself to get this question asked because it's always bugged me.

"When my dad died, you left food at my house."

Her smiles falters as her brows twitch. "Yeah, so?"

"You drove all the way up here to leave it and didn't make any for my brothers. Just me. Why did you do that when you hated me?"

"I still cared," she replies with an indignant huff. "I can have issues with someone and still want to show that I care."

I frown, my eyes searching her face for more because it feels like there must be more to it than that. She was married at the time. We weren't speaking. It had been years since her home reno disaster.

I could see her showing up for Max and her best friend . . . but not me. Not after everything we'd been through.

"Seeing you at your dad's funeral killed me," she adds, her voice catching in her throat. "You were just sitting in the back of the funeral home by yourself, and I wanted to walk over and hug you so bad, but I knew you wouldn't want that from me."

Dakota's eyes are red-rimmed and shining in a way that I feel in my gut. Warmth spreads through my chest. Even with all our bullshit, all our bickering, our huge blowout . . . she still cared about the shit that mattered. It makes me feel seen in a way I haven't ever felt seen.

"I'll take that hug now, if you're still offering."

Her brows pop up, and a grateful smile lifts her cheeks as she moves across the water and wraps her arms around my neck, shifting so she's sitting on my lap with her legs around my waist.

I squeeze her waist, burying my face in her neck and breathing in the scent of her, the feel of her, the essence of her. I spent so many years hating Dakota Schaefer and her hating me, and it all feels so fucking petty now. We had real life shit happen the past seven years—the death of a parent, a divorce, heartbreak on both sides. Why did we waste so much of our energy being assholes when we could have been friends?

She pulls away and holds my face in her hands, her fingers raking over my beard before she leans in and kisses me. It's a gentle kiss, different than any other we've had before. It's not lustful or dirty or exploratory or angry.

It's comforting.

It feels like the sweetest, most sincere form of connection I've ever experienced with a woman, and my throat stings with the importance of it. Our tongues caress each other, my hands mapping her back before gripping her neck to deepen the kiss, siphoning every bit of goodness out of her that I can get. We've kissed hundreds of times by now in all our hooking up, but somehow this one feels like our first.

When we finally pull apart, we press our foreheads together, our breaths heavy, chests rising and falling as steam billows up between us. She runs her fingers through my hair, her lips quivering as she says, "I don't think I ever really hated you, Calder. I think I just hated that you pieced something together about my marriage before I did, and that was humiliating. How did I not see how wrong Randal was? How did I not know it was a mistake?"

My muscles tighten as I squeeze her to me, trying hard to take that pain away from her. "Hindsight is always twenty-twenty."

"But you knew it." She pulls away so she can look directly into my eyes. "And I knew you knew it. So I just kept being awful to you because you felt like a constant reminder of a bad life decision I was stuck in. I was married, and it felt like every time you saw me, you knew I was unhappy and lying to myself. I was waiting for you to scream *I told you so*."

"I wasn't judging you, Ace." I slide my hands up her back, massaging her shoulders to calm her down. "Never."

"It was easier to label you as the asshole who ruined my perfect wedding and my perfect house, but you were just a scapegoat to my bad life choice." She licks her lips and tugs the lower one between her teeth. "I'm sorry I iced you out so hard. Truly. If I could go back in time, it wouldn't be to not work with you. It would be to just have the guts to call off that wedding. Deep down, I knew I shouldn't have married him."

I move my hands up to cradle her face, my thumbs drawing a line along her jaw. "If it's any consolation . . . I've never seen a more beautiful bride."

Her head jerks back. "What are you talking about? You weren't at my wedding."

"But I saw you in your dress . . . before it was ruined."

Her lips part as she lets out an audible gasp. "When?"

"At your house. It was the week before the pipe broke, and you were with Cozy and your mom. Cozy had Ethan with her. He was just a baby then. I came over to do some plumbing, and your mom let me in. I had just got in the door, and you were walking down the stairs in your dress."

She inhales. "I remember this now."

I lick my lips and shake my head in awe as I recall every little detail about her on that day. The dress hugged her in all the right places, and her skin glowed like an angel. The dress was simple but stunning, and her blue eyes sparkled under that veil she had on. She was a fairy tale.

"I couldn't speak," I confess, looking down and then back up at her awestruck expression. "I forgot what I was even there for. I couldn't take my eyes off you."

She frowns, her eyes flicking back and forth between mine like she's trying to work out a puzzle. "I thought you hate weddings."

"I do. But I liked you in that dress." My shoulders shake with silent laughter.

She licks her lips and sighs. "It was a great dress."

"I'm sorry I ruined it." I tip her chin up to look at me.

She frowns and shrugs. "I'm not. In the end, Randal didn't deserve that dress. Maybe no man did. That dress is a fantasy . . . and this . . . this is reality. Sex. No strings. No feelings. This is all I'm worth."

My heart sinks at the words that have just spilled out of her. I open my mouth to tell her something that makes this not sound so cheap, but she cuts me off.

"Calder, it's fine. It's easier to just accept it. It makes life more tolerable to just call it what it is. Who knows if I'll ever find my happily-ever-after again? But at least I can have some good sex along the way. Right, Killer?"

Using my nickname stings in this moment, and I feel my body tensing with irritation, my mouth opening to pick a fight. But I stop myself because maybe I need to hear it. Maybe I need to be reminded of what this is before both of us get in too deep.

Chapter 32

HOW DO YOU LIKE THEM APPLES?

Dakota

My heart races as I sit at the bar of The Mercantile in Jamestown where Calder told me to wait for him after work. I sip my appletini, which the older female bartender gave me a weird look for ordering, as I admire the atmosphere. I've driven by this place plenty of times in my journeys up to Calder's, but this is the first time I've stopped in. I can see why he comes here so much. It's cozy and relaxed and exactly where I would expect to see those Fletcher mountain men stop after work.

I eye the appletini she served me in a rocks glass because she didn't have any martini glasses. It's kind of ruining the aesthetic of my character, but I'll be damned if I break now.

A deep, husky voice whispers from behind me as a hard object pokes into my back. "Miss, I need you to turn around slowly and show me what's in that big bag of yours."

I take a deep breath and freeze with my neon green drink at my lips. "Who are you?"

"You know who I am." The object pushes deeper into my back causing a stirring in between my legs. "Now, what's in the bag?"

My tummy trembles as I fight back a giggle and turn to face the man with an ominous looking umbrella in his hand. Not exactly a threatening object, but I'll roll with it. I part my lips and blink coyly up at him. "Tell me who you are first, and then I'll show you anything you want."

His brows tip, and I notice him fighting back a smirk behind his beard. "I'm LaRon, and I own the cider house up the mountain, and someone's been stealing all our good apples."

"Oh no, that's awful." I gasp doing my best to give Betty Boop vibes. "But I'm allergic to apples."

LaRon's brows furrow as he seems to struggle with what to say next. "Um . . . you're drinking an appletini, though."

"That drink isn't mine." I hold my hand up over my mouth in the shape of an O, nailing this character.

He frowns again and asks, "How about them apples?" He taps my boobs with the umbrella, and we both burst out laughing as I whack his umbrella away.

"This is serious apple business," he gruffs, horribly fighting away his smile. "I saw you hiding behind the stone mill, and I know it was you I chased through the tasting room last week. I have my fermenting exams coming up, and I need those stolen apples or I'm going to have to call the police."

"Wait." I break character and frown up at him. "I thought I was the one with the fermenting exams. You're the orchard owner."

Calder's face falls. "Shit, you're right."

"I told you we got too plot-heavy."

"I know, all right, just go with it." He clears his throat and resumes his character. "You don't need to take that fermenting exam. I'll teach you all about my hard cider."

My eyes flash down to his groin. "I promise I can be such a good apple slut."

"Calder!" a loud voice barks from behind me, and I swerve in my stool to see the lady who made me my drink. "Get away from that nice girl right now."

"Judy, it's fine. She's my—"

"No, it's not." The woman looks down at me. "Sweetie, I'm sorry to tell you, but this guy is not the one for you." She cuts menacing eyes back up at Calder. "You boys promised me you wouldn't hit on anyone at my bar."

"Judy, this is Dakota. She's my . . ."

I tilt my head and smile, enjoying the panic and awkwardness all over this normally confident mountain man's face.

"What am I, Calder?" I blink coyly up at him.

He frowns at me and then smiles. "She's my brother's wife's best friend. We go way back."

I roll my eyes. "Nice save."

Calder looks back to Judy. "I promise this is consensual."

"I know all about this animal," I confirm, turning back around and grabbing a menu off the bar. "Thanks for having my back, though."

Judy puffs out a noise. "Okay, sweetie. You just let me know if he gives you any trouble, okay?"

"Will do." I wink at the sweet lady, who smiles and then shoots Calder a dirty look. "I like her."

"Can I get a beer at least?" he calls down the bar to her, and she waves him off.

Eventually a pint appears in front of Calder before Judy murmurs under her breath, "If you ask me for cider, I'm throwing you out."

When she walks away, we both burst out laughing again, horrified that she heard more than we intended her to.

"I take it you know her?" I ask, glancing back.

Calder sighs. "Yeah. Judy is good shit, and she doesn't take any shit. She helps me out with Milkshake when we're ever out of town."

"Oh, that's nice." I smile at her. She gives me a dubious look like she's trying to warn me off about Calder, but I feel pretty well informed about this mountain manwhore already.

"Sorry I got off track on our script there," Calder says taking a big drink of his beer.

"Oh my God, it's fine. Role-playing is so fun, though. I'm sure we'll do better next time."

"Next time?" Calder eyes me curiously.

My cheeks heat as I realize what I just suggested. As much as I love experiencing these new things with him, I hate that it means checking off another box. Another box checked means another step closer to our little arrangement being over. I press my lips together and eye the menu, trying not to let my mind wander.

"I'm starving. Can we eat here before we head up to your place?"

"Absolutely," Calder replies with a delicious glint to his eye. "Let's see if they have any apple pie."

We order burgers and have a second round of drinks, talking animatedly about our days. It feels shockingly comfortable being immersed in Calder's world like this. Hanging at his favorite bar, eating a meal with him, talking about work. It's not the first meal we've eaten together, but it's the first meal we've eaten in an establishment, and I can't help how my mind wanders to wondering what it would be like if we did this more often.

What will it be like when we're done with the list? Will we really just go back to how we were before? When I see him around Max and Cozy, will it really be like we haven't had mind-blowing sex?

It is mind-blowing for Calder too, right? It sure seems like he's not losing any steam on things, but maybe he's like this with every girl he's slept with, and I'm just another warm body.

My mind is racing so much that I don't hear the question Calder asks me.

"So, can I?"

"Can you what?" I ask around a french fry.

"Can I be your plus-one to this award thing?"

My chest swells with emotion over that question. We haven't talked about this for a few days, so it's surprising to me that he's remembered and wants to go. That's a little date-ish, isn't it? "You really want to?"

"I know I don't want you to go with anyone else," he replies, reaching over and placing his hand on my thigh. "You're mine until we cross this finish line, right?"

"Right," I tut as a knot forms in my throat. At this rate it's shaping up to be quite a finish, and I have no idea how I feel about that.

Chapter 33

SEX SHACK

Dakota

"Name something you might hurt yourself riding on," Steve Harvey says on the TV in Calder's shop.

"A cactus! A tree stump. A budget airline seat!"

Calder stops varnishing a piece of furniture in his workshop and hits me with a look. "You get that it's answers that are most common, right?"

"Yes." I pop a kernel of popcorn in my mouth, my legs swinging from where I'm perched at the butcher block countertop.

"But you're always wrong. Like every time. You haven't guessed a single answer correctly this whole evening."

"So?"

"So . . ." He sets his paintbrush down and wipes his hands off on his jeans as he walks over to me. He grips my legs to spread them out and he positions himself squarely between my thighs, his hands scoring my flesh as he hits me with a devastatingly sexy look. "You should probably be embarrassed."

"Shut up." I reach for a handful of popcorn and toss it in his face.

We've grown far too comfortable with each other ever since our hot tub confessions over a week ago. It's turned into a bit of a free-for-all in our enemies-with-benefits department. He sends me dirty texts during the day that usually make it impossible for me to not drive up the mountain to see him that night. He even stopped by my store one day for lunch, and let's just say . . . I put the Be Back in 10 Minutes sign up on my front door real damn quick. There's something completely irresistible about Calder when he's in his dirty clothes from working on a job site all day.

And shower sex has been checked off the list like three times now with all the sleepovers I've had up here.

Sleepovers were never specifically listed in our plan, but they weren't ruled out either. Trista seems to be enjoying watching me do my drive of shame as I make my way back down the mountain in the mornings. The one downside of sleeping with a man in a very interconnected family, I suppose.

But we haven't even discussed the PowerPoint checklist in a few days, and I'm pretty sure we only have one thing left before we head back to the sex club.

Have sex at my house.

For some reason, both of us seem to be avoiding that challenge. I'm not sure what Calder's reason is, but I know mine, and surprisingly, it has nothing to do with Randal.

I'm afraid if I bring Calder back into the scene of the crime, we're going to backslide into the miserable people we were seven years ago.

I like who we are on Fletcher Mountain. We're carefree but focused. Yeah, we bicker and pick at each other, but we actually hear one another, and the sex is incredible. I'm not ready for the finish line.

Steve Harvey's voice cuts into my musings confirming that not even one of my guesses were right. I stick out my tongue at Calder. "Better to try and fail than never try at all."

His forehead lifts knowingly, and my head jerks when I realize I've just possibly admitted that marrying Randal could be perceived as a good thing. That is not a parallel I want to draw today. Although I did get a very good email from my lawyer a couple days ago telling me that Randal was withdrawing his request to reopen our divorce settlement to change my payment schedule, so that was some good news. And thankfully, Randal hasn't called to complain about it or gloat about his new girlfriend. And even more thankfully . . . I don't give a flying fuck about his new lady. How's that for growth?

Among some other good news is the fact that Calder has sold three of his furniture pieces from my website. When I told him about the orders, he looked like a kid on Christmas morning. He instantly started stressing about the fact that they needed a fresh coat of varnish before he could take them to my fulfilment facility where the crew was going to work on how best to package and ship them.

"I can't believe someone in Canada bought this giant porch swing," Calder says as he steps away from me to get back to work. "The shipping cost is insane. Who has this kind of money?"

"People know a good thing when they see it," I reply with a smile. "Have you given any thought to that email I forwarded you?"

He blows out a long breath. "Nah, not yet. Not really. I mean . . . a little."

A boutique home-goods store in Denver reached out to my website to see if they could feature Calder's furniture in their showroom. They have a decent consignment split, and what Calder would lose in direct sales he'd gain in exposure and being able to sell locally.

"It sounds kind of nice to just drive all my pieces over there and dump them off when they're done," he says, gripping the back of his neck. "I could really use the space in here, and I feel bad free-loading off your fulfilment company. If this became a long-term thing, I'd need to figure out something more permanent. If I say *yes* to this offer . . . I wouldn't have to mess with any of that."

"That's definitely a perk." I try to keep my opinion to myself as he works through this, which is crazy hard. When Calder told me the profit margin he'll make on this stuff, my head exploded. This is what he's meant to be doing with his life!

"But I'd also have to commit to providing a set number of pieces every month based on supply and demand." He runs his hand through his hair, his mind whirring with information over-load. "That's a bigger commitment that I'm maybe not ready for."

"Why aren't you ready for that?"

"Cuz of my dad's construction business. Wyatt and Luke can't operate without me."

"Have you asked them?"

He rolls his eyes. "I know what they'd say."

I purse my lips and glare at him. I wish Calder believed in himself half as much as he believes in me. My eyes drift over to my two shelving units that are glossy from the fresh coat of varnish he applied earlier tonight. They are going to look so good in my store, and I already have new inventory to fill them up. And I had no notes for him when he showed them to me tonight. He kept asking me over and over, telling me that he assumed I would have tweaks. But he assumed wrong. I love them. And I love him for making them for me.

My face heats with the words in my head. I don't love *him* . . . obviously. I just love what he did for me. What he continues to do for me. He's become a genuine friend through our little PowerPoint sex-periment, which is unexpected and so appreciated. Hopefully we'll be able to stay friends when we end this so when we inevitably see each other around, it won't be horrible.

"I'm picking you up at six tomorrow, right? You're sure that's early enough? I can ditch work earlier if I need to," Calder asks, redirecting my attention from the TV back to him.

"Yes, but you really don't have to come," I whine, my stomach swirling with anxiety. "You have to wear a suit and pretend you like me."

"Oh God . . . what a nightmare," he mock-grumps.

"I will be a nightmare." I pull my legs up to sit crisscross. "I'm going to be nervous and awkward and stressed and probably take it all out on you."

He shrugs. "So basically . . . how you act most days of the week."

"Shut up." I roll my eyes and chew my lip nervously. "I really don't mind going to this awards ceremony alone. That was always my plan. It's so businessy and lame. It's barely a thing."

He sets his paintbrush down and walks back over to me, guiding my legs down to resume his space between them. "But if I'm not there, who will heckle you when you accept your award and make sure you stay humble?" He presses a soft kiss to my lips that has me seeing stars before he says, "We don't want all that success going to your head so you think you can actually fuck the patriarchy."

Clenching my teeth, I slide my hands forward to wrap around his neck and shake him. An odd noise bubbles up from him as he laughs and squeezes my sides, sending me into a fit of giggles.

"Is everyone decent? I'm not going to see any body parts that will haunt me until the end of time, am I?" Trista calls out, walking in with her hand over her eyes.

"We're not naked . . . yet," Calder murmurs the last part, shooting me a heated look as Trista walks in, taking in the workshop with wide, eager eyes.

"So, this is the sex shack I've been hearing so much about."

"Sex shack?" I exclaim, turning a confused look to Trista.

She holds her hands up defensively. "That's just what Wyatt told me."

I cut a look to Calder, silently screaming at him for talking about our sex life with his brothers. Two nights ago, Trista would have got an eyeful if she'd walked over here. Calder had me bent over the sawhorses, and I fear I may have told him to keep his tool belt on.

So much cringing.

I give Calder a push to get him out from between my legs, but he doesn't budge. He just turns around and presses his back against me, crossing his arms over his chest like it's totally normal for us to be touching each other in front of his family in our sex shack.

God, he's a stubborn ass sometimes.

"Wow . . . I had no idea you had so many pieces done, Calder. They're all so beautiful." Trista walks around inspecting them all. "But I'm partial to the chair you gave me last year, of course."

"I know. I see you sitting on it outside the barn every damn day," Calder teases, but I can hear the pride in his voice. He likes seeing Trista sit in that chair. It validates his passion.

"Did I interrupt a deep discussion?" Trista asks, hooking a thumb toward the door. "I'm sensing a little tension here maybe."

"Dakota was just trying to uninvite me to this award ceremony tomorrow night." Calder makes a loud, obnoxious noise with his throat.

I shove him in the back, but the big lug doesn't budge.

Trista's eyes light up. "That's why I came over, actually! Johanna said she can watch Stevie, so I was just letting you know we're good to come."

"Come where?" I ask, frowning at her.

"To your Best of Boulder thingy. We all want to see you get your big award."

"Wait . . . who is *we*?" I blink rapidly, struggling to make sense of the words coming out of her mouth.

"Cozy, Max, me, Wyatt, Luke . . . I'm not sure if he's bringing a plus-one. Calder too, of course."

Calder nods like all of this makes perfect sense.

"Why would you guys all want to come?" My eyes dart from Trista to Calder and back to Trista.

"It was Calder's idea, and I think it's a great one." Trista smiles brightly at him. "We didn't realize you could bring guests until he told us."

I pinch Calder's side viciously.

"Ouch, Ace! That hurts!"

"What are you doing?" I hit him with a punishing glower.

"Nothing," he replies with a laugh as he turns on his heel and hits me with a sexy smirk that makes my stomach do flips.

"Bullshit," I scold. "Fess up."

His hands squeeze my thigh in a reassuring caress. "I just think you've had a hell of a year, and you deserve to be celebrated by those who love you."

My cheeks heat at that word that just slipped out of Calder's mouth so casual like. He obviously didn't mean love love. He just meant love like *friendship love*. Cozy and Trista love me of course, because they're my friends, but Calder Fletcher is not in love with me.

He told me when this all started that love would never be on the cards for him. And for a man like him to love someone as stubborn as me? Not a chance in hell. But I can appreciate this enormously kind gesture. He really has more heart than people expect. Me included.

I shake my head, willing my brain to stop short-circuiting. "So I went from going alone to having an entourage of people?" They both nod at me, and I feel a bit lost for words, so I finally shrug and say, "I guess I'll see if I can get us a whole table."

"Great." Trista claps her hands. "I'm so excited. I even have a dress that I think will fit." She stops in her tracks and frowns. "On second thought, I better go try it on again. See you both tomorrow."

"See you tomorrow," Calder calls back cheerily.

I cut a menacing look at the mountain man in front of me. "You're going to pay for that."

He waggles his brows. "That's what I was hoping you'd say."

Chapter 34

Calder

Wyatt, Trista, Max, Cozy, and Luke all sit at an opulent round table at a banquet hall in downtown Boulder. Finishing off our large table of guests is Kate and Miles, friends of Max and Cozy's that I've known for years now. Miles is a partial owner at the Tire Depot in town and a regular at our monthly poker nights. He smiles as his Kate continuously has the whole table in stitches regaling us with stories of her career as a self-proclaimed smut writer. Pretty sure some of the activities Dakota and I have been getting up to these past few weeks could be book-worthy, but since I value my own life, I will keep those stories to myself.

White flowers and candles are spread all over the tables. People are dressed in suits and gowns, sipping cocktails, and mingling with fellow Boulder business owners. It's definitely a who's-who of Boulder here tonight. Max knows everyone of course, and even me, Wyatt, and Luke have run into a fair share of people we've worked with as fellow local business owners.

Though, I haven't been very interested in idle chitchat with acquaintances because I'm too busy staring at the hottest woman in the room.

Dakota's blonde hair glows in the dim banquet lighting as she sits back in her chair and sips her champagne. My eyes drink her in for the hundredth time tonight. She's wearing a one-shouldered fitted little black dress that hugs every damn curve of her. It has a sexy cut out along her collarbone that I have been fighting the urge to press my lips to all night long. The thick gold link belt she added cinches her at the waist, giving her that hourglass figure that makes my dick press against the zipper of my slacks.

When I picked her up earlier tonight and she walked outside before I could get to the door, I damn near stroked out at the sight of her. Her heels are sky-high, her ass is unreal, and the faint remnant of a tan line on her exposed shoulder caused the strangest word to tumble from my lips . . .

Mine.

That tan line is mine, those curves are mine, the way her long blond curls tighten throughout the night from the humidity of the room . . . *mine.*

I adjust myself in my black suit pants yet again as I picture my hand tangled in her hair while her red lips wrap around me. It's an image I would very much like to make a reality, but this evening isn't about sex. It isn't about our PowerPoint checklist or her quest for sexual awakening. It's about Dakota and everything she's accomplished in her life. Her divorce is merely a footnote to all that she's achieved this year, and I need to listen to my upper head, not my lower head.

The sex can wait.

However, I do have big plans for her later. We're planning to spend the night at her place finally, and by the time I'm done with her, all memories of her ex-husband will be gone for good.

Dakota's long red nails skate along my thigh as she leans over to whisper in my ear. "Should we go for some extra credit tonight?"

My brows wrinkle as I pull back to look at her, my vision hanging on the sexy pout of her red lips that she's currently tugging between her teeth. "What did you have in mind?"

She leans in again, and her hot breath tickles my ear as she replies, "Maybe a little more exhibition action. I saw a family restroom with a door that locks, and we could . . ." She nods toward the door, and my cock reacts instantly.

To take her into a bathroom and bend her over the sink sounds fucking divine. I could shove that tight dress up over her ass and mess up her hair while I fist it and drive into her from behind. I could even take my tie off and wrap it around her mouth to help muffle her cries of pleasure, so no one hears the filthy things I do to her. My dirty girl likes a little bondage. And I like the idea of her walking up on that stage with her cunt stretched out from my dick. Her lips raw from my beard. It all sounds really fucking good.

But my upper head has different ideas than my lower. I swallow the knot in my throat, fighting back the erection growing in my slacks as I lean into her. "I don't want this evening to be about that."

"About sex?" She gapes at me like I'm speaking in tongues. "When do you think about anything but?"

My brows furrow as I fight off the sting of that remark. "I want it to be about you and only you."

"Okay, sorry," she murmurs, and a puzzled look casts over her face as she pulls away from me. She shifts in her seat and crosses her legs, her cheeks flush as a wave of insecurity clouds her gorgeous face.

When I lean in to whisper in her ear again, I feel how tense her shoulders are. "To be clear, Ace . . . I want to fuck you."

"Then, what's the problem?" she hisses, her voice thick with hurt and rejection.

My lips thin as I stare deeply into her eyes. "I want tonight to be about more than that."

Her chin quakes as she nods and offers me a weak shrug. "Whatever you say."

Trying to lighten the mood, I squeeze her leg. "I like when you let me be the boss on occasion."

She rolls her eyes, looking sexy and pouty, and I hate that I made her feel anything other than amazing on her big night. But this isn't the time for her to be working through her checklist. This is the time for her to be a boss-ass bitch even if I'm just as surprised as she is that I want that for her.

Not sure where my balls have gone to during this whole arrangement, but I expect they'll be back soon enough.

Dakota

A hush falls over the audience as the emcee of the night takes the stage, speaking about the Boulder Business Bureau and its long-standing commitment to creating the culture in our town. I do my best to listen and live in the moment, but my mind is relentlessly drifting back to Calder.

He passed up sex with me.

Calder Fletcher said no to sex.

I know he said he just didn't want to do it because he wants tonight to be all about me, but isn't giving me an orgasm pretty much all about me? And it's my night, so shouldn't what I want count for something?

A heaviness presses down on me as I consider the fact that he might be getting sick of me. We've been doing this arrangement for a few weeks now, and we don't have much left to check off the list. Maybe he's counting down the days until this is over. He's made it very clear he's not a relationship guy, and we're venturing very close to that territory. And as rejection prickles into my mind, I start to remember the things Randal used to say to me.

Your thigh dimples show in those shorts. I think you should wear jeans instead.

Maybe if you joined my gym, you could get back those abs you had when I met you.

You should talk to my nutritionist. A lot of the stuff you eat is bloating you.

You hate everything in your closet because you don't look like you did the day we got married.

I'm just being honest with you. If your own husband can't point out your flaws, then who can?

Was Calder looking at my stomach just now?

I shake my head and turn to focus on the speaker. It doesn't fucking matter, Dakota. Calder is one of many men that will judge you. What matters is that you don't give a fuck what they think. You're here to get an award for your business tonight, so just focus on that.

A deafening round of applause erupts, and Cozy reaches over to nudge me, clapping and smiling. "Get up there, girl!"

My blood pressure skyrockets when I realize I missed them calling my name. On wobbly legs, I stand, smoothing down my dress and fighting to hold my head up high as my mind spins with a million different thoughts. As I make my way across the stage, I look out at the audience all clapping for me. For what I've done. What have I done?

A glass statue is placed in my hand, and I look at it, frowning at the words etched into it. *For Excellence in Business* stands out the most. The emcee gestures to the microphone, and suddenly, the speech I had prepared evaporates from my mind. Guess I'll be speaking from the heart tonight.

"Thank you so much," I say, and everyone sits down, quieting around the room for me to continue. I pause to look at the object in my hand once more and can't stop the laughter rising in my throat. "It feels so weird to get a trophy as a grown-up."

The audience chuckles, and I bite my lip, shocked that I just said that out loud.

"My business isn't rocket science." I swallow the knot in my throat before I continue. "I literally called it The T-shirt Shop because when I filled out the grant application for the building, I was a senior in college and cared more about afterparties than what I was going to do after college."

More laughing from the crowd, and my eyes find Cozy and

Trista and Kate. I glean strength from those powerful women I'm lucky to call friends and force myself to continue.

"But somehow, the Boulder Business Bureau awarded me with that grant, taking a huge chance on me, and somehow, miraculously, I've managed to stay in business for over ten years now."

Someone in the audience whoops, and I smile when I see it was Kate.

"I don't write best-selling novels or build houses or fix people's cars or open up rescue centers for abandoned wildlife. I just . . . sell cute T-shirts that I hope people feel good in."

My eyes land on Cozy, and she's grinning so big it makes my chest ache with happiness.

"It's important to feel good . . . about yourself. *Confidence* is such a big word that is tossed around like you either have it or you don't. But I think we'd all be lying to ourselves if we said we felt confident in every part of our lives . . . of our businesses. Outside influences are constantly trying to tear us down. Things that aren't in our control. It's a tough world out there, and no one is short of opinions."

My voice trembles at the end of that sentence, and I clear my throat, feeling my hands grow slick with sweat as I clutch the glass award.

"But maybe insecurity can be a strength too. Maybe not feeling confident in yourself is what keeps you hungry. It keeps you evolving and changing and trying new things. Self-doubt encourages self-reflection, and when you really start to look at yourself, maybe you see something that can push you in a new and exciting direction . . . like tie-dye classes."

Light chuckles roll through the crowd, and my mind flashes to the countless groups I've had cycle in and out of my store. It's a pain-in-the-ass mess, but it makes me a part of this community that I love so much.

"In a lot of ways, I'd say it was my lack of confidence that got me here. The mistakes I made along the way helped me find where I was meant to be.

"But I'll tell you this. If you can surround yourself with good, kind people, whether that's colleagues, employees, friends, or family . . . people who want to raise you up instead of drag you down . . ." I take a moment, a deep breath, and my eyes lock with Calder as I state the last part ". . . you can feel safe in your insecurities because there will always be someone there to call you out on your shit. Thank you."

Chapter 35

Calder

"Great speech, baby," I say when I finally have Dakota alone in my truck. She was swarmed by people after the presentation was complete, including my family and her friends, and I've been itching to tell her how much her words moved me.

"Thanks." She offers me a wobbly smile that has me frowning back at her.

"I mean it. That speech . . . it was so inspiring. Did you just come up with that on the spot?"

She nods, not giving me much to work with.

"Well, it was fucking good and funny. Just the perfect mix of heartfelt and so very you. You should feel so proud."

"Yeah, I am." She licks her lips and wrings her hands on her lap, looking out the window and avoiding my eyes.

"And you looked so fucking beautiful up there."

"Did I?" Her head snaps around, and she hits me with a curious look.

"Yes, I told you multiple times. Did you not hear me?"

I laugh, and she tilts her head, eyeing me with a look of contempt. "Oh, I heard you. Just still a little confused on why you didn't take me up on my offer."

My hands tighten around the steering wheel as I release a groan of frustration. "I knew you were in your head about that."

"I'm not in my head," she snaps, her shoulders rising with tension. "I'm just saying for a guy who loves sex so much, why would you pass up something like that?"

"I told you it was because I wanted the night to be about you."

"Yeah, thanks for that." She folds her arms over her chest. "You know what? If you just want to drop me at my house and go home, I'm good with that. It's been a long night, and we could both use some sleep before we go to the sex club tomorrow."

"You want me to drop you off?"

She nods, her eyes facing straight ahead. "Yeah, we can just forget about that last checklist item. I can still revise the PowerPoint any time I like, right?" She reaches into her clutch and pulls out her phone like she's actually going to edit the file right now.

My jaw clenches at the flippant tone in her voice. Neither of us have brought up the PowerPoint in days. Last week we made a loose plan for the sex club on Saturday night, but I guess I thought maybe things were changing. She still wants to go? Dammit, this woman always keeps me on my toes.

And she's not dumb. She knows what she's doing. She's backing me into a corner. Forcing me to call this what it is: more than sex.

But a pressure builds in my chest every time I think of that. Flashbacks hammer into me of Robyn and her spiderweb of lies and deceit and how she fucked with me and my brothers. I don't want to go through that pain again. It's not worth it. I'm not worth it either. I'll break Dakota's heart and be just as bad as her shitty ex, and Dakota will break mine and be just as bad as my shitty ex. Who needs that fucking trauma in their life?

For what? For some good sex? Why bother? I know what's out there. I could reactivate my fucked-up dating apps and find a million other girls that are ten times easier than the grumpy blonde sitting next to me. We could end this right here, right now, and I could have someone else in my bed by tomorrow night.

A knot forms in my throat over that thought. I've gotten too used to Dakota's wants, Dakota's needs, her noises, her curves. Her softness. Her scent on my sheets. I know exactly where to touch her to get her revved up, and I like that I know that about her. And she has absolutely learned what sets me off. Who would have thought I'd enjoy being flogged? I'd have never let a hookup try that on me. But her? Why the fuck not?

This connection we have? It feels like a secret between the two of us that no one else in this world knows. I could find someone else, possibly, but if it's not Dakota, I know without a shadow of a doubt I would be bored out of my fucking mind.

Dakota Schaefer and her stubborn, nagging, moody ass has ruined me for other women.

"Fuck this shit," I growl and yank the wheel to pull my pickup over on the side of the road, checking the curb with my tires as I do.

"What are you doing?" she exclaims, grabbing onto the handle above the door.

I throw the truck in Park and thrust a finger into her face. "You are such a pain in my ass sometimes."

"The feeling is mutual!" she snaps back.

I unbuckle my seat belt and lean across the console of my car to grab her face with one hand.

"Let me go, Calder."

"No, dammit. Not until you listen to me."

"What?"

I exhale to contain my tension, my hand sliding down to her neck as I hold her possessively, forcing her to hear the words from my lips. "For the past fucking month, I can't think of you without getting hard. But for once in my whole damn life, I cared about more than just sex. I cared about making you feel special. I cared about watching you shine. I cared about my family and friends seeing you in your element because I was proud as fuck of you. So proud I felt smug . . . like . . . look at this chick I get to call mine. Be fucking jealous, universe."

Her brows furrow as she tries to look away, but I clutch her jaw, holding her eyes as her breathing picks up pace.

"But make no mistake, baby," I murmur while pressing my fingers into the back of her neck to angle her face up at me. My thumb lifts and drags down her pouty lower lip, a harsh breath escaping her lungs as I add, "I've wanted to fuck you all night long. On the drive to your house I wanted to fuck you. I wanted to fuck you the moment you stepped out of your house. And I desperately wanted to fuck you when you were on that stage making your big speech. You, Ace. It's all about fucking you, because despite being a pain in my ass, you are all I want."

I pause, releasing her jaw as our eyes hold each other with a million unspoken words.

"If you want me to go home tonight, I will. If you're done with me, that's fine. But if it's up to me, I'd rather you just sit on my face until I leave this great magnificent world because I can think of no better way to go."

Her serious expression morphs into one of irritation as her eyes roll to the roof of my car. "You are so dramatic."

She shoves me away, and the tension in my shoulders instantly lifts as I lean on the console and hit her with my dazzling smirk. "I learned from the best."

She glares at me while fighting back her own smirk that makes my cock hard. "Just drive the truck, Tomcat."

A smug smile spreads across my face as I put the car back in Drive. "You got it, Karen."

Dakota

"Take off your clothes for me," Calder commands, his voice deep and husky in the dim lamplight of my bedroom. "But do it slowly."

My heart flutters in my chest as I turn on my heel and offer my back to him. "Little help here?"

He chuckles, and his breath is heavy as he steps up behind me and slowly drags my zipper down. The cadence of it in this moment is one of the most erotic sounds I've ever heard.

When he's done, he walks around me and sits down on my bed.

He ditched his suit coat and shoes downstairs, and now he's before me in his black slacks and white dress shirt. He slowly loosens the tie around his neck, his legs spread wide as he stares expectantly at me. "Now strip."

I jump slightly, my nerves tingling as I ease my dress down my shoulder. It's a tight, formfitting fabric, but luckily it has stretch, and I manage to wiggle it down over my hips. I kick out of it and stand in a pair of black panties, a black strapless bra, and my heels before this inky mountain man.

"Such a good fucking girl." He lets out a deep, audible noise while his eyes score over my entire body and cause heat to flood into my core. He stands up and walks toward me, reaching out to brush his fingertips along my belly as he circles me. Goose bumps follow in his wake and my entire body vibrates toward a needy ache right between my legs which is all his damn fault after those heated words in his truck.

I can't think of you without getting hard.

Make no mistake, baby. I've wanted to fuck you all night long.

You are all I want.

Those words alone are the best aphrodisiac. Not to mention the way he held my neck—as if he couldn't help but control me.

I could melt into the floor just thinking about it.

His breath is hot in my ear when he whispers, "Do you think you're beautiful?"

I twitch at that question. I know what my answer should be. It should be a resounding *yes*. I just gave an acceptance speech about confidence. And after what Calder just said to me in his truck, the word *yes* should tumble out of my lips without pause.

Yet, the word doesn't come.

Calder growls as he steps up behind me, his fully clothed body brushing against my sensitive flesh. "Do you feel this?" he asks, pressing his groin into my back.

The hard ridge of his cock digs into me, and I gasp as the yearning shoots straight to my core.

"You do this to me. No one else." He grabs my hand and pulls it behind me to grip his shaft. My fingers squeeze his hard length as I rub him over his pants, my body trembling with need.

I want more. I want skin on skin, I want him inside of me, wrapped around me, everything.

"I'm not going to lick your beautiful pussy until you tell me you're beautiful."

I wonder why I'm fighting to answer this so much. Yes. It's just a word. A short word that I believe.

I do think I'm beautiful.

But a realization dawns on me . . . one I've never had before.

"I don't have to tell you I'm beautiful," I croak, my voice thick with arousal.

Calder stops in front of me and stares intently back at me.

I bite my lip and narrow my eyes at him. "I don't care what you think."

The corner of his mouth twitches, but he remains silent as I press my hand to his chest and walk him back toward the bed. He flops down, bouncing on the soft mattress as he looks up at me.

"Whether I'm beautiful or not is irrelevant." I reach back and unclasp my bra, the cool air causing my nipples to pucker in front of his face as I drop the fabric to the ground. He glances at my nipples, but his eyes snap back up to me, a desperate look on his face that causes my insides to clench.

"My body and my beauty will change over time." I grip the band of my panties and push them down to my ankles, stepping out of them with my strappy heels still on. I prop one foot on Calder's leg, my eyes glancing to the strap. He immediately moves his hand to the buckle, undoing it with deft precision before tossing it to the floor.

"But my worth will never change." I lift my other heel up, and Calder quickly undoes that strap as well, pressing a soft kiss to the top of my foot before I lower it to the ground.

I stand ten toes down and completely naked, reaching my hand

out and slicing my fingers through Calder's hair, feeling more powerful than I have in my entire life. "The time for me to let a man
have any control over what I feel in the bedroom or out is over."

His eyes are dark pools of desire as he stares up at me, a hint of
a smile teasing his lips. "Then, what do you want from me, baby?"

I quirk one brow up and bend so I'm eye level with him. "I
want you to lie back so I can ride your face and give you the death
you so long for."

Fire sparks in his eyes as I push him back, and he pulls me with
him onto the bed. I slowly crawl over his fully clothed body letting my breasts rub against him. He latches onto my right breast
circling his tongue over the tight bud, sending sparks straight to
my needy center.

"Fuck, I love when you do that," I whisper-moan as he sucks
hard letting my nipple go with a slight nip of his teeth. His rough
hands slide down to my ass encouraging me to keep moving
upward.

"I love the sounds you make when I do it." He growls and it
sounds primal and animalistic as I move to straddle his face. I hover
over him, pausing to glance down at him and make sure he still
really wants me to do this.

I've never actually sat on a man's face before. Randal was never
into it. But the way Calder looks at me is intoxicating.

He lifts his head off the bed and swipes his tongue across my
slit, causing me to gasp out and shudder at the contact.

"So wet for me." His deep voice vibrates off my tender skin as
his fingers dig into my ass, encouraging me to rock forward. He
doesn't hesitate, answering with another hard lick. "God, I love
how you taste."

A flush rushes through my face at his illicit words, and with a
shaky breath I lower myself onto his mouth, circling my hips gently
over him. With a huff of irritation, he yanks me down, forcing me
to brace myself on the headboard until all of my weight is seated
firmly on his face.

"Fuck." I cry as white blinding pleasure erupts through me with that single movement. I throw my head back and moan as the friction of his facial hair sends small tendrils of electricity all over my skin. His head squirms beneath me as his tongue laves my clit, making me shudder with each swipe, causing me to grind my pussy onto his face.

My breasts sway as I thrust against him over and over, losing total control as I fuck his mouth. I hear a muffled grunt and gasp when I realize I could be hurting him and pull back quickly to give him a breath.

"Don't you dare fucking stop," Calder snarls, his eyes flashing up at me with dark pools of passion. He pulls me back down onto him murmuring against my flesh, "Take what you need from me. Use me. Lose yourself and let go. Come all over my face, baby."

His groan vibrates inside me as I press onto him, and he hardens his tongue to thrust deeper as his nose grinds onto my clit, making me scream and white-knuckle the headboard.

The sharp tightening feeling building in me has me swiveling my hips faster and faster, chasing the impending orgasm that's coming so fast and yet not fast enough. He gasps for air quick and yanks me down again so fast my mind barely registers what he did. His grip is punishing as he nips at my clit before his tongue delves back into me. I can hear him lapping at my wet core, the sound echoing off the walls along with my moans.

I lose my breath completely when I feel a digit pressing against my puckered asshole. I grip a fistful of his hair, not sure if I want to push him away or actually kill him by pulling him unbelievably closer to me. The coiling tension building inside me is faster than I can wrap my mind around, has my hips thrusting forward harder onto his mouth and back into the finger that presses into my untouched hole as I gasp for air between each moan—till an eruption of ecstasy bursts through me like a tidal wave I can feel all the way down to my toes.

Slowly I come back to my senses and rise on shaky knees as I loosen my grip on his hair, not realizing how hard I had been pulling on it as my numb fingers tingle with awakening. I let out a small laugh looking to see if I pulled any strands out before I ruffle it and unceremoniously flop off him. I inhale a deep breath, my entire body weak and jellylike as small tremors still wrack my system.

I look over and see Calder staring at me, wet-faced, smug, and foolishly happy. He rolls over to face me, his eyes blazing with lust as he runs his hand over my belly, his gentle touch speaking louder than his words ever could.

I reach down and hold his hand to my stomach as emotion swells in my chest. This feeling coursing through me isn't just orgasm aftershocks. It's my final awakening. It's the realization of what I've been missing my whole life. Missing the confidence to be with someone who trusts me as much as I trust him. Missing the ability to fight for what I know I deserve. This feeling is worth more than I ever imagined, and it's worth never giving up on.

And even though I know I found this confidence in myself . . . I have this grinning bearded bad boy beside me to thank for helping me rediscover the girl I thought I'd lost forever.

God, I love being a woman.

Chapter 36

Calder

I stand in the shower at Dakota's house the next morning, my head hanging low as I brace myself on the tile wall. I placed these tiles myself one at a time, piece by piece. I had hired a subcontractor to do it, but the guy left after one day with Dakota, so I was stuck doing the work with her nagging over my shoulder.

Only she wasn't nagging. She was just being herself. Caring about something so much she pushed herself into the middle of it, just trying to make everything the best it could be.

Like my fucking furniture. She no more than snapped her fingers, and suddenly, I have a tab on her website, and I've made four thousand dollars on shit that was just collecting dust in my shop. Not to mention the other opportunity I'm still mulling over. She really is a freak of nature how she manages to get so much done.

And last night, in her bedroom . . . I've never been more turned on in my life. She didn't tell me she thought she was beautiful. She showed me, in ways I didn't expect. She's magnificent.

This enemies-with-benefits agreement and sex conquest PowerPoint checklist were just the catalysts to helping her heal from the bullshit Randal put her through. And I got a front row seat for all of it. She's going to be unstoppable now.

"Don't tell me you're jerking off in the shower again like you did in Mexico," Dakota's voice reverberates off the tile walls as she opens the glass door and walks into the steamy space with me. Her hair is a fucking disaster, and her face looks young and innocent since she washed off all her makeup last night after I fucked her for over an hour.

I wanted it to last all night. I wanted to break our record and give her more than three orgasms. But when you have a woman like Dakota in your bed, who rides your face like a champion bull rider, you hold on for dear life and last as long as you can.

"No need to jerk off when I have the real thing right here." I move to her, capturing her mouth with mine as I tug her bottom lip with my teeth. I pull her under the spray of water, pressing her up against the cool tile. She gasps into my lips, and I growl when I feel her nipples pebble against my chest.

She breaks away, breathless and invigorated, just like my cock bobbing in between us, needy for another release. God, will I ever get enough of this girl?

"Maybe I can help you with your little problem," she says as she looks down at my hard-on with a wicked glint to her eye. Her lips curl into an O as she drops her chin and spits right on my dick.

I grunt and splay my hand against the tile as she wraps her fingers tightly around me, spreading the slickness of her saliva over my length, mixing it with the shower water and causing a dizzying friction between the two moistures.

She strokes me into a state of ecstasy, and I'm ashamed at how easy it is for me to come all over her stomach. She slides my white pearly seed around her belly and smiles up at me, drunk with arousal.

I make a move to drop to my knees to return the favor, but she stops me in my tracks. "I don't have time."

"There's always time for oral, baby," I murmur against her breasts.

"No . . . I have to open the shop."

I frown. "You're working today?"

"Just for a couple hours this morning until my other staff member can release me."

I grumble as I press into her, sliding our wet bodies together.

She feels so fucking good against my skin. "If I knew that, then we would have started with you."

"But you're quicker than me," she moans as my cock catches her moist center.

"That's because you spit on it," I deadpan, zero shame in my voice. "Fucking hell, woman. That's two attempted murders you have on me now. One when you rode my face last night, and now this."

She giggles and reaches for the shampoo, and I stop her, squirting it into my hand and rubbing it into her hair. If she won't let me give her an orgasm, I can at least do this.

"So what time do you want to head over tonight?" she asks, tipping her head back to rinse the bubbles out of her hair.

"Tonight?" I glance down at her.

"Yeah, what time do you think we should go to Lexon? Is there a good time people go? I'm so curious to see if I could be into voyeurism. I never really gave it a try the first time I was there. And I haven't watched a lot of porn, so I don't know if this will be my thing or not. It could be!"

My heart sinks as I realize she's still fully planning to go to the sex club to check this box off her fucking list. I know I didn't explicitly say that I want her beyond this PowerPoint bullshit last night, but I thought I showed her. I thought my declaration in the truck was obvious. Wasn't it?

Insecurity niggles at my gut, and I hear myself reply, "I don't know. I guess. Probably ten?"

Her eyes move away from mine quickly as she reaches for the conditioner and does that one herself. "Works for me."

"Does it?" I ask, a sour mood overwhelming me.

"Yeah. Why wouldn't it?" She lifts her chin, and her eyes search mine for a long, awkward moment, like she's waiting for me to say something.

Normally, I don't hold back with this woman, and I'm pretty sure she doesn't hold back with me. It's why we fight just as much as we fuck. Everything is always on the table. But something is stopping me from telling her I don't want to go tonight. And it will be a cold day in hell before I let her go back to that place on her own.

So I guess we're doing this. We're going back to the sex club, and we're going to check that final box on her list.

And I'm going to try not to lose my fucking mind while we're there.

Chapter 37

Dakota

I didn't have to open the store today. I just needed to get out of my house with Calder. I didn't want to cuddle him in my bed or make breakfast. I didn't want to notice how good he looked standing in my living room or have him watch me do my hair and makeup or bring me up a cup of coffee.

The shower was bad enough. Doing anything more domestic would freak me out because I am in way over my head, and the fact that we're headed back to the sex club tonight has me freaking the fuck out.

I park outside of my store and open my phone, needing to talk this out with someone before I explode. I can't discuss it with Cozy or Trista because they would both encourage me to be open with Calder and tell him how I'm feeling. That's how it worked out with their Fletcher men.

But Max and Wyatt are so different from Calder. Max was married once before, so obviously open to love, and Wyatt was ready for a family so much that he was willing to hire a surrogate. They both clearly have different end goals in life than Calder—the perpetual, self-proclaimed playboy.

I need to confide in someone who doesn't know both parties and who is unequivocally Team Dakota.

"Hey, girl, hey!" Tatianna's voice peals into the phone. "Good morning to you."

"I'm having tons of casual sex with Calder Fletcher and we're checking kinky experiences off a PowerPoint presentation that he put together after I asked him to be my sex club wingman and he told me I wasn't ready for it and tonight we're supposed to go back to the sex club for the first time after weeks of mind-blowing, incredible sex with him and I am freaking the fuck out."

I exhale heavily and hear nothing on the other line. "Tot? Tot, are you there?" I pull my phone away and see the call is still connected so I put it back to my ear. "Tatianna?"

"Tatianna has passed away, and you are now speaking to her celestial spirit."

I groan and scrub my hand over my face. "Be fucking for real, please."

"I am!" she squeals. "I just poured creamer into my coffee, and you come at me with that? Of course I died and went to heaven. What the hell is going on up in those mountains?"

"A lot of sex. Like a lot a lot. Like I'm insatiable, Tot. I hardly recognize myself anymore. I used to think good sex was only for smutty romance novels. It's not. It exists out there for real."

"Don't tell me that," she tuts, and I hear her set her coffee down. "I cannot believe that these fictional men can be real. I'm delulu enough without that sick fantasy."

"I know, it's upsetting to me too."

She releases a long sigh that I feel in my bones. "So what is the problem, exactly?"

I shake my head, my chin trembling instantly as I let reality settle in. "I don't want to be done with Calder."

She pauses for a moment, and her tone is serious and sincere when she asks, "Has he given you any indication he doesn't want to be done either?"

"Not really, not fully."

She harrumphs into the line, and my chest tightens with anxiety. "I don't think you're going to like what I'm about to say, but Dakota . . . when a man tells you what he is, believe him."

I close my eyes and feel the burn of two hot tears sliding down my face. "I know."

"Randal told you what he was, and you didn't believe him, and look how that turned out."

"I know," I croak again, and press my forehead to my steering wheel. "I hate that I'm doing the same damn thing I did before. My God, it's like I learned nothing from a divorce that cost me half a million dollars."

"You did learn something," she says, and my head pops up. "You phoned a friend. You didn't phone any friends when you were in your Randal era. You dove into that mess without a second thought."

I nod woodenly, willing myself to really listen to what she's saying. I can't let myself believe a man is anything other than what he's shown me he is. Randal showed me what he was on day one, and I ignored the red flags. I have to refocus on what my initial goals were with this arrangement with Calder . . . no matter how much it hurts me.

"So, what do I do about tonight, then?" Chills crawl over my skin because there is no part of me that still wants to go, especially when it most likely means it will be my last night with Calder.

"You go to that club with him, and you act totally good. You let him spank you in front of strangers or whatever nasty shit your kinky ass is into. Be totally chill, like you've been training for this like the motherfucking Olympics, okay?"

I garble out a laugh. "I kind of have. Seriously, my vagina is probably never going to look the same."

"That's disgusting and appealing all at the same time."

"Right?"

Chapter 38

POKER FACE

Dakota

"I feel like a different person here tonight," I say proudly as I perch on a barstool at Lexon Club with a cosmo in my hand.

Calder nods, sipping his water in brooding silence. It's odd that he didn't order a beer, but he's been weird all night. Quiet and withdrawn. So different from last night.

I continue talking in hopes that his mood will shift, doing my best to channel Tatianna's advice. If this is the end of Calder and me, I want to walk away with my head held high.

"Maybe your PowerPoint challenge could be a real thing for people looking to boost their confidence. You could market it to the divorcée crowd. That's a huge audience, I'm sure. You could publish it as a book. Like the new age *Kama Sutra*. Kate could teach you anything you need to know about self-publishing so you wouldn't even have to find an agent or anything. Are you any good at writing?"

Calder looks at me with the same surly pout he's had since he picked me up an hour ago.

"What is your problem?" I snap, feeling exasperated by his mood. "This is no fun if you're just going to be grumpy all night."

A figure appears out of the corner of my eye, and I look over to see a man in a black suit standing right beside me. He smiles and says, "Hey, baby girl," and I'm jostled on my stool when Calder leans across me and thrusts a finger in the man's face.

"Keep fucking walking, pal," he growls, his voice deep and threatening.

The man's head jerks back. "What's your problem?"

"Right now, it's just you." Calder's eyes are menacing slits as he stands up, towering over the guy in all his big mountain man glory. The man shuffles away, chancing a glance back at us. Probably to make sure Calder isn't chasing him.

My brows lift. "Well, okay then."

"This is stupid," Calder grumbles, pinching the bridge of his nose as he drops back down onto his stool.

"This was on the PowerPoint." I grab my glass to take another drink, trying to hide the tremble in my hand. "It's our last challenge, so why don't we just get to it? You're not even drinking, so why are we sitting down here? Let's go upstairs and find a room to watch some action."

After a moment, Calder stands up, lacing his fingers through mine in a way that feels so affectionate, it makes my stomach hurt. He's so good at this, and he doesn't even know it. He runs from commitment because of what that Robyn girl did to him, but that relationship wasn't even real. She was a head case. If he tried it with someone who had more to offer him, maybe caring about someone wouldn't be so scary.

Why did I just consider myself for that role? Is that what I want? Do I want a longer-term situation with Calder Fletcher?

Something tells me that if I do, I'm about to get my heart completely broken.

I hate that he's the one who says no to relationships because that puts all the power in his hands. My cards are out there on the table. He knows what I'm looking for. Right?

He leads us up the stairs to the various playrooms with his hand pressed against the small of my back. I glance around at the other patrons and can't help but notice all their eyes on Calder and the urge I have to thrust my own finger in their faces.

I'm doing my best to act like I'm cool with what we're doing here tonight and that we are still very much casual, but my stomach is in knots. What will happen with us after we leave here? Will he go back to hating me?

I hold my chin up high and try to muster up the confidence Tatianna told me to show. It's not a lie either. In the past few weeks I've grown through this arrangement. And hell, if I can survive seven years with Randal, I can survive a few weeks with Calder. I'm strong enough for this.

We stop at the theater room, and it's swarmed with another large group session. I glance around, wondering if Mr. Scat Man is back, but thankfully I don't see any sign of him. To think I was just strolling through there over a month ago without a care in the world is wild.

I was clearly not in a good headspace to be here weeks ago. It was reckless to just dive into this community after browsing a few Reddit threads. Maybe it was good Calder found me when he did, or who knows what would have happened?

And interestingly enough, as I look around here right now, I don't feel myself wanting anything in particular. My original hope with going to sex clubs was to have new experiences and explore various kinks. Now that I've had some time with Calder, I feel like my cup is full. My goals have changed. I think I'm ready to look for love again.

"See anything you like?" Calder murmurs, leaning against the glass window with his arms crossed. He looks completely bored staring at the multiple people going at it down below.

My face scrunches up as I scrutinize everyone in various throes of passion. "You know, when I originally came here, I was search-ing for something. A kink that would just click in my mind and tell me *Yep, this is what you've been missing. This is why you were boring in bed and didn't have any confidence. You never found your kink.* But I feel like after everything . . . I'm just good."

"You're good?" Calder asks, his brows furrowed intently.

I nod and continue peering down at everyone. "Yeah, there's nothing here that I'm interested in exploring anymore. What about you?"

"What about me?" Calder blinks, his expression unreadable.

"Well, is there a kink you still haven't discovered that you want to find?"

His Adam's apple slides down his throat as he watches me with a severe look in his eyes that I cannot understand.

"Let's keep walking and look around, then. Maybe we'll find it." My legs are shaking as I grab his arm and pull him away, my stomach churning over how I'll feel if he finds whatever he's looking for. Because I know that whatever he's looking for is not me.

He follows me, albeit a bit begrudgingly, and I glance in the rooms we pass by, nothing really drawing my attention until my eyes snag on a couple in a private room. Last time I was here, this glass was black so you couldn't see inside. It must be a room where you can either choose to have the window open or not. Clearly this couple wants to put on a show.

And what a show it is.

A middle aged–looking woman with an incredible, curvy body is strapped over some type of bench, not horribly dissimilar to the sawhorse in Calder's workshop, but maybe with a bit more padding. She's naked and tied down by her hands and feet, and a man with a head of thick silver hair is wielding a leather flogger.

Calder releases my hand to reach over and twist a nob, and suddenly the sounds from the room are being played through a small speaker next to the window.

"You were a bad, bad girl, Lacey," the man bites out, his voice thick with arousal as his erection strains in his pants. "And you know I hate to have to punish you. But you make me do this."

My insides squirm as I hear the woman apologize, her voice breathy and hoarse. The woman cries out and gasps as he rears back and strikes her bottom with the leather flap. He commands her to count with him, and their voices are heady as he works her over with harsh, punishing slaps. Over and over and over again. Her ass cheeks are bright red, and her face full of lust and longing.

I feel myself moving closer to the window, pressing my hand

against the cool glass as desire pools in my belly. The man pauses his assault on her and swipes between her folds, rubbing his two fingers together before putting them into his mouth and sucking them clean.

A moan escapes my lips, and I clap my hand over my mouth, mortified at how publicly turned on I am watching these two pleasure each other. And make no mistake, the woman is finding pleasure in what this man is doing to her. Maybe I found my kink after all.

A large hand grips my elbow and tugs, and I turn around to find Calder staring at me with a heated look in his eyes that sends shock waves through my stomach. His breath comes faster than it should for us just standing there, and he nods toward a hallway behind us.

My legs tremble as moisture collects in my panties while we walk quickly down the darkened hall that looks familiar. When Calder opens the door at the end, it's then that I realize we're back in the same closet he dragged me into the first time we were here.

His lips are on me before I can catch my breath, his erection digging into my belly as his hands grope all over me. My hair, my back, my ass, my breasts. He can't move fast enough.

"Tell me that turned you on, Ace," he murmurs against my lips, his tongue thrusting into me as his hands slide up my skirt.

"Yes," I pant, my body aching for release.

"I wasn't even watching them," he says against my neck, his lips kissing their way across my collarbone, his beard scratching my skin and turning everything inside of me to fire. "I was watching you. God, you are so sexy."

I moan loudly, my hands slicing into Calder's hair and gripping firmly at the roots. He slips his hands under my legs, hoisting me up and pressing harshly into my center. We're both still fully clothed so there's no penetration, but the grinding action between us is sending me through the roof.

"Let's get out of here," Calder says, biting the lobe of my ear. "I want to take you home and fuck your brains out. I want to fuck you to sleep. I want to fuck you until you can't take anymore."

"Do it now," I beg, my body aching for release, my breasts heavy inside my bra.

I feel Calder's head shaking against me. "Not here."

"Why?"

"Because."

"Why?" I cry out again.

"Because I said so!" he barks, pulling away from me, anger replacing the desire on his face. "Dammit, Dakota. I don't want you here."

Humiliation shudders down all around me as I drop my legs from his body and press my hand to the wall, struggling to catch my balance. He moves toward me, and I hold my hand up, stopping him in his tracks.

"Fuck, what now?" he snaps, his tone visceral. "What did I do now?"

My throat aches with an emotional reaction that I am trying really hard to hide. "I'm just really getting tired of you rejecting me. Twice in two days is pretty telling."

"Telling of what?" he asks, his voice gruff.

"That you're ready to be done with me. With this. With our little arrangement." My eyes find his as I hold my chin up high, refusing to crumble in front of him.

"Is that what you think?" he huffs out, his face taut with stress. "Jesus, Dakota, for a smart girl, you can really be fucking clueless, you know that?"

"What the hell does that mean?" I cry, my head spinning with lust and anger and pain all at once. So much it hurts. "What is clueless about you saying you don't want me? What could I possibly not understand?"

"I don't want you here," he roars, thrusting a hand through his hair. "Not here. Not like this. I want you in my bed, in your bed, in a place where I can tell you . . ."

"Tell me what?" My heart feels like it's going to explode out of my chest. "Tell me that we're done? That you've had your fun and now it's peace out?"

My body trembles with the reality I just laid out on the table. I've been holding so much back from Calder. From myself. I want him to want to keep me. There are so many feelings confusing me, and I think . . . I think I want more with him. A future. But I don't know what he feels. I can see now that I've been holding back because I can't fully tell if he's really in this with me or if I'm just another one of his conquests. A pet project that will be just another notch on his belt because Calder Fletcher doesn't take anything seriously. Not his work, not his art, not his relationships. Why would I be any different?

He presses his lips together and shakes his head, and it's like we're playing a game of chicken. It's the Mexican palapa all over again. Neither of us would give up the room because we refused to let the other one win. No one will admit their true feelings in this moment because no one wants to be the loser.

Well, he can win this time.

This closet is all his.

Chapter 39

Calder

I stare slack-jawed at Dakota's back as she storms out of the small room, leaving me standing here with a raging boner and a fucking mess of anxiety swirling all around me. That anxiety manifests as a heaviness in my chest when I finally realize something.

My kink is Dakota Schaefer.

I drop my head into my hands, my mind reeling with that new bit of information that I probably should have figured out fucking days, hell maybe weeks, ago. And she's not just my kink.

I'm in love with her.

Holy fuck, I'm in love with her. *Holy fucking fuck.*

All these years of looking for excitement, for a thrill, for new experiences to mask the old, are because I wasn't with this person.

She is my person.

My feet feel like they're stuck in mud as I struggle to chase after her, hating the fact that she's walking this place alone, hating that she's here at all. I've been a miserable asshole since we arrived because I can't handle everyone looking at her like she's up for grabs. She's not.

She's mine.

And just as soon as I find her, I'm going to tell her that once and for all and stop dancing around the bullshit. She feels it too. She has to. There's no way I got here on my own. There's no way she looked at me the way she did last night and didn't feel it. Right?

Finding my footing, I jog through the hallway and make my way down the long staircase, breathing a sigh of relief when I spot

Dakota's blond hair. Good, she's still here. She didn't jump in a cab and leave me with my heart on my sleeve and my dick in my hand.

My dick, however, deflates instantly when I see the person standing next to her. He has a man bun and a lame-ass fucking mustache, and he goes by the name of *Randal*.

Dakota's eyes find mine, looking cornered and desperate as I beeline straight for her, protectiveness vibrating through my entire body. Randal must feel my approach because he turns around, and his eyes go wide when he spots me.

"What is this, a Boulder theme night?" Randal laughs as I move over and stand next to Dakota, putting my shoulder slightly in front of her to create some space between her and this fuck-wit.

Randal's face morphs from surprise to realization as he points between me and Dakota. "Wait, are you two here together?"

Dakota's hand sneaks up, lacing her fingers with mine, and that's all the answer Randal needs as he barks out a riotous laugh. "Oh my gosh, I did not see that one coming."

"There is nothing to see." My jaw cracks as I clench my teeth, my muscles tightening all over my body. "Why don't you just go about your business and leave us alone."

"No, no, this all makes more sense now." Randle steeples his fingers in front of him, a positively tickled expression all over his face. "I thought when I saw Dee here by herself, she was finally trying to get her freak on at last. But I should have known it took a guy like *you* to break her out of her shell."

Randal pokes me in the chest, and I swing my hand out, swatting him away. "Don't touch me, Randal."

He laughs again and turns his beady eyes back to Dakota. "This is kind of serendipitous, isn't it?"

"What is?" Dakota asks, and I hate the emotion I hear in her voice. I don't know if I put it there or Randal, but I hate it with every bone in my body.

He turns a grotesque sneer from me to Dakota. "Well, you never liked him just like you never liked yourself, so you really are probably perfect for him."

In one breath, I eliminate all space between us, so we're nose to chin as I tower over his five foot ten height. Dakota grabs my arm, trying to hold me back as I pitch my voice to be casual and controlled. "Have you ever been stabbed, Randal? Cuz I'd like to show you what that's like."

"Oh, you don't want to just give me a black eye again?" Randal holds his hand up, and I feel the blood in my veins run cold. "We've upgraded to weapons now?"

Silence descends over us as I internally cringe at what he just revealed.

Dakota's voice is soft as she asks, "*Again?* What does he mean?"

Randal moves his attention to the woman beside me as he tsks. "You let a guy take you to a sex club, you should probably know him a bit better, don't you think, Dee?"

"What is he talking about, Calder?" Dakota snaps, yanking me around to look at her. She blinks back tears and shakes her head as the puzzle pieces begin clicking together. "It was you who gave him the black eye he had at our wedding, wasn't it?"

I drop my head in surrender.

"But why?"

I step closer to her, my heart racing as I try to grab her hands, but she yanks them away. "I was going to tell you the day I saw you in your wedding dress. But you looked so beautiful and so happy. And I just couldn't bring myself to hurt you like that."

Her eyes swim with emotion as she frowns up at me, still not understanding. "But what were you going to tell me?"

"Yeah, Calder . . . what were you going to tell her?" Randal's voice is like nails on a chalkboard, and I clench my fists fighting the urge to knock him out.

"Randal, you need to back the fuck up, or I swear to God I will end you." I turn back to Dakota, guilt slicing through every part of my body as I say the words that I've wanted to say for the past month. "I saw Randal coming out of a bathroom with a woman at Pearl Street Pub two weeks before your wedding."

She inhales sharply and her eyes move to Randal, but I continue. "I wanted to tell you to call off the wedding, but I didn't think I had the right, so I decided to fix the problem directly."

"How?" she snaps, her voice cracking at the end as her eyes swerve back to me. "How did you fix my problem?"

I swallow the knot in my throat. "I was working in your bathroom later that week when Randal was moving his stuff in. He walked past me to put stuff in the closet, so I took the opportunity to call him out on his shit. I told him if he ever fucked around on you, I'd kill him. It got physical."

Her eyes widen, and her lips twitch as she processes everything I've just said.

"You fucking sucker punched me," Randal bellows, crossing his arms over his chest. "And with no proof that I actually cheated. You are certifiable."

"I didn't know we damaged a pipe during the scuffle," I say, hating the look of betrayal written all over Dakota's face. "I can't believe that's something I would have missed, but I know back then I wasn't the best at details."

Dakota's hands run through her hair, her eyes swimming with so much emotion, she looks like she's going to be sick. "You knew he cheated on me and didn't tell me?"

"I didn't have any proof, but it looked bad." I shrug, having no good defense for my actions.

Her eyes move from me to Randal, her jaw tight with rage as she asks, "So did you cheat? We're divorced now, so it really doesn't matter, but I have to know now once and for all. I've always wondered."

My chest feels like it's caving in, because I hate that she wants to know the answer to this question. It wounds me on some level, and I don't fully even understand why.

Randal's expression is smug as he slides his hands into his pockets like this is just a casual Saturday night conversation. "I never cheated, but . . ."

"But what?" Dakota asks, hanging on his every word.

He cuts his eyes to me, and an evil smirk plays on his lips. "I did bust the pipe in the bathroom. I was pissed and took a wrench to it after Calder had left. When it started gushing, I got the hell out of there and let him take the fall. He fucking deserved it, and I would do it again—"

Randal's body thumps to the ground as I pull my fist back and shake it out, the sting of hitting his cheekbone burning up my fucking wrist.

"If I'm going to be accused of sucker punching someone, I'd better make it true," I grumble, anger radiating through my entire body. Not because he let me take the fall, but because he so callously ruined something that was important to Dakota. She was the woman he was going to marry, and he sabotaged her house with no remorse? What kind of twisted fuck does something like that?

Randal howls, rolling onto his back and clutching his face. "You goddamn animal!"

I look up to see Dakota running out of the club just as two security guards come barreling toward me.

"You're done, Fletcher," one thunders in my ear. "You're banned for life."

"Fine by me." I hold my hands up, allowing them to yank my arms back behind me as they manhandle me in the same direction as Dakota. I wouldn't give a fuck if I never came back to this place again. Especially if a guy like Randal is allowed to darken its doorstep.

They ram me out the door, slamming it closed behind me. I rub my shoulder where the glass framing hit, and the silence of the outside feels ominous. The sound of a garbled cry turns my head, and I find Dakota leaning against the side of the building, her face in her hands and her shoulders shaking.

I want to sucker punch myself now.

My feet crunch on the concrete as I move to embrace her. "Don't cry, baby."

"Don't *baby* me!" she screams, her face blotchy with tears as she yanks away from my hands like I burned her. "Don't touch me. Don't even look at me!"

"Dakota, please calm down."

"How can I calm down?" she cries, breaking my heart. "I just found out my ex-husband possibly cheated on me, and you knew and have been lying to me about it for the past seven years."

I exhale a heavy breath. "It wasn't any of my business."

"Not your business?" she screams, her voice hoarse. "Human decency isn't your business?"

"You would not have taken that news from me well. You couldn't stand me back then. You would have laughed in my face or punched me, and then I would have had the black eye."

"Better than me having wasted seven years of my life with a lying asshole." She stares accusingly at me, like this is all my fault when I know better.

I thrust my finger at her. "Hey . . . you picked him, not me."

She shakes her head and wipes at the mascara running down her cheeks. "And in the past four weeks we've spent together, there was never a time when I was pouring my heart out to you where you were like *Hmm, maybe I should tell Dakota about that big, awful secret I've been keeping from her for almost a decade*?"

"You're divorced! What does it matter? You're not even with him anymore!" My head feels like it's about to explode. She shouldn't care about Randal. She shouldn't give a fuck about him. She's so far past him that she shouldn't even remember his name.

"I'm obviously still messed up over him. I mean . . . you found me at a sex club for Christ sake, Calder. A sex club!" She lets out a maniacal laugh. "What the hell is wrong with me? Better yet, what the hell is wrong with you?"

"People look for connection in all sorts of places," I argue, feeling her judgment pointed directly at me.

"Apparently even my ex-husband! God, what is wrong with men? Why do you guys do this shit?"

My nostrils flare as rage simmers in my veins over her lumping me into the same category as Randal. I'm nothing like that fucking clown in there. "I'm sorry for not telling you what I saw, but you have to take some accountability for choosing that ass fuck to begin with. That's on you. You wanted to call that wedding off and you didn't. That is something *you* have to live with . . . not me."

"At least I actually got married," she snaps, crossing her arms over her chest. "At least my relationship was real. You didn't even know a woman was pinning you against your brothers. You're not exactly talented at picking winners either."

My spine straightens at how casually she just weaponized my past against me. A past that I don't talk about with anyone. Only her. "You don't know what you're talking about."

"Yes, I do." Her chin trembles as tears fall down her face. "I know you, Calder. I know that you just people-please and do whatever everyone else wants you to do because you're too afraid to do anything on your own in case you fail."

"Oh, is that right?" I let out a dry laugh.

"Yep," she chirps with an audible pop. "And your fear of failure has arrested your development, so now you're stuck in a constant state of never growing up. Going to sex clubs, living on a mountain with your brothers, working the same job that was handed to you by your dad, never opening yourself up to relationships. I'm surprised one of your self-help books didn't help you see you're just a passenger in your own damn life."

Her words cut deep as she points a mirror at me, forcing me to see my life through her eyes. No wonder she can't admit any feelings toward me. I'm a joke to her, just like I am to everyone else in my family. She doesn't see me as anything more than a casual fuck, like everyone else.

My voice is grave and detached when I reply, "I must have missed that chapter."

"Guess so."

Silence grows between us as I watch her stand before me, her shoulders under her ears as she visibly turns back into the judgmental, controlling Karen I knew her as before. "But what about you?"

"What about me?"

"What about that big, grand speech you gave last night about wearing your insecurity as a badge of fucking honor and allowing people to lift you up? Was that all bullshit? Because from my perspective it just looks like you don't know how to stand up for what you want."

"What do I want, Calder?" she screams, her eyes wild and manic. "Since you seem to know me so well, what the hell do I want?"

"Me!" I roar, my muscles tight over every part of my body as I say the quiet part out loud. The part that terrifies the fuck out of me because the last time I put myself out there with a woman, I almost lost everything. My brothers, my family, my work, my home. "You fucking want me, and you're using this goddamn PowerPoint challenge as an excuse because you're too insecure to go for what you really want."

She releases a haughty laugh and chews her lower lip. Her nostrils flare as she nods aggressively. "That may have been true before, but I promise you it's not true now."

I expel a huge breath, feeling like I just got the wind knocked out of me. One bump in the road, and she's done. Jesus fucking Christ, she is crazy.

Dakota's phone buzzes, and she glances at it before turning to make her way to the vehicle that's approaching.

"So that's it? You're done?" I'm still unable to truly accept this as over.

She pauses at the car door and looks back at me. "Too much has changed now, Calder. Your mask came off . . . and what a coincidence . . . it only took seven years to show the real you."

Chapter 40

THE HACKER

Calder

"What the actual fuck are you doing?" a high-pitched voice shouts into my phone line.

"Um . . . hello to you too, Everly," I reply, my brows furrowed because I have no idea what kind of greeting this is from my sweet niece to her uncle from across the pond.

"What are you doing with your dating apps?"

I frown at the dating profile that I logged into for the first time in months. I don't know what I was doing exactly, other than just trying to find my former self again. But looking at the various conversations I've had with other women literally makes me sick to my stomach. I hate who I once was.

Then it dawns on me. "How do you know I'm doing anything with my dating apps?"

She groans in frustration. "Because I'm logged into your accounts, and I can see you updating them! You better not make your profiles live again, Uncle Calder, or I swear to God!"

"Hey," I bark into the phone, causing Milkshake to jump from her end on the couch. "Those are my profiles, and I'm changing my damn password now that I know for certain it's been you messing with them."

"Like it'd be hard for me to guess your new password. *Milkshake111?*" My head jerks because that's exactly what I would have changed it to.

"Why are you messing with my shit in the first place? You're in a different country. Don't you have homework to do or something?"

"Yes, but I swear, it's a full-time job dealing with you three."

"Who three? Me, Wyatt, and Luke?"

"Yes!" Everly growls into the phone. "You guys make it damn near impossible to help, do you know that? All I'm trying to do is find you three someone to love and care for in your old age so you don't die alone, and I can have some cool aunties. Why do you have to make that task harder than it already is?"

"None of us asked you to do that," I state, my face twisted in confusion. "Wait. Are you telling me you had something to do with Wyatt and Trista getting together?"

"Um . . . duh!" Her voice rises in pitch again. "You think Uncle Wyatt would have found a surrogate as perfect as Trista on his own?" She lets out a laugh. "Of course that was all me. You guys are so clueless, I swear. And now you're over there sabotaging all my good work."

"What work? My dating apps? That shit you put in there was crazy. No way was that going to bring in a decent woman—"

"Not the apps, the palapa!"

My lips part. "You had something to do with that?"

"Good God, yes. There was an open room at the villa for you, but I had Carlos lock it up and tell everyone it was under renovation. Getting you and Dakota to share that little grass hut is some of my best matchmaking work to date, and I'm still very impressed by my work with Dad and Cozy."

I stand up, my chest expanding with this very irritating intrusion on my goddamn life. "You don't need to matchmake me, Evie. I'm good over here."

"Oh sure . . . so good you take your cat for walks in a cat carrier multiple times a week."

"What's wrong with caring about my cat?"

"Nothing, but being a cat daddy isn't as hot a flex as you think it is, Uncle Calder."

My throat tightens at the humbling truth falling out of my sweet, innocent niece's mouth. Except she's not so sweet and innocent. She's a fucking demon child who's lost her ever-loving mind.

"I don't know what shit you're trying to pull, Everly, but just stop it, okay? Dakota and I are not what you think we are. We're just . . ." I can't even bring myself to say the word *friends* because it hurts too much ". . . enemies. She literally hates me, just like she has for the past seven years."

"There's a fine line between love and hate."

Her words jab into a place that I am trying not to feel right now. I can't believe I actually thought I loved Dakota. Love is not kicking someone in the teeth when they've screwed up. Love is not harnessing someone's fucked-up past against them as a weapon. It's unconditional. It's bigger than the moment. It's something a person can say out loud, and that word is not something either of us have said to the other.

And your fear of failure has arrested your development, so now you're stuck in a constant state of never growing up. Going to sex clubs, living on a mountain with your brothers, working the same job that was handed to you by your dad, never opening yourself up to relationships. I'm surprised one of your self-help books didn't help you see you're just a passenger of your own damn life.

She's made it clear what she really thinks of me. How much she hates me. Love is a fucking lie.

"I'm afraid it's just hate between us, kid. I'm sorry if you got your hopes up, but trust me . . . Dakota is not my end game. Direct your matchmaking hopes to Luke, and just leave me be."

I sigh and end the call before chucking my phone at the wall, chipping the drywall, and cracking my screen in the process. Milkshake meows, staring at me like I'm an idiot.

"I know, Fuzz. I know."

Chapter 41

FRIENDS IN LOW PLACES

Dakota

"Hey Trista, it's Dakota." I say, pressing the phone into my shoulder at my shop on Monday morning.

"Hey girl! How's it going?" she answers, and I hear the sound of a goat bleating in the background.

"Fine, fine. I was just calling to let you know that your Mount Millie T-shirts came in, and they are super cute."

"Oh my God, awesome!" she squeals excitedly. "This is making it all feel so real. I still can't believe Wyatt is going to let me build my rescue center on his land. Let the rebrand from Fletcher Mountain to Mount Millie commence!"

"Congratulations." I wince as I force the smile that I know I should have for my good friend right now. This is a big moment, but my heart just can't fake it. "You can stop at the store to pick them up anytime."

"Can you just run them up the mountain next time you come up?"

My pulse quickens as I set the shirt down and hold the phone in my hand. "Um . . . I won't be coming up the mountain anytime soon."

"What? Why?"

I clear my throat and blow out a long breath. "Calder and I aren't speaking at the moment."

"Oh please," she laughs.

Silence stretches across the phone.

"Wait. Are you serious?" Her voice turns grave. "I will be right there."

"Trista, you don't—"

The line cuts off, and I drop my elbows onto my checkout counter and cover my face with my hands, hating that I have to do this. I have to tell my friends . . . again . . . that something didn't work out with a guy.

When I told everyone about me and Randal splitting up, no one seemed surprised. I suppose the countless stories and cry-fests I had throughout the last few years of our marriage prepared them for the news. In fact, when I told Cozy, the first words out of her mouth were *Thank God*.

It's amazing how many people hold their opinions back on your love life when you're married.

Even go as far as not tell a soon-to-be bride that her fiancé was cheating on her. Fuck. Was he? Did he do that all throughout our marriage?

I'm sorry for not telling you what I saw, but you have to take some accountability for choosing that ass fuck to begin with. That's on you. You wanted to call that wedding off and you didn't. That is something you have to live with . . . not me.

He was right about that at least. Randal was a facade. If I really look at our early days, there were red flags that I ignored. The fact that we would stay out late on the weeknights all the time, and he never cared that I had to get up early the next day to open my store. The fact that he spoke endlessly about his job and never asked a thing about mine. The fact that he didn't attend a lot of the things involving my friends and family because he always had other stuff to do. He even blamed his coworkers for why he'd smell like women's perfume.

So many red flags I just turned a blind eye to.

All because I was excited to be married? Gosh, how humiliating. How desperate. Cozy was marrying Max, and I wanted to join my best friend in the next steps of our lives together. I was ready for the happily-ever-after. What a joke.

Maybe there's red flags I chose to ignore with Calder too. His surly moods that came out of nowhere, the way he argued with me about everything he disagreed with. How he managed to lie to me for the entirety of our relationship.

Red fucking flags.

There's a knock at my store door, and my head pops up to see both Trista and Cozy standing there, concern etched all over their faces.

"Oh God, tell me you didn't tell her," I groan, as I let them in and lock the door again since it's still not time to open.

"Why didn't *you* tell me?" Cozy snaps, propping her hands on her hips as she hits me with a pointed look.

I sigh and lead them back toward my point-of-sale counter. I've got about twenty minutes before I need to turn my Open sign, so we better get this annoying girl-power pep talk over with.

I slouch over the counter and shrug. "There's nothing to tell. I told you guys when we started this thing that it was casual."

"That is the biggest load of bullshit I've ever heard." Cozy's eyes narrow. "No one at that award ceremony thought that you two were casual. Not even Luke, and he's super jaded these days."

My brows raise. "He was just my plus-one for the thing. It's not that deep. You guys were all there too. It was a group thing."

"Only because Calder rallied us all up to come. That was his idea, not yours."

"I didn't ask him to do that."

"No, he did it because he cares about you."

"That doesn't change the fact that he's been lying to me for the past seven years!" I exclaim, a wave of emotion swelling in my body over that fact. How pathetic he must have thought I was all those years, being with someone who he thought cheated on me. "Calder knew Randal was doing shady shit and never told me."

"Oh, get over it. We all knew Randal was a pig, and we kept our mouths shut too," Cozy snaps, her tone completely unapologetic.

"I resent that on behalf of Sir Reginald," Trista chimes in to defend her potbelly pig.

"I like your pig more than I liked Randal."

My jaw drops. "Cozy, you were my maid of honor!"

"I know! It sucked. Randal only cared about himself always. It was awful."

"How could you not tell me how you felt about him?"

"Because you were my best friend, and I loved you too much to risk losing you." Her anger morphs to one of tenderness as she leans against the counter. "It would kill me to lose you as a friend, just like it would have killed Calder to hurt you."

My eyes sting as I shake my head, refusing to believe this about Calder. "You're wrong. He's not into me like that. Like I believe he cares about me, but not in the ways that matter. He cares about me like he cares about his cat. He likes me for company, but beyond that . . . I'm still just an expendable pet."

"Spoken like someone who doesn't have a pet." Trista sputters out a laugh and slaps her hand over her mouth. "Sorry, but that is the most ridiculous thing I've ever heard."

"Why?"

"*Just a pet* isn't a phrase you can use with someone like me. Saying *just a pet* is like saying Stevie is *just a baby*. There are people who would kill for their pets, Dakota. And I'm telling you . . . Calder would kill for Milkshake. My God, he takes her for cat walks."

"I know! That's crazy!" I exclaim like somehow that makes my point.

"That's love!" Cozy bellows, splaying her hands out on my counter. "And I'm not sure you can recognize it when you see it, because you never truly had it."

I wince and shake my head, rejecting everything she's implying. Randal loved me in the beginning. Otherwise, why would he have proposed and moved in with me and married me?

Although, when I think about it long and hard, his love was conditional. When my appearance changed, he changed. In the beginning, when I was thinner, I was this prize he liked to escort around town on his arm. And as I gained a little weight . . . he pulled away, and we started doing things separately more often. Was it because he didn't like how I looked, and that's why he didn't want to have me with him? It certainly would track with all the comments he made about my body.

He really was a pig.

"None of this changes anything about me and Calder," I argue, feeling bone-tired with my own thoughts. "If he loved me, I'd know it. All the nice things he did for me were probably because he felt guilty for not speaking up about something that could have changed the course of my entire life."

"Is your life really that bad that you aren't happy with exactly where you are?" Trista asks, her voice firm as her eyes pierce me with challenge. "You have a beautiful home, a successful business, great friends. I would have killed to have a fraction of this success just a year ago. Plus, you just won an award. All signs point to you being exactly where you are meant to be, Dakota. Life has a funny way of shoving us in directions we never would have expected to go. Hell, I never planned to have children. I was so certain of that, I thought I could be a surrogate and save some money. And if I was a surrogate for any other man, I would have been fine giving the baby up. But Wyatt changed all of that for me. He made me feel safe enough to begin a new journey with him and Stevie."

"But I don't feel safe," I cry, tears running down my face as I say the most gut-wrenching words that I haven't had the guts to say out loud. "I don't feel safe with him. I feel terrified."

"Of what, exactly?" Cozy asks, her eyes red-rimmed as she looks at me with so much sympathy, I feel myself crack down the middle.

"Of truly being in love for the first time in my life." I cover my face as I admit the ugly truth. The truth that I've never even admitted to myself until now. "With Randal, it was simple. My heart wasn't as deeply involved. I was in my *fuck the patriarchy* era when I met him, and I always kept him at a safe distance. So much so, the divorce didn't really shake me. I was sort of excited to pick up the pieces of my life and take steps to find myself again. But with

Calder . . ." My voice cracks as an ache blooms through my chest that feels like it could take my breath away. "If he breaks my heart, I don't know if I'll recover."

Cozy reaches out and grabs my hand, her face bending in a way that's so mothering and so nurturing, the tears just flow harder. "You will recover because you have us."

I drop my forehead onto our clasped hands, desperately trying to soak up all the strength she's sending me when she adds, "Just keep being the stunning woman I saw on stage Friday night, and continue fucking the patriarchy one mountain man at a time, okay?"

"What does that even mean?" An unexpected laugh escapes me and I sniff my running nose.

She giggles back. "You'll figure it out."

Chapter 42

SPECIAL DELIVERY

Calder

"Hold your fucking end up, Luke!" I growl at my brother as he helps me lift the giant shelving unit down from the bed of my pickup. "Goddammit! What's wrong with you?"

"All right, fuck this," Luke growls, dropping his end and letting it smack down onto the concrete. "I'm not going to help your moody ass move this shelf one more inch."

He flings his hands up in the air and stomps away, walking down the sidewalk next to where I'm parked in front of Dakota's shop.

I turn my eyes to Wyatt who's propped on my truck watching the show like he's just missing his popcorn.

"Little help here?" I bark, and with a heavy sigh Wyatt walks over and takes Luke's place.

Thankfully, Luke makes himself useful and opens the door so we can maneuver the giant custom piece into The T-shirt Shop. I direct us over to the corner where I know it's going to go, and we set it down, both sweaty and out of breath and irritated beyond belief.

After we've brought the second one in, I glance over at the checkout counter and spot the young girl I've seen in here before. She looks at us like she couldn't give a flying fuck what we're doing in here.

"Is Dakota here?" I snap, annoyed that the girl has nothing to say.

"She's in the back." She goes back to flipping through her magazine, and my teeth clench in irritation.

"Guess I'll go get her," I murmur under my breath as I stomp my way around the counter, heading through the back door to retrieve the woman whose face I can't get out of my damn head.

The last time I was here, I fucked her on the worktable where customers make tie-dye T-shirts. I somehow ended up with blue dye all over my arm, and we laughed our asses off and considered doing a Papa Smurf role-playing exercise. Anything to add a checkbox to that PowerPoint we were so infatuated with.

I remember the day I was here suspecting that, maybe, Dakota was trying to add things to our list to prolong our arrangement together. The more things to explore, the more fun we got to have.

I was good with that.

I didn't want us to end.

I wanted us to go on forever.

What a fucking moron I am.

"Hey," I call out, and Dakota jumps a foot in the air at the sound of my voice.

Her cheeks flush a deep crimson, and she presses a hand to her chest. "Calder, what are you doing here?"

"Can you come out here and tell me where you want these shelves?" I turn away, unable to make eye contact with her because just the glimpse of her in my peripheral hurts something deep inside of me.

"I didn't know you were bringing them today," she says, walking over toward me. The smell of her perfume makes my chest ache with a deep need that fucks with my head.

"I didn't know I needed to call ahead."

She stops, and I can feel her staring up at me, silently willing me to look at her, but I refuse.

With a frustrated noise, she walks past me out into the shop, uttering a clipped *hi* to Wyatt and Luke before standing in front of the giant shelf, arms crossed, head cocked, eyes tight, and lips pinched.

"They're fine where they are."

I cut her a look. "Just tell me what you want."

"I said they're fine. They look great."

"Bullshit, they're not fine. Just tell me." I stomp over to the shelf and prop my hand on it. "An inch to the left? Three millimeters to the right? What do you want adjusted?"

My brothers' eyes both widen, and their shoulders inch up under their ears as they prepare to duck and cover from the mighty wrath about to unleash. I'm poking the bear, but I don't give a fuck. These shelves are heavy, and Miss Bossy Boots here always has an opinion, so I'd rather just get it over with than deal with her throwing her back out trying to move them after we leave.

Dakota's eyes narrow as she steps closer to me, her chin raised high as she hits me with those striking blue eyes of hers that still make me weak in the knees. "I know you want me to go all *Karen* on you so you can fulfill the prophecy you have in your head about what an evil bitch I am, but I'm not going to give you the satisfaction, Calder. The shelves are great exactly where they are. In fact, they're perfect. I can't thank you enough for how much work you did on them. I'll go write you a check right now and include a nice big tip for the delivery."

"Don't fucking bother." I storm toward the door.

Our fingers brush as our paths cross, and I flex my hand, stung by the brief contact, and irritated by the urge I have to reach out and grab her whole body and press myself against her. I miss the feel of her against me. I miss her fucking touch. Her fucking voice. Her fucking everything. I miss her.

"Thank you!" she calls to my back with a cheery fake tone.

"You're not welcome."

"I'm not surprised!"

I slam open the door of her shop as I step outside, my heart racing a mile a minute when the cool spring air hits me in the face. God, that woman makes me crazy. She knows how hard I worked on those shelves, and she's being a brat about it just to get back at me.

Well, never again. My days of doing anything for Dakota Schaefer are fucking over.

I take several deep breaths in my truck, my body shaking over the fact that the entire time she was reaming me out, I just wanted to grab her face and kiss her. She's so stubborn, she can't even admit the truth and see that the bigger picture is so beyond this bullshit from our past. We are both different people now. She's better. I'm better. We're better.

Right?

Fuck, maybe I'm not better. I'm sitting in my truck steaming mad waiting for my brothers to get their dicks out of their hands so we can go. Maybe I'm no different than the fucking screwup I've always been. I'm in no position to love anyone right now. I can't even get my damn life together. Killer Calder strikes again.

By the time my brothers join me in my truck, I'm breathing a little easier, and the time alone has allowed me to get control of myself.

As we drive back to Fletcher Mountain, Luke kicks my seat from his place in the back. "Can I state the obvious?"

"What?" I grumble through clenched teeth as I glance at a silent Wyatt beside me.

"No one fights like *that* with someone they aren't madly in love with." Luke arches a knowing brow at me in the rearview mirror.

I blink away the painful truth behind his remark. "She doesn't love me."

Wyatt does the Wyatt thing and says a million words without saying a single sentence.

"She doesn't fucking love me," I growl. "You guys don't know what you're talking about. The girl is crazy. She'd rather hold on to the past than admit she might be wrong about something."

"Well, are you good at admitting when you're wrong?" Wyatt asks, his voice rough from lack of using it.

"What does that mean?"

He clears his throat and stares ahead as we make our way out of town. "It would seem to me you're more focused on punishing her for being hurt than doing what you need to do to mend whatever hurt you may have caused."

"I wasn't trying to hurt her," I argue, my throat tight as emotion swells inside of me. "I was trying to protect her. I'd do fucking anything for her. Anything. Even if she's being annoying or nagging or controlling or overbearing . . . God, none of that bothers me. Weirdly, that shit is what I love most about her. I fucking . . ." My voice breaks, and I fight against the sting in my eyes and the swelling of my heart.

I decide to lay it all out there. "I love her."

The silence is heavy in the cab of the truck as those words hang in the air and fully sink in. I haven't said it out loud until this very moment. I've been fighting the feelings all week and hoped that seeing her today might help me realize it was all in my head. She's not my person.

But she is.

I love her just as much today as I did when she was screaming at me from the parking lot of a sex club.

"I love her," I say it again for good measure, and it feels good to get it out. Like relief. Like I'm no longer fighting something inside of me that I needed to let out.

"Then, you have to prove that to her, man," Luke says leaning over the back seat.

"How?"

"I don't know. I'm single as fuck," he replies with a laugh. "And apparently horrible at relationship advice if you ask Addison, so maybe I should shut the fuck up."

"What is that supposed to mean? What's up with you and Addison?"

He laughs, and I hear him shift in his seat. "She's off her rocker. She's literally looking for a husband so she can take over her dad's lumberyard."

"She needs a husband to do that?" I ask, frowning over that random addition.

"I don't know. I'm at my wit's end with her." He sighs and I hear him murmur under his breath, "If you and Dakota work things out, I'm about to be lonely as fuck on Fletcher Mountain."

"I wouldn't be so sure about that." I glance at him in the rear-view mirror. "Everly might have some plans for you."

"Everly?" He frowns, looking completely confused, and I can't help but laugh. I'm guessing Luke will discover Everly's extracurricular activities in due time.

My smile falls when I realize this is the first time I've cracked a grin since Saturday, and it doesn't feel good because I don't want to be happy without Dakota. I don't want to do anything without Dakota. I'm done being a passenger and letting her call the shots. Luke is right: I have to prove to her that we're bigger than this bullshit.

"We have poker at Max's Saturday night, right?" I glance over at Wyatt who nods. My mind starts to race with ideas, and I feel my mood lightening by the second. "Maybe we should invite the ladies to come and play with us."

Wyatt nods slowly, and Luke pats my shoulder. "Whatever you need, I got you."

"That's really good to hear because I also need to talk through some work stuff with you guys this week if possible." I take a deep breath before I say the next part. It's something I've been pondering for quite some time, and it's now or never. "Do you have time to meet after work tomorrow at The Mercantile?"

Wyatt nods but cuts me a concerned look, and I fight back the nerves crawling up my back. I have to trust that my family will have my back on this, no matter what it might change for all of us. I'm in the driver's seat of my own life now.

Chapter 43

YOU'RE BLUFFING

Dakota

I try to keep it together as I drive the short distance from my house to Cozy and Max's place. Cozy invited me over for a girl's night with her and Trista, and I could use a drink. I've been in a foul mood since Calder stormed through my shop on Thursday and dumped those shelves without a look back.

And the attitude he brought them over with still has me seeing red. He was moody, dismissive, and everything that drives me nuts about him. Why does he get to be mad at me right now? I wasn't the one who lied and withheld valuable information. What else has he lied to me about? How well do I even really know him?

And why the hell did I ever think it would be a good idea to enter an enemies-with-benefits relationship with him? When do situations like that ever actually work out and everyone parts ways with no harm done? Never. At least I didn't lose a friend through all of this. We started as enemies and we'll end as enemies. As it should be.

And a sex club? Jesus. That was so unlike me. I can't believe I didn't realize how raw I was after my divorce. How unstable and impulsive it was of me to go there alone.

Thankfully, going back there last weekend with Calder did at least show me that I no longer need a kinky sex club to feel good about myself or push myself out of my comfort zone. I can do it on my own.

But it was a whole lot more fun with Calder. I hate how much I miss him.

I ring the doorbell of Max and Cozy's house, steeling myself to not be a sorry sack all night long. I need to laugh again. Need to have a drink and stop thinking about the inky mountain man who looked so good in my bed last Sunday.

The door swings open, and I glance down to find Ethan greeting me. His dark hair is tucked under a backward cap, and he has a white tank top on with some unusual art on his tiny arms.

"Did you get some fresh tats since I last saw you, Ethan?" I ask, laughing at the temporary nylon tattoo sleeves he has covering both arms.

"Yeah, my uncle took me to the tattoo shop last night." He rubs his hands over his arms and attempts to flex. Gosh, he really does look like a miniature Calder.

"Wow, did those hurt to get?" I touch the designs on his arm.

Ethan looks up at me like I'm a complete moron. "They're not real, Dakota."

I huff out a laugh through my nose and ask, "Is your mom home?"

"Yeah, come on in. I'm just getting your chips set up."

"My chips?" I follow Ethan through the entry way and around the corner where the house opens to the living room and dining area that overlooks Max and Cozy's back deck.

I glance at the table and see various spots set up for a poker game. A lot more than three people it would seem. Are Max and Ethan joining us? Not exactly what I had in mind for a night with the girls, but I guess it might be nice to take my mind off—

"Here you go, Ace," Calder's voice causes me to jump three feet.

I whirl around, and my eyes lock on the big brawny sight of him, my stomach swirling with nerves. He's dressed in jeans and a black-and-white flannel shirt rolled up to his elbows, revealing that alluring ink of his, and he has a backward baseball cap on, similar to Ethan's. It's a new look for him, and one that I do not mind one bit.

I glance down at the money he's holding out to me. "What's this?"

"Your buy-in." He shoots me a crooked smile that I feel squarely between my legs.

"My what?" I'm suddenly distracted by several voices coming from the kitchen around the wall.

I walk over and see Cozy, Max, Trista, Wyatt, Luke, and Johanna all eating snacks around the island. This looks like the opposite of a girl's night. This looks like a family reunion.

"Why are there so many people here?"

"We invited some extras for our poker night," Calder answers with a shrug, like it's totally normal for him to be here and we didn't just get in the worst fight I've ever had with a man I'm sleeping with.

"Are the ladies participating in the poker playing?"

"Yes, that's what this is for." He thrusts the cash into my hand. "I know you like to fuck the patriarchy by letting a man pay for your buy-in, and I aim to please."

"What does *fuck the patriarchy* mean?" Ethan asks, shoving a pretzel into his mouth.

Calder waggles his eyebrows at me. "You want to answer that one, Blondie?"

Ethan stares at me, waiting for my answer, and I gasp at the memory of a different Fletcher child asking me this same question many years ago. It was in this very room with this very mountain man looking at me just like he is now.

And he called me Blondie.

My throat feels tight as the group from the kitchen descends upon the dining area. I'm still a bit frozen as Cozy spots me and smiles brightly. She walks over, and my face morphs into something a bit less friendly.

"What the hell is going on?"

"It's poker night!"

"I really need people to stop staying that." I pinch the bridge of my nose. "Are we staying here for poker night?"

"Yes, we are."

"Why are we staying for poker night?"

"Because I think it could be fun."

I hit her with a punishing glower because something is seriously up, but there's too many people around for me to throw a fit about it. So I accept the giant glass of wine Trista hands me and head over to the table, sitting directly across from the man whose face I can't stop picturing, and do my best to go with the flow.

"What are these cards?" I ask as Ethan deals out two cards to everyone.

"Calder's baby pictures!" Johanna answers with a laugh, but she's not playing poker. She's walking around the table while feeding a bottle to Stevie. "Wasn't he the cutest baby?"

"Yeah, Ace. Wasn't I the cutest baby?" Calder waggles his brows at me suggestively, and I start to wonder if perhaps I dreamed about our big fight and him punching Randal and me riding home in a cab crying.

Or maybe right now is a dream, and I'm about to wake up any minute. Either way, I'm glad he's calling me Ace instead of Blondie. That was a horrible nickname he slapped me with all those years ago.

As everyone begins placing their early bets, Calder has me nearly spitting out my wine when he says, "Hey Dakota, did you know in seventh grade I shit my pants?"

I sputter and cough and hit my chest, struggling to catch my breath as Cozy slaps my back from her seat next to me. "No . . . Why?"

He shrugs. "Just wanted to share that with you."

I frown and do my best to focus back on the cards.

"Wyatt, how many fights would you say I've been in?" Calder asks, propping his bearded chin on his hand and staring at his older brother.

Wyatt scrunches his forehead in thought. "I want to say five."

"Six," Luke corrects, pulling his baseball cap down low over his face. "We brawled with those guys that talked shit about Trista last year at the Merc."

"Oh, that's right!" Trista gasps, pressing a hand to her heart and sticking her lower lip out. "You guys were the sweetest little assaulters."

"We were, weren't we?" Calder says with a smile and turns his focus back to me. "I've been in six fights, Dakota. Seven if you count me knocking out Randal last weekend."

Okay, so that wasn't a dream, but that doesn't rule out the idea that this could be a dream. "Good for you?" I reply like it's a question because I don't know what is happening.

"Mom, remember that time I got arrested for going to that party in the woods?"

"When you were seventeen? Yes, I remember," Johanna responds, her face surly and scowling. "Your father had to pick you up at the cop shop and go to juvenile drug-and-alcohol education classes with you for two weeks."

"Dad was so pissed about that," Luke says with a laugh.

Calder winces. "Yeah, it's still a weirdly good memory I have with Dad, though." A thoughtful look spreads across his face before he looks at me again. "That's the worst legal thing I've ever been involved with . . . for now, at least."

"Can I go to a party in the woods when I'm seventeen?" Ethan asks, to which the entire table responds *No*.

"Tell her about your favorite TV show," Trista says, chiming in out of nowhere. I jerk an accusing glare her direction, still trying to figure out what the hell is going on, and she just smiles coyly back at me.

Calder loses all humor on his face. "You swore you wouldn't tell anyone, Trista."

"I'm not going to say it! You are." She giggles and hides behind her two cards.

With a heavy sigh, Calder turns his menacing glower from her to me, softening as he looks at me. "My favorite TV show is *Gilmore Girls*. There. I said it. I love that small-town shit. Come at me, you assholes."

Wyatt, Luke, and Max all tear into him about his love for the show, and I still can't understand this Calder theme-night thing happening. It seems like everyone is in on it, but it still doesn't explain to me why it's happening.

"I'm just fucking the patriarchy, guys." He winks at me, and I swear my stomach gets butterflies. Why the hell is this working?

"Calder once picked a fight with a mannequin when he was drunk," Max says, slapping the table.

"It's true. Also, when I was eight years old, I stole a pack of Bubblicious gum from the gas station, and I still have it in my dresser to this day. I felt too guilty to eat it but also too embarrassed to return it."

"Also, no one wants almost thirty-year-old gum returned," Luke deadpans.

Calder's head snaps back to me. "I was at a lake once, and there was sign that said not to feed the ducks, but I fed them. I'm sure that upsets you because of your sincere hatred for birds, but it's better you know this side of me now."

My eyes swim with confusion as I process everything he's saying. "Calder, what are you doing?"

"I'm telling you anything from my past that I think you should know. So there's no more hidden truths like the Randal thing."

I cringe, feeling awkward about bringing up all of that in front of everyone at the table. "Why is everyone participating?"

"Because we like you two together," Trista adds with a smile.

"Calder told me the night you two met when I was little that you were the prettiest girl he'd ever seen!" a scratchy voice says from somewhere unknown, and I look around, frowning curiously.

Cozy holds her phone up and reveals Everly on a FaceTime call, stunning me into a rare silence. Everly in Ireland is in on this too? What time is it even, over there?

"Oh, Dakota—" Calder starts, and I hold my hand up to stop him.

"No more, Calder, please!"

"This isn't a confession." He pins me with a serious look, and I calm down, hoping he's finally going to tell me what the fuck is going on. "I was just going to tell you that I need you to take down that tab on your website that lists my furniture."

"What?" I snap, my lips parting in shock as I fight back the sting of that request. It somehow feels harsher than anything else he's said to me.

"You can go ahead and take my furniture off your website. I'm done with all that."

I sit up straight and lean across the table. "Are you taking that deal from that store in Denver?"

"It doesn't really matter, does it?" Calder's eyes narrow, his nostrils flaring slightly as he looks at me. "You don't want to know anything else so . . ."

I release a laugh as chills run down my body. He's right. I don't want to know anything else. I don't want to know what a damn fool he's being or how his crazy friggin' family just lets him waste his life away.

I look down at my cards, murmuring something under my breath, while Luke says, "Hey, Calder, want to grab me another beer?"

He stands to go get it, and I smack my cards back down on the table, stopping him in his tracks. "So you just want to *not* make money, then? Cool, Calder. Way to be a tough guy. Who likes doing something they love for money, anyways? I'll get your tab on my website taken down right away. We wouldn't want to not waste your potential, right?"

Silence descends, and I feel everyone's eyes on me, but my brain is too fired-up to give a shit. I pick my cards back up and tap them on the table, my legs bouncing viciously as I look around at everyone awkwardly staring at their cards. "And it's funny how all of you can get on board with helping him mess with me tonight, but you're unwilling to help him where it actually matters."

"What are you talking about?" Wyatt asks, his mouth puckering as he glowers over at me from his place beside Calder.

"You use him to do all the grunt work on your job sites because he doesn't have a kid or he's doing less of the business side that Luke manages, but the shit you have him doing could be easily subcontracted out. Hire a drywall guy. Hire a part-time employee. There are better things Calder can be doing with his limited free time."

"Like what?" Luke asks, his eyes piercing into me.

"Have you ever been inside his shop?" I snap, knowing I'm completely crossing a family boundary here but unable to stop myself. "Have you seen what he's capable of? What he makes with his bare hands? It's beautiful and has your dad's essence all over it. You all should be so proud of him and this talent he honors with your dad's memory."

I look up to see Calder's eyes red-rimmed and burning a hole straight through me. And then I see that Johanna is tearing up too. And Max. And hell, I even got Wyatt and Luke. Dammit, this isn't what I wanted to happen. I'm going way overboard here, but I can't just stop caring about this infuriating man because he screws up.

I inhale a shaky breath and try to compose myself better. "I apologize if I'm speaking too personally about your dad. It's not my place."

"You go ahead and keep talking, hon," Johanna says, her eyes fierce on mine. At least someone seems to be hearing me.

"I'm just trying to get you guys to realize that the furniture Calder builds is so incredibly special. It makes the crap out by Max and Cozy's pool look cheap and basic."

"Hey, I picked that out!" Cozy chirps, her voice thick with emotion.

"Well, it sucks compared to Calder's work, and I have a feeling Steven would agree," I reply with indignation over a man I am desperately trying not to care about. "How all of your houses aren't filled with his furniture is beyond me. You guys treat this like it's a hobby, and it's not. It's his passion. It's his therapy. It's his greatest life's work and could be an extremely fulfilling career for him." I turn and thrust a finger up at Calder who looks completely stunned. "Tell them about the high-end boutique in Denver that's interested in featuring you."

"It's not that big a deal," Calder replies, his eyes locked on mine with a look of longing that I feel squarely in my gut.

"*It's not that big a deal?*" I volley back, my chair scraping on the floor as I stand up. "They want to feature his work in their showroom. It's a really cool thing! God, Calder. This is so typical you. You just . . ." I let out a frustrated growl as I turn and walk toward the kitchen, desperate for some space.

"Talk to me outside for a moment?" Calder asks, moving toward me.

"I'm too mad to talk." I pull away, holding my hands up.

"Walk your ass outside or I will carry you out. You know I've done it before." He points to the door with a sharp commanding tone that makes my entire body flush with desire. I'm getting sex club flashbacks in front of his whole family, which is not good. Licking my lips, I make my way through the expansive sliding glass door that leads out to the deck overlooking the pool, grateful for the cool night air to help clear my head.

My heels clomp loudly as I pace and stew over all the stuff his whole family spewed at me about Calder's past when they are missing the point. His future is so much bigger than this fight between me and him. Why don't they see that?

"Can you stop pacing so we can talk?" Calder's voice is stony serious, halting me in my tracks.

I turn and cross my arms over my chest, glaring at him before glancing at the giant windows that reveal the entire dining room like a living art tableau.

Everyone sees me glaring and turns away quickly, trying to make themselves look busy, like they're actually playing cards and not just eavesdropping on our whole conversation.

"What are you trying to pull in there?" I snap, my tone acidic. "This is such an ambush."

Calder's eyes are downcast as he licks his lips and takes in a deep breath. "I'm trying to prove to you that I'm trustworthy. I'm telling you my truths."

"By telling me you shit your pants in seventh grade?"

He grimaces and grips the back of his neck. "Okay, I was going for *funny and relatable* on that one . . . Maybe it didn't land."

"You need to take yourself more seriously, Calder," I cry, my soul radiating this truth to help him see himself more clearly. "When are you going to see yourself as amazing as I do?"

He blinks rapidly as his lips part, his gaze growing tender in the soft light pouring on him from the house. "You think I'm amazing?"

"You know you're amazing."

"I didn't know you thought that, and your opinion is the only one I care about these days." His brows furrow as he looks at me like he's seeing me for the first time. "I thought you hated me."

My face twists as emotion swells inside of me. It's easier to hate him. I'm familiar with hating him. What I feel for him right now as I look into his green eyes that stare back at me with so much hope and adoration . . . is terrifying.

"I'm trying really hard to hate you," I croak, my voice wobbly and uncertain.

The corner of his mouth tugs up. "How's that going?"

"Not good!" I squeeze my hands into fists as my mind swims with the memories of the first time we met, right here at Max's house. "I forgot you called me Blondie."

"Ace suits you better."

"It's better than Karen."

He chuckles softly as he steps closer to me, reaching his hands out to grab mine. I let him because I miss the way his rough, calloused hands feel in mine, how warm they are, how every time I see him in a flannel shirt I want to cuddle into him like he's my own heated blanket.

"I'm taking that Denver-store deal, by the way."

"You are?" I gasp.

He nods and gets a sheepish look on his face. "I had a big talk with my brothers, and we're going to bring on more guys to give me time to pursue the design thing. I'll still be a part of the family business but not working near the hours I have been. I'm negotiating contract terms with the store next week."

My lips turn down as I fight away the proud smile threatening to spread across my face. "Calder, that's incredible."

"Thanks," he murmurs, looking shy. He stares down at our hands, rubbing his thumb over my knuckles and sending shocks of longing through me. "I think my dad would have loved you."

My throat tightens as tears fill my eyes. "I think your dad would have thought I was crazy."

"Probably." His chuckle is soft and feels like a hug to my heart. "I have one more truth to tell you."

I close my eyes and breathe deeply out my nose, preparing for the worst. "Okay . . ."

"I'm in love with you."

I open my eyes, and the sweet, soft expression on his face takes my breath away. "You are?"

"Obviously, Ace." He smiles and looks away, giving me a profile view of his beard and jawline. "I don't tell just any ol' girl I shit my pants."

I shove him with our clasped hands. "Please be serious."

"I am," he says, turning back to look at me as he steps in closer. He releases my hands to cup my face, and my whole body tingles as his thumbs glide softly over my cheeks. "The guy who kept that truth from you seven years ago is not the man standing in front of you right now. I'm sorry I didn't tell you about Randal, but I'm not sorry you married him because it put us right here, right now, and made it possible for me to say I love you, baby. As it turns out, true love is my kink. And I've never loved anyone the way I love you."

My body trembles as I grip his flannel shirt in my hands. "I love you too, you infuriating asshole."

His face lights up as he leans in and kisses me so utterly perfectly, I think my whole body could melt into the ground. I wrap my arms around his neck and accept his apology, his love, his truth, and his kiss with all the confidence in my body. And, it turns out, there's plenty.

I break away for air, my heart thundering in my chest, my eyes seeing stars as Calder pulls me in close, his hands sliding down to my bottom as his lips brush against my neck.

"You know your entire family have their noses pressed to the glass and are watching us make out right now, right?" I murmur into his shoulder and feel his body shake with laugher.

"I guess you're not the only voyeur in the family."

Chapter 44

TWO FAVORITE PUSSIES

Calder

I wake early the next day and reach over to find the other side of Dakota's bed empty. Frowning, I look at the clock to see it's only seven. Where the hell is she? I get up to go look for her, my cock shamelessly poking through my boxer briefs as I walk into the bathroom and see the light on in the closet.

I find her standing on her tiptoes in my Colorado Rockies T-shirt, holding the hanger of a large white garment bag. It's unzipped, revealing the infamous stained wedding dress that was trashed all those years ago during the house reno mishap. I clear my throat and lean against the door, fighting away the painful flashback I am having right now.

Her head turns to look at me, and her cheeks flush crimson. "I could never bring myself to get rid of this dress. The one that I married Randal in, however, went right in the trash can."

My shoulders shake with silent laughter. "I bet it felt good to dump that one."

"It really did," she replies with a heavy sigh. "But you know what I've been thinking about all morning?"

"What?"

"I was so pissed at you about that flood, and you never once thought about ratting Randal out. He was just as much a part of the accident as you. In the end, he was fully responsible. Why didn't you say anything even then?"

My lips thin as I stare at her looking so stunning with her sleep-tousled hair and bare face. "I wanted to protect you."

"But why? I was so awful to you during the reno even before the accident."

A heaviness builds in my chest as I consider whether or not to say the next part out loud. It could scare her away. Then again, I told her I wouldn't keep any more truths from her . . . so here goes. "I think I wanted you even then."

She frowns back at me. "What are you talking about?"

I scrub my hand over my face, shocked that I'm actually admitting all of this to her and myself. "You marched into my brother's house on poker night all hot and spicy and poking at all of us like you owned the place. You were exactly the kind of girl I would go for."

She smiles curiously. "So why didn't you?"

"You were Cozy's best friend," I reply, gripping the back of my neck. "She was getting serious with my brother, and I knew the only way I could try to be with you would be if I was willing to marry you."

Her expression shifts, and a terrified look streaks across her face. "Wait. Does that mean now you want—"

"I don't want to marry you, Dakota," I reply with a laugh, and she looks relieved until I add the last part, "yet."

"*Yet?*" she exclaims, propping her hands on her hips like she's about to scold me. "My divorce was final a couple months ago, Calder."

"Oh, I know," I huff, pushing off the frame of the door to eliminate the space between us so I can wrap my arms around her waist. I press a chaste kiss to her forehead as she grips my bare shoulders. "I'm not saying marriage now. But I am saying that I don't hate the idea of you walking toward me in that exact dress someday. It made me breathless seven years ago and that was before I even realized how I felt about you."

Her body tenses beneath my hands so I try to soothe her with a soft kiss to her lips. "I'm not trying to rush you, baby. I'm just trying to show you that this is real for me. And you are the only woman in my life that I have ever felt like this with, and I will do whatever I can to keep you right here."

I squeeze her hips and pull her in close, feeling her heart race against mine. This is perhaps an even bigger declaration than the love bomb I dropped on her last night. But fuck it, once you start letting yourself feel shit, it kind of feels fucking awesome.

"I'm happy to call you my girlfriend for now, and we can see where the future takes us."

A bright, teasing smile sparkles on her face. "Did you just call me your *girlfriend*?"

"Would you prefer I call you *my woman*? Cuz I like the sound of that too."

Her brows pop up, and a heated look crosses her face. "You can call me whatever you want as long as you keep doing whatever you did with your tongue to me last night."

"Oh, did my woman like that?" I growl, dipping my lips to her neck and nibbling her supple flesh. "My tongue is at your service, but I need something a little sexy from you too."

Her hands slide down my chest, and I let out a deep groan as she strokes my cock over my briefs. "Name it," she whispers.

I shake my head and laugh. *She's going to fucking kill me.*

"I'm not sure this thing works with boobs," Dakota says all trussed up in my living room with her arms stretched out wide.

"It works great with boobs," I reply, walking over to her and adjusting the straps. "But it might work better if you were naked underneath."

"Oh, is that right?"

I chuckle softly and a memory of her at the sex club flashes in my mind. "Hey, I can get you a matching mask if you like. It might be a little dirty from the girls who wore it before you, though."

A loud thwack sounds as Dakota hammers me in the stomach with an adorable look of righteousness.

I hold my hands up in surrender. "Lambchop! Lambchop! No masks."

She laughs and shakes her head as Milkshake bellows for the tenth time from the door, sick of our shit. I turn back to Dakota, and her breath is heavy, and her eyes are full of arousal from the poking and prodding I've been doing to her. My woman likes it when I tie her up.

"Listen to me, baby." I grip the straps up around her shoulders and yank her to me. "I promise you that no woman has ever worn this carrier. Only you."

Her nose wrinkles, but she gets a touched look on her face as she tips her chin up and offers me her lips.

I chuckle through my nose as my lips find hers, catching her in a deep, drugging kiss. Finally, I pull away and slap her on the ass to head toward the door.

"What do I do?" she asks, holding her hands out awkwardly.

"Just stand there, and Fuzz will jump up into your—"

She squeals loudly as my cat does exactly what I promised she'd do. I help get her legs situated in the holders and open the door for us to step onto my front porch. Dakota walks down the steps, her hands awkwardly bowing out from her body while I lean on the railing, taking in the view of her in front of the mountain vista.

She turns around and pushes her hair out of her face. "How do I look?"

"You look damn fine on my peak." I smile and cross my arms over my chest, knowing this is a sight I could get used to. I waggle my brows at her. "My two favorite pussies."

She rolls her eyes. "I hate you sometimes."

"That's just fine because I love you."

Her cheeks flush. "I love you too."

I smile and join her as we do our very first cat walk as a couple who has a hell of a lot more love for each other than hate.

Epilogue

CALDER GETS HIS DOMESTIC ON

Dakota

A Few Months Later

"Well, hey there," I say as I swing open the front door of my house to find my man standing there all hot and tattooed and bearded and shooting me one of those smiles that makes my knees weak.

His smirk sends a surge of desire through me as he moves in, pulling me into his arms for a deep, all-consuming kiss. We've been doing this whole boyfriend–girlfriend dance for a few months now, and it's going surprisingly well for a couple of people who used to hate each other with the fire of a thousand suns.

He stays at my place regularly. I stay at his place regularly. I have clothes at his place. He has clothes at mine. I even set up a litter box in my house so he can bring Milkshake over when he wants to. That's love, baby!

But there's been something weighing on my mind that I wanted to present to him today before we head over to Denver to finally see all his furniture pieces displayed in the boutique. Something that I know will make this man who changed my outlook on life very, very happy.

And that's what Calder has done. He's prevented me from becoming a bitter divorcée by showing me what real love looks like. I feel safe with him and seen. There's a beauty to fighting and bickering easily with the person you love. No one has a chance to harbor secrets or resentments. Everything is always on the table so you can work through it, one infuriating argument at a time.

That passion translates very well to the bedroom too. We fight hard, but we make love harder. The confidence I feel in myself by having a man who hears me and respects me and loves me the way I always wanted to be loved makes the sex so much more meaningful. There is no finish line in sight because Calder Fletcher is my end game.

"I have something I need to show you before we leave for Denver," I murmur as Calder's lips find my neck and he trails soft kisses along my collarbone.

"Please tell me it's your bedroom," Calder growls against my skin. "We have about twenty minutes before we need to leave, and I know I can make good use of that time."

I close my eyes, and my insides do flips. My bedroom with this man does sound good. Extremely good. But no. I have a plan, and I will not let this sexy man derail me. Using all my strength, I push Calder away, creating some space between us so I can hear myself think.

He's breathless, and the dark look of hunger in his eyes is making my stomach continue with the flips.

"I made a list," I state and turn on my heel to walk into my house where my laptop is on my coffee table.

"Oh God, what? Do you want to redo this house again? I knew it was coming. It's been seven years, and the styles are changing, and you just can't fucking sit still, can you, woman?" He flops onto the sofa beside me and scrubs his hand through his hair. "Come on, show me what I need to get working on."

I smile and shake my head at him. "You better watch your tone, mister. You're going to like this list, I think."

I open up my computer to reveal my presentation. Calder isn't the only one with PowerPoint skills.

Title: Calder Gets His Domestic On

His laugh is soft and warm as he puts his arm around me and moves in close. "What is this?"

"You'll see," I say excitedly and flip to the next slide.

Primary Objective: To live happily ever after.

"Too late," he says, kissing my shoulder and sending goose bumps all over me. "I'm already there."

Secondary Objective: To have more great sex.

"I really like where this is going, Ace."

PROPOSED PLAN:
#1: More Cat Walks

"Already loving this presentation." His voice is thick with giddiness as I click to the next slide.

#2: Family Feud in the Workshop

He eyes me skeptically. "Is this a list of all my favorite things?" I giggle and remain silent because it's all of my favorite things too.

#3: Weekly Hot Tub Dates

"Baby, you know I don't need a presentation to see you in a bikini more. Count me in."

#4: Dinner Together Every Night

"Okay, I think we can figure that one out."

#5: Move In Together.

"Seriously?" Calder asks, and his body goes tense beside me.

I nod and smile. "You've been so patient with me, and it means so much to me that you're not pressuring me to do anything until I'm ready. And while I'm still in no rush to get married again, this . . . this I can do. If it's something you want, of course."

"Fuck yes, I want it!" He leans in and presses a chaste kiss to my lips. "I'll start packing this week."

My lips part in shock at that very unexpected response.

"What did I say?" he asks, his brows furrowed as he notices my change in demeanor.

"You'd move into my house?" I ask, feeling my eyes sting with tears.

"Well, yeah, I thought that's what we were talking about. I know how much this house means to you. You worked hard on it and have big dreams for it. I don't want to take that away from you."

"But your brothers," I croak, my voice thick with emotion.

He shrugs. "I'll still see them all the time. I'm not worried. The cabin can be like our getaway place."

"You would actually move off the mountain for me?" I ask, entirely stunned by this unexpected development.

He eyes me seriously, his head shaking back and forth. "When are you going to get it through your head, Ace? I'd move mountains for you. Hell yes, I'd move off the mountain for you. I love you."

Tears fall down my face because this is supposed to be my grand gesture, my big moment to make him happy. But he just continues flipping the script and changing my plans in the best way possible.

I sniff loudly and refocus. "But what would you say if I wanted to move into your place?"

Calder's face drops, lips apart and eyes wide, and I think he even stops breathing for a second. "Are you serious?"

"Yeah, would you not like that?"

He moves in closer to me, his entire body tense as he holds my face and hits me with so much earnest excitement, it's like he's a kid in a candy shop. "I just always assumed with your business and the house, you wouldn't ever be able to move out of Boulder."

"It's not like you live hours away. It's like a forty-minute drive."
I shrug dismissively. "And I've been thinking about this a lot lately.
If I sell my place, I can pay my settlement to Randal all at once
and be done with him for good. Plus, I love your place and so does
Milkshake. She's not as happy here."

Calder's eyes are red around the edges as they swim with emotion and a tender look sweeps across his face. "This is one thing I
will not fight you over, baby. I would love to have you move onto
Fletcher Mountain with me. Hell yes."

He eliminates the space between us and kisses me, healing
something in me that I didn't even know needed healing.

I've been so stressed about having this perfect home and perfect marriage and perfect life, but nothing is perfect. Not me, not
Calder, not even his mountain. And it's the imperfections, the
messiness, the unconventional grit of it all that make it a real, full
life. Living happily . . . that's it. Feeling safe . . . that's it. Feeling
good in my skin . . . this is the ultimate end goal, and everything
else will fall into place.

Calder

I am one smug motherfucker as I make my way through the busy
Denver traffic, on our way to the furniture boutique to finally see
my work on display. I've been a nervous wreck about this big life
change for me. It will mean more hours spent in my workshop,
potentially doing custom orders, working more with customers
and not just for myself.

But suddenly, I feel cool as a cucumber. None of that stresses
me out as much as it did twelve hours ago.

Because Dakota is moving in with me.

I didn't realize having her on the mountain was even a remote
possibility, and to know that it was her idea and not mine . . . Like
I said. *Smug.* No one is wiping this smile off my face today.

We pull into the parking lot of the store located in a swanky part of town. There are luxury stores all over, and I feel like a total fish out of water clomping around on the sidewalk in my boots and jeans.

"I wish they'd let me haul it all here," I grumble, holding Dakota's hand as we make our way toward the building. "What if they damaged some of them?"

"You have to chill out," she says, wrapping her other hand around my arm. "You watched the guys load everything up. They were very careful. They don't want to ruin your stuff either. They're pricing this stuff way too high to be careless!"

I exhale heavily. She's right. Maybe I am a little nervous still. I just need to remember that I signed a deal with these guys for one year, and if we don't sell anything, I can get out and go back into the family business. No harm, no foul.

But I'd be pissed if this didn't work out after all the work we've done. I had to create an LLC and put up a website and have professional photos taken of my shit and start an Instagram page. It's weird. I'm not managing any of it either. Everly is, and the little shit is making all sorts of viral videos already. She's been home for the summer only two weeks, and she's going full steam ahead on my new business endeavor.

Milkshake Designs is a real original name for a furniture line too, let me tell you. I'm pretty sure the Denver store wanted to back out when I finally told them what I settled on for a name. But it was at least better than Fuzz's Furniture which got Ethan's enthusiastic vote. We considered naming the line something after my dad, but I don't want the work I do to feel like a memorial to him forever. It feels more fitting to keep him as my silent inspiration.

Dakota helped me hire a logo designer, and now we even brand an emblem of Milkshake's face on every piece that leaves my workshop. Who would have ever thought I'd know a thing about marketing and branding? Not me.

But Dakota sure as hell did.

All I know is, I get to sit in my shop several days a week and make stuff with my hands. Stuff I'm proud of and that would even impress my father if he was still around. And now my woman will be right there on the mountain with me. Smug motherfucker.

Dakota presses a firm kiss to my lips before we walk into the glossy store covered in fancy marble flooring and sleek modern lighting. We hang a left and walk toward the corner of the store where they are displaying my stuff, and my chest contracts when I see my mother, Luke, Wyatt, Trista, Max, Cozy, Ethan, and Stevie all huddled over there.

"What the hell?" I ask, my eyes drifting from their faces to their shirts as we approach. It's images of my cat. But not just my cat, it's Milkshake and *me*. I'd noticed Dakota taking photos of me and Milkshake the past couple of months . . . particularly ones where I'm holding her with my shirt off. I figured it was just her kink and my woman wanted some content for her spank bank. No shame in that kind of game.

But no . . . no, no, no. My woman is a demon. She plays with dark magic and delights in the misery of others.

Wyatt steps forward, stopping me in my tracks with his grumpy, zero-humor face. My eyes move down his chest, and it's a photo of me in my underwear with Milkshake snaked around my neck as I sleep, her butthole dangerously close to my lips.

I feel violated.

Wyatt glowers at me and then looks to Dakota. "Can I take it off now?"

"No! We're doing a family picture," Dakota replies with a laugh.

"Wave to the camera, Uncle Calder . . . We're live on Instagram!" Everly peals, appearing out of nowhere and shoving her phone in all our faces. Wyatt continues to scowl, and I can't help but laugh as I glance at the image on her shirt. It's me with Milkshake in the cat carrier, but my eyes are closed, and I look like I'm mid-sneeze.

"Okay, guys . . . Milkshake Designs are available now, pop on over to the store to check it out. Link in bio!"

Everly ends the live and reaches up to give me a giant hug. "Your stuff looks amazing, Uncle Calder! I'm so proud of you." She moves to Dakota and gives her a big squeeze next. "And the T-shirts were a perfect touch. Well done."

"Why, thank you," Dakota bows shamelessly.

"I don't like you two being in cahoots with each other." I glare as I point between the two of them. "You both have a dark side, and when you combine those forces, scary things can happen."

Everly laughs, and her gaze drifts down to my hand wrapped around Dakota's. She gets a starry look in her eyes, so I reach over and ruffle her hair, impeding her view.

"You didn't bring Milkshake?" Ethan asks, staring up at me. He's wearing a photo of me with Milkshake in the cat carrier on one of our cat walks.

"Nah, man . . . they don't let pets in here. Sorry."

His lower lip sticks out. "I wanted to walk her."

"Well, I'm not sure she would have let you walk her anyways."

"Why not?"

"Because last time you screamed in her ear like a little psycho and she scratched you, remember?" I reply cheerily.

Ethan scratches his head. "Oh yeah, I forgot." He sighs and turns on his heel to go join his parents who are seated on a couple of my pieces.

I walk over and admire the setup, accepting praise from all of my family. And I have to admit, everything looks really good. The lighting, the staging, the various home furnishing accents the store has tossed on my stuff. It really gives the designs a completed look that I wouldn't have been able to achieve myself. Maybe this is going to all work out.

Everly sets up a camera on a tripod as she begins arranging all of us for a picture, and I notice that Dakota has opened up her jacket to reveal her own photo of Milkshake. But in this one Fluff's not with me, she's with Dakota. I smile big because I took that picture. They were cuddled up on my couch, and I was having another smug moment of *I am one lucky motherfucker.* And that was before we decided to move in together.

I press a chaste kiss to her temple and turn around to see what's taking everyone so long to set up for this picture. Oh . . . Stevie shit her pants. And Trista is currently changing that mess on one of my brand-new tables. Lovely.

"You're going to get so many more of these lovely family moments now that you're moving in with me, Ace," I murmur, ignoring the fit Ethan is throwing about the smell of Stevie's shit.

"What?" Everly squeals, and I see everyone's eyes on us, and I glance over to make sure my table isn't covered in baby shit. "Dakota is moving in with you?"

I turn my attention back to my girlfriend, and she nods with a sheepish smile.

"Finally, more feminine energy on Mount Millie!" Trista lifts her hands up in celebration.

"Fletcher Mountain," Wyatt gruffs, causing me to laugh.

"Oh God," Luke drawls hanging his head low. "And another one bites the dust."

"Oh, don't look so glum, Uncle Luke," Everly says with a sly smile. "Something tells me you might just be married before the end of the year."

Bonus Epilogue

CAT FAMILY

Dakota

A Few Years Later

"I am swimming in pussy," Calder says as he sits down on the filthy concrete floor of the rescue center that Trista recommended while a swarm of cats climb all over him.

"And you've never been happier." I laugh and kneel down to scoop up an orange one currently gliding along my leg.

"Oh, I don't know about that." Calder shoots me a wicked look. "I was pretty damn happy last week."

Heat fills my cheeks as I flash back to the trip we returned from a few days ago. We've been doing a fair amount of recreational travel the past couple years and on our last journey we stopped at a sex club that we'd read about. It was . . . an experience.

Don't get me wrong, our sex life has been incredible the past few years, so it's not like we needed this to spice things up. But there was something so electrifyingly naughty about being back in that scene with my boyfriend. All that pent up arousal that surged through me as we watched other couples required an outlet that I could use. And Calder was all too happy to satisfy my every need. Turns out, we both enjoy a bit of voyeurism on occasion. Though I think Calder watched me more than any of the other patrons at the club.

And as hot as it was, I don't think we'll be going back to another club anytime soon. It was fun, but we both agreed it was just for a visit. We both seem to prefer the company of just each other.

It's pretty remarkable to be so open and secure in a relationship that we can try new things and keep it spicy while also feeling free to say enough.

I love it.

I love *him*.

The talk of marriage and kids has come up a handful of times, but neither of us are desperate to do either. We're both happy as we are, managing our flourishing businesses, and enjoying a bit of travel here and there. We even went back to our little Mexican palapa last winter and made some new memories that still make me weak in the knees. What happens in Mexico stays in Mexico indeed.

And when we want to feel a little domestic, we're so lucky because we have wild little Stevie right next door. She's almost four now and comes skipping over all the time. Calder even built her a little dollhouse that he keeps at our place to encourage her to come play anytime she likes. She is spoiled on Fletcher Mountain with only adults around her, but the way Wyatt has been looking at Trista lately makes me think it won't be long before they add another to the peak. My guess is Calder will be just as smitten with that one too and I can't wait. It's beautiful watching him be an uncle. He's so proud of everything Stevie does.

That's the perk of compound living. We don't miss a thing and we get to spend as much time with his family as we want and still curl up in our beautiful cabin every night just the two of us . . . and our soon-to-be two cats.

Life on Fletcher Mountain is good. Why mess with perfection?

"Damn, I want to take them all home," Calder says, pulling me out of my happy musings as he scoops a third cat up into his arms. "They all seem like they're friends. We can't split up a pack."

"Just one, Cat Daddy." I sigh and smile, hating to be the practical one, but it's going to be a big task to get Milkshake used to a new friend. I don't want to shock her with more than one.

I've grown attached to that little furball and am protective over her. She needs to approve of this new addition to the cabin just as much as I do. Thankfully, Trista is an expert at this stuff so we'll have plenty of help to make it as painless as possible.

"I just love cats so much," Calder groans as a black cat paws at the gauze wrapped around his left hand. Apparently, he hurt himself in the workshop today, though he refuses to let me look at it. I'm guessing he needs stitches so I fully plan to look at it before we head back to the mountain.

The orange cat in my arms purrs and nuzzles into my neck. "I'm good with being a childless cat lady, but I draw the line at becoming a cat hoarder."

"I like this black one," Calder says, as it tugs on his bandage. "She's got some fight in her. Reminds me of someone I know."

My eyes narrow. "You better not be referring to me, Calder Fletcher."

"Never." He waggles his brows at me and butterflies erupt in my stomach. Bearded and holding three cats at a time is a good look on him. I must stay strong. *I must stay strong.*

The black cat manages to find success loosening the gauze, and Calder's too busy with the other two to notice that his wound is now exposed. I set the orange one down and walk over to him to inspect what happened.

"Calder, what is this?" I gasp as I pull the bandage off the rest of the way and see black ink etched around his ring finger.

"Fuck," Calder says, carefully setting the cats down and holding his hand with his other to conceal whatever is on his finger. He looks stressed as he glances around nervously. "I wasn't planning on doing this here."

"Doing what here?" I ask, grabbing his hand to see what he's hiding.

He conceals his hand behind his back and stares down at the cats having a full conversation with himself before nodding firmly. "Fuck it . . . this is better."

"What is better?" I exclaim, feeling irritated and confused and slightly worried. "What is going on?"

Calder gazes down at me and the grave look on his face causes my heart to sink, but when he lowers himself down on one knee, all the air whooshes out of my lungs.

"Calder? What are you doing?" I feel myself sway so I reach out to hold on to his shoulders for balance as the cats all seem to scurry away, likely sensing the elevated emotions radiating off of me.

"I'll be the one asking the questions here, Ace." He winks at me and my heart begins hammering in my chest as I stare at him with so much love and adoration, I think I could burst. And he hasn't even done anything yet!

"There's a lot of things we don't do like other people," Calder says formally as his eyes glitter up at me. He looks so young and boyish and hopeful, my heart swells at the sweet sight of him. I could look at him forever. I want to look at him forever.

"Our unconventional life is what I love most about us." He reaches into the front pocket of his flannel and pulls out a sparkling diamond ring on a silver band. He had that in there the whole time?

"But this thing. This ring. I guess you could say it's conventional, but listen, I don't care if we never get married. If you don't want to walk down an aisle again, you don't have to. But I want you to wear something that says you're mine forever. I want you to know you're mine forever. And I'm yours. That's why I did this."

He reveals his hidden hand to me, holding it out, and I stare down as I read my named scrawled in black ink around his ring finger. My eyes well with tears.

"You tattooed my name on your finger?" I feel like I need to say it out loud for confirmation.

"Yeah, well, I wanted to put your name on my ass, but Everly said this would be more romantic."

I laugh and shake my head. That kid is still pulling strings in this family. One of these days, we're going to pull them back and she won't know what hit her.

"But my ass is yours too, just so we're clear," Calder adds, causing me to giggle more.

"You are crazy."

"I'm crazy in love with you, Ace. I'm crazy in love with this life we're living together and I want to do it forever. So, Dakota Schaefer, will you please wear this ring and do forever with me?"

My heart swells at the insecure look on his face, like he thinks I could ever say no to him. Like he doesn't know that I never knew what love was until I met him. Like he doesn't realize he makes my life infinitely better just by being his stubborn, silly, always surprising self. Does he really not realize how he saved me by helping me believe I could save myself?

I drop down onto my knees and cup his face, my fingers brushing against his coarse beard. "Hell yes I'll do forever with you."

"Yes?" he exclaims his brows shooting up to his hairline.

"Yes!" I laugh and brace myself as he yanks me into him, covering my mouth with his and kissing me like it's our first time. Tender, sweet, and sinfully sexy.

When we pull apart, I'm out of breath and shaking as he slides the round diamond onto my finger. "It's beautiful."

"Everly picked it out."

I erupt in a fit of laughter. "You Fletcher brothers would be lost without that girl."

"Tell me about it," Calder huffs.

I inhale sharply when an idea comes to mind. "I think I'm down for a tattoo also."

Calder loses all humor on his face as his eyes flash back and forth between mine. "Are you serious?"

I nod slowly. "It would be my first but yeah, I want your name on me too."

A low groan vibrates his chest. "Just when I thought you couldn't get any sexier."

He attacks me with more kisses, pressing our bodies together and running his hands down to my ass in a way that gives these cats quite a show. I break our kiss and press a finger into his chest. "You're still only getting one cat."

"For now," he husks and presses his lips to my neck, sending goose bumps down to the tips of my toes.

I sigh and roll my eyes to the sky. "For now."

★ ★ ★ ★ ★

Thank you so much for reading! If you loved these mountain men brothers, Luke and Addison's fake marriage of convenience, friends-to-lovers book Honeymoon Phase *is next! Coming soon from Amy Daws and Canary Street Press wherever books are sold.*

If you're curious about older brothers Max and Wyatt, read on for excerpts of their spicy romantic comedies Last on the List *and* Nine Month Contract!

Excerpt from
Last on the List

Max Fletcher

A light knock on my door has me straightening in my desk chair. Everly doesn't knock, so I can only assume it's the nanny. I smooth down my new tie for the day and attempt to look busy as I call out, "Come in."

Cassandra walks into my bedroom, dressed in a long tie-dyed T-shirt and a pair of black leggings. She glances briefly at my bed and then forces her eyes on me.

"Can I have a word with you, Mr. Fletcher?" she asks, her hands playing with the hem of her shirt as she approaches my desk.

"Yes, of course. Where's Everly?"

"She's reading upstairs," she replies quickly, tucking her damp hair behind her ears.

The smell of coconut invades the room, and I wonder if she's just gotten out of the shower. Not that I should be thinking of my nanny in the fucking shower.

"I was wondering if maybe we could tell Everly I quit?" Cassandra quips, her tone sharp and contained.

My heart rate increases as I repeat her words in my head before I can mutter them out loud. "Quit?"

"Yeah . . ." she responds, her eyes staring down at the floor. "I'd rather she think I quit than blame herself for getting me fired. She keeps apologizing about the accident today, and I know it's breaking her little heart that she hurt me. If she thinks you let me go because of the pool incident, she'll never forgive herself."

I sit back in my chair, processing everything Cassandra has just said to me. She's known my kid for one freaking day, and she's willing to take the fall for her? I'm rarely speechless, but this situation makes forming a coherent sentence difficult.

I clear my throat. "Do you want to quit?"

"Not at all." Cassandra's round eyes lift to meet mine. The sunlight pouring in the windows behind me makes her eyes look greener than ever. "But I know that what happened today was terrifying for you and Everly. We were lucky you were here. I mean, I don't think I was going to drown. I was getting up to the top of the water before you jumped in. But I fully admit that it wasn't safe. Yes, it's true I'm not a great swimmer. I mean, I think I can save my own life, but if something like this happened to Everly, I'd be terrified of what that could look like. And with how much time you want us to spend in the pool this summer, I realize this makes me unqualified for the job I accepted. Therefore, I take full responsibility and will tender my resignation, Mr. Fletcher."

My head jerks back. *Tender her resignation?* That's pretty official language for someone whose past employer involved making footlong subs. I inhale a deep breath and stand, propping myself on the edge of the desk. "Let's take a breath here, Cassandra," I say, crossing my arms over my chest.

She nods and tucks her hands behind her back, her chest jutting out toward me. I flinch as I recall the feel of her extremely full breasts in my hands. How is it possible to be completely fucking terrified and half hard at the same time? That's really something I should talk to a therapist about someday. But not Josh's wife, Lynsey. Patient confidentiality or not, I don't need my best friend's wife to think I'm lusting after my kid's nanny.

"The truth is, Everly is an excellent swimmer," I continue, refocusing on the task at hand. "An incident like this never should have happened. Everly feels awful because she knows what she did was wrong. She usually has better impulse control than that, but I think she's really excited about hanging out with you this summer, and she got carried away."

"Hey, I've been there," Cassandra huffs with a laugh, her hand pushing into her dark hair as she gazes out the sliders behind me. "I remember pushing my sister off the dock at the lake once. She whacked her ankle on the boat hoist and screamed bloody murder for hours. Even had to get stitches."

I fight back a smile at that very random overshare. "Ouch."

"Yeah . . . the whole lake heard her battle cry. It was Awkward City. I immediately regretted my life choice that day."

I cringe knowingly, thankful for the turn in the conversation as the tension relaxes. "Kind of like your new boss regretting accidentally grabbing your chest as he attempted to save your life?" My shoulders lift with embarrassment.

"I mean, I was a kid, and you are a full-grown man, but I guess you can still relate." She lets out a soft giggle, and the tension eases between us as I watch her with downcast eyes.

"Awkward what?" I frown and watch her curiously, wanting to know more about her.

"City. Awkward City." The teasing smirk on her face makes it hard to keep scowling.

I click my tongue and sigh, trying to figure out the best way to resolve this. Giving up, I gesture toward her chest, trying hard not to look at it. "Well . . . I am sorry about that."

"It's fine. My tits get in the way a lot." She closes her eyes and shakes her head. "I shouldn't have said that. Can we stop talking about my breasts now?"

"Please," I agree because now I can't stop looking at them and recalling how the weight of them felt in my hands. Fucking hell . . . Awkward City indeed.

"Okay then." She pulls her shirt away from her chest as if she's trying to conceal her completely unconcealable breasts. "So are you saying I'm not fired?"

★ ★ ★ ★ ★

Last on the List *is available now in ebook and audiobook, and the trade paperback will release from Amy Daws and Canary Street Press in September 2025 with exclusive bonus material!*

Excerpt from
Nine Month Contract

Help Wanted: Grumpy Mountain Man seeks baby momma to grow his seed. Uterus a must. Ovaries negotiable. Boobs not required but a nice bonus. Job is an incubator position only. No parenting allowed. Surrogate must be impervious to grunting in the form of communication and impartial to goat droppings. Rustic mountain range housing available upon request. Interested parties can text 555–5456. Murderers need not apply. Expect sizable payment and signed legal contracts before insemination commences. Also, must be cool with brotherly neighbors . . . and no, that isn't code for Why Choose.

Wyatt

Pet Goats: 1
Annoying Brothers: 3

"You fucking fuckers!" I roar as I slam my foot on the brakes in front of my brother's cabin, sending a dust storm of gravel swirling around my truck. Jumping out of the driver's seat, I charge up the steps toward my two siblings sitting on Calder's front porch and come to a stop between them. I glare at their relaxed frames stretched out on a couple of wooden rocking chairs with tin cups of coffee in hand.

Like it's just a normal Saturday fucking morning.

I hold up the piece of paper in my hand. "Which one of you posted this at the bar?"

"Easy there, Wyatt . . . you don't want to hit your daily word quota all before lunch." Calder laughs and sets his cup down on the end table beside him and snaps his fingers. "Although I guess 'fuck' was redundant, so you have a few more words to burn."

Without warning, I reach out and grab his collar, yanking him out of his chair. I knew it was Calder. It's always fucking Calder. "Is my life some kind of joke to you?" I seethe, feeling every muscle in my arms flex as I hold my six-foot-three brother up on his tiptoes. I'm only an inch taller than him, so it's no easy task.

"How do you know it was me?" Calder's eyes dance with mirth. Mirth that I am two seconds away from punching off his smug face.

I glance over at Luke, the youngest of us, who seems perfectly at ease as he scratches his short beard and enjoys the show. I slant my gaze back to the most typical middle child on the face of this earth—never mind the fucker is thirty-five now. He was a pain in the ass when we were young, and he's a pain in the ass now. The only difference now is he has more disposable income and more "inspired" ideas for his shenanigans.

My voice is growly as I crumple the sheet between us. "'Impervious' was your word of the day last week, and you used it incorrectly for hours."

The corner of Calder's mouth tips up. "Pretty sure I got it right in that ad, though, didn't I, Papa Bear?"

Rage spikes in my veins now that he's confirmed his guilt. "I'm going to throw you off this mountain and burn your cabin down."

I drag Calder's floundering body down the front steps of his porch toward the lookout point in front of my cabin, ignoring his raucous laughter that echoes off the foothills. I spent weeks clearing trees from this mountain vista when I bought this land to create this view before I even built my home. I wanted a place to quiet my thoughts and bring me peace.

This is the opposite of peace.

"Whoa, whoa, whoa," Luke calls out, his boots crunching on the gravel as he jogs past me to press a hand to my chest. "It's way too early in the day for manslaughter and arson threats."

"No shit," Calder scoffs, extricating himself from my grip. He steps back and straightens his flannel, concealing the ink scrawled across his chest. "This violent behavior will make finding you a Momma Bear very difficult, Papa Bear."

"Stop calling me Papa Bear," I hiss, ruing the day I ever thought it'd be a good idea to have my brothers build on this secluded mountain with me.

I fist the ridiculous ad in my hand and glance up the hill at the three cabins we all built together almost ten years ago. Three brothers living on a mountaintop I bought in rural Colorado sounded like a dream back then. We all worked side by side to develop this stretch of land and build self-sustaining cabins to survive up here on minimal energy resources. Even in the snowiest of winters, we have everything we need to survive for days without contact from the outside world. Weeks even.

Sounds like fucking heaven.

Or it did . . . until something started to feel different for me. *As though something was missing.*

"This isn't a fucking joke," I grumble, running my hand over my short hair.

Calder's expression shifts from cocky to damn near somber as he pins me with a serious look. "I didn't make that ad as a joke, Wyatt. I made it because you're a damn fool for going back to that agency in Denver that's going to charge you six figures for a surrogate when there are decent women right here in Jamestown who will grow your baby for a fraction of the price."

"It's not about the cost, Calder," I boom for the hundredth time. "I'll pay whatever it takes to become a . . ." I hesitate to say the word out loud, my voice getting caught in my throat as the weight of it presses down on me.

Dad.

When will that word ever stop being difficult for me to say out loud? My eyes move over to the memorial bench Calder built and placed at the lookout point two years ago after our father passed unexpectedly. Our dad's favorite saying is inscribed on it: *We're not here for a long time, we're here for a good time.*

Dad was the salt of the earth—hardworking, protective, and challenging in all the best ways. I can close my eyes and still feel his presence all around me—his signature scent of Brut cologne, his chastising tone when my brothers and I were late to a jobsite, his bark of a laugh, or the way he never sneezed just once. It was always an attack of eight sneezes in a row. Fuck, I miss him.

And let's not even think about how hard it's been for my mom, who was just about to celebrate their forty-fifth wedding anniversary before he passed. Now, she's a widow who still cries at family events.

Dad was the definition of patriarch, and when we lost him, we lost our guide, our anchor, our voice of reason. The world got a little darker.

Now, I want to bring some light back into our lives. I want to see my mom hold my kid for once instead of my niece or nephew. I'm proud of what my brothers and I have built on this mountain, and I want to share that with a child of my own.

And I'll be damned if I let Calder fuck with my plan.

★ ★ ★ ★ ★

Nine Month Contract *is available now in all formats from Amy Daws and Canary Street Press wherever books are sold!*